*Natalie —
Thanks
Dark Nights is
fun! Happy Reading.*

FIREBRAND

Bound TO *Seduction*
Slave TO *Passion*
Possessed BY *Desire*

ELISABETH NAUGHTON

Elisabeth Naughton

Copyright © 2013 by Elisabeth Naughton

This book is a work of fiction. References to real people, events, establishments, organizations, or locations are intended only to provide a sense of authenticity, and are used fictitiously. All other characters, and all incidents and dialogue, are drawn from the author's imagination and are not to be construed as real.

All rights reserved.

No part of this book may be reproduced, scanned or distributed in any printed or electronic form without permission. Please do not participate in encouraging piracy of copyrighted materials in violation with the author's rights. Purchase only authorized editions.

ISBN: 1482659727
ISBN 13: 9781482659726

Titles by Elisabeth Naughton

Firebrand Series
(*Paranormal Romance*)

POSSESSED BY DESIRE
SLAVE TO PASSION
BOUND TO SEDUCTION

Eternal Guardians Series
(*Paranormal romance*)

BOUND
ENSLAVED
ENRAPTURED
TEMPTED
ENTWINED
MARKED

Stolen Series
(*Romantic Suspense*)

STOLEN SEDUCTION
STOLEN HEAT
STOLEN FURY

Single Titles

WAIT FOR ME
(*Romantic Suspense*)

Anthologies

BODYGUARDS IN BED
(*with Lucy Monroe and Jamie Denton*)

Careful what you wish for...

Bound to Seduction

A Firebrand Novella

USA TODAY BESTSELLING AUTHOR

ELISABETH NAUGHTON

*For my good friend,
Darcy Burke,
Who's always looking for a little more smexytime.*

Chapter One

THE CLANK OF THE CELL door opening echoed like a thousand cannons exploding across the night sky.

Tariq lifted his head and gazed through the strands of hair covering his eyes, only to experience the rush of blood boiling in his veins when he saw the condescending face peering down at him through the bars.

"Sleep has not done you well, Tariq," Zoraida mocked, the opulent blue silk of her gown swishing as she moved into his dingy cell. Behind her, three guards, armed to the hilt, remained outside the bars, ready to strike at a moment's notice. "I fear your will to live hangs in the balance."

His arms ached from being held above his head as he'd leaned against the stone wall and tried to sleep, and he was weak from lack of food, but he pushed to his bare feet, the chains cuffed to his wrists rattling against the bar embedded waist high in the cold stone at his back. With some unseen force of will, he contained the fury whipping through him at the sight of the sorceress who'd imprisoned him in this hellhole. But smiled to himself at the knowledge his misery would soon be over. And with it, her reign.

"The only life that hangs in the balance is yours, *sayyeda*. I'm willing to die for my cause. And when I do, yours goes with it."

Her superior grin faded. Those emerald eyes, as dangerous as chipped glass, narrowed with a hatred he felt burn all the way to the depths of his soul. "You will continue to do my will. As you have for ages. That is the command of your *sayyeda*."

"Fuck your command," he growled. "I'm done being your slave."

She moved closer, until the sweet, powdery scent of her assailed his nostrils. Close but not close enough for him to reach. Even with his powers bound in this dungeon, she knew better. "Such aggression and hostility from a fierce Marid warrior is not unexpected. But I wonder this. How long will your resolve last when the lives of all you love are on the line?"

"You hold no power over my tribe. My kingdom will persist. Your immortality dies with me."

Her gaze traveled the length of his bare chest, hovered on the amulet against his throat, then dropped to the scrap of dirty cloth tied across his hips. She looked down his bare legs at the food he refused to eat, still sitting on the tray on the hard, stone floor at his feet, then back to his face. A malicious grin spread across her bloodred lips. "No, djinni. My immortality will continue to thrive. And you will continue to fuel it." Without looking away, she called, "Guards?"

Shuffling echoed behind her. Tariq's attention slid from her to the dark corridor outside his cell and the two men being dragged across the dungeon floor. Both wore nothing but scraps of cloth, like him, and both were bloodied and bruised as if they'd been beaten to within an inch of their lives. Long, dark hair fell across their faces, shielding their eyes, but on each, a fire opal—similar to the one he wore around his neck—reflected light into the dank room.

"Bring them closer so he gets a good look," Zoraida said, still focused only on him.

Both men grunted as they were shoved face-first up against the bars. Then the guards grasped their hair and lifted their heads so Tariq could see his brothers' bloody, dirt-streaked and swollen faces.

The fury born into his tribe from the beginning of time erupted inside him. He lurched forward, ready to tear Zoraida's throat out with his bare hands, but the chains clanked again, stopping his momentum. "Release them, you bitch!"

Zoraida stepped so close he could see every tiny pore on her disgustingly perfect face. "You will not stop me, Tariq. And you *will* do as I command, or I will slit their throats and end their meager existences. The Kingdom of Gannah now rests in *my* hands, not yours. Continue down this road of so-called honor and everything you hold dear will fall to ruin."

Blond hair fell over her bare shoulder, the soft curls brushing her milky cleavage as she lifted a finely manicured finger and ran it down the length of his cheek. She was beautiful—blindingly so. But her beauty was a farce. Underneath, she was aged and decrepit. As aged and decrepit as Tariq felt from the years of his imprisonment.

Her expression shifted from enraged to amused. "Of course, if you were to cooperate, I might be amenable to releasing... one." She shot a look over her shoulder toward his brothers. "Even if he is now...stained."

The need for revenge enflamed Tariq from the inside out, but he let his gaze drift past her to his brothers. Both were strong djinn warriors, princes of their kingdom, as was he, but they weren't ruled by fate. They exercised free will. And as such were open to corruption, as he had been. If he—the eldest and strongest of the brotherhood—had fallen prey to the seductive sorceress, then he'd been a fool to think his brothers were safe.

Nasir's chest rose and fell with his labored breaths, but in his eyes, Tariq saw determination. And the unspoken words: *Do not break, brother.* His gaze shifted to Ashur, who could barely keep his eyes open. He would not last through another beating by Zoraida's guards.

Tariq ground his teeth and looked back toward the sorceress. And though it took every ounce of strength he had left, he forced the words past his teeth when he said, "What would you have me do, *sayyeda*?"

Nasir opened his mouth to protest, but the guard kneed him in the kidneys. Nasir groaned and slid to his knees.

"Eat," Zoraida said, watching Nasir writhe on the ground as if it pleased her. "Regain your strength. And when you are called upon, service your mistress's wishes in the manner in which she is accustomed." She threw a victorious grin over her shoulder toward Tariq. "Without hesitation."

Bile churned in Tariq's stomach as he looked toward Nasir's pain, unable to help or even avenge his brother. And every muscle in his body screamed *No!* to what Zoraida was offering. But if this were the only way to ensure his brothers did not die—for at least one to be free—for them he would agree. He would once again become the pleasure slave Zoraida had condemned him to be. And every soul she sent him into the human realm to corrupt would fuel her immortality that much longer.

But by all that was holy, he would never stop looking for a path to his own freedom. He would find it. And one day soon, he would see her blood stain the ground at his feet.

"As you will it, *sayyeda*," he said through clenched teeth.

She stepped to the bars, ran her fingers down Ashur's cheek, and harrumphed. To the guard holding him upright, she said, "See to it he does not die. At least not yet." As she moved through the cell door, she added, "You will have your new assignment tomorrow, Tariq. And this time, use all within your power to make sure the woman is satisfied. My immortality and your brothers' lives depend on it."

※

Mira Dawson drew in a deep breath in the hopes it would settle the nerves bouncing in her stomach.

It didn't.

Stop being so nervous. You're just shopping.

Shopping. Yeah, that was it. Just an ordinary, everyday shopping trip.

The lie swirled easily in her mind, and though her subconscious screamed *turn the hell around*, something more primal urged her on. Running her sweaty hands down the front of her T-shirt, she steeled her nerves, then pushed the shop's doors open.

The bell above jangled. Vintage clothing hung on the wall to her left. Racks of capes and corsets and short, flirty skirts filled the small central space. Hats decorated with feathery plumes hung on hooks all along the left, rows and rows of stiletto-style boots lined the floor, and ahead, a glass counter filled with antique jewelry finished off the cramped room.

She felt as if she'd stepped back in time. To when women were sex objects dressing to please their masters. Apprehension slid through her, and she was just about to turn around and leave when a woman pushed aside the curtained doorway behind the counter and said, "May I help you?"

Too late to bolt.

Mira forced a smile as her pulse picked up speed. She stepped toward the counter. "Yes. Um, maybe." She glanced around the shop, making sure it was truly empty, then lowered her voice and added, "I've come to inquire about the Firebrand opal."

The woman's eyes hardened behind wire-rimmed glasses. She looked to be in her mid-forties, round in the face, plump through the hips, more motherly than madam. But her eyes… her silver eyes…were assessing. And knowing. And hinted of dark, seductive secrets.

Mira swallowed the lump in her throat. As the uncomfortable silence stretched out, she realized hightailing it out of this place really was the best idea after all. But before she could move her feet, the woman motioned with her hand and said, "Come."

Curiosity got the best of her. It was her biggest flaw. She always needed to know how and why things worked, and when she'd heard about the Firebrand opal, she hadn't been able to think of anything but the—supposed—magical stone. She knew that was the reason she was here now.

Part of the reason, at least. Or so she tried to convince herself.

Mira's hands shook as she made her way around the counter and stepped through the curtained doorway. The back room was nothing special. An old box-style TV sat on a chipped table. A love seat covered by a blanket was pushed up against the far wall, and inventory boxes were scattered through the small space. When the woman pointed to the couch and barked, "Sit!" Mira did as she was instructed, not sure what to expect.

The woman opened a curio cabinet Mira hadn't noticed, extracted a wooden box and brought it to the couch. She sat next to Mira and studied her with those weird, silver eyes once more, her hands resting on the top of the aged wood as if protecting an ancient treasure. "How did you hear of the Firebrand opal?"

"A…friend told me about its…unique…properties."

"And what do you seek from the opal?"

Mira's pulse beat like wildfire as she remembered what Claudette, the woman who was most definitely not a friend but who'd been seated next to her at the salon, had said about the opal.

Wicked pleasure, mind-numbing fantasies, your heart's every secret, sinful desire come true.

Though Mira wouldn't mind experiencing a few X-rated fantasies brought to life, it wasn't what she wanted most. "I seek…a man."

The woman's brow lifted.

"Not just any man," Mira corrected, feeling suddenly foolish as she tucked her hair behind her ear. "A specific one. Devin Sloan." Her face heated. "I work with him at my architecture firm. He's gorgeous." Defeat rushed through her. "And he doesn't see me as anything but a friend."

"The opal does not have the power to make someone fall in love with you."

Mira knew that. Claudette had said as much. Though Claudette hadn't actually used the necklace, she claimed she knew someone who had. "I don't want him to fall in love with me. I mean, I do. Eventually. But I wouldn't want him to fall in love with me because of a wish. I want him to fall in love with me because he wants to." Her cheeks literally burned. God, she felt foolish. "All I really want is for him to notice me. I want to… learn…how to gain his attention. And then how to keep that attention, once I've got it."

Because that was the real issue here. She met lots of men, and she dated. She wasn't locking herself away somewhere. But she'd yet to find one who was as interested in her as she was in him. Which was why none of her relationships ever seemed to get off the ground.

The woman's eyes narrowed once more. "Are you a virgin?"

Mira couldn't help but laugh. But it came out stilted and awkward, not confident as she'd hoped. "No. Definitely not." She was thirty-two years old, for crying out loud. "I'm just not…" Okay, now she sounded pathetic. She drew a deep breath. "For whatever reason, I've yet to meet a man who is enraptured by me. And I'm thinking that's got to be related to the way I react to them. Dating is one thing. Taking a relationship to another level and keeping a man's interest for more than a couple of dates is something completely different. I guess I just want to learn to be more desirable."

She thought of Devin. His sandy blond hair and devastating smile. He definitely didn't see her as desirable, even though she'd had a crush on him forever. He saw her as any other girl in the office. And that chapped Mira's ass more than anything.

The woman smoothed her hands over the box. Seemed to debate…something. Just when Mira was sure the woman was going to boot her out of the building, she said, "The opal's power is not to be underestimated. It will burn through you, tempt you, and if you are not careful, it has the power to destroy you."

Mira didn't like the way that sounded. Claudette hadn't said anything about being destroyed. She'd simply said the opal had the power to grant wishes.

The woman opened the box and extracted a silver chain before Mira could ask what she meant. A tear-shaped fire opal, alive with red and orange hues and edged in silver, hung from the bottom of the chain. Light from the opal seemed to glow throughout the room, sending shimmering ribbons of color across the walls. Mira's eyes widened. The woman held it out to her, and before Mira could stop herself, her fingers were brushing the stone, its warmth searing her skin.

"When you leave here, put this around your neck," the woman told her. "Once you make your wish, do not try to remove it. You will not be able to until your wish is fulfilled. But heed my warning: Choosing to wear the Firebrand opal opens yourself to consequences you may not yet foresee. Be sure it is a risk you are willing to take."

Mira held the opal in the palm of her hand, stared down at the red and orange colors dancing like fire as her entire arm warmed. Though the woman's warning made her pause, the longer she stared at the opal, the less worried she grew.

She'd never seen anything so beautiful. Couldn't seem to look away from the stone. An uncontrollable urge to keep it with her…always…consumed her. "Wh-what happens to it when my wish is fulfilled?"

"The opal will find its way into the hands of another. That is all you need to know." The woman rose as if in a hurry. With the box tucked under one arm, she gestured toward the curtain.

"Now go. And do not put the talisman on until you are far from my store. I'll not have its magic unleashed here."

In a fog, Mira found her feet. She was still having trouble looking away from the stone. When the woman pushed her toward the curtain and out into the store, though, Mira finally snapped out of her trance and tucked the opal into the pocket of her jacket. "What do I owe you?"

"Nothing."

"Nothing? That doesn't seem right. This necklace has to be worth something."

The woman's silver eyes narrowed once more. "You will discover its price soon enough."

Before Mira could ask what that meant, the woman disappeared through the curtains, and a chilling silence settled over the shop.

Chapter Two

Mira bit her lip as she stared at the opal laid out on her kitchen table an hour later. It wasn't glowing anymore, and looking at it now, she was pretty sure she'd imagined that to begin with. The thing was nothing but a pretty necklace, really. A trinket.

And yet, she couldn't get the shop owner's warning out of her head. *Choosing to wear the Firebrand opens yourself to consequences you may not yet foresee. Be sure it is a risk you are willing to take.*

She pushed out of her chair, went into the kitchen, made herself a cup of tea. On the street below, cars honked in the Pearl District of downtown Portland. She should be at work, but she'd taken the afternoon off after visiting that shop, and she knew there was no way she could work from home right now. Not when the opal was all she could think about.

The microwave beeped. She pulled the steaming cup out, dropped the tea bag inside. Looked back at the necklace on the table and tried to think logically.

What consequences? What kind of magic did it really have…if any? Mira had a degree. For a while in school, she'd been pre-med. She knew all about the placebo effect. About sugar pills tricking patients into thinking they were receiving medications that were helping them. In her head she didn't doubt this necklace was the same sort of mirage. If someone who wore it believed it had power, it gave them a confidence they wouldn't otherwise have.

She blew on her tea. Winced when her subconscious said, *Okay, then why did you go all the way down to that shop? And why do you now have the gemstone?*

She brought the tea back to the table. Didn't sit but stared down at the necklace as she debated her choices. Just because she was aware of something didn't mean she wasn't open to trying it. After all, she was also "aware" that the power of persuasion was a big one. And she wanted Devin. Had wanted him for a while now. She'd finally just reached a point where she was tired of waiting for him to realize she was his perfect match. If wearing this silly necklace somehow gave her the confidence to take things with him beyond friendship, then she was willing to give it a try—whether it had real power or not.

She set her tea on the table, lifted the necklace. And told herself to stop being such a pansy. As she slipped the chain around her throat and closed the clasp, then brushed her fingers across the opal nestled just above her cleavage, she reminded herself that she was a smart woman. A successful architect. She wasn't desperate. She didn't need a man to complete her, but she wanted one. And if this didn't work, well, it wasn't the end of her world. Nothing *bad* was going to happen, as that shopkeeper had cryptically led her to believe.

"Your wish, my command."

Mira whipped around at the sound of the deep voice and stared through the archway at the man standing in the middle of her living room. Fear raced through her chest. She took one step back toward the kitchen counter behind her and the knife block she knew was there. "Wh-who are you, and how did you get into my apartment?"

A slow, mesmerizing smile slinked across his deeply tanned face. "My name is Tariq. And you wished for me. That is how I came to be."

Mira's heart pounded so hard beneath her ribs, she was sure he had to hear it. She bumped into the counter, inched her hand backward until her fingers knocked into the knife block. "I—I didn't call for anyone. Leave. Now. Or I *will* call the cops."

His gaze dropped from her face to her chest. "Did you not put on the necklace?" He stepped into the kitchen, and Mira's eyes widened when she took a good look at him in the light streaming through her kitchen window. Shoulder-length dark hair, ebony eyes, a strong, square jaw covered in a dusting of scruff, and a body sporting jeans and a light blue T-shirt that didn't hide the fact it looked as if it were carved from marble. "*Azizity*, I am from the opal."

Holy hell, the guy was psycho. Mira stared at him with wide eyes. He didn't make another move toward her, only stared back with a knowing and heated expression, one that, for reasons she couldn't explain, shot warmth straight to her center.

No way this was real. She glanced past him to the door, which was still locked, the chain exactly where she'd left it when she'd come home, then to the windows that didn't show any evidence of having been opened.

"What...? How...?"

"Have you ever heard of a race known as djinn?"

Mira's eyes grew even wider as they swept back to him. "As in Arabic folklore? Are you saying you're a genie?"

Correction, not just psycho. This guy was off the flippin' charts *insane*.

"Folklore to humans," he said with only the slightest narrowing of his fathomless eyes. "And genie is such a derogatory word."

She looked around again, knowing she was either about to get sliced and diced by some escaped mass murderer, or that she was hallucinating. Big-time.

She had to be hallucinating. "I—I don't see a lamp."

One corner of his lips turned up in amusement. "We don't use lamps. Another myth." He took one small step closer to her, and even from across the distance, she felt the heat of his body stir the air around her. "I am Tariq from the Marid tribe and the Kingdom of Gannah. And I am here to fulfill your wish."

※

Tariq waited for the woman to say something—anything—but she only continued to stare at him with those unbelieving eyes. Eyes that were a unique mix of green and brown, rimmed in gold.

As those pretty eyes grew wider and she still didn't say anything, he fought from frowning. *She* had summoned *him*, dammit. She was the one who had gone looking for the Firebrand opal, and now she was standing stock-still before him as if she'd seen a ghost? He would never understand humans. They wished for things they didn't want, and then when they had them, they wished for something else.

Bile churned in his stomach over the fact he was being forced to do this yet again, but he reminded himself what was at stake here. For his brothers, he would seduce again. As many times as he had to until they were both free. This one wouldn't be a total hardship, he realized as he took in the strawberry-blond hair that fell to her shoulders, the high cheekbones, the small mouth, and seductive mole just to the right of her lips. But he'd done this too many times during the long years of his imprisonment to be anything more than only slightly intrigued by the woman in front of him. And until she cooperated and stopped looking at him as if he'd sprouted a second head, he couldn't get this thing started then finished so he could focus on a plan to destroy Zoraida for good.

"*Azizity*?" he asked, careful not to touch her, at least not yet. "Are you all right?"

"I—" Her gaze raced over his features; then her face paled, and her eyes rolled back in her head just before her whole body went limp.

"Humans." Tariq wrapped his arms around her before she hit the counter and fell to the floor. The scent of peaches assailed his nostrils. Smooth skin and sensuous curves filled his hands as he lifted her into his arms. She was lighter than he thought but still deadweight against him as he carried her into the living room and laid her out on the couch.

No, he would definitely never understand this race. Even with the shock he was used to seeing on their faces when he first appeared, he'd never had one pass out on him.

He wasn't sure what to do, so he went back into the kitchen, grabbed a towel from the drawer, and ran it under a stream of warm water. After ringing it out, he came back to the living room and sat on the edge of the couch next to her.

Soft waves fell across her cheeks. He brushed them back, felt the satiny strands against his fingers, and marveled at the contrast between his dark flesh and her much paler skin tone. Long lashes feathered the skin beneath her eyes, making her look almost angelic. And her mouth—plump and pink—drew his attention. A mouth he would soon be taking, soon be licking, soon be tasting.

A wicked shot of heat rolled through his groin. A dark desire he usually had to work to conjure. But this came suddenly, without force, without the magic he always needed to become aroused. The realization caught him off guard more than the fact she'd passed out on him.

It would make things easier, he told himself. It didn't mean anything. Pushing the thoughts aside, he ran the damp towel along her forehead. "Wake up, *azizity*. I'm not here to hurt you, only to pleasure you with your wish."

And corrupt your soul to feed the immortality of one evil sorceress.

He ignored that thought too. Dwelling on it would get him nowhere. And he was as much a victim in this as she was. More so, because she'd asked for it.

Slowly, her head rolled to the side, the muscles around her eyes tightened; then she blinked several times before opening those mesmerizing eyes and looking up at him. It took several seconds before recognition dawned, but when it did, her eyes flew wide all over again. She pushed up on her arms and scrambled back into the corner of the couch. "Oh my God."

"Relax, *azizity*. All is well."

Her gaze shot from him to the kitchen and back again. "I wasn't hallucinating."

He chuckled. He sorta liked this human. Even with her odd reactions. "No, you most certainly were not."

"I… You… This…"

Still scared, he realized. There was only one way to fix that. Even though it was a risk, he sensed unless he took this chance, they were going to circle around each other and never get down to business. And that wouldn't help his brothers.

"Listen to me, *azizity*. You have the power here. I have none. I'll show you. Brush your fingers over the opal at your chest." When she only continued to stare at him, he added, "Go on. Nothing bad will happen. I promise."

Cautiously, she brought her fingers toward the opal, then touched it gently, caressing the stone in such a way he felt the vibration in the very center of his chest.

Which was weird. Because even though he was bound to the stone, he wasn't connected to it physically.

Before he could ponder what that meant, he was flying across time and space, then materializing back where he'd started.

Sunshine-laden walls and comfy feminine furnishings gave way to drab gray, cold stone, and iron bars. The guard outside his cell whipped around when he heard Tariq appear, narrowed his eyes, and shot a look toward the chains in the wall.

Contempt brewed in Tariq's chest. Even in his cell, they didn't trust him. Not after he'd attacked Zoraida's guards upon return from his last assignment. And this guard had to realize he was back sooner than anticipated, which meant he'd failed.

Hopefully not. Hopefully his assignment possessed that human characteristic that made his job possible, even if she was different from all the rest.

Curiosity.

The guard took a step toward the door, his jaw hardening. Metal clanged as he pulled the sword from the sheath at his hip. But before he could get the key in the lock, Tariq was flying again.

Relief whipped through him. As awful as it was to be forced against his will, spending time with the woman was a thousand times better than being locked in that cell. Or punished.

He materialized again in the middle of her living room. She was sitting up on the couch, her eyes still wide, a lock of hair brushing her cheek. But like he'd hoped, her fingers were once again brushing the opal near her breasts.

"Where…where did you go?" she asked.

"To my world," he answered, not moving from his spot. Not yet. He didn't want to do anything to spook her. "My realm exists on another plane. The opal is the doorway through which I cross. And you, *azizity*, are the key master who either summons or sends me back."

"Whoa." She pressed a hand to her head. "I feel like I've fallen into a twisted version of the *Ghostbusters* Only I don't remember any of the actors looking like you."

He chuckled again. Because her reactions were not at all what he expected. "You seem surprised by this. Were you not instructed in what to expect from the Firebrand?"

"Yes. I mean, no." She raked a hand through her long hair, the soft strands falling against her cheeks and shoulders like waves of silk. "I mean"—she looked up at him— "all I knew was that the opal had power. That it could make wishes come true. Not that it housed a gen—" Her cheeks brightened. "I mean… you."

Shocked and cautious but observant. Another interesting reaction. "And now that you know, do you wish you'd made a different choice?"

"I don't know. How does this work? You're djinn. Isn't that like…a demon?"

Add smart to her list of attributes. He sat on the ottoman of a nearby plush chair. "Djinn are as old as angels. We are spiritual beings who take on solid form. Like humans, some are good, some are evil, and still some are benevolent. My brothers and I hail from the Marid tribe. We are the most powerful djinn, but we are also the ones you want on your side."

"Do other djinn…besides you…cross into the human world?"

"Yes. Frequently. Many are fascinated with human behavior. They camouflage themselves, allowing them to remain unseen as they cause trouble. As spirits, it's easy to influence humans to do one thing over another. Think of it like the devil sitting on your shoulder, whispering in your ear. You can't hear him, but he's there."

"Well, that's comforting," she mumbled, glancing toward the floor.

He smiled again. He did like this human. He normally didn't feel compelled to give this much information, but she was truly interested, and he also sensed without it, they'd never be able to move on. "Some of us don't relish causing havoc. We grant wishes. Which, you have to agree, is a good thing."

Her eyes slid to his, and he saw the hesitation in their hazel depths. And for the first time in all the years he'd been doing this, a shot of guilt spiraled through his stomach.

"So how does it work?" she asked. "The wish? Do I tell you what I want and that's it?"

Guilt was replaced with another wave of heat rolling through his groin. A heat that was again a surprise. "Yes, *azizity*. Your wish is my command."

He knew what was coming. Some twisted female fantasy where she had all the control and he was forced to pleasure her in whatever perverse way she wanted. The scenes changed from woman to woman—sometimes he was ordered to act as a Viking, other times a soldier, even others a pool boy—but the end result was always the same. He did whatever, wherever, and however they wanted. No matter how humiliating it may be for him.

Her cheeks turned pink, and she looked back down at the carpet again, twisting her fingers together. "Oh."

As he sat in silence, waiting, he couldn't help but be taken aback by her reaction. Why wasn't she telling him what to do? Why wasn't she already commanding him? Her embarrassment was so different from the other females who had summoned him. By this point, most were already naked, laid back like an offering, waiting for him to get on with it. And yet she sat across from him, embarrassed by what she wanted.

"There's nothing to be apprehensive about, *azizity*. I am yours to command."

Her eyes grew wide just before she covered them with her hands. "Oh, boy," she mumbled. "This is so not what I was expecting."

Heat arced through his pelvis again, and this time...the thought of acting out those fantasies didn't turn his stomach. In fact, thinking about acting them out with *her* excited him in a way that left him feeling the slightest bit...confused.

"Fear not, *azizity*. Tell me your wish, and we will commence at your speed. For however long it takes until you are thoroughly satisfied."

She dropped her hands into her lap. Frowned. "Why do you keep calling me that? *Azizity*?"

"It's a term of endearment where I'm from. It means 'my darling.'"

Her frown deepened. "I'd rather you call me by my name. Mira. Mira Dawson."

"Mira," he said slowly. "It is an old name. Latin. It means peace." Interesting. Since he couldn't remember the last time he'd had any kind of peace. Not that it mattered, since he was a slave. He pushed the thought aside. "I am Tariq."

They stared at each other across the room long seconds. And he sensed she wanted to rise, to cross to him, but didn't know how. It was his job to push her. To influence her thoughts and actions so Zoraida could feed from her soul's corruption. But somehow he knew if he pushed, this one would back far away. And there was no telling how long it would be until the Firebrand opal fell into another's hands. Time his brothers just didn't have.

Reluctantly, he pushed to his feet. This action would enrage Zoraida, but in the long run, he hoped it would pay off. "Think about what you want, Mira. And when you are ready, summon me back."

Slowly, he stepped toward her, giving her plenty of time to see he wasn't about to hurt her, and reached for her hand. Her skin was soft where his was rough, pale where his was dark. Lifting her fingers to his mouth, he skimmed his lips over her knuckles. Sparks of heat raced all through his body at the simple touch. Heat, he saw from the way her eyes darkened, she felt too.

Again, not what he expected. Not what he was used to. Nothing he even knew how to react to.

Brow wrinkling at what it all meant, he placed her hand at her chest, right over the opal, and for the first time in forever found himself torn between hoping she called him back and wishing she wouldn't. Before he changed his mind, he said, "Now, send me home."

Chapter Three

Mira spent the rest of her day doing anything she could to take her mind off what had happened.

As she scrubbed the inside of her fridge, she knew only one thing for certain: Tariq was real. She hadn't imagined their meeting or his poofing in and out of her living room. He was real. He wanted to grant her a wish. And he was a genie.

Her hand paused against the glass shelf. Holy hell. He was a genie. Even if he didn't like to use that word, that was exactly what he was. The poof of black smoke when he'd disappeared and reappeared was as much an indication of that as was the fact he was bound to the opal.

She lifted her hand, *almost* touched the stone at her chest, then stopped short. She wasn't ready to call him back. Not yet. She needed to think.

Forget thinking. She tossed the sponge into the sink across the room and ripped off her yellow latex gloves. What she needed to do was research.

She wound into her home office, sat in the chair behind her desk, and opened her laptop. An hour later, after filling her brain with enough djinn mythology to make her head ache, she was still confused.

He'd said some djinn were good. That they granted wishes. Yet her research said otherwise. It was the last few lines about his tribe—the Marid—that she couldn't stop thinking about:

Few in number, very powerful. According to folklore, Marid have the ability to grant wishes to mortals; however, they usually only do so when forced by a master.

Mira sat back in her chair, fingered the chain at her neck. Remembered Tariq standing proud and warrior-like in front of her. Why would a djinni from the Marid tribe—which, according to her research, was the most powerful, the most proud, the most conservative of the six tribes when it came to interactions with humans—grant any kind of wish to a mere mortal? Everything she'd read said members of his tribe stuck together. Why would he care about her wants and needs? About *any* human's wants and needs?

Her fingers drifted down the chain, hovered just above the opal. She'd taken it off earlier, then put it back on. The shop owner had said once she made her wish she wouldn't be able to take it off until her wish was fulfilled. While the thought of it being locked around her neck for any extended length of time made her more than a little claustrophobic, she felt safe in the fact she controlled the situation. And that it was up to her to call Tariq back or not.

He wasn't going to hurt her, of that she was sure as well. But was he offering her this deal because he wanted to? Or because he was being forced…for whatever reason?

Her thoughts drifted to Devin. Yes, she wanted him to notice her, but she wasn't willing to do just anything to get him. Before she decided if she was really going to go through with this whole wish-fulfillment thing, she needed to find out more about Tariq.

Slowly, she pushed out of her chair, then paused in the doorway. Her bedroom sat to the left, the living room to the right. Darkness pressed in through the windows, telling her night had fallen while she'd been researching. A smart woman would go to bed, sleep on this decision before acting. But every time she thought about moving into her bedroom, she remembered Claudette's claims.

Wicked pleasure, mind-numbing fantasies, your heart's every secret, sinful desire come true.

Followed by the image of Tariq. Tall, broad, so very muscular. Dark and dangerous, radiating a sexuality even Devin couldn't compete with. Then she heard Tariq's deep, sexy voice when he'd said, *I am yours to command. For however long it takes until you are thoroughly satisfied.*

Her blood warmed. Shot sparks of need through her limbs, into her abdomen to spread rolling waves of heat across her hips and between her thighs. She gripped the doorframe for support.

"Oh God." She would not survive a night fantasizing about him and *that*. She needed to know more. *Now.*

On unsteady legs, she made her way out into the living room, flipped on a lamp, and sat on the edge of the couch. Thankfully, it was Friday, and she didn't have to go to work tomorrow. So it didn't matter if this "discussion" lasted awhile or not. She didn't have to be up early. And if the discussion turned into something else…

She swallowed hard at the erotic visions taking shape in her mind. The ones not of her and Devin, as she'd often dreamed, but of her and Tariq. Both naked and sweaty and breathless.

Her pulse picked up speed, and she swiped a hand over her suddenly damp forehead. Told herself to get a grip. That wasn't why she was calling him back. Before she could change her mind, she brushed her fingers over the opal and held her breath to see if he'd appear.

A cloud of black smoke filled the center of the room then slowly dissipated, leaving Tariq standing in the same clothes he'd worn earlier. Only this time, those obsidian eyes, that fall of dark hair that just brushed his shoulders, and that insanely sharp jawline covered in scruff shot a thrill to her very core, not fear and apprehension as it had before.

"Mira," he whispered, the corners of his lush lips curling ever so slightly. "Your wish, my command."

Heat and need rippled right back through her abdomen, brought a flush to her cheeks. Every time he used the word *command*, she seemed to grow hotter.

She cleared her throat. Could tell from his waiting expression that he thought by calling him back it meant she wanted to begin their…what? Deal? Wish? Yet she hadn't even told him what she wanted. And when she did…

Her blood went white-hot when she thought of what she wanted. And how he would work into that wish.

On shaky legs she stood, and when he took a step toward her, that thrill turned to excitement, but she held up a hand to stop him—and her. "Wait. I have some questions first."

His eyes narrowed in speculation. But his expression cleared and settled before she could wonder what he was thinking. "Ask me anything. I am yours to command."

Command. There was that word again. Only this time it didn't sound sexy as it had before. It sounded…forced. She dropped her hand, swallowed the nerves, feeling both foolish and a little disturbed. But this was important. She didn't want to be with someone—even if it was just a wish—who didn't want to be with her. Even if he was a super-hot genie sent to fulfill her every desire.

"I did some research while you were gone," she said. "And I believe you. What you told me…it's crazy." She looked around the room, only half-believing she was saying this. "Twenty-four hours ago, I never would have thought this was possible, but now…everything is different." She looked back at him. "But before we move on to my, ah, wish, I need to know one thing."

When he only stared at her, she shifted her feet and forced herself to go on. "Are you here by choice? Or are you being forced by some…master…to fulfill my wish?"

Her heart thumped hard. So hard she was sure it had to be bruising a few ribs. And under his heated stare, she couldn't read him. Didn't have a clue what he was thinking. Or feeling—if anything. Did djinn even *have* feelings?

"You researched me," he said slowly, still staring at her.

"Yeah. Well, not you specifically," she managed, though her throat was thick with nerves. "But your tribe. And everything I read says those from the Marid tribe keep to their own realm. They don't cross over into the mortal world like the Jinn and Jann tribes do. Like the Shaitans and Ghuls." She swallowed back the rising sickness when she remembered what she'd read about the last two djinn tribes. While the Jinn and Jann were mostly just curious about humans, the Shaitans and Ghuls preyed on both the living and the dead, loved to torment and destroy whenever they could. She'd been so relieved Tariq was not one of them.

"You researched me," he said again.

"Yeah," she repeated, twisting her hands together. "Does that bother you?"

"No, Mira," he said softly. "It does not bother me. It…surprises me. No one in all my long years of servitude has *ever* gone to the trouble of trying to learn more about me."

His admission sent pleasure through her chest, and a smile curled her mouth. But the elation was dampened when she realized he'd used the word servitude.

The warmth dimmed. "So you are being forced to be here with me."

He took a step toward her and, before she could think to stop him, ran his palm across her cheek, cupping her face and looking down at her with eyes that were soft inky pools of… confusion.

Heat rushed in again.

He brushed his thumb across her cheek, the simple touch sending tongues of wicked fire licking through her torso. "You are unlike any mortal I have ever met." His gaze drifted down, and he ran the fingers of his other hand across the opal nestled in the top of her cleavage. "While it is true I am bound to the Firebrand and am forced to serve, for the first time in forever, I feel…tempted."

Tempted was good, right? It meant at least part of him wanted to be here with her. Or so she hoped.

She held her breath. Waited. His gaze lifted back to hers. And someplace deep inside her went dark with desire at the longing she saw reflected in his sinfully wicked eyes. Longing *she* had put there.

"Who are you, Mira Dawson? And why do you have this strange effect on me?"

Tariq wasn't sure if he was dreaming, fantasizing, or just plain finally going nuts after all the years Zoraida had kept him locked up. But even if this was some schizophrenic hallucination, he didn't care. Mira had researched his tribe. She'd truly cared whether he was forced to be with her or not. No one—not a single human he'd granted wishes to in all those years—had once thought of him. What he wanted, what he needed. Not a single one had looked at him as anything more than a lowly genie.

But not her. Right now, staring up at him with those hypnotic hazel eyes, she was looking at him as if he was a man.

Which was a huge misconception he should remind her of. He was not a man. Had never been a man. He was djinn. The heir to his kingdom. A lethal warrior who had commanded armies. One who had eventually been captured, tortured, and condemned into slavery. But none of that mattered right now— not even his failures. All that mattered was her. And this tiny moment of relief he'd found because of her.

"I'm…no one special," she said softly, breaking his train of thought. "I'm just…me."

She was more, though. Something in the center of his chest said she was much more.

"Tell me your wish, Mira."

She looked down at his T-shirt. And again he watched a blush creep across her cheeks. A blush that excited him with each passing second. "I…it's a little embarrassing."

"Nothing you wish for will shock me." Especially because he was already starting to think of all the ways he could pleasure her. And was actually looking forward to them. Which was a first for him. A big first.

"This might," she mumbled. Then, drawing in a breath, she looked back at his face. "I want to learn about…seduction."

When he opened his mouth to ask how she wanted to be seduced, she held up a hand, stopping him. "Before you ask, no, I'm not a virgin. I've had boyfriends. And I like men. I like sex. But…"

She hesitated. Bit her lip. Looked back down at his shirt. And he waited because he sensed this was hard for her. And because the way her top teeth sank into her bottom lip was so damn sexy, he had a wicked, all-consuming urge to take a bite out of her himself.

"Oh, man," she said. "This is so embarrassing." Then she squared her shoulders and met his eyes again. "Okay, here's the deal. I'm the first one in my family to go to college. My parents were both blue-collar workers who couldn't afford to send me to school and worked extra jobs so I could go. I sacrificed partying and boys in favor of studying so I could make them proud. Then, when I graduated, I was focused on getting a job to prove to them their sacrifices were worth it. And I did. I got a great job. I love my job. And it was enough. Until my dad got sick a few years ago. I found myself torn between work and helping my mom when I could, but all the while I was starting to feel as if something was missing. Yeah, I've had boyfriends, but no one special, you know? I guess a relationship didn't matter much to me before, so maybe I didn't try hard enough. Then my dad died last year, and my mom went to live with my aunt in Idaho, and suddenly I found myself…"

"What?" he asked before he could stop himself, mesmerized by her words, her voice, that she was sharing something so personal with him.

She looked back up at him. And there was such regret in her eyes, he couldn't look away, even if he'd wanted to.

"Alone," she said softly. "I'm alone."

His heart thumped as she closed her eyes, shook her head. Opened them with a look of longing that speared straight to the center of him. The same longing he felt on a daily basis.

"I don't want to be alone," she said, "but I've a feeling something I'm doing consciously or subconsciously when I meet men is sending the impression I'm not interested, even though I am. I'm not asking you to turn me into some Playboy bunny, I'm just asking you to help me learn how to be more…desirable. I want to know that when I do meet that right man—if I haven't already—that I'm confident and skilled enough for him to want me just as much."

His pulse picked up speed. Was she asking him to…?

"I'm assuming that, typically, you're the one who does the"—her cheeks turned red all over again, and she swallowed, looking at his throat rather than his face— "pleasuring. But if you don't mind—and you're up for it—I'd like to be the one to do that. Maybe you can tell me what I'm doing right. Or wrong. If, that is, it's okay with you…"

She finally met his gaze full on, and his breath caught at the hope he saw reflected in her eyes.

"So your wish," he managed in a voice that didn't sound like his own because he was still too surprised to think clearly, "is to…?"

"Yeah," she said softly. "My wish is to pleasure you. What do you think?"

Chapter Four

TARIQ COULD BARELY BREATHE.

She wanted to pleasure *him*. And she wasn't ordering, she was asking. For permission.

No one had asked his permission for anything in longer than he could remember. No one but her.

"Well?" she asked again. "What do you think?"

What did he think? He thought he had to be hallucinating. But he wasn't. He was in the human realm, and she was real. Real and so completely unexpected, he knew he needed to thank her. To show her just how much what she'd wished for—*how* she'd wished for it—meant to him.

"Mira," he said in a raspy voice. "Close your eyes."

She hesitated. Assessed. But when her lashes fluttered closed, he found himself touched again at how easily she trusted him.

He stepped close, wrapped one arm around her waist, drawing her flush up against him. She sucked in a breath but didn't open her eyes, and his pulse picked up speed because she felt so sinfully good. Smelled like heaven.

He shouldn't be enjoying this, not when his brothers were suffering, but he couldn't help himself. He pictured their destination. Gathered his powers. And when Mira felt them flying and gasped, he tightened his arm around her and whispered, "It's okay. Just hold on to me."

Her eyes popped open as soon as their feet met solid ground. And he watched with amusement as she pushed out of his arms, whipped around, and those mesmerizing eyes of hers grew wide all over again. "Where...? "How...?"

He smiled as she took in the swaying palms above, the turquoise water lapping the sandy beach, as the warm breeze blew her silky hair across her cheeks. He normally didn't transport humans when he crossed into their realm. It could be risky. Especially if they moved during flight. But after what Mira had done for him, he wanted to do something special for her.

"Where are we?" she asked.

"A little island in the Tahitian chain."

"No way."

"Close your eyes again, Mira."

This time she looked at him as if he'd grown a third eye, and the expression was so damn sexy, he laughed. "Trust me. No more flying. Not yet, anyway."

"I don't know what to expect around you," she said, but she closed her eyes once more.

"And I with you, Mira."

He lifted his hands, called up a simple spell. Then he turned a slow circle and spoke the ancient words.

When he was done, he said, "Okay, you can open your eyes again."

Her lashes fluttered, and she looked down, gasped to see herself dressed in a thin white cotton dress with cap sleeves, a gathered bodice with ties open at her cleavage, and a flouncy skirt. A dress that accentuated her breasts, her curves, even her skin tone. One that looked as if it had been made just for her—which it had.

"How did you do that?"

"Magic."

Her gaze darted past him to the hut he'd also conjured. "Wh-where did that come from?"

He would never tire of this woman's reactions. So unexpected. So...honest. He reached for her hand. "Come."

She let him draw her toward the hut with its thatched roof and bamboo porch. Gleaming hardwood floors spread beneath their bare feet. Gauzy curtains blew in the breeze as they stepped inside. A sitting area filled with pillowy white furnishings opened to a four-poster bed covered in dreamy white netting.

Mira tensed beside him. Perspiration coated the palm of her hand against his. And for the first time, unease settled in. Unease he never felt. Not with anyone. "Do you not like it?"

"No, I..." Her cheeks turned pink as she looked around. "It's beautiful. I just..."

She was nervous. Again, not the reaction he was used to.

He stepped in front of her, blocking her view of the bed, and brought his hands up to frame her face. "Before we start your wish, I have one request."

"What?"

"For you to trust me. In order to give pleasure, you must first experience it yourself. Has a man ever pleasured you, Mira?"

A flush rushed over her cheeks again, and she looked down at his chest covered in the thin T-shirt. "I told you I'm not a virgin."

"I didn't ask if you were a virgin. I asked if you had been pleasured. Thoroughly. Completely. By someone who knows how to focus solely on you."

Her blush deepened. "Um…"

Just the fact she had to think about how to answer told him no. At least not in the way he meant. He tilted her face up to his, forcing her to meet his gaze. "Then let me."

"That's not part of my wish," she whispered.

"No. It's mine."

Her eyes darkened. And in their depths he could see that his words relaxed her. Excited her. Aroused her. But she was still hesitant.

He needed to do something to ease her stress.

He slid his hands down to hers, clasped her fingers, and drew her around, walking backward out onto the porch again. She followed, her brows drawn low, questions swirling in her glittering eyes. "I thought—"

"There is no rush. Only time. Only this. Turn around."

Hesitation swirled in her eyes, but she turned to face the double chaise that appeared on the porch. "What's this for?"

"For you." He muttered words in his language, and the chaise dropped flat, the thick, plush cushion smoothing out before her. "Lie down on your stomach."

She looked over her shoulder with *are you for real?* eyes. Eyes that brought a smile to his lips and warmed the chill deep in his chest. "I promise, nothing will happen that you do not want to happen. Lie down and let me rub the tension from your shoulders."

She hesitated, then finally climbed onto the chaise and stretched out. He handed her a throw pillow, which she tucked under her head and wrapped her arms around. "You don't have to massage me."

"Shh," he said as he smoothed the back of her dress across her hamstrings. "Just enjoy."

She drew in a breath, let it out, relaxed into the cushion. He moved around the front of the chaise, knelt down, and brushed her hair to the side, then began kneading the muscles of her shoulders.

She exhaled a long breath, relaxed even further, and as he felt the tension begin to ease, he moved his hands over the back of her dress, down to her waist, and up again, never touching her bare skin, never pushing her farther than she wanted.

"Do you like that?" He trailed his hands up her spine, pressed fingers into the muscle as he worked his way down to her lower back.

"Too much. You have magic hands."

He moved to her ribs, slid his hands up her sides, felt her suck in a breath when his fingertips barely brushed the outsides of her breasts.

She was soft where a woman should be soft, firm where she should be firm, and as his gaze strayed to the hem of her dress, resting just above the backs of her knees, he had a wicked, erotic flash of dragging the skirt up with his teeth, of massaging the soft, rounded globes of her backside, of lifting her hips and sinking into her from behind.

Blood rushed to his cock, hardening him with only the thought. It had been years since he'd wanted a female as much as he wanted this one. He'd lost his desire when he'd lost his freedom. But with her, here, now, he felt as if he was regaining a tiny piece of himself.

She pushed on her hands, straightened her arms and looked up at him. His fingers stilled against her upper back as he gazed down at her face. The warm breeze ruffled her hair against her cheeks, and the way the sunlight fell across her skin, she almost sparkled. Want and need and desire swirled in her eyes. The combination left him hard and achy. And though he knew for her this was merely a wish, for him it was so much more.

"Roll over," he said in a raspy voice.

Her gaze held his, then slowly she complied and rolled onto her back.

Light hair fanned out beneath her. Her breasts pressed against the thin cotton of her dress, her nipples visibly hardening in the slight breeze. He swallowed pushed to his feet, and moved around the chaise to sit at her side, his hip brushing hers, his gaze running down the length of her body. "Close your eyes again."

She breathed deep and did as he said. At her sides, her fingers grasped the edge of the cushion.

He started gently, running the tips of his fingers along her bare arms, down and back up again, watching the slight rise and fall of her chest as she breathed. Watching the muscles around her eyes tighten as he traced his way up to her throat, then back down, moving over her dress to her legs, then all the way to her feet and back. As his hands stroked her body, she relaxed inch by inch once more, easing deeper into the cushion, turning herself over to him one wicked touch at a time.

His gaze slid to her lips as he stroked her—plump, pink, so perfectly made for kissing—then to her collarbone, over the Firebrand opal at her chest, just like the one he wore but which she couldn't see in this realm, then finally down to the front ties of her dress, hanging against her creamy cleavage.

He wanted to know what she looked like beneath that dress he'd conjured. What she felt like, her skin against his. When he brushed his fingers against the base of her neck then lower, stopping on the ties and pulling until her bodice loosened, she sucked in a breath and held it but didn't push him away.

Her breaths quickened. She wasn't wearing a bra, and he watched in rapt attention as her lush, firm breasts were slowly revealed to him, one agonizing inch at a time.

He went slow. Gave her every opportunity to stop him. But she didn't. And by Allah, she was beautiful. Dusky pink areolas, so tantalizing he wanted to lower his head and draw each one into his mouth. Firm, high breasts he knew would fit perfectly in his hands. He had an overwhelming urge to rip the dress from her skin, to part her thighs and press inside her until they both cried out in ecstasy. But more than that, he wanted her to want him. As much as he suddenly wanted her.

He leaned forward, marveled at the way her body trembled when he pressed his lips against her collarbone. When he kissed the soft skin of her throat and trailed his mouth up to breathe hot against her earlobe.

"Tell me what you want, Mira. I'm yours to command." Her skin was silky soft, so damn sweet against his tongue. "Yours to use in any way you want. This is all about you."

Slowly, hesitantly, Mira's fingers slid into his hair, and she moaned as she tipped her head to the side, granting him access, showing him the first sign that yes, she wanted this too.

Desire bunched in his stomach, shot straight into his groin. He licked the tender column of her neck, latched on, and suckled.

She moaned when he found an extra sensitive spot. And, drawing one leg up, she pressed her naked breasts against his bare chest, rubbing herself against him in a way that was so sinfully erotic, he didn't know how much longer he could last.

"Tell me, Mira," he whispered.

"I—I want you to kiss me," she whispered.

Yes. Finally. "Where?"

"My—my throat."

Disappointment flowed that it wasn't her mouth, but he moved to the other side, breathed hot against her skin until she shuddered, then closed his lips around the column of her throat once more. She'd beg for his mouth on hers later. He'd make sure of it.

"Where else?" he asked against her skin.

"My ear." He trailed his lips up to her lobe, felt her shudder beneath him, loved the way her naked breasts pressed into his chest.

"My collarbone," she added before he was done. One corner of his lips curled at her enthusiasm, and he answered by licking the spot, swirling his tongue around a mole, then sliding lower to trace his tongue along the very top of her cleavage.

Heat gathered all along her skin, penetrated his and amped his desire to a full-blown inferno. "Where else?"

"My...my breasts."

He breathed hot against her right nipple. She trembled, moaned, arched her back, and closed her eyes, and as her breast came closer to his mouth, he groaned himself, then licked at the tip and finally drew her into his mouth.

"Oh God," she muttered. Her updrawn knee pressed against his side. The hem of her dress fell to her hip, exposing her long, toned thigh, dragging his attention from what he was doing.

He wanted his mouth there. Wanted to brush her skin from hip to mound. To trace the line of her sex with his tongue and stroke her deeply until she came in his mouth.

His heart beat fast and hard as he moved to her other breast, as her fingers tightened in his hair, as she arched and offered more of her luscious body to him. Her nipple hardened in his mouth, and she groaned in pure pleasure. He answered by circling the tip with his tongue and asking, "What else?"

"Touch me," she said. "I want you to touch me."

"Where?" He scraped his teeth across her nipple ever so slightly. "Tell me where."

"Oh…" Her whole body shook. She lifted her hips, lowered them. Aching, he knew, for his touch between her thighs. And he wanted to give it to her. That and so much more.

"Tell me, Mira." He sucked harder on her breast, drew a long, shuddering groan from her throat.

How on earth did this woman think she was not desirable? Her reactions alone had him lingering on the edge of control. There was passion inside her long denied and dying to be set free. A passion he was bound to corrupt with his wicked, lascivious ways.

His arousal began to dim, but he forced the thought away. Today was not about guilt. It was about pleasure. About making her feel good. The corruption…what it would do to her…what it would do to him…he'd worry about that later.

He brushed his fingertips across her updrawn knee and licked her nipple again. "Tell me, Mira. Should I touch you here?"

Her knee fell open. "Yes. God, yes."

He skimmed his fingers up her thigh, to the hem of her gown resting against her hip, just barely covering her sex, and breathed heavily against her naked breast as he looked down her body. "Here?"

"Yes, yes."

"Tell me," he whispered, feathering his touch along her inner thigh. "Tell me where."

She groaned in frustration, lifted her leg higher, and as she did, her dress fell against her mound. He drew in a breath as her white, cotton panties came into view. Even through the thin fabric he could tell she was swollen. Hot. Wet. And he groaned himself because now he knew for sure she wanted him. Wanted him with the same burning desire that was consuming him.

He looked back at her face. Her eyes were tightly closed, but her lips parted in pleasure as he traced his fingers down her inner thigh, stopped short of touching her overheated flesh, then back up again. "Tell me, Mira."

"I want you to touch me between my legs," she managed, a flush rushing over her cheeks with her words. "I want you to touch me everywhere. Anywhere." She lifted her hips closer to his hand. "I want you to make me come. Right now."

Yes, yes. Finally, yes.

Chapter Five

Mira barely believed the words spilling from her mouth.

But she didn't stop them. She was too swept up in some all-consuming desire she couldn't remember feeling before. Not for her ex-boyfriends. Not even for Devin.

It had to be the magical effects of the opal. That was the only thing that made sense. The heat from the stone burned against her chest, warming her skin. But she really didn't care how or why it was happening. All she could focus on was the sinfully erotic way Tariq's fingers were finally—*finally*—skimming her sex, sliding beneath her panties and into her wetness, then back up again to circle her clit and drag a moan from her throat.

She wanted to pry open her eyes, to see if he was watching her reaction, but she was almost afraid to look. Because if she didn't see desire in his eyes…if this was only duty…

The heat began to dim, the arousal dampen. He'd said he wanted her, but that could just be a line. Like the guy who pretended to have a good time on a first date, promised to call, and then never did.

This is not a date.

"Stay with me, Mira." Tariq's husky voice cut through her musings, pulled her back from the edge. "Lift up."

Eyes clenched tightly closed, she lifted her hips. Sucked in a breath as he dragged her panties down her thighs.

"Open your eyes and look at me, Mira. Look at me pleasuring you."

The erotic vision his words conjured sent heat careening through her veins once more, and she blinked in the sunshine and looked down her body, only to experience that rush of heat all over again when his fingers brushed her sex.

Lust darkened his eyes. Sweat glistened on his brow. And the way he was watching her—as if he wanted to taste her right where he was touching her—made her whole body tremble.

He palmed her breast with one hand, slid one finger of his other hand lower, inside, and she tightened around him as he knelt on the ground between her legs, as he slid his finger out, then back in deeper, as the warmth of his breath rushed over her clit.

"Do you want me to taste you, Mira? Do you want my mouth here?"

He nuzzled her sex, and she was so caught up in the lust, she couldn't look away even if she wanted to. She pushed up to her elbows, marveled at his dark head between her thighs, tightened around his fingers as he pressed back in with two. "Yes. Yes, I want that."

He lowered his head, laved his tongue along her clit, circled and swirled as he thrust in and out with his fingers, drawing her closer to oblivion. She groaned, dropped her head back, lifted her hips so he could stroke her deeper, so he could taste more of her. His fingers were thick, his tongue wet and so damn salacious flicking her most sensitive spot. Her climax raced closer. She wanted to delay it, wanted to prolong the pleasure but knew she wouldn't be able to. This whole day was more erotic than anything she'd experienced in her whole life.

"Come for me, Mira. Come in my mouth. Let me taste your release."

Electricity gathered in her pelvis and exploded in a burst of lightning, lancing through her limbs to steal her breath. Every muscle in her body spasmed as the orgasm hit. Her elbows went out from under her. White-hot ecstasy consumed every part of her.

Her back landed against the chaise. She spiraled through an abyss of sensations, then slowly sound returned, followed by the warmth of the sun against her skin, the brush of the warm breeze, the feel of Tariq, whispering hot words against her sex she didn't understand. He smoothed his fingers through her wetness, bringing her down slowly, pressing his lips to her hip, her lower belly, her breasts all over again.

Her chest rose and fell as she tried to suck air. Stars fired off behind her closed eyelids. She blinked several times, finally pulled her eyes open, and stared up at the thatched roof above.

Tariq moved up her body and into her line of sight. She looked into his dark eyes, saw satisfaction and heat. A heat that reignited a burning passion she thought he'd quenched.

She lifted her hand, brushed it across his rough cheek and, before she thought better of it, lifted and pressed her mouth to his.

This time, he drew in a surprised breath, and she wondered if she wasn't supposed to kiss him, if it was against the rules. Then he opened for her, groaned into her mouth, and whatever worry she'd had fled. He wrapped his arms around her, pressed his body into hers and stroked her tongue deeply, roughly, as if he'd been wanting to kiss her from the start. As if he couldn't get enough and didn't want to let her go.

Her fingers rushed up into his hair, fisted. Her mouth turned greedy against his. She opened her legs, felt his erection press against her already overheated sex, and couldn't wait to feel him inside her.

That—what he'd done for her...the way he'd pleasured her—had been amazing. No, not amazing, electric, incredible, like nothing she'd ever experienced. He knew exactly where to touch a woman and what to say to make her come apart. But it wasn't enough. She wanted more. She wanted all of him.

"Tariq..." She kissed him deeper, changed the angle of the kiss, lifted her hips to show him what she wanted. He answered by pushing up on his hands, rubbing his very aroused erection between her legs, making her moan with the promise of ecstasy all over again.

But before she could find a way to free him of his pants, he broke the kiss and stared down at her, his chest heaving.

His face was flushed with desire, his lips swollen from her mouth, his eyes as dark as she'd ever seen them. She knew he wanted her. She could *feel* that want swelling against her sex. But there was something else in his gaze, something that stopped her from ripping his clothes off and having him.

"*Hayaati*... I can't. Not like this."

She didn't know what he was talking about. Didn't know what that word meant, but she loved the sound of it falling from his lips. Loved the way he was looking at her, as if he couldn't control his desire. As if she was dragging him to the edge as he'd done to her. "Tariq—"

"Did I pleasure you?" He cut her off so quickly, she faltered.

"Yes. *Yes*," she managed, trying to ignore the look. Trying to ignore the shot of worry it sent spearing into her chest. He'd pleasured her more thoroughly than anyone ever had. She lifted her hips again, tried to get him to move against her. Grew hot at the thought of returning the favor, of drawing him deep into her mouth and swirling her tongue over his cock until he exploded in her mouth. Then she wanted to ride him until they both came a second time. "I want to taste *you* now. I want to make you feel as good as I do."

He pushed back farther from her body. "That is not part of the deal."

Deal? *Deal*? Screw the deal. She didn't care that she'd never felt this kind of desire before, that she'd never needed to be the one giving the pleasure instead of the other way around. But it was all she could think about. All she could feel. She wanted to be the one to make *him* shudder in release, to feel *his* orgasm consume him, to know *she* was the one who'd given him pleasure as no one else had ever done.

She lifted her hips, grew more frustrated when he eased off her body. When he put space between them. He shook his head again, brought her fingers to his lips, kissed each one gently. "Not now, *hayaati*," he said as if he'd read her mind. "I'll never survive. You have to go back before it's too late."

She didn't know what he meant. She just knew she wanted him. But when he lifted her hand toward her chest, fear replaced worry. "Tariq, wait—"

"Rest. Recover. And when control has returned, think about what is right. Think about what is wrong. I do not want to see you destroyed by the opal. Your wish hasn't begun. There is still time to save yourself from my curse."

He pressed her fingers against the Firebrand opal before she could stop him, brushed them slightly over the stone, and then the world swirled around her, a vortex of smoke and fire and heat and flame. She felt herself flying, felt her hair tumbling across her face, the wind brushing her cheeks. And then everything darkened and cleared, and she looked around to find herself lying on the couch in the middle of her apartment.

She gasped, sat up. She was wearing the same jeans and T-shirt she'd been wearing before, but somehow she knew everything she'd experienced had been real. Knew she hadn't imagined what had happened, because her breasts still tingled from Tariq's kisses, her sex was still wet from his mouth, and the desire she'd felt was still zinging through her nerves, making her want with a blinding fierceness.

She stood on shaky legs, checked the kitchen, her office, the bedroom. But he was nowhere to be found. Disappointment rushed in on a wave, consumed her from the inside out.

Sitting on the edge of the bed, she tried to make sense of what had just happened. He didn't want to see her consumed by the opal? What did that mean? Her fingers grazed the chain, circled around to the back of her neck. And as her fingertips brushed the clasp, it opened as if on cue. The necklace landed in her lap with a soft thud.

Surprise registered. The shop owner had said she wouldn't be able to take off the necklace until her wish was fulfilled. Was Tariq releasing her from her wish? Could he *do* that?

Then his last words registered. Words that sent a chill down her spine.

There is still time to save yourself from my curse.

Darkness surrounded Tariq. The cell was cold, the floor covered in a layer of dirt. As he slid to the ground, leaned his back against the frigid stone wall, and closed his eyes, he told himself he'd done the right thing. Leaving before he corrupted Mira's soul was the only choice he *could* have made.

It was one thing to corrupt the soul of a human who went looking for trouble. But Mira was different. If he tainted Mira's soul, he'd be no better than Zoraida. And even he wasn't willing to become like her. Not even for his own brothers.

He wasn't sure how long he slept, but when he awoke, he knew a visit from Zoraida was inevitable. She had to be pissed over what he'd done. She could see—through the opal he wore—into the human world and watched his targets. But he was willing to take the risk. Because for the first time, something besides his own suffering mattered.

Footsteps echoed outside his cell. He opened his eyes just as metal clanged against metal, and the cell door swung outward.

"You've a visitor," the guard barked.

The guard shoved a half-naked man into the cell. Long, dark hair covered his face. He tripped, started to go down, but Tariq lurched to his feet and caught him before he hit the floor. "Nasir?"

The cell door clanged shut again as Nasir lifted his bruised face toward Tariq and tried to smile. His bottom lip was split and bloodied, and he was missing a tooth. "You recognized me even with my makeover? Guess Zoraida's guards aren't doing a good enough job."

Carefully, Tariq lowered his brother to the floor. Disbelief and rage whipped through him. "What did she do to you?"

Nasir grimaced as he scooted back to lean against the wall. His skin was dirty and bruised, and he was thinner than Tariq remembered. As if he'd not only been beaten but starved as well. "Nothing I can't handle."

"How did she find you?" It was the first time Tariq had talked to his brother in nearly ten years. Not since the day he'd been captured by Zoraida's goons along the Jagged Coast and brought to this hellhole.

Nasir lifted a shoulder, dropped it. He shook his hair back from his face, a move he'd been doing since they were kids, and for the first time, Tariq saw a flicker of the warrior he knew his brother to be in the battered djinn at his side. "We got a request for help from the Wastelands. Ghuls were reportedly ravaging villages. My unit was moving through the Red Desert when we came across a small settlement, still smoking. They were lying in wait. Ghuls. Wreaking havoc. A battle resulted. I heard a scream, went looking. Came across an innocent about to be raped. I tried to help. Turned out she wasn't so innocent."

"Zoraida?"

Nasir nodded. "The Ghuls were hers. They jumped me before I even realized what was happening."

Nasir's explanation made perfect sense. His protective streak was legendary. He hated injustice, and when it involved a female, there was no keeping him sidelined. Not if he thought he could help. Tariq knew that protective streak was a result of guilt. The war between the tribes had been going on for hundreds of years, but Nasir had always been the pacifist in the family. The one who thought negotiations and treaties were the way to end wars, not battles. Their father disagreed. As prince, a military career was required, but being a general, commanding legions, had never been part of who Nasir was. Until, that was, his betrothed was killed.

She'd lived in a small coastal village. One that built ships for the kingdom. Ships used in the Gannahmian army. The attack came at night. On a holiday. When most inhabitants were home, asleep in their beds. The entire village was burned to the ground. Every resident killed. And Nasir, who was supposed to be visiting his love for the holiday and wasn't because he'd been called out on patrol, had never forgiven himself for not being there to protect her.

Tariq leaned back against the cold cement wall, rested his forearms on his updrawn knees. "And Ashur. How did she find him?"

"You know Ashur," Nasir said with a ghost of a smile. "Can't stand to be left out of the fold."

Tariq would have laughed, but the situation was anything but funny. As the youngest brother, Ashur did hate being left out. But he'd never willingly turn himself over to Zoraida. "How did she…?"

"She used me," Nasir said, all humor gone from his voice. "Said she was willing to make a deal. That she knew where to find you."

Shit.

"We didn't even know you were still alive," Nasir went on. "Father thought you'd perished on the Jagged Coast. We mourned you, Tariq. They held a funeral rite."

Tariq stared at the bars. So his family had already buried him. Ten years in this hell and they thought he'd died exploring some stupid coast in their kingdom's name. No wonder no one had ever searched for him.

He looked to his brother as the thread of hope he'd been hanging onto since being brought here solidified. "Surely Father's looking for you and Ashur now."

"I'm sure he is," Nasir said on a sigh. "But he won't find us. Ashur didn't tell anyone where he was meeting Zoraida. She warned him to keep it secret. She's good at disguises, as you know. Ashur didn't suspect a thing either. Until it was too late, that is."

Tariq looked back ahead as that thread snapped. He thought of the guards holding Ashur against the bars of his cell the last time he'd seen Zoraida. The way his brother had barely been able to stand. The way his eyes had been glazed and not focusing. "Where is she keeping you both?"

"In a cell. Not far from here."

"And how long have you been here?"

"I'm not sure. Weeks. Months. It all seems to roll together in my head. They brought Ashur to me a few days ago. But he..."

Tariq's head snapped around at the hesitation he heard in Nasir's words. "He what?"

Nasir rolled his head against the stones until he met Tariq's gaze. "He's not doing well, brother. They keep pulling him out. And when he returns, he's even more bloodied and bruised than before. He's not done anything to deserve the beatings. He barely even moves or talks. I've tried to get them to take me." The good corner of his mouth curled, just a touch, drawing Tariq's attention to Nasir's newly split lip. "Works every now and then. But they keep going after Ashur." Nasir's smile faded. "He's—"

Fury consumed Tariq all over again. "He's me."

Nasir lifted his head. "What?"

"Zoraida can't punish me because it would delay her ultimate goal, so she's taking it out on both of you. And she knows Ashur is weaker. So she's using him to get to me first."

Rage rippled through every muscle. She wouldn't stop at Ashur. She wouldn't stop until Tariq completely gave in.

He thought of Mira. Of the gift she'd given him. Of her wish. Of his backing away and warning her off that wish. Zoraida had seen what he'd done. The Firebrand opal granted her a bird's-eye view. And instead of taking her fury out on him, she was doing it to his brothers. Because she knew that would leave a bigger mark than any lash against his skin.

"I don't know how much more he can take," Nasir said softly. "And if all three of us die in here…"

Tariq clenched his jaw. This suddenly wasn't just about Mira's soul. If they all died, there'd be no heir left in their kingdom. Their father wouldn't be able to rule much longer. He'd been ready to pass rule to Tariq ten years ago, but Tariq had wanted one last exploration. One last bout of freedom up the Jagged Coast before he was mired in the duties of court. A selfish decision he now regretted.

"She can't win, brother," Nasir said into the silence. "If she destroys us, she'll turn her attention to Gannah. With the Ghuls under her command, her strength the way it is, and us not there to lead the army…"

Nasir's voice trailed off, but he didn't need to finish his thought for it to register with Tariq. If what his brother said was true—if Zoraida had aligned herself with the Ghuls—then it meant the war was heating up. With all three princes—generals in the Gannahmian army—dead and the king ailing, what confidence would their soldiers have? How long could Gannah realistically defend itself without a ruling monarchy?

Consequences of his actions swirled behind Tariq's eyes. Decisions he never should have made filled his thoughts and mixed with images of Mira on that Tahitian beach. And through it all, he knew Zoraida was smarter than he'd given her credit. Torture was one thing. Deciding between life and eternal death was something else altogether. Especially when you were the one forced to choose condemnation for one versus thousands.

"What are you going to do?" Nasir asked into the silence.

Tariq ground his teeth against the injustice building inside him. "The only thing I can do."

Chapter Six

M IRA WAS PISSED.
Not just at the way Tariq had left her but at his dire warning.

Curse? What curse? She dumped a laundry basket full of clean clothes on her couch as she stewed.

At first, she'd been horrified by his rejection of her. Then wigged out over his warning. But the longer she thought about it and the more time that passed, the angrier she became.

Screw him for making her stress and worry like this. Screw him for disappearing on her in the first place. There was no way her little "wish" was going to "destroy" her, as he wanted her to believe. That was a mile of bullshit she definitely wasn't buying.

This had nothing to do with a stupid curse. It had to do with him. Maybe he just wasn't interested in her. Her hand stilled on a shirt mid-fold as the thought hit. She probably wasn't as exotic as the women in his world. Definitely not as aggressive. What had she done during their last encounter? She'd lain there like a lump and let him have all the power. Wasn't her "wish" about taking charge of some of that power? Wasn't it *his* job to teach her how to do that?

She tossed the folded shirt in the basket, picked up a pair of capris as her temper spiked. Well, next time she wasn't going to sit back and be the docile wallflower he expected. And he wasn't scaring her off with his mindless threats. So what if he wasn't attracted to her? This was her wish, dammit, and she wasn't backing away from it or any challenge.

She finished folding the laundry, put it away, then went into her kitchen and opened a bottle of wine. As she stood at the patio window looking out at the city's sparkling lights and downed her first glass, she reminded herself that it didn't matter what Tariq thought of her personally. She wasn't interested in him. She was doing this for Devin. So that when it was over, she'd have the confidence to snag the only guy she truly wanted.

And she deserved him, dammit. She'd spent way too many years alone. She deserved to have a man fall at her feet.

She poured herself another glass of wine and took it and the bottle to the coffee table in her living room. As she sipped the cabernet, she forcibly relaxed her muscles, breathed deep, and eased onto the couch. To her right, a fire roared in the fireplace. From outside, city lights beat in to illuminate the room. Her confidence grew with every passing second, swirling with the anger still bubbling inside her, any fear or misgivings she'd had drifting to the wayside. She was in charge here, not Tariq. It was his duty to do what she wanted. It was his place to fulfill her wish.

She brushed her fingers across the Firebrand opal resting against her chest, sipped her wine again, and waited. A cloud of smoke filled her living room, followed by Tariq's muscular body, shoulder-length dark hair, and chiseled features.

Yeah, he was sexy as hell, but who cared? This was about her. She looked up at him, sipped her wine again. Waited.

His face was a mix of emotions she couldn't read. Not that she cared. He took a step toward her. "Mira—"

She pushed to her feet, set her glass on the coffee table, and crossed to him. "I don't want to hear you say anything but 'Yes, Mira.'"

She stopped in front of him, pressed a hand against his chest, and marveled at the corded muscle and heat beneath her palm. "And I don't care if you're attracted to me or not, Tariq. This isn't about you."

His eyes widened. Surprise registered in their dark depths. And a smug smile flitted across her mouth because yeah, she'd surprised herself too. And damn, but she liked this surge of power.

"Show me how you like to be kissed," she told him. When he hesitated, she added, "'Your wish, my command.' Remember?"

His gaze drifted to the Firebrand opal nestled in her cleavage, and her anger built because she sensed he was going to come up with some lame excuse as to why he couldn't go on. "You're bound to fulfill my wish, djinni. Kiss me now."

His dark gaze shot back to hers, narrowed—which only pissed her off more—then skipped past her and swept the room.

What was left of her patience snapped. She grasped his face, tugged it down to hers, and pressed her mouth to his.

He froze, his eyes open wide. She didn't let go, kissed his plump, masculine lips again, and pressed her body flush against his.

He was hot. Everywhere. Tingles erupted in her breasts, in her hips, anywhere they touched. Dark flashes of arousal rushed through her mind as his hands settled at her hips. She tightened her arms around his neck, tipped her head, slid the tip of her tongue along the seam of his lips, waiting, *hoping* he'd take the hint and open to her.

"Tariq, dammit," she said against his mouth. "Kiss me. Kiss me like I want right now."

For a moment, he didn't move, not a single muscle. And then a growl erupted from his chest. His arms closed around her with stunning force. He opened to her, slid his warm, wet tongue along hers, drawing out her desire and replacing it with a wicked need that consumed every inch of her body in a rush of flames.

Her muscles went lax. Her body thrummed with need. Her legs ached to slide around his hips.

She groaned as he walked her backward toward the couch, nearly cried out in ecstasy as he lowered her to the cushions. His kisses drove her mad, his tongue so slick, so firm, so delicious stroking her own. She wanted that tongue laving her breasts as it had before. Wanted to feel it slide along her sex until she came. Then she wanted it back in her mouth as she straddled his hips and lowered, taking him deep for the very first time.

Wicked, erotic images of the two of them tangled naked filled her mind. Him holding her head between his legs, forcing his cock into her mouth. Her on her knees, her ass in the air, his hand pushing her face into the floor as she struggled while he thrust into her from behind again and again and again. Him pinning her to the wall face-first, fucking her from behind, pulling her back against him and forcing her to look to the right toward another naked male body, this one hazy but clearly turned on, the face masked, the strong legs eating up the distance as he headed their way with a riding crop in his broad hand.

The last image jolted her out of the kiss. She pulled back, stared up at Tariq's flushed face. Tried to catch her breath.

Whoa. Wait. What the hell was that? The whole multiple partners/BDSM thing definitely wasn't something she'd ever fantasized about. She gave her head a swift shake, tried to clear the image from her mind. Only it didn't work. The images were still there, circling, flashing, growing darker and more perverse.

She shoved Tariq away, sat up, and rubbed both hands down her face, more shaken than she wanted to admit. That wasn't a turn-on for her. Neither was forced sex or pain. So why was she thinking of both now? Why couldn't she get those pictures out of her brain?

"Mira?" Tariq asked, concern in his voice. "Are you okay?"

"I—" She drew a deep breath. It didn't help. "I—can't breathe."

He moved off the couch and back a step. She pushed to her feet, stumbled by him. Stopped in the middle of the room and tried to suck back air. Her lungs felt three sizes too small. When he came up behind her and reached for her hand, she tried to push him away, but there was no strength in the shove.

"Breathe, *hayaati*," he whispered.

She squeezed her eyes tight. Shook her head again. "I—I can't get them to stop. The pictures won't go away."

"Ghuls," he growled.

She had no idea what that meant, but even as the images assaulted her all over again, she heard him muttering words in a foreign language. Words she didn't understand. Slowly, the images fled, leaving behind nothing but mist and fog. And before she could ask what he'd just done, her muscles went lax, and darkness spiraled in.

Mira blinked several times. She had no idea how long had passed or what had happened, but when she finally pulled her eyes all the way open, she found herself looking up at the dark, vaulted ceiling in her bedroom.

"There, *hayaati*," a male voice whispered—Tariq's voice. "Don't move too much just yet."

Something cool brushed across her forehead. She blinked several times again, realized she was lying on her bed. The bathroom door was ajar, letting in just enough light to illuminate the room. Shadows played over Tariq's face, but even with them, she could see the concern.

"Wh-what happened?"

"You were being influenced," he said with a shot of anger in his normally calm voice.

"Influenced?" That didn't make sense. By who? By what?

"I told you last time I was here that there are good and evil djinn. That some prey on those in your realm, force humans to do things they wouldn't otherwise do? They showed up because of me. I should have expected this."

As he spoke, Mira thought back to what he'd told her before, then to the way she'd demanded Tariq kiss her only a few moments ago. Embarrassment rushed through her, followed by the memory of those images. And the desire to be the center of each wicked, naughty, X-rated scene.

Her cheeks heated. She looked away from his face. But his finger tipping her chin back toward him stopped her.

"You are safe now, Mira. I banished them."

"Them?"

"There were two. Ghuls. The most perverse of all the tribes. I didn't sense them when I first appeared because you…distracted me." This time, it was his turn to blush. But the color faded from his cheeks before she could register anything other than surprise. "There's no telling how long they were here tormenting you. But they're gone now. You have nothing to worry about."

Nothing to worry about except him and this insane desire still rushing through her veins. Was that a result of the Ghuls? Of her? Of Tariq? And what would happen when he left? Would those things—those Ghuls—come back?

She swallowed hard, for the first time realizing she was dabbling in something way outside her expertise, then looked at his strong chest covered by the thin black T-shirt. Maybe he was right. Maybe she did need to rethink this whole wish thing. She was opening herself up to some pretty weird shit here.

But even as she debated, she knew she didn't want to go back on her wish. Her need for Tariq was still as strong as it had been before. And deep inside, she knew that had nothing to do with those Ghuls. She'd wanted him since the beach. No, since before that. Since she'd first seen him standing in her living room. Yes, that whole influencing thing was pretty freaking nuts, but the images were now gone, and those *things* weren't preying on her anymore. As long as Tariq stayed with her, she knew she'd be safe. He'd said they'd showed up because of him. When her wish was finished, those Ghuls wouldn't care about her anymore, would they?

The key was keeping Tariq with her. And finding a way to make him want her as much as she wanted him.

Unease rippled through her. The same unease she felt whenever she passed Devin in the halls at work or tried to come up with a reason to run into him after hours. This was what she wanted to change. This lack of self-confidence. She wanted to be desirable. Strong. Craved.

Except…yeah, that was easier said than done. And even though she'd wished for it, he didn't seem very eager to teach her.

She closed her eyes, rolled her head on the pillow as a lump grew in the center of her throat. Maybe she was just destined to be alone. Maybe love and marriage and the whole happily-ever-after thing wasn't in the cards for her.

"It's okay, Mira."

His hand brushing her shoulder brought her eyes open. She looked up at him. At his deeply tanned skin, at the scar above his left eyebrow she hadn't noticed before, at those dark, dark, haunting eyes. Eyes she wanted to lose herself in. Even if it was just temporary.

"Do you think I'm pretty?" she asked.

"What?"

"Are you attracted to me?"

Color tinged his cheeks once more as he moved back an inch. "I—"

She pushed up to sitting, brushed her hair back from her face. There was no sense going ahead with this if he wasn't at least a little attracted to her. She couldn't just use him as some so easily did. And if she didn't ask, she'd just drive herself nuts wondering. "Tariq, you said you wanted to be with me before. Do you still?"

"Mira—"

"Because here's the deal." She drew in a deep breath. Let it out slowly. Knew it was now or never. She could take a chance, go after what she wanted or…not. In her business dealings, she was a go-getter. In her personal life? Not so much. It was time to change that. "I'm not naïve. I've dated plenty of men, but I've never felt confident with them, and I think that's why I'm still single. I want to learn...how to touch without wondering if I'm doing it wrong. To experience desire without the fear of rejection. And I called *you* back because for some strange reason—even though you are djinn, which is totally out there for me to even say—I feel comfortable with you. I want *you* to be the one to teach me. If you're not attracted to me, though... If you're just going to run again or come up with excuses why I should 'think' more about what I want, then this isn't worth it to me. I'll take the Firebrand opal back to that shop and tell the shopkeeper my wish didn't work."

She stared at him. Waited for an answer. But he didn't say anything. His eyes were blank, his expression neutral. And in the silence, Mira's hopes and dreams crumbled at her feet.

She'd taken a chance. She'd gone after what she wanted. And in the end...it didn't matter.

She was right where she'd started out.

Alone.

Chapter Seven

Tariq stared at Mira as her words sank in, and his pulse picked up speed.

She was willing to give up her wish all because she had standards. She wanted him—he could see it in her eyes, read it in her words—but she wasn't going to force him. *She* was giving *him* an out, if he so chose.

Awe, admiration, and wonder swept through him once again. For a woman who was unlike any other he'd ever met.

All the resolve he'd come back here with, the intent to fulfill her wish, corrupt her soul as Zoraida wanted so he could move on and free at least one of his brothers, withered and died. How could he value one life over another?

Options raced through his mind as he stared at her. It was too late for him to free her from her wish. By calling him back, he was bound to her now until that wish was fulfilled. But…maybe there was a way to prolong it. Until, at least, he could come up with a better solution for all of them. Zoraida wouldn't kill his brothers so long as he was here. Not when she needed Mira's soul to strengthen her powers. And if he stayed with Mira, the witch couldn't send Ghuls to influence Mira's thoughts.

Staying took on a whole new appeal. Maybe they could just sit here and talk until he figured out what to do next.

"Tariq?"

Mira's soft voice jolted him out of his thoughts, and he brushed a finger down her cheek before he thought better of it. "In my language, the word for teacher is *mu'allim*."

"*Mu'allim*," she repeated, drawing the word out. "I like that. But you didn't answer my question."

Her skin was silky smooth, and so pale next to his hand. Captivating. "You are beautiful, *hayaati*. And yes, I am extremely attracted to you. So much so that I left before not because I wasn't interested, but because I knew if I didn't leave then, I wouldn't be able to stop touching you, stop tasting you. I knew I wouldn't be able to stop taking you."

Heat flared in her eyes. Heat and desire and need. A need he could sate, right here and now. If, that was, he planned to corrupt her, which he couldn't do anymore.

Keep talking. He had to keep talking so he didn't reach for her.

"So much so," he went on, thinking any words were better than none, "that the thought of you wanting to know how to please a man fills me with a jealous streak I've never experienced before. Djinn are not jealous creatures."

A slow smile spread across her face, one that turned her from beautiful to downright gorgeous. She eased up on her elbows, maneuvered to sitting, and pulled her legs out of the way. "Is that so?"

"Yes, *hayaati*, it is."

She moved before he even realized her intent. Pushed against his chest, sending him back onto the mattress. Then she leaned over him until her strawberry-blond hair fell around his face like a curtain. "I want to make you feel as good as you made me feel."

Holy Allah in heaven. No one had ever cared about pleasing him. In all the years he'd been Zoraida's pleasure slave, his assignments had only ever cared about their own desires. His weren't even an afterthought. "Mira—"

She brushed her lush lips against his throat. Tingles rushed through his body, speared straight into his cock. "Do you like to be kissed here?"

His resistance wavered as his eyes slid closed. "Um…"

"How about here?" She trailed her mouth up to his ear, laved her tongue across his lobe as he'd done to her.

Yes, yes. Allah, yes, he liked that. But he shouldn't. He shouldn't be letting her kiss him or touch him at all. He should be trying to distract her. Words. He needed to use words to get things back on track.

He slid his hands to her biceps, pushed gently. "Mira—"

She ignored the move, kissed his jaw, his chin, worked her way back up to his mouth instead. "And what about here?" Her index finger trailed across his lips. "Do you like to be kissed here as well?"

Desire rippled through his chest, spread lower to engulf him in flames. "Yes, *hayaati*," he whispered before he realized what he was saying. "By you, always there."

Her mouth closed over his, just as he wanted, just as he'd dreamed. And though he knew he shouldn't, he opened to her, stroked his tongue against hers, grew hot and achy at the need for her to touch him elsewhere. Everywhere.

With her it wasn't forced. With her it was natural. With her it was not duty, but pure, erotic bliss. A bliss he hadn't realized he'd missed until right now.

A ribbon of guilt wove through him. He thought of his brothers locked in their cells. Of Ashur being beaten. Of Nasir's split lip and malnourishment. Why had he complained about his imprisonment? Their torture was a thousand times worse than his. Especially now, when he was being kissed by the most amazing creature he'd ever met.

She skimmed a hand down his chest while he explored every corner of her lips, her mouth, her teeth and tongue. Her fingers tangled in his shirt as he cradled her face. She tugged the shirt up, breaking the kiss long enough to drag it over his head, then closed her lips over his once more.

She threw the cotton on the floor at her back. Smiled down with that sexy, heated, all-consuming look. And desire bunched in his stomach as he watched. Followed by a swift slap of reality.

Words weren't going to work anymore. She wanted him. As much as he wanted her. If he tried to stop things now, it would only result in her feeling rejected.

He never wanted to hurt her.

Indecision rippled through him. Power was something he'd been forced to relinquish long ago to Zoraida. But even with his assignments, he still maintained control. He gave them what they wished, but he did so at his leisure, tempted them in a way he knew would corrupt their souls just as Zoraida wanted. This time, though, he could give that control to Mira. If he played his cards right, he could give her what she wanted *and* protect her soul from Zoraida at the same time.

She slid down his body and pressed her lips to his chest before he'd even made up his mind. "I love how smooth your skin is here. I love how muscular you are."

He closed his eyes as she kissed his pecs, as she lowered and laved her tongue across his left nipple, then his right. Electricity arced through his body, shot into his groin, made him harder than he was sure he'd ever been.

"Do you like this?" she asked, trailing hot, wet kisses down his abdomen. "Do you like my mouth on you?"

Allah, did he. "*Hayaati*—"

She moved lower, pushed her fingers into the waistband of his jeans. Then tipped her gaze up so seductively, a wicked shot of desire made him lift his hips and rub his aching cock against her breasts. "I want to taste you, Tariq. I want to feel you harden against my tongue. Is that okay?"

Okay? *Okay*? She wanted to know if that was okay?

He ground his teeth against the raging need but couldn't stop himself from pressing up on his elbows so he could watch while she slid to the floor and maneuvered between his legs. Somehow, he found the strength to say, "I am yours to do with as you wish, Mira. Anything. Everything."

Confidence burned in her eyes. A confidence that hadn't been there before. She popped the button on his jeans. Slid the zipper over his erection. Looked up again with that sinful, sexy, seductive expression. "I want you to tell me what pleases you. Right now, I want to learn how to make you come."

Just her words was enough to make him do nearly that. His erection twitched as she pressed her hands inside his jeans, ran them down his hips, pulled the garment from his legs, and let it drop to the floor.

She sucked in a breath when his cock sprang up, hard and pulsing and hot. Then licked her lips as if in anticipation of a wicked taste. "Commando. I like that. Tell me what to do, *mu'allim*."

The word sounded dirty on her tongue. Nasty. Hotter than hell. His pulse grew faster.

This was about her, he reminded himself. About letting her have control, letting her take what she wanted. It wasn't about him.

"Touch me," he managed.

When her hand closed around his length, he nearly jumped. Her fingers were so dainty, her skin like silk. She moved her hand up, tightened at the head, then stroked him slowly.

"Do you like that?" she asked.

He nodded.

"Do you want more?" she said as she circled the head again, and tremors ran through his flesh. When he nodded once more, she added, "Tell me."

He was in so much trouble here. He pushed his hips against her hand, groaned as her fingers slid down his length. "Taste me, *hayaati*."

She smiled again, that Cheshire-cat grin he was growing to enjoy. And pleasure gathered in his groin as she leaned close, as her tongue flicked out to lick the tip, as the warm wetness of her mouth closed around his cock.

His eyes slid closed. He dropped his head back. Shuddered as she lowered and drew him deeper. Her tongue stroked the underside of his cock, her lips closed tight around his length. And when she suckled, he saw stars. He didn't have to show her what he liked; she instinctively knew. Her hand stroked the base while her lips and tongue drove him completely mad. Then she drew him so deep he brushed her throat. He groaned in pure ecstasy.

"Allah, Mira. Just like that. Deeper."

Her mouth was like nothing he'd ever felt. And the fact she was doing this for him, when she didn't need to be, only amped his arousal. Her free hand brushed his thigh while she suckled, moved to his lower belly. The touch sent shards of electricity racing along his nerve endings. His balls tightened, and pleasure zinged down his spine. And when she groaned around his cock, sending vibrations through every bit of his flesh, he knew he wouldn't be able to hold back much longer.

"Mira..." He threaded his fingers in her long hair, rubbed her skull as she continued to push him closer to the edge. Her free hand slid down his hip and brushed his inner thigh, then gently squeezed his balls.

"Mira—"

He tried to pull free of her mouth, but she clamped on tighter with her lips, sucked harder. And then it was too late. He couldn't do anything except shudder and groan as pleasure slammed into him and stole his breath.

The pressure eased around his cock. She continued to stroke him slowly as he came down the other side of the best orgasm of his life, her teasing tongue flicking the head, making him shudder all over again. When she finally let go, he blinked several times, looked up, and watched as she swallowed, then grinned with the wickedest of smiles.

"Did I do a good job? Did you like that?"

He answered by levering up off the bed, closing his arms around her, taking her down to the mattress, and kissing her flushed, swollen, insanely erotic lips.

She groaned as she opened to him, as she wrapped her arms around his back and eased her legs apart so he could sink against her body. He tasted himself and the wine she'd sipped earlier. And a hunger like nothing he'd tasted before.

Thought fled. Need consumed him. He pushed her shirt up, palmed her breast. Loved that she wasn't wearing a bra under the thin cotton T-shirt. She arched her back, kissed him harder. But she was wearing too many clothes. There wasn't nearly enough skin.

"Mira." He pulled back, dragged her torso off the bed, and stripped the shirt over her head, then threw it on the floor. "Need you naked."

She giggled, reached for him as soon as her shirt was gone, and brought her mouth back to his. "Yes," she whispered against his lips, lifting her hips as he pushed his hand into the waistband of her jeans and slid it around to cup her ass. "Naked."

He kissed her again and again, squeezed her ass, pressed his renewed erection against her mound. He wanted to draw out the foreplay, to make her writhe as she'd made him writhe, but all he could focus on was getting inside her. Finding out if she was as tight and wet as he knew she'd be.

He dragged his mouth from hers, kissed her ear, her throat, breathed hot against her breasts as he flipped the button on her jeans and dragged the denim from her legs.

She was as beautiful as he remembered. Pale, soft, her hips flared just right, her waist trim, her breasts the perfect size for his hands. For his mouth.

He closed his lips around her right breast, suckled the tip. Shuddered when her fingernails scraped his skull and she dropped her head back, arching toward him and groaning all over again.

"Have to be inside you, *hayaati*." He moved to her other breast.

"Yes," she whispered.

"Want to feel you come around me."

"Oh yes." She lifted her hips.

"I want you on your hands and knees, offering yourself to me."

She trembled, groaned, squeezed her knees against his sides. "Yes, yes, yes."

He was too far gone to think. To stop. To wonder why she was willing to do anything he wanted. He eased away, flipped her to her stomach. Brushed her hair to one side and pressed his lips to the nape of her neck.

She shuddered, moaned. Pulled her knees up under her and pushed up to her hands. And when she looked back over her shoulder with nothing but lust in her eyes, the last of his resistance broke.

He knelt on the bed behind her. Trailed his hand down her spine. She closed her eyes, pushed back against him. He wrapped an arm around her waist, pulled her upper body back flush with his. His cock pressed against the cleft of her ass as she gripped the wrist at her waist to balance herself. He kissed her ear, nipped at the lobe. Whispered, "Spread your knees."

She did as he asked, and he skimmed his free hand down her stomach, into her curls, then finally brushed his fingers across her sex.

He'd given lots of pleasure during his years in prison, but this was the first time giving pleasure brought pleasure to him. He felt every wicked burn of desire as he slid his fingers along her wetness, circled her clit, then dipped lower to press inside.

"You are so tight, *hayaati*," he whispered in her ear as he pushed in with one finger, felt her clamp on tight, then slid out again. She dropped her head back against his shoulder, moaned, and rocked her hips against his hand. "Do you like that? Do you like me fucking you like this?"

"Yes, yes. God, yes."

"Do you want more?"

She swallowed. Nodded. Gripped his wrist tighter at her waist.

"Tell me."

"I want all of you, Tariq. I want you inside me."

He closed his mouth over hers, kissed her deep, then let go. She fell to her hands on the mattress. He moved in closer, palmed her ass with one hand while he stroked her sex with the other. When she moaned and pressed back against him, he wrapped his hand around his cock and guided it toward her sex, stroking her with the tip until she shuddered.

Heaven. It was the only thought he had as he sank into her wetness. As he pulled out, then pushed in again. Her whole body tightened. She shifted back to meet his thrusts. Groaned again and again as their coupling picked up speed.

He felt himself slipping. Felt his control loosening. And knew—for the first time ever—what it was like to be on the other side. To be the one who was tempted, influenced, driven to do things he wouldn't otherwise do. A blinding desire to take her harder, to use her in any way he wanted overwhelmed him. To disregard her wants and needs in favor of his own. This was what he did to the humans he granted wishes. This was the way he corrupted. By giving them a taste of something erotic, then twisting it until that desire consumed them.

The realization slammed into him, stole the air from his lungs. He gasped, pushed away from Mira, tried to slow his racing pulse as he dropped back to sit on the side of her bed.

Mira turned, looked at him with half lust, half surprise. "Tariq? Is everything okay?"

No, everything was most definitely *not* okay. His chest was strung tight as a drum, his ears were ringing, and he was pretty sure those were spots firing off behind his eyes. Not to mention, every soul he'd ever corrupted was flashing in his brain. "I...I'll be fine. In a minute."

Mira scooted closer. Soft fingers brushed his bare thigh. "Did I do something wrong?"

"No, you didn't do anything. It was me. I—"

His words cut off when he looked at her—*really* looked at her—and saw her for the first time. So honest. So real. So unlike any other person he'd ever met. It was as if he could see her soul for what it was. And it wasn't tainted. It wasn't black. It was...pure.

"You what?"

"I..." His brow dropped low. "Who are you, Mira Dawson?"

A slow, winsome smile spread up her face. "I'm just a woman."

But she wasn't. She was more than that. For whatever reason, she was special.

He kissed her. Slowly. Gently. Unable to do anything but touch his mouth to hers. She groaned against his lips, slid onto his lap, and wrapped her arms around his shoulders.

He opened to her, didn't try to stop her when she pushed him to his back, when she levered herself over him. When her hand stroked his cock and she positioned it back at the entrance to her body.

"Mira," he whispered.

Slowly, she sank down, and they both groaned as he filled her. Arousal flushed her cheeks a warm pink. She rocked against him, pressed her hands to his chest. Never once looked away as she rode. And as his orgasm barreled close, he brushed the hair back from her face and knew, wherever he went, no matter how long he was chained to Zoraida, he would always remember this moment. Of finally being wanted. Not for what he could do but for who he was. Of finally doing the right thing in the sea of all the bad he'd ever done.

"Tariq…" Her rocking picked up speed. She grew tighter, hotter, wetter.

He sat up so he could taste the pleasure from her lips when it hit. "Yes, *hayaati*. Ride me. Take me. Come for me."

Her mouth dropped open. A long groan echoed from her chest. He captured it with his mouth, kissed her deep again and again as he lifted his hips, as he thrust deeper, as he tried to milk every inch of desire from her before it was over.

Electricity raced through each cell in his body while she rode the wave. And before he realized it was coming, his own orgasm slammed into him. Stole his breath. Made those stars he'd seen earlier explode in a mountain of fireworks. Everywhere. Until want and need and dreams and wishes all condensed into a hot, burning point of light that sucked up everything in one giant vortex of pleasure.

Mira collapsed against Tariq and tried to drag air into her lungs. His chest rose and fell with his own rapid breaths, and both their bodies were coated in a sheen of sweat. Sweat that felt way too good.

Pleasure still radiated everywhere—even in her fingers and toes—and she smiled as she remembered how easily she'd made him come with her mouth. How easily he'd made her come with his body.

"I…I hope I didn't hurt you."

Tariq's voice vibrated from his chest into her ear, and she pushed back, smiled down at him. Her heart turned over as she stared into his eyes. A reaction that both surprised and confused her. "No, you didn't hurt me. In fact, I think you might have fixed me."

He darted a look around the room, and the way his eyes changed from lazy to on guard brought a rush of worry that chilled her skin. Were those Ghuls back? Had he seen something?

He rolled her to her back, pushed up on his hand. A wave of disappointment washed over her as he slid from her body. "Don't say that. Not yet, *hayaati*."

She still didn't know what "hayaati" meant. She'd have to look that up. And she wasn't sure why he didn't want her to say he'd fixed her. But as he climbed off the bed and pulled on his jeans, the fear in his voice registered. Followed by an understanding that dawned bright in her mind.

If her wish was complete, their time together was over. He didn't want it to be over.

Warmth replaced the chill. She slid to the end of the bed, reached for his T-shirt from the floor before he could pull it on. "I didn't say I was done with you, Tariq." She tugged the shirt over her head, let it drop to her thighs. Loved how it smelled like him. "I said you *might have* fixed me. Not that you did."

He stopped. Looked back at her. Then a relieved smile spread across his face, just before he eased down and kissed her, pushing her to the mattress once more and driving her wild with his mouth. When he eased back, she saw approval in his dark eyes. "You are unlike any woman I have ever met."

She liked that. Liked it a lot, actually. She fingered his bicep. He was so muscular. Cut. *Hot.* "I think there's still lots more I need to learn. This was great and all, but I don't think I'll be done with you until I know I can pleasure you without you having to tell me what to do."

"That could take a while," he teased.

"Could take a long while." She smiled. "I'm thinking we might need another session right now."

One dark brow lifted. "Right now? Are you ready for that so soon?"

She brushed her hand down his spine and gripped his ass through his jeans. "I'm definitely ready for it. The question is, are you? You've already had two orgasms. You might need to gather your strength."

He chuckled. "I am djinn, *hayaati*. Can't you feel that I am ready?"

She did feel it. He was hard against her thigh already. Arousal tingled between her legs once more.

She lifted her head. Pressed her mouth to his. Mumbled, "You dressed way too quickly."

He chuckled again. Slanted his mouth over hers and kissed her deeper. She opened to him, drew his tongue into her mouth. Groaned at the slick, dark taste of him all over again. "I want you to stay with me tonight, Tariq. All night."

His eyes flashed in approval, and he pushed his hips against hers in a wicked way that made her downright crazy. "I'm yours. Anything you want. Everything. You only have to ask."

She smiled. Lifted to kiss him again. But as her lips met his, something changed. She felt it in the way he pulled back. Saw it in the surprise in his eyes. Smoke spiraled in the room. He looked down as it whipped in a tornado around his body.

"Tariq?" She pushed up from the mattress as he was lifted off her.

"It's all right, *hayaati*," he said in a calm voice. A too calm voice. "I'm being called back."

Called back? No, that wasn't part of her wish. "Tariq—"

"I will return, *hayaati*."

She reached out to him, but the smoke rose over his head, covering him from view before her fingers could reach his. And then it spun so fast, the force of the wind blew her hair back from her face.

In seconds, he was gone. Nothing to show he'd ever been there except for the thin blue T-shirt she was now wearing.

That and the ache between her legs. The one that only left her wanting more.

Chapter Eight

Footsteps echoed in the hallway. Several. Since being back in his cell, Tariq had finally managed to relax. Hours had passed with no visit, no explanation as to why he'd been called back. But he could guess.

He lifted his head just as the cell door swung open and Zoraida swept into the room, her royal blue gown swishing in the air behind her. Fury coated her features, her eyes blazing with a rage he'd never seen before. No sooner had he climbed to his feet than her arm connected with his jawbone in a blow that sent him staggering into the wall.

Pain shot through the left side of his face. His hands hit the stones behind him. Her magic had grown these last few years—thanks to him—and with it her strength as well. Pushing away from the wall, Tariq refused to rub at the pain, instead leveled his narrowed gaze on her, then the three guards close at her back.

He could take her, he didn't doubt that. But they had swords, and without his magic, he'd never get by all three without losing his life.

"You will not defy me," Zoraida growled. "*I* am your *sayyeda*. *You* are my slave. And you *will* do my bidding. Guard?" she called over shoulder.

A guard outside dragged a bloodied and beaten Nasir into the room. "Yes, mistress."

"Send him to Jahannam."

"No!" Tariq jerked forward. The Pits of Jahannam were fighting rings set up for the entertainment of Ghuls. Few condemned there survived its horrors, and those who did came out forever changed.

Zoraida's fist jammed into his jaw, sending him crashing into the rock wall again. "Stand down, djinni, or I will send your other brother there as well."

Blood ran across Tariq's tongue, trickled down his chin. Frantic, he looked for Nasir behind Zoraida as guards rushed in and grasped Tariq's arms so he couldn't lurch at her. They'd beaten his brother severely. Nasir's face was black and blue, and he was barely able to stand on his own two feet. "Nasir—!"

"Don't fight her," Nasir said in a weak voice as the guard dragged him out. "I'll be okay. Save Ashur. Find a way to save Ashur, Tariq. He won't last much longer."

Nasir's empty voice echoed from the passageway until he was gone. Rage whipped through Tariq as he turned his glare on Zoraida.

"You will not defy me, djinni. I am your *sayyeda*," she said again, as if saying it would make him submit.

But he wouldn't. Never willingly again. Fury and disbelief swirled through him, but he didn't answer. He was too busy plotting all the ways he would turn his vengeance on her when the time was right.

"The whip," she called over her shoulder, her icy gaze never leaving Tariq's face. As a guard handed her the weapon, she barked, "Secure him!"

The guards shoved Tariq face-first toward the stones, chained his wrists to the hooks mounted high in the wall.

He knew not to fight, knew it was useless. But he wouldn't give her the satisfaction of seeing him break.

"You *will* do my bidding," Zoraida repeated as she snapped the whip back, then brought the tip forward to slice into his skin.

Fire erupted across his back, pain so intense it stole his breath. His body jerked, and he slumped forward against the wall, gritting his teeth. To keep from crying out, he thought of Nasir. Of Ashur. Of his father and their kingdom. And of the retribution he would rain down on Zoraida and her Ghuls when he was free.

"No one controls my will except me," Zoraida said through clenched teeth, snapping the whip back again. "Do you understand?"

The whip cracked. Leather bit into his flesh. A red burn exploded all along his spine. He sagged against the cuffs as she pulled the whip back again and again, as the leather sliced open his skin and darkness beckoned from the shadows.

He lost track of the number of times he was hit. But as the leather bit into his skin, reality spread out before him like the river of blood pooling at his feet. She could make him feel pain as he'd never experienced, but she wouldn't kill him. She still needed him to corrupt Mira's soul. For whatever reason, her Ghuls couldn't do it. Which meant Mira was safe. At least for now.

His hazy mind drifted back to all the souls he'd corrupted for Zoraida. Most of the time, he'd succeeded in fulfilling his targets' wishes, but there were a few times he hadn't. When even he hadn't been enough for the women who'd summoned him. Those souls hadn't mattered to Zoraida. Yes, she'd punished him, but she'd just sent Tariq out on another mission when he'd failed. But something was different this time. Mira's soul was vitally important to Zoraida. And he was the key to getting it.

Who was she? Why was she so important? And was it possible she could somehow be instrumental to Zoraida's downfall?

His eyes drifted closed. He tried to push the pain to the back of his mind. Tried to think clearly. But the bite of leather, the burn of each lash was too much to ignore. And before long, darkness threatened.

You can't save them all. Nasir, Ashur…Mira. You'll have to choose. Them or her.

Sound drifted away. Darkness closed in. And then there was nothing but silence. Not even a choice.

Mira hadn't seen or heard from Tariq in three days. She'd tried to call him back with the opal, but he either wasn't listening or whoever controlled the stone wasn't letting him through.

The last thought circled loudly in her mind as she sat at her computer and skimmed her e-mail, searching for one from a professor she'd located online who supposedly knew all there was to know about djinn. She hadn't been able to focus on anything but Tariq this week, so she'd finally cashed in some vacation time. With nothing else to do but worry and stress over the way he'd left, she'd gone looking for more information on his race and had finally found Dr. Claire Sampson, a professor of folklore and history at the University of Florida.

They'd e-mailed back and forth several times. The woman had heard stories of djinn being trapped or bound by certain objects, and in her last e-mail had said she'd do some more research to see where historical records showed those objects turning up. Just the fact she hadn't thought Mira was a complete kook when she'd started peppering the woman with questions was a major plus as far as Mira could see.

Silently rejoicing when she saw the subject line: RESEARCH, she hit open and started reading.

Mira—

Historical documents show that djinn can be bound only by a powerful master—a sorcerer, a priestess, a wizard, etc.—someone who has studied a grimoire, or magical textbook, and knows how to bind a djinni without negative repercussions. They're not bound to the object itself but to the energy within an object, which means they can be bound to anything, really, but more often than not, they're bound to magical objects like talismans and amulets...rarely lamps like you see in popular culture. King Solomon reportedly used a magical ring made of copper and iron with a fire opal set in the metal to command the djinn he enslaved. (Djinn are severely weakened and drained of magical abilities in the presence of iron.)

I'm still looking into ways to break a bond between slave and master—I don't know if it can be done, but if it can, all parties—slave, master, exorcist—have to be in the same realm, and ideally, in the same area. A colleague recently mentioned the Key of Solomon—a grimoire King Solomon reportedly wrote containing all his secrets regarding djinn. When I know more I'll pass it on to you. In the meantime...

I've read numerous accounts of human interactions with djinn, but I've never heard of a djinni wanting to stay with a human by choice. Yes, they can mate with them, but it's rare. And they aren't known to fall in love with humans...at least not often. They're tricky creatures, even when bound to an object. Be careful you're not reading something into the situation that isn't there. This isn't just about your peace of mind; it's about your safety as well. There are powerful entities out there—magical entities—that prey on djinn and use them to get what they want. Sometimes that's as simple as wealth, but usually it's something more nefarious. Like the destruction of a human soul. I'll keep looking, but in the meantime, my advice would be this: do NOT do anything to summon this djinn back. If he's gone, let him stay gone forever and consider yourself lucky you escaped unscathed.

—*Claire*

Mira sat back from the screen as the professor's last sentence sank in. Let him go? The woman wanted her to pretend as if the last week hadn't happened? Mira couldn't do that. And she didn't believe *all* djinn were bad. They had free will, just as humans did—or so her research said. But more importantly, her heart told her Tariq wasn't bad. He couldn't be. Not after the way he'd protected her from those Ghuls and the way he'd tried to get her to change her mind about her wish in the first place.

Slowly, Mira's mind circled around to her wish. And spun right back to Dr. Sampson's e-mail.

There are powerful entities out there that prey on djinn and use them to get what they want...like the destruction of a human soul.

Dread welled inside her. Was that why Tariq had come to her? Because some master wanted her soul? That made no sense.

But then she remembered the shopkeeper's warning when she'd gone looking for the Firebrand opal: *Choosing to wear the opal opens yourself to consequences you may not yet foresee. Be sure it is a risk you are willing to take.*

She lifted her fingers, ran them against the stone at her chest as she had numerous times since Tariq had left her in a puff of black smoke. Was that what he'd been trying to warn her about? Was that why he hadn't made love to her on that Tahitian beach and had sent her back, telling her to think long and hard about what she really wanted?

She thought of the way he'd acted when he'd returned. Reserved. Unsure. How she'd point blank asked him if he wanted her or not, and how he'd finally admitted that he did. But he hadn't seemed happy about that knowledge. In fact, he'd seemed…saddened by it.

Then she remembered the way she'd teased him after they'd made love, how she'd told him maybe he'd fixed her. And how panicked he'd looked at the thought.

Reality chilled a space in her chest. He'd known. From the very first. He'd known that by fulfilling her wish, he was damning her soul in some way. He'd tried to stop her wish, and when that hadn't worked, he'd tried to prolong it. And he'd been dragged back to wherever he was now by whomever was controlling him because of that attempt.

Fear surged through her, rippled through her limbs, stole her breath. But was quickly replaced by a determination that spread a calm along every quivering nerve ending. There was still time. Nothing had been decided yet. Nothing that couldn't be changed. And because nothing was final, she knew Tariq would be back. He hadn't completed whatever task his master had sent him here to do. She had one last chance to make all of this right.

She hit reply on the e-mail and furiously typed her response. And her remaining questions. When she was done, she clicked send, sat back and prayed Dr. Claire Sampson could help her. Because suddenly, her wish—finding a way to make herself more desirable to Devin—didn't matter. All that mattered was uncovering a way to free Tariq from his bonds. And maybe, if she was lucky, save her own soul in the process.

※

Exhaustion weighed heavy on Tariq as he crossed the portal into the human world. His wounds had healed over, but they were still tender. And he was weaker than he should be from the beating. But instead of giving him time to fully recuperate, Zoraida was antsy for him to finish his assignment.

A poof of black smoke encircled him; then his feet hit solid ground. Through the dissipating haze, Mira's excited voice drifted toward his ears, but he couldn't tell what she was saying. Then he didn't care. Her body hit his, nearly knocking him off his feet, her arms wrapped around his neck, and then her lips… her sweet and succulent lips…were closing over his, parting to let him in, dragging him toward a temptation he didn't want to give in to. Not until he figured out how he could protect both her and his brothers…and bring Zoraida down for good.

Impossible. You have to make a choice. Her or your brothers. You can't save them all.

She pulled back from his mouth, looked up with hazel eyes that sparkled like diamonds. "I wasn't sure when I'd see you again. I'm so glad you came back to me. I missed you, Tariq."

Warmth spread through his chest. And words choked in his throat.

How could he choose between her and his brothers? He loved his brothers, felt responsible for what had happened to them, but Mira... She'd truly missed him. He could see it in her eyes. And not just the wish he could grant her or the fact he was a prince and a warrior. But she'd missed *him*, the person.

"Mira—"

She grasped his hands, pulled him forward as she stepped back toward a U-shaped couch. "Come here."

He stumbled, the heat of her hands warming his palms, sending electrical vibrations all along his nerve endings. He looked around as she tugged him down to the couch, as she snuggled close to him on the soft leather, as he closed his arms around her and her head rested against his chest.

Teak furnishings, floor-to-ceiling cabinets, a galley kitchen, high-tech electronics, and ahead, a raised bed. This wasn't her house. This wasn't anywhere he recognized. Water lapped somewhere close. Water that indicated...

"Mira," he said quickly, excitement building inside him. "Are we on the water?"

"Yes," she said against him. "On my boss's boat. He let me borrow it. I haven't been able to focus since you left, so I took the rest of my vacation."

They were on a boat. The tension in his muscles began to relax, and relief spiraled through his whole body. Zoraida couldn't hear them on a boat. Water interfered with her ability to see through the opal he was wearing and monitor what he was doing. It was a loophole she hated. And he was forbidden from taking any mark on a boat, into water period. But he hadn't brought Mira here. She'd brought him.

A slow smile twined its way across his mouth, and he tipped her chin up to his so he could see those mesmerizing eyes again. "You, *hayaati*, are amazing."

"Why?"

"Because you are."

He brushed his fingers through her long hair, lowered his mouth to hers, and kissed her the way he'd restrained himself from kissing her earlier. Her lips parted easily, and he stroked his tongue against hers, tasted her sweetness, her goodness, her wetness and need. Reveled in just being close to her. Even if he knew it could never last. For the first time in ten years, Zoraida couldn't see him. She couldn't hear him. She couldn't touch him. Not so long as they were on this boat. And before he had to decide what to do next, he planned to show Mira just what her gift meant to him. Even if she didn't know it was a gift in the first place.

He pushed her down to the cushions, braced his hands on the leather as he climbed over her and changed the angle of the kiss, as he tasted her deeper, as her arms came around him and she pulled him close. His chest brushed hers; her legs opened to make room for him. And when she groaned, when her fingers dug into his shoulders and she pulled him even closer, all the worry rushed away.

He'd never been in love before. Not even with a female from his world. He'd never had time. And then he'd been imprisoned by Zoraida, and love had been the furthest thing from his mind.

But here he was. With a female. A *human* female. One who gave and gave and didn't ask for anything in return. One who had *missed* him, even knowing what he really was.

"Mira—"

She lifted her knees on each side of his, drawing him toward her heat, kissing him again and again and cutting off his words. Then she pressed her full, luscious breasts against his chest until all he could think about was stripping her naked and showing her with his hands and mouth and body how much she meant to him.

"Mira—"

"Don't talk, Tariq," she whispered, kissing his lips, his nose, his cheeks. "Just kiss me again. God, I missed you."

They were words no one ever said. Words he'd longed to hear. Words that touched a part of him he'd closed off from the world. He sank into her mouth, pushed his erection against her mound, groaned at the contact, just as she did. But when her hands traveled down his back and her fingers pressed into his still-healing wounds, he jerked back from her mouth and ground his teeth against the shot of pain igniting like fire in his flesh.

"What's wrong?" she asked. "What happened?"

"Nothing," he managed, wincing as the burn slowly faded. "I'm...fine."

"You're not fine," Mira said, pushing him up and climbing onto her knees on the couch. "You're hurt. Turn around."

"Mira—"

"Turn around, Tariq."

One glance at her determined features told him she wouldn't drop this demand until he complied. And though he didn't want her to see the lash marks, he knew they weren't going to finish what they'd started until he appeased her.

He turned his back toward her.

"Take off your shirt," she said.

He unbuttoned the shirt he wore, shrugged out of the short sleeves, and let the rayon fabric fall around his waist.

Mira gasped.

He looked over his shoulder. Couldn't see anything but Mira's shocked eyes and her hand covering her mouth. "That doesn't sound encouraging, *hayaati*. You're supposed to say, 'It's not that bad.'"

Her heartsick gaze shot to him. But there was no humor in her voice when she dropped her hand and said, "Who did this to you?"

He looked away, at the bed across the salon he still wanted to tumble across with her. But that clearly wasn't going to happen until they talked. And he had a feeling once they did and she learned the truth, tumbling anywhere with him was going to be out of the question.

You have to choose. Her or your brothers.

"Tariq," Mira said again when he didn't answer. "Who did this to you?"

"Zoraida."

"Who's that?"

"My master."

Mira sank back to sit on her heel. "The person who controls you. The one who sent you here to me."

He tugged his shirt back on, turned to face her. Knew that she had to be wondering how and why and what it all meant. Knew, when he looked into those glittering hazel eyes, that he was going to tell her. "A sorceress. One who used magic to break down the walls between our worlds. One who"—and here was where it got sticky— "tricked me."

"How?" Mira asked, tucking her feet up under her as he pushed to his and started pacing.

Moving at least gave him something to do besides wonder what she was thinking. But the salon was so small, there was very little room to move. He raked a hand through his hair. "I'm the eldest of three sons. My father, the king—"

"Wait. Your father's a king?" Shock ran across Mira's face, slowing his feet. "That makes you a—"

"Prince. Yeah. Or at least, I was one. Once." He shook off the thought, resumed pacing. The open shirt flapped against his stomach. "War is constant in our realm. The tribes are always fighting, seeking power. My brothers and I were all soldiers in the army, but as the eldest, it was my duty to assume the throne. I didn't really want it. I liked being with the troops more than I did commanding them. But our father hasn't been the same since he was injured in battle several years ago, and it was time. I was selfish, though. I asked for one last mission. He agreed—reluctantly—and sent me and a handful of soldiers up the Jagged Coast. Several villages had been ransacked by Ghuls. We were supposed to eradicate the Ghuls, restore order, and return me to my throne a hero."

"What happened?" Mira asked quietly.

"Zoraida fooled me." He thought back to how naïve he'd been. How young and easily coerced. How stupid. "She was in a bar in one of the first villages we freed. The soldiers were celebrating. There were females from the village there that night. Lots of females, ready to show their appreciation for what we'd done. She was one of them."

"She seduced you."

Was that jealousy in her voice? Tariq couldn't tell. And he couldn't dwell on it, because in a minute, it wouldn't matter.

"She used magic over me," he said. "I didn't know it at the time, but I realized it as soon as it was over. When the magic wore off, I saw her as she truly is. Not beautiful and magnetic as I'd envisioned her to be, but frigid and deadly. The raids on the villages—they were all traps. She commands the Ghuls, has since she came into our realm, only we didn't know. She knew my father would send one of his sons to oversee the battles, and she needed a royal djinn from the strongest tribe to complete her goal: to become the strongest magical being in all of the realms."

"What happened next?" Mira asked in a quiet voice.

"She bound me to the Firebrand opal, made me her slave. Sent me out into the human world to…" He swallowed, glanced down at the floor because he couldn't meet Mira's eyes. Not this time. "…corrupt souls to fuel her power."

When Mira didn't say anything, he resumed pacing. Okay, so now she knew the truth about the whole wish fulfillment thing and why he was here with her now. And she hated him, just as he'd known she would. But that space in his chest chilled faster than he expected, and what had once been warm and full of life earlier turned cold as a blackened cinder.

He thanked his luck they were on a boat. That he was blocking her only escape. That she couldn't get away, at least not yet. He needed her to hear the rest, even if she didn't want to.

"I've been her slave for ten years. I've done what she commanded because I was always looking for a way to freedom. But just before I met you, I realized there isn't one."

She still didn't speak, and he still couldn't look at her. He just needed to get it all out. "I went on a hunger strike. I figured starving myself was the easiest way to end my life and her quest for power. But she manipulated me again. Somehow, she captured both of my brothers, and she brought them to me. She'd beaten them. Threatened their lives. They'd been looking for me. It wasn't their fault they'd been captured. It was mine."

He drew a deep breath, let it out. Finally stopped pacing and faced her, because she deserved to see his eyes. "I knew you were different, right from the start, Mira. I knew as soon as I took you to that island that this time I couldn't go through with my task. I couldn't corrupt your soul for Zoraida." He pressed his fingers against his temple. "I know it means nothing to you, but I've been racking my brain, trying to come up with a solution. Trying to find a way to break the Firebrand opal's hold on you. To free you from this nightmare I've sucked you into. I want you to know that I'm not giving up. That no matter what, I'll find a way to make sure Zoraida doesn't get your soul."

Holy Allah. He'd made his choice. He hadn't realized it until the words were out of his mouth, but now he didn't want to take them back. He chose her. He loved his brothers, but he couldn't condemn one soul just to save another. And even if Mira hated him for all eternity, that didn't change anything. She didn't deserve this any more than he did. Any more than his brothers' did. She didn't deserve anything but happiness.

He was so caught up in his thoughts, he didn't see her push off the couch. Didn't hear her cross the floor. Didn't even know she was next to him until her soft voice said, "I love you, Tariq."

His head came up. His eyes widened. "You...*what*?"

A gentle smiled curled her kiss-me mouth. "I love you."

Disbelief rushed all through him. "Mira, I'm a monster. I came here with the intention of—"

"Damning my soul. Yes, I got that." She stepped closer, rested her palms against his bare chest. Warmth seeped from her hands into his body, easing the chill deep inside. "But you haven't yet. And you don't want to. And since you've been gone, I've had several days to research and think things through, and there's only one thing I know that really matters."

"What's that?" he asked before he could think to stop himself.

She lifted her hand, brushed it against his cheek. And he leaned into her touch without even realizing he was doing so. "I made my own wish. I brought you here. I didn't have to do that, Tariq, so you shouldn't feel guilty about anything that happens to me. It was my choice."

"Mira—"

She rose on her toes. Wrapped her arms around his neck. Brought her body flush against his until the chill was nothing but a memory and her heat was all he felt. "I would do it again too. Even if it was only for a few days. Even knowing everything I know now. I would do it again to spend these hours with you because they've been the best of my life. I thought I wanted to know how to be desirable, but I realized…I already am. I just hadn't met the right man."

"Mira," he whispered, unable to stop himself from closing his arms around her. "I am not a man."

"No, not technically, but it doesn't mean you deserve what was done to you. I can't even begin to try to understand your world, but I know what's in your heart. I know that you care about your brothers. About your father and your kingdom. And

I know from spending time with you that you have a gentle soul, regardless of what you think. You tried to stop me from following through with my wish. You protected me from those Ghuls. And when I wouldn't change my mind about wanting to be with you, you did everything you could to prolong my wish so I wouldn't be hurt. Even knowing that witch could punish your brothers in the meantime. And then you come back here with these marks on your back, and I…"

Her voice caught with so much emotion, it radiated through his entire body. "That's not something a monster does, Tariq. That's something an honorable man does."

He didn't know what to think. She loved him. A slave, sent to condemn her. Really loved him.

She looked down at his chest. "I know that in your own way you care about me, because you wouldn't have done all that if you didn't. Even if it isn't—"

"Mira, I care more for you more than I've ever cared for anyone else."

Her eyes lifted to his, brightened at his words. "You do?"

He nodded and brushed his thumb over her cheek. Even as his heart pinched at what that meant. "More than I ever thought I could."

A slow, sexy smile spread across her lips. Lips that were plump and lush and tempting as they skimmed across his. "Show me," she whispered. "Forget everything else right now, and just show me."

Chapter Nine

Mira's skin tingled with excitement and nervousness. Not the same nervousness she'd felt the last time they were together. No, she wasn't worried about pleasing him; she was worried about what came after. What she and Claire had discussed. What she had to do when it was over.

Don't think about that now. Think about Tariq. Think about being with him. Think about this last moment together.

He lowered his mouth to hers, and she opened to him without hesitation, tasted the hunger on his tongue—the same hunger she knew was on hers. His hand slid down her spine, pressed gently against her lower back, drawing her body even tighter against his. She moaned into his mouth, tangled her fingers in his hair, and kissed him harder. Wanted to kiss him as no one had ever kissed him before. As she hoped no one would ever kiss him again.

He hadn't said he loved her, but that was okay. She didn't need the words. She knew he cared about her. And that was enough.

She took a step forward, forcing him back. When his butt hit the raised bed, she slid her hands down his chest, smiled as his arms closed around her and he lifted her feet off the floor, then laid her out of the mattress just as she wanted.

He was all solid muscle and chiseled angles. She watched in wonder as he shrugged out of his shirt, kicked off his boots, as he climbed over her. Desire darkened his eyes, brought a flush to his cheeks that superheated her blood. She reached for him, was careful not to touch the wounds on his back, then lifted to meet him, pressing her lips against his with a fierceness that stole her breath. He lowered his body to hers, and she loved the beat of his heart against her own, loved the heat radiating from his skin. Loved how they fit together as if they were made for each other.

He kissed her jaw, her earlobe, trailed his lips down her neck, and nibbled at the tender column of flesh. She moaned, arched into him. He slid his hand across her belly, under her shirt, and up to palm her breast. Electricity rippled across her skin as she lowered her back to the mattress again. As she found his mouth and kissed him once more while his fingers teased her nipple into a hard point beneath the satin of her bra.

She broke away from his mouth. Breathed heavily. "Tariq—"

"Lift up, *hayaati*." He eased off her so she could sit up, then tugged the shirt over her head and tossed it on the floor. Eyes locked on her satiny bra, he flipped the front clasp and tugged that off as well until her breasts spilled into his large, more than capable hands.

"So soft," he whispered. Her nipples tightened under his heated stare. As he cupped each one and ran his thumb across the tip. Then she nearly came out of her skin when he lowered his head and laved his tongue across her nipple.

Groaning, Mira dropped her head back in pleasure and arched into his mouth. She'd had lovers before, but none had been like Tariq. None had known where to touch her to make her lose control. Dark flashes of arousal pulsed through her. She wanted to taste him on her tongue again. Wanted to feel his cock deep inside. Wanted him limp and sated in her arms when it was over then begging for more. And she wanted to be the only one to satisfy him, just like this, every day, for the rest of his days, however long that may be.

Don't think about the future. Just enjoy right now.

She knew that was what she had to do. She knew it was the only way she'd survive. But it didn't stop her from wanting. From needing. From dreaming about a future she knew they could never have.

He flicked the button on her jeans as he brought his mouth back to hers, slid the zipper down. When she lifted, he pushed his hand inside her jeans and around to cup her ass, grinding his erection against her mound until she saw stars.

"I love the sounds you make, *hayaati.*"

She loved the sounds he made too. Loved when he groaned against her. When he rubbed that glorious erection between her legs as he was doing now. Just when she thought she'd go mad from the grinding, he broke away from her mouth, dragged her jeans and underwear down her hips, tore them from her legs, and dropped them on the floor near her shirt. Then he peeled off his own jeans and climbed back on the bed, smiled in that sexy, lazy way of his that heated her blood to near-boiling levels.

Her gaze slid over his perfect body. She could stare at him for hours and never tire of the view. But right now she wanted more than just looking. She wanted him.

He cupped her left breast, then slid his fingers lower to her stomach, and finally into all her moist, wet heat. She groaned again, lifted her hips. Needed him everywhere. Anywhere. "Tariq…"

"You're so wet, *hayaati*." He lowered his head, nibbled at her neck, teased her with his fingers.

She closed her eyes and rode his fingers as he stroked her, gave herself over to his wicked touch. Tingles spread out from her sex, loosened her limbs, made her achy with need. She turned her head, found his mouth, kissed him deep while he circled her clit with his thumb, while he slid his fingers lower and finally inside her.

She groaned, tightened around him. Gasped when he stroked her deep. But it wasn't enough. She wanted more. She wanted all of him. "Tariq, I need you now."

His eyes were as dark as she'd ever seen them when he pulled back from her mouth, and stared down at her. He shifted his body over her, pushed up on one hand, then filled her in one fluid movement that drew a gasp from her lips and sent pleasure spiraling through every cell.

Yes. *Yes...*

She tightened around his length. Tried to hang on to his shoulders as he drew back out and in. As he slowly picked up his pace, that pleasure grew in intensity until it was all she could feel.

"Mira," he moaned. "Allah, I love being inside you."

She loved having him inside her. She met each thrust with her own. His lips closed over hers. She moaned into his mouth, wrapped her arms around his shoulders as she lifted to meet him. And she kissed him again and again while he made love to her. Wanting to draw this moment out. Knowing it was going to be their last.

Tears burned her eyes, but she forced them back, didn't want anything to ruin the moment. They rocked gently against each other on the boat. Water lapped at the hull. But she knew he was getting close. She could tell by the flush of his cheeks, by the way he thickened inside her. By the way he hit that spot again and again, driving her closer to her own release.

"Open your eyes, Mira. Come with me."

She blinked several times, met his gaze. And his eyes…God, they were the most beautiful things she'd ever seen. Not sharp or brilliant in color but vibrant. Fathomless. Alive. Everything she felt when she was with him.

Her orgasm rocketed through her, sending electrical sensations all through her body that robbed her of breath and thought and focus. It went on and on as he thrust harder, deeper, as he filled her as no one ever had before. And when he roared through his own release, long moments later, she was still shuddering, still jerking, still moaning at the most intense orgasm she'd ever experienced.

He fell against her. Aftershocks continued to ripple through her body, but thought returned. And with it, a feeling of completeness, of belonging. Of home.

Slowly, she sifted her fingers into his damp hair, kissed his temple. "That was better than last time," she said. "Think you can do that again?"

He chuckled, and the vibrations spread all through her chest, warming her deep inside. "This time, I might need a moment to recover, *hayaati*."

She rolled her eyes even though he couldn't see her. "So much for being an all-powerful supernatural being, huh?"

He smiled as he pushed up on his arm and looked down at her. A devilishly sexy grin that heated her blood all over again. "Are you mocking me?"

"No, I was just stating an observation." She hooked one leg around his thigh and rolled him to his back, keeping him locked tight within her. He went easily, smiling at her joke the whole time. And she took that as a sign that his back didn't hurt nearly as much anymore. Or maybe she'd taken away the pain. "What if I promise to do all the work?"

She pushed up to sitting. Tightened her sheath. Grinned down at him with all the confidence she hadn't known was inside her. His eyes darkened again as he rested his hands at her hips and she rocked slowly against him. He hardened quickly inside her, as if all he needed was that tiny bit of coaxing.

"And what if I want to help?" he asked, lifting to thrust deeper inside her. "Just a little?"

She grew wet and hot and achy all over again. Bracing her hands on each side of his head, she leaned close. "I guess a little help won't hurt, djinni. But this time, my wish is to pleasure you. So you have to let me do whatever I want."

His lips curled as she closed her mouth over his. As she lifted and lowered. As she slid her tongue along his and tasted his hunger all over again.

"Your wish, *hayaati*. My command."

Chapter Ten

Tariq was pretty sure he'd never been so satisfied.

Mira lay draped over him, her chest rising and falling with her labored breaths, her hair a wild tangle of silk all across his sweaty skin. He ran his fingers through the thick blond mass, loving the feel of it—and her—against him as she tried to slow her breath, as they both came down from another rocking climax.

His heart pinched when he thought of what would happen next. They were safe out here on the water, but as soon as they went back to shore, Zoraida would expect results. And when he refused, the sorceress would become enraged. He didn't want to lose his brothers, but he couldn't damn Mira. She was as innocent as they were. And he could no longer sacrifice one for the good of others.

"Where are we?" he asked as he stared up at the ceiling.

"On a boat," she said, her voice vibrating against his chest, sending tendrils of pleasure all through his skin. "I already told you that."

He smiled, even knowing all the danger that loomed ahead for both of them. With her, he felt light, alive, loved. And that's what he'd hold on to. Even when his brothers were gone and Zoraida took her fury out on him. He'd remember this moment with her and everything she'd given him and know his choice was worth it. "That's not what I meant, smartass. I meant, where is the boat?"

She pushed up on one arm and looked down at him. Her eyes sparkled in the low light, and his heart cinched down even tighter as he looked into her beautiful face. "You need to be more specific, djinni. I'm not a mind reader, you know." She grinned again. "On the Columbia. Off Sauvie Island. Don't worry, we aren't drifting. I dropped anchor."

He wasn't worrying about that. He was worrying because they didn't have much time. They needed to get out of this bed and strategize. He needed to teach her to recognize the influence of Ghuls so she could defend herself when he was gone. But he didn't want to do that yet. He just wanted to stay here and be close to her, even though doing so was only prolonging the inevitable.

He brushed a lock of hair back from her face. "It's been a long time since I've been on the water. I miss it. Thank you for this."

"Your kingdom is near the coast, isn't it?" When he nodded, she said, "You sail a lot?"

"I used to. Not much lately."

"I guessed," she said, pushing up to sit on his legs.

He loved that she wasn't self-conscious about being naked with him anymore. Loved the way she trailed her hands down his chest. "Let me guess? Your research?"

That Cheshire-cat grin returned once more. "Something like that. But I didn't bring you on this boat just because I thought you might be missing the water."

"You didn't?" She shook her head, and his brow lowered as he tried to read her expression. "Then why?"

Resting her hands on his chest, she leaned down and kissed him. "Because I love you."

His heart turned over, and he opened to her, drawing her tongue into his mouth one more time, hoping it would be enough. Knowing it wouldn't.

She ran her hands over his shoulders as she kissed him. Down his arms and back up again. He lost himself in her kiss. In the sheer perfection of her. In all the love he'd never had before. Her fingers trailed down to his wrists. She grasped his arms, tugged them above his head. He smiled as she kissed him. As his desire built all over again.

Okay, one more time. Then he'd get serious. So long as they were out on the water and she still needed him, he'd let her do whatever she wanted. For however long it took. When she was finally sated, then he'd refocus.

"I love when you touch me like this, Mira."

She pushed his hands together over his head. "Good. Because I have a feeling in a minute, you're going to be really mad."

His brow dropped as she pulled away from his mouth. And then something cold and metal snapped over both his wrists.

He jerked his head back, looked up. But before he even saw the cuffs, he knew they were iron. Knew because it zapped his energy and made him weaker than he'd been in years.

His gaze shot back to Mira. She quickly climbed off him. A guilty look ran across her face. "What are you doing? Mira, uncuff me right now. Iron—"

She winced. "I know. Iron makes you weak. But trust me, Tariq, there's no other way."

He watched in shock and disbelief as she tugged on her clothes. Of course, she knew. She'd researched his tribe extensively. He jerked on the iron cuffs with what little strength he had. But they were secured to a hook in the wall, and all his efforts did was jangle metal against metal. "Mira. What…? Why…?" He pulled hard again. Knew he was growing weaker with each second. "You have to let me go."

She tugged the comforter over his naked body. Then leaned down so she was close to his face. "I know she can't see us on the water. Or hear us. But I also know you'd never let me do what I'm about to do, so I had to cuff you."

She ran her fingers over his jaw, and instinctively, he leaned into her touch, even as anger pushed up his chest. "Mira, listen to me—"

His words cut off when her fingers moved down his throat; then both hands spread across his collarbones as if she were feeling for something.

Panic spread through his entire body as she began uttering words in an old language he'd only heard once. Words Zoraida had spoken when she'd bound him to the opal. And his eyes grew wide when the opal he wore in his realm—the one that was just like Mira's but invisible here—materialized against his chest.

Her fingers closed around the opal, and she muttered more magical words that broke the clasp.

"Mira," he gasped, eyes wide with disbelief. "How did you—?"

"Find your brothers, Tariq," she whispered against his lips, just before kissing him one last time. "My wish has been fulfilled."

No. *No!* "Mira!"

A vortex of black smoke materialized in the room. Horror enveloped Tariq as the smoke cleared and Zoraida stood in the center of the salon. Tariq jerked on the cuffs, but he was so weak now, he could barely move. "Mira, run. Get out of here!"

She had no idea what she'd just done. By voicing her wish was fulfilled, she'd brought Zoraida's wrath down on her. He couldn't protect her cuffed to this wall. Panic made him yank and pull and do anything to break free.

"Water," Zoraida announced, glaring toward Tariq. "Clever, djinni. Remind me to punish you for that."

She turned her icy gaze on Mira. "Your wish is fulfilled, human. That means your soul belongs to me."

Mira didn't even flinch as a wicked grin spread across Zoraida's face. Did she know Zoraida was a sorceress? That she could torture Mira, enslave her, kill her at any moment? That panic morphed to a full-blown terror that whipped through Tariq like a hurricane. "Mira, run!"

"Maybe," Mira said in a calm voice, ignoring him. "Maybe not."

Zoraida's eyes narrowed. "What do you have behind your back?"

Slowly, Mira pulled her right hand forward and opened her palm. Tariq's opal glimmered in the low salon light.

Fury flashed in Zoraida's eyes, shot from the opal to Mira's face. "How did you get that?"

Without answering, Mira tugged a curved bottle made of yellow glass from behind her back with her other hand. One Tariq had seen sitting on the shelf near the bed when he'd first come onto the boat. Gaze locked on Zoraida, Mira held Tariq's opal over the bottle, then said, "Your hold on him ends here. By the magic in the Key of Solomon, I free him from his chains."

No. He wouldn't be able to protect her. Zoraida would kill her for sure for this. *No!* "Mira!"

Zoraida's eyes grew wide as saucers. Before she could lunge forward, Mira dropped the opal into the bottle.

Zoraida screamed. The liquid in the bottle fizzled and popped, and then the opal disintegrated. Fire erupted all through Tariq's body, exploded out his fingertips. His body lurched off the bed as if he'd been shocked with a ten-thousand-volt electrical current. Voices echoed in his ears. Mira's. Zoraida's. But the black smoke was already circling in. Already pulling him back. The cuffs broke free of his wrists. His vision blurred. Through a haze, he reached out for Mira, but the roar of the vortex swirling around him was too strong, the force too great. And then, before he could stop it, he was flying across time and space, heading…he didn't know where.

Mira swallowed hard as she stared into the face of the enraged sorceress. Power radiated from her body, churned in the air. But the hatred in her eyes… It was like nothing Mira had ever seen before.

She couldn't wonder where Tariq had gone. Couldn't focus on the hurt she'd seen on his face when she'd cuffed him. He was safe now. He was free. That was all that mattered.

"You," the sorceress growled. "I will make you pay for what you've done."

Mira took a step back. Braced herself for the sorceress's fury. She didn't have a weapon, nothing to protect herself. What little magic Claire's research had garnered had already been used to free Tariq. She'd known it would come down to this. That she'd be left alone with an irate magical being when all was said and done, but she hadn't realized just how frightening that would be.

"It was worth it," Mira managed in a shaky voice, trying to stay tough. Trying not to let this…thing…see her fear. "To get him away from you, it was worth it."

The sorceress's eyes turned red. She lifted her hands and threw them forward. A burst of electrical energy sizzled from her fingertips, flew through the air. Mira screamed. She knew she did. But the blast never hit. It went right through her and slammed into the wall of the boat, opening a hole in the side that rocked the boat from side to side.

Mira stumbled, hit the wall of the boat. Frigid water poured into the cabin, seeped around her feet. But she was too focused on the sorceress's eyes, growing wider with disbelief and fury, as she glanced from her hands to Mira's face.

There was nowhere for Mira to go. Panic spread through her chest, threatened to overwhelm her. And then she thought of the Firebrand opal.

Her wish was fulfilled. It wasn't bound to her anymore.

She quickly reached up and flipped the clasp on the chain around her neck. Excitement speared through her when it opened and the opal fell into her hand.

Across the cabin, the sorceress yelled, "No!"

But Mira didn't hesitate. She dropped the opal into the bottle, just as she'd done with Tariq's stone. Only this one didn't sizzle and pop. It bobbed in the liquid she'd enchanted with magical words Claire had given her, then seemed to hover, suspended inside.

Firebrand

The sorceress screamed, and Mira looked up just as another vortex of light and smoke and energy spun through the room. But this one didn't disintegrate. In a roar so loud it shook the boat, the sorceress, her magic, every bit of her twirling tornado was sucked into the bottle.

Barely able to believe what had just happened, Mira slapped the top down on the bottle, securing the clasp. Inside the yellow-tinged glass, the Firebrand necklace still floated, but there was no sign of the sorceress. Just a crackle and sparkle of magic that told Mira she and her power were in there somewhere.

"Holy shit," she breathed. She'd done it. She'd saved Tariq, she'd managed to save herself, and she'd trapped the sorceress.

Her hands shook. Her heart raced. Slowly, sound returned. And a shiver racked her body. She looked around the salon, half filled with water from the gaping hole in the side, and realized the boat was sinking.

She scrambled for the stairs. The boat groaned and jerked to the side, knocking her off balance. The bottle slipped from her fingertips. She went under the steadily rising water, kicked hard to come back up. Sputtering, she looked around for the bottle. It was floating on the steadily rising surface of the water. Heading for the hole in the side of the boat.

She had to get to it. She couldn't lose it!

She swam hard for it. Her fingertips grazed the glass, but she couldn't reach it. Before she could get her hand around the neck, it was sucked out of the boat and disappeared into the river.

Mira's head went under. Water swirled around her. Lungs burning, she kicked hard to get air. When her head popped up, she gasped, so close to the ceiling. Oh God, she wasn't going to get out. She was going to drown down here.

She swam as hard as she could. Finally reached the stairs, now at an angle as the boat filled. Water poured over the deck, into the salon, but she fought against the current and pushed through until she was on the drastically sloped deck. She didn't bother looking for a lifejacket, knew there wasn't time. Hands on the grab rail, she struggled to the edge and pushed off, sailing into the river, hoping she'd jumped far enough out so the boat didn't suck her down with it. Praying she'd live.

Because as much as she'd been willing to sacrifice herself for Tariq, she didn't want to die this way. Not when they were both finally free.

Chapter Eleven

Mira drew a deep breath, lifted her hand, and knocked on the office door. Three days had passed since the events on the boat. After being rescued by a passing ship, she'd filed a report with the harbor police about the "electronic malfunction" on board that had caused the sinking, apologized to her boss for wrecking his boat, then cashed in the rest of her vacation time. She needed a couple of weeks to chill out and recover mentally from what had happened, and she had one person she needed to thank in person.

A voice inside the room called, "Come in," so Mira turned the handle and stepped into the cramped office on the University of Florida's campus.

The woman with auburn hair and wire rimmed glasses at the desk near the window looked up from her computer. "Can I help you?"

"I'm Mira Dawson. We chatted via phone and e-mail."

Claire Sampson's eyes widened, and she pushed out of her chair with a smile, holding out her hand in greeting. "Oh my gosh, it's so great to meet you in person."

Mira shook the other woman's hand—or hands, as the woman closed both of hers over Mira's—and felt the first real smile since the accident slide across her face. "You too. I wanted to come and thank you in person."

"No thanks needed. If anyone should be doing the thanking, it's me. You provided me with incredible research." As if realizing she was still holding Mira's hand, she quickly let go and motioned to a chair next to her desk. "Please, sit."

"Thanks." Mira lowered to the seat, set her purse on her lap.

Dr. Sampson was tall, close to five ten, and she had the prettiest blue eyes. As brilliant as polished sapphires. But the glasses, the loose-fitting slacks and white blouse with what looked like a mustard stain on the buttons and the smudge of ink across her cheek screamed nerdy professor to Mira.

She smiled again, more relaxed than she'd expected. The fact Claire seemed as dedicated to her job as Mira had hoped, settled her nerves. If she'd been some stuffy, know-it-all professor, Mira would have felt intimidated.

"I know it must have been extremely overwhelming for you," Claire said, "but…wow. I can't wait to hear all the details."

They'd chatted via phone after the incident, but Mira hadn't been ready to give away the nitty-gritty then. She'd still needed time to absorb what had happened. But she owed Claire because she'd been the one to help her. And that's why she'd made the trip all the way to Florida so they could talk in person.

As Claire pulled out a tape recorder, Mira took another deep breath and launched into the entire story. From the moment she'd met Tariq until she'd been pulled from the water. And as Claire listened, those gemlike eyes grew wider and more excited with each juicy detail.

"Amazing. Completely amazing," the professor said when Mira was done. "I've always suspected that djinn are just like us—that there are good and bad ones and that they live by free will—but your story is the first that actually confirms this for me."

There definitely were good and bad, and just as she'd done every hour since that day, Mira wondered where Tariq was, if he'd found his brothers, if he was happy now that he was finally free.

She shook off the thought because she knew dwelling on where and what and how would only drag her down. And even though she loved him, she knew he'd only been with her because of the curse. She'd hoped and prayed that he'd come to her on his own now that he was free—he'd said all djinn could cross between realms, so she knew he didn't need the opal to do so—but so far, he hadn't. And that was the other reason she needed to emotionally recover from everything that had happened—because she missed him more than she'd ever missed anyone in her whole life.

"There's just one thing I don't understand," Mira said. "Why didn't the sorceress's energy kill me? It was strong enough to blow a hole in the side of the boat. How come I'm not dead?"

Claire looked at her as if it were totally obvious. "Because you were pure of heart."

Mira frowned. "I'm not pure of heart. I wished to be desired by a man. That doesn't make me pure. Heck, that's about as selfish a wish as anyone can ask."

Claire smiled as if she were explaining things to a child. "I didn't say you were pure of heart in the abstract way. I said when you sacrificed your life for Tariq's, *at that moment*, you were pure of heart. It doesn't mean that you were before or even that you are now. It just means you were when it mattered most. The sorceress's magic couldn't touch you then because it's laced with evil. Evil energy can't destroy something that's pure."

Mira considered that for a moment. "So you're saying I'm not special."

Claire's smile widened. "Special in the fact that you stood up to an extremely magical entity and lived? Sure. Special in the fact you could do it again? Probably not. I hate to break this to you, Mira, but you're just like everyone else on this planet. Normal and very unmagical."

Mira chuckled. Unmagical was fine with her. She'd had enough magic to last her a lifetime. "I can't thank you enough. For helping me. For all the research you did. For finding those spells in the Key of Solomon—"

Claire clicked off the tape, glanced toward the door, and lowered her voice. "About that…let's keep that under wraps. I had to go to great lengths to find that text, and between you and me, I wasn't even sure it would work. Since it did…well, I don't have to tell you there are numerous people who would want that kind of power if they knew about it. In fact, I'd appreciate it if you and I never speak of it again."

Mira nodded slowly, unsure just what Claire was getting at. But she understood that kind of power in the wrong hands could do nothing but harm.

"The only regret I have," Mira said, "is that I lost the bottle. I'm afraid of what will happen to it."

Claire sighed and leaned back in her chair. "Unfortunately, I've a feeling it'll eventually turn up. But it could be years before that happens. And the good news is…that's not your worry. If someone does eventually find it, the sorceress will be more focused on that person than on finding you because the opal will most likely be bound to them. So long as you keep all of this quiet, you're safe. And speaking of you… How are you doing…really?"

Mira knew Claire was asking how she was doing emotionally. And a host of feeling washed through her, none of which she wanted to linger on too long. But she appreciated the fact the woman had asked. "I'm fine. I lived, right? I won."

"What about Tariq?" Claire asked quietly.

Mira's heart pinched. "I'm just glad he's finally free."

A knowing smile spread across Claire's ink-smudged face. "You are a rotten liar, Mira Dawson."

Smiling herself, Mira pushed out of her chair. She liked Claire. In fact, all this magical stuff aside, Claire was the type of person Mira could see herself being friends with. She held her hand out. "I'll get out of your hair and let you get back to work. Thank you so much for everything."

Claire waved off her hand and instead wrapped her arms around Mira in a tight hug. "If you need anything, I'm only an e-mail away."

Tears stung Mira's eyes as she nodded. Knowing her emotions were dangerously close to the surface, she said goodbye and let herself out.

When she stepped into the midmorning sunshine, she drew a deep breath of humid Florida air. Claire was right. It could be years before anyone even found that bottle. She couldn't spend her life worrying what was around the next corner. If her time with Tariq had taught her anything, it was that she was a vibrant woman with a bright future ahead of her. It was far past time she stopped hiding behind her job and started living.

She moved down the steps of the history building and onto the sidewalk. Ahead, a man pushed up from a bench sheltered by a large oak and looked her way.

Her heart jerked, and the air rushed out of her lungs on a wave. One corner of Tariq's lips tipped up in the most devastatingly handsome smile. One Mira felt all the way to her toes.

"Oh my God. Oh my God," she breathed, running toward him.

She threw herself against him, hardly able to believe that he was here. His arms closed around her back, his warm, solid chest pressed against her front, and then his face was sliding into the hollow between her neck and shoulder, his breath warming her from the outside in.

"Oh my God," she said again, still unable to believe he was real. "You're here."

He eased back, smiled down at her. "You are a hard woman to find without magic."

He leaned down and kissed her before she could ask what he meant. Before she could *think* to ask. And then his lips were against hers, his tongue sliding into her mouth, his arms tightening around her until he was all she saw and heard and felt…everywhere.

Her head was spinning when he finally broke the kiss. "How did you…? What happened when you…?" Tears burned her eyes. "I was so afraid you were mad at me about what happened and that's why I haven't seen you."

He brushed a tear from her cheek she hadn't known had fallen. "I wasn't mad, *hayaati*. I was afraid. For you."

Hayaati. She'd finally looked up the word, knew it meant 'my life'. "I knew you would be. That's why I didn't tell you what I had planned."

"We'll have to work on your communication skills. But to answer your other questions… After you freed me from my chains, I was sent back to my realm. I was still weak from the iron, so it took me a while to recover. But when I did, I went home. I saw my father. My mother. I cannot tell you what that meant to me."

That space around her heart warmed when he spoke of family.

"We knew when you trapped Zoraida. The Ghuls fell into a state of disarray. Since then, our army has been able to get an upper hand, and the Ghuls have been driven from our kingdom entirely. We have you to thank for that."

Her heart warmed even more, but she remembered Claire's comments in the office and wanted to make sure he understood. "I wasn't trying to save anyone but you."

"I know, *hayaati*, but you saved a kingdom just the same. We—my entire tribe—are forever in your debt."

A thrill rushed through her. A thrill she wasn't sure what to do with. "What about your brothers? Are they happy to be home as well?"

Tariq's expression shifted from soft to sad. "We can't find them."

"Oh, Tariq…"

"They both wore opals like mine. They're still bound to the Firebrand opal and Zoraida as I was. We don't know where they went."

That thrill she'd felt moments before withered and died. And the consequences of what she'd done spiraled through her. "I didn't know. I'm so sorry. I put my necklace in the bottle. That's how I trapped the sorceress. But the bottle slipped out of my fingers into the river, and I couldn't reach it. I didn't realize—"

"Shh…" He placed two fingers over her lips. "It's okay, *hayaati*. No one's blaming you. Zoraida enslaved my brothers, not you. You have nothing to feel bad about. You freed me. You freed my kingdom. And you gave me a chance to someday free my brothers."

"I don't understand."

"Your spirit was stronger than most females Zoraida sent me to corrupt. That's why she needed your soul. It would have fueled her powers that much more. But it was your strength that drew me. I felt a connection to the stone—through you—I never felt with anyone else. And even though I was no longer bound to the opal after you freed me, I sensed when you were released from its hold. We have djinn searching for the necklace. It will be found. And so will my brothers."

"What about the sorceress?"

"When we find the bottle, we'll figure out a way to contain her."

It sounded logical. And she knew with all the magic in his realm, if anyone could find a way, it would be him. Then she remembered his first words.

"Why did it take you so long to find me?" she asked. "What did you mean, 'without magic'?"

That toe-curling smile warmed his lips again. "I asked my father to let me come back here, to search for the necklace myself. To be with you."

Her heart leaped, and tears stung her eyes all over again. "You did?" she asked on a whisper.

He nodded. "There's a catch, though. The longer I stay, the more human I become. My magic will fade until it's finally gone. I figured I should get used to being human, so I tried looking for you without it. But I didn't expect to look for you clear across the country. I eventually gave up and used just a little. I needed to find you."

She could barely believe what she was hearing. "You mean if you stay with me, you'll eventually lose your immortality?"

"Djinn aren't immortal. We just live a very long time."

And he was giving that up for her. Those tears burned hot all over again. "Why would you do that?"

"Do you really have to ask?" He cupped her cheek. "Losing my magic is a much smaller sacrifice than what you were willing to give up for me. I would rather spend one human lifetime with you than a thousand without you. You complete my soul—a part I didn't even know was missing. I would go through all of Zoraida's torture again just to end up with you here, right now. Mira...*hayaati*...I love you."

Mira's chest was so tight she could barely breathe. She threw her arms around his neck, held on with everything she had in her. She'd wanted to be desirable. She'd wanted to find a love that would last the ages. She had. It just hadn't been at all what she'd expected.

"I love you too, Tariq. I—" She couldn't get the words out. She couldn't do anything but hold on for the rest of her life.

He chuckled against her neck. "Oh, I'm glad to hear that, because I'm going to need you to teach me all about life in the human world. I think I've a lot to learn."

She eased back. Smiled up at him in the early afternoon light. And knew the wish she'd made weeks ago was the best wish of her life. "You want me to teach you something? Wish for it, djinni."

His grin warmed the last cold space inside her. "My only wish is for you."

"Your wish, my command," she whispered as his lips lowered to hers once more.

Pleasure is the best revenge...

Slave to Passion

A Firebrand Novella

USA TODAY BESTSELLING AUTHOR

ELISABETH NAUGHTON

*For Rachel Grant,
Plotting queen extraordinaire and a whiz at
all things title-related.
So thankful to have you in my writing corner of the world!*

Chapter One

Pain rippled through every inch of Nasir's body.

Muscles in his arms and legs quivering, he pushed up on his hands. Gravel and sand embedded in his palms, stabbed into his knees covered by the threadbare pants. Through bloody and sweat-drenched hair, he looked toward the Shaitan across the arena. The djinni's chest rose and fell with his heavy breaths, and dirt and blood coated his skin from the fight, but he didn't even seem fazed as he lifted his axe, ready to hurl the killing blow.

Roars from the crowd dragged Nasir's attention. His gaze shifted to the stands, to the Ghuls—one of the six main tribes that made up the race of djinn—waving their fists, chanting "*Kill! Kill! Kill!*" as if he were nothing more than an animal.

He ground his teeth, pushed up on one knee. Refused to groan at the blinding pain in his shoulder. He wouldn't go down like this. Not on all fours in the fighting pits of Jahannam, as entertainment for the most base and depraved djinn tribe. He wasn't afraid to die, but he wouldn't do it as a coward. And if he was going out, he planned to take the Shaitan out along with him.

Fire cut across his ribs. His muscles ached as he found his feet. He swayed but somehow managed to steady himself. Blood dripped from the gash in his side, ran down his torso to dampen his waistband. His vision blurred.

He tried to focus on the djinni ahead. Hair he guessed had once been blond but now looked as dirty as the sand beneath them hung to his shoulders. Sweat dripped down his angular and scarred face. As a slave, the Shaitan's powers were bound, just as Nasir's were, but the bastard didn't seem to mind. He had size and brute strength on his side. And the shit-eating grin curling his split lip said he knew Nasir was fading fast.

"*Kill! Kill! Kill!*"

The roars grew louder. The Shaitan growled and charged. Nasir gathered what was left of his energy and ducked beneath the swinging axe, thrust out his sword, and caught the Shaitan across the back.

Blood spurted, spraying across Nasir's face and chest. The Shaitan arched and howled. Nasir's adrenaline surged, empowering him with a fresh source of strength. He whipped around before the djinni could strike again and stabbed his sword into the Shaitan's back.

The bastard's eyes flew wide. The axe fell from his hand as he dropped to his knees. Blood gushed beneath his body, staining the sand of the arena. Breathing heavily, Nasir yanked his blade from the Shaitan's back and beheaded him in one clean move.

The djinni's head hit the ground with a thud, followed by his hulking body. Gasps echoed through the arena, then the chants fell silent.

Nasir's chest rose and fell in an uneven rhythm as he looked up into the stands. Disgust rolled through him. They were savages. Every single one of them. Ghuls held no allegiance to any other race. They didn't care if the winner of this battle was Marid or Shaitan. All they wanted was to be entertained by a gruesome death. But now that he'd given them that, they didn't utter a sound?

Fuck them. Fuck them all. Their thirst for blood and death had shaped him into the brutal *sahad* he'd become. Though it sickened a place deep inside him, he knew he'd go on giving them exactly what they wanted. But not for glory or fame or even the miniscule hope that one day he could win his freedom. No, he'd kill again and again because staying alive was the greatest act of rebellion he could thrust upon those who had imprisoned him in this hell.

His arms shot to the open sky, and he roared.

The crowd exploded in excitement, their earlier apprehension forgotten. Females jumped up and down, clapping, waving vibrantly-colored scarves in his direction. Males cheered at the bloodbath at his feet.

Adrenaline pumped through Nasir's veins. He turned a slow circle, clenched his empty hand into a fist, stabbed his sword higher into the air as he drank in their ovations. He was a Marid warrior, son of the great king, and he'd decimated every single thing those barbarian Ghuls had thrown at him.

"This is not who you are."

The voice hit him out of nowhere. Soft. Feminine. Sweet. So familiar it stole his breath.

He dropped his arms to his sides. Turned to glance behind him. But he was alone on the sand. With cheers ringing in his ears, he looked up into the stands, his gaze skipping from one exuberant face to the next, searching for her. But all he saw were hundreds of Ghuls, eyes and hair and the clothing of his enemy blending together in a wash of color until he couldn't focus on a single one. Until the arena spun around him.

Something in his chest cinched down tight, followed by the memory of Talah's face. Her smile. Her gentle spirit. The way she'd brushed her hand against his jaw and looked at him with tenderness that last day, when he'd left her to fight his father's war.

When he'd left her to die.

"This is not who you are, Nasir."

She would not support this. She wouldn't be awed by his victory. Though she'd hated what the Ghuls were doing—pillaging the Wastelands and threatening their kingdom—she'd despised death more.

The adrenaline waned, leaving him empty and cold. Leaving him feeling as dead as the Shaitan on the sand at his feet.

His gaze drifted to the mutilated body, and for the first time since he'd been imprisoned—for the first time since he'd lost Talah, really—he didn't recognize himself. All he saw was the monster he'd become.

Kavin pulled back on the hand gripping her upper arm. "There has to be someone else."

Zayd turned to face her, stopping in the dank hallway of the dungeon beneath the arena. His features were tight, his short, dark hair only slightly mussed from the dank air that had blown through it in the corridor. Cries of agony echoed through the walls around them, making Kavin's stomach churn at the torture she could only imagine. The scent of rotting flesh was ever present, but Zayd didn't seem to notice. He was as focused as she'd ever seen him, and his fingers pressing tightly into her bare skin were a stark reminder that he was in control, not her. "I choose who, female, not you."

Kavin swallowed hard as she looked up at the Ghul who was, technically, her master. He was born of the aristocracy and could have chosen any female as his latest mistress, but he'd picked her. The fact her family had offered her up without protest still burned in the pit of her stomach. "I…I just think there must be one of better breeding. The Marid is an animal. He—"

Zayd stepped close, tightening his grip around her arm until pain shot up from the spot, cutting off her words midsentence. "Which is exactly why he must be the one. To appreciate all that I have to offer, you must first experience the dreck at the bottom of society."

Horror washed through Kavin. He really was going to hand her over to that…that thing. "But he could kill me!"

Something dark sparked in Zayd's eyes, as if he enjoyed the thought of that thing touching her. "He won't. The Marid has a strong will to live. And he knows if he brings death to you, he'll be executed. This is the test of all *jarriah*, my dear. This is *your* test."

Bile rose in Kavin's throat. *Jarriah* was just another word for concubine. A female sex slave. One of many Zayd kept within his walls.

This is not my life.

The words revolved in her head as he pulled her down the dingy corridor. Her peach gown, the one she'd worn to the arena today in the hopes of pleasing him, was now dirty and wet all along the hem from the water that seeped through cracks in the stones. How had this happened? How had she come to be in this wretched place?

After the initial shock of her family releasing her to Zayd, part of her had been excited. It was customary for highborn males to pick and take the females they wanted. The fact he'd chosen her? A commoner? It was practically unheard of. She'd been blinded by his status and wealth and handsome good looks. Had dreamt of marriage, even knowing most Ghul males took multiple wives. But that had been okay with her, so long as he was kind. And if one day he grew to love her...then nothing else would matter.

But that was before he brought her to his harem and she realized he didn't want her for his wife. There would be no love between them now, no home or family or future. He looked upon her as nothing more than the slaves who battled to the death in the pit of the arena. As entertainment to meet his depraved needs. And he was now handing her over to the worst of those slaves as a test. To be broken in by a monster, so that when she went back to him, he would look like a shining knight.

He tugged her to a stop in front of a heavy steel door. Two guards stood outside, looked from him to Kavin and back again. The one on the right tightened his grip around the spear he held braced against the floor and said, "The *sahad* has been chained, my lord, per your instructions, but not prepared."

"This will not take long," Zayd answered. "My *jarriah* is not here for a sample but to simply meet the mighty champion and congratulate him on his latest victory." A wicked grin curled Zayd's lips. "Sampling will come later."

A sickening chuckle echoed from both guards, and Kavin's skin crawled as they both leered in her direction. She brushed her hair over her shoulder and tried not to let her fear show.

The guards stepped aside. The one on the left unlocked the door and pushed it open. "Scream if you need us."

Scream?

Kavin's pulse raced as Zayd pulled her into the cell behind him. She felt the guard's licentious gazes follow as she stepped past them but was more concerned with the monster that lurked in the dark. Zayd's footsteps echoed across the stone floor, his fingers pressing deeply into her arm as he jerked her along. A chill slid down her spine, and as her eyes tried to adjust to the darkness, she squinted, unable to see anything but Zayd.

For the first time since they'd left the arena, Zayd released his hold on her arm. Silence echoed through the dark chamber, ratcheting Kavin's anxiety up all over again. Then the heavy cell door clanged shut, causing her to jump and take a step closer to her master.

"Light!" Zayd called.

A scraping sound echoed, then a shaft of light speared into the room from a rectangular hole in the door, illuminating the space enough so she could look around.

There were no windows. Nothing hanging on the walls. Just a single, unmade bed that looked stained with blood and sweat, and a small, wooden table, holding an unlit, dripping candle.

It was a hole. Worse than that, it was a dungeon where hopes and dreams were ground into dust.

"Rise, Marid," Zayd barked.

Kavin's heart pounded against her ribs. She stepped behind Zayd as she looked around wildly for the monster she sensed lurking in the shadows. Silence echoed through the darkness like a vast cavern of nothingness, and just when she was sure there was no one there, metal clanged, and a shuffling sounded to her left.

Kavin whipped that way, her eyes wide, her muscles tight and ready to flee. She tried to move farther behind Zayd, but he blocked her, pushing her forward instead. She stumbled. Reached out for Zayd at her back. But he moved out of her reach.

"Come into the light, Marid, so that my *jarriah* may get a good look at what waits for her."

Kavin froze. She didn't know where he was. How close. What he would do to her. She didn't know anything except terror for the male hidden before her and bitter hatred for the one at her back.

The shuffling echoed again, followed by the clink of chains. And then his big body moved into the light directly in front of her.

Kavin sucked in a breath. Eased back a step until she hit Zayd. He grunted his disgust and moved away once more, making it more than clear she wasn't finding any safety with him.

But Kavin didn't try to move again. Fear kept her feet firmly locked in place. The Marid was bigger than he'd seemed in the arena. Still covered in grime, there was a scent about him—sweat, blood, death—one that rolled through her stomach until the desire to gag overwhelmed her.

She held it back, knowing doing so would only enrage him—and her master—and stared at the hulking beast mere feet away.

Chains were cuffed to his wrists. Chains Kavin hoped were locked tight to a wall or bar or something strong enough to restrain him. Dark, stringy hair brushed his bare shoulders. His arms were massive, his naked chest and stomach so hard it looked as if he were carved from stone; his thighs like tree trunks. He wore nothing but filthy, thin black pants that were frayed at the hem, and an opal. A fire opal, strung from a chain around his neck, the stone resting at the hollow of his throat.

It was the fire opal that drew her attention, reflecting an orange-red glow into the room, like flames from a blazing inferno. She'd seen it in the arena. It was all the talk amongst the females who followed the fights. Why did he wear it? Where had it come from? And why had his master not yet removed it?

Questions swirled in her mind as she looked from the opal to the wounds on his flesh, still oozing with blood. Then, finally, to his face.

A square jaw covered in dark stubble, lips set in a hard line, a nose slightly crooked as if it had been broken more than once. With the jagged red scar across his right cheek and the bruises marring his forehead, he looked hulking, feral, menacing. And his eyes... His eyes were dead pools of obsidian staring straight at her.

She stumbled backward, hit Zayd's chest. But instead of shoving her forward as he'd done before, both of his hands closed around her upper arms, steadying her against him.

"My *jarriah* does not like what she sees?" A smile wound through Zayd's words. "That pleases me. Greatly."

This is not my life. This is not my life! Tremors raced down her spine.

Zayd pushed her forward, this time moving with her. Her shoes scuffed along the floor as he forced her closer to the monster. "Take a good, long look, *jarriah*. See and smell what will soon be touching you."

Tears burned Kavin's eyes. A sob caught in her throat. Though she leaned hard against Zayd, she knew not to fight him or turn her head away. Knew if she did, he'd only lengthen the time she'd be sent to this hell with the monster.

The scent of death wafted in the air around her. That and the bitter bite of blood and sweat. She kept her focus on the opal, tried to breathe through her mouth and not her nose so she wouldn't get sick, but knew Zayd was waiting. He wanted to feel her fear. Wanted to make her writhe because he was a sick son of a bitch who got off on that kind of thing. Her skin grew tighter, her legs weaker as she fought from giving him what he wanted. But he wasn't letting go. And knowing it was the only way he'd release her, she finally chanced a look up.

The monster's gaze was fixed on the wall over her shoulder, not on her. But this close, she could feel the heat rolling off him in waves, see the muscles flex beneath his skin with coiled restraint. He wanted to hurt her. She saw it in the way his jaw clenched, in the way his hands curled into fists at his sides. He hated her simply because she was Ghul and he was Marid. Because her race had enslaved him here in these pits. Before she could stop it, the way he'd beheaded the Shaitan in the arena flashed in her mind. How he'd so easily decapitated the djinni with such violent ferocity.

He wouldn't kill her? How could he not? His sheer size, his obvious strength, and his bitter hatred made her impending death so obvious it shook her to her core.

She turned her head away, slammed her eyes shut. Tried to curl into Zayd at her back.

This is not my life!

A menacing chuckle echoed through Zayd's chest. Then his hands softened at her arms, and he took a step back, tugging her gently with him until, finally, there was space between her and the monster. "Guard!"

Metal clanked metal, followed by a whoosh of air spilling into the room as the door opened. A burst of light rushed into the dark space, blinding Kavin. But all she could focus on was the blessed air and the fact she was safe.

For now.

Zayd gripped her hand and pulled her toward the light. Relief spiraled through her veins. To the guard, he said, "Contact me when the slave has been prepared."

And just that fast, with one simple sentence, the relief she'd felt fled like a thief in the night. Until all that was left was a rolling sickness in her belly over what horror she'd find waiting when her master forced her to return.

Chapter Two

Kavin stared at the layer of bubbles floating on the surface of the water, feeling as if she were floating right along with them. Warmth enveloped her limbs as she lay in the marble pool, but she was cold to her very core. And the memories of the monster in that cell…

A shudder ran through her.

"*Jarriah* is cold?" Hana, the servant girl tending to Kavin, moved around a column that soared to the intricately carved ceiling and poured more steaming water from the large bronze pitcher in her hand into the bath. The aromatic scents of roses and orange blossoms wafted in the warm air, but Kavin still shivered.

Hana's sandals clicked along the polished stone floor as she moved up the wide steps and knelt at Kavin's back. She reached for a sponge from the side of the pool, dipped it in the water, then dragged it across Kavin's shoulders and upper back. "*Jarriah* is tense, too. I take it your meeting with the *sahad* did not go well."

"The word *sahad* makes him sound like some romantic gladiator." Kavin sat upright, the water sloshing against her bare breasts, the girl's voice cutting through her frenzied thoughts for the first time since she'd been sent to the baths to prepare herself. "He's not. He's a repulsive monster. He's…"

Bile rose in her throat, but she forced it down, just as she'd done before. This was what was expected of her—to go willingly to meet her fate and complete her test—but every muscle in her body screamed *Run! Escape! Disappear before it's too late!* Only she couldn't. Her djinn powers were bound, and even if they weren't, she'd never developed them. If she fled Zayd, he'd find her before she even reached the city wall. She'd be captured and executed. And even though something in the back of her mind whispered death might be better, she didn't want to die. She wanted to live.

Tears burned her eyes. Tears of injustice and rage and disbelief. When she'd been with her family, she'd been free. Now she was nothing but property. A slave. Soon to be a *jarriah*. Her stomach rolled over at the thought. Soon her only worth would be in fulfilling the lascivious needs of her master.

If, that was, she survived her test.

Anger threatened to run over in a hot wave of tears she just barely held back. She covered her face with her hands, hating that she couldn't just scream out her frustrations alone. That this servant was here to witness the last moments of her freedom.

"Shh, *jarriah*," Hana said as she ran the sponge down Kavin's bare back and smoothed her wet hair from her face. "It could be worse. He could be Shaitan. Or Infrit. Or one of the Ghuls from the Wastelands. He is Marid. This is a benefit to you."

"A benefit?" Kavin shot over her shoulder. "I don't see how any monster raping me for the sick pleasure of some highborn is a benefit, regardless of his tribe."

Hana harrumphed, then scrubbed the sponge down Kavin's arm rougher than necessary. "You only focus on the negative. Not the positive. You must accept the fact you are a slave now, *jarriah*. No different from me or even that djinni you call a monster. Choice is no longer yours. The sooner you accept your fate, the easier your life will be."

Her life? Easy? Despair washed through Kavin as she stared at the marble along the far edge of the rectangular pool that could easily accommodate ten and, knowing her lecherous master, probably did, routinely. There was no such thing as easy anymore.

Hana moved around the corner of the pool so she could reach Kavin's right arm and gentled her touch as she trailed the soapy sponge between Kavin's fingers. "You also overlook the fact the *sahad* is Marid."

Kavin glared at the dark-haired girl, her despair angling right back to anger. "What does his being Marid have to do with anything?"

"Do you not know?" Hana's fingers stilled against Kavin's, and an amused expression lit her dark eyes. "Marid view females quite differently from Ghuls."

"I find that hard to believe."

Hana refocused on her task. "They do not treat females as property but as treasures. The *jarriah* test is Ghul alone."

"How do you know this?" Kavin asked skeptically.

Hana stepped over the side of the pool and eased into the water, the thin fabric of her simple servant's dress soaking up the aromatic liquid as she lifted Kavin's other arm. "When I first came here, I was told of a *jarriah* who was Marid. She'd been captured during raids on the Kingdom of Gannah."

"Who told you about her tribe?"

"My mentor. The slave who trained me. She served the Marid female briefly. They gave her to a Shaitan for her test.

Shaitans, as you know, *jarriah*, do not regard females of any tribe as treasures."

Kavin swallowed hard as she eyed the Ghul slave marking wrapped around Hana's left bicep—a serpent emerging from black flames. A marking Kavin would soon bear herself, once her test was complete. No, Shaitans were nearly as debased as the wild Ghuls who roamed the Wastelands. She knew her tribe had a bad reputation amongst other djinn, because those in the Wastelands weren't policed—they raped and pillaged without remorse—but that didn't mean *all* Ghuls were bad.

Unease rippled through her when she thought of Zayd and the other highborns who took whatever they wanted without regard for anyone else's wants or needs. They dressed better than the Ghuls in the Wastelands, were educated and came from noble lines, but were they really any different? Then she thought about her parents, who'd taken the money Zayd had paid them as if it were a blessing. They'd not once tried to find her since they'd sold her. Finally, her mind drifted to what could have been—and probably was—done to a Marid female enslaved by Ghuls during a time of war.

Unease morphed to illness in the pit of her stomach. She looked away from Hana's tattoo.

"She lived through her test," Hana said, dropping Kavin's arm and running the sponge across Kavin's collarbone. "But she came back changed. Though she still spoke of her mate with hope, as if he could—someday—rescue her, the light was gone from her eyes. My mentor advised her to let her old life go and accept her new fate, but she couldn't. She did not survive life as a *jarriah*."

Shock rippled through Kavin. "The highborns killed her?"

"No, *jarriah*. She killed herself."

Dread pooled in Kavin's soul as she looked down at the soapy water, the bubbles slowly dissipating around her, much as her own will to live. Would that be her fate? If she survived her test, would she ever be able to accept her new role? Or would she slowly wither and die on the inside until there was nothing but a cold, empty shell of her former self left behind?

For the first time, she thought of the *sahad* in the dungeon of the arena not as a monster but as djinn. What had he been like before his imprisonment? Before being sent to the fighting pits of Jahannam? Had he always been a monster intent on death and destruction? Or had he been something—some*one*—more?

"Tip your head back, *jarriah*."

Kavin did as Hana said and closed her eyes while questions swam in her mind. Warm water trickled down her hair to dribble along her shoulders. A click resounded as Hana set the pitcher on the edge of the pool, then the water rippled as the servant girl moved behind her. Strong fingers massaged Kavin's hair into a lather.

Long moments of silence echoed through the vast room. Finally, Kavin said, "You mentioned Marid view females differently. That they don't employ the test. Surely they have other means of keeping their *jarriah* in line."

"They don't keep *jarriah*."

"Not at all?"

"Not at all."

Kavin pondered that as the girl's fingers moved down the length of wet hair at her back. "Then they must have many wives."

"Only one."

Disbelief rippled through Kavin, and she turned her head to the side, expecting to see humor on the slave girl's face, indicating she was joking. Only, Hana's face was stoic as she went about her duties. "You can't be serious."

"Completely. I told you before. Marid males mate for a lifetime. With only one female."

Kavin could barely believe what she was hearing. "And what if the female dies?"

Djinn were known to live for a thousand years, but they weren't immortal. Though they were generally immune to most illnesses, they could be killed, just like humans.

"That," Hana said as she reached for the pitcher from the side of the pool and filled it with water, "is the only thing that could turn a Marid from civilized to barbarian."

Kavin's chest tightened as Hana rinsed her hair. And images of the *sahad* raining down death and mutilation in the arena, then later standing hulking and menacing in his cell, flashed in front of her eyes all over again.

Hana wrung the water from Kavin's hair. "You are lucky your master is sending you to a Marid for your test. Considering their instinctive nature, you'll most likely be safe, even if he is a *sahad*."

She rose from the water and lifted a towel from the edge of the pool, which she held open for Kavin. Slowly, Kavin pushed out of the water and stepped into the bath sheet.

Hana wrapped the soft cotton around her naked body but didn't move away. Instead, she leaned close. "Though, if he's already lost his mate…" Her breath sent a shiver of foreboding down Kavin's spine. "Then, if I were you, I would be afraid. I would be *very* afraid."

Three males tattooed with the Ghul slave markings—just like the one Nasir sported on his left arm—treated his wounds.

They didn't speak as they went about their duties, and Nasir stood still and unmoving as his cuts were stitched, just as he always did. But something was off. Unlike the normal treatment he received after a match, this time the slaves weren't bathing the grime of the arena from his skin. In fact, the most cleansing they were doing was wiping the dripping blood, then covering the wounds thin bandages.

He didn't know what that meant, but since he'd been sent to the pits nearly four months ago, not a whole lot surprised him. He stayed alive by staying alert. And right now, his senses were buzzing that something was up.

His gaze drifted from the wall across the room to the slaves around him. Each wore the traditional slave attire—loose gray pants, no shirt, sandals on their feet—and not a single one was more than half Nasir's size. He knew he could take them if he wanted, but there was no reason. The threat wasn't in this bathhouse but outside its rock walls. Where guards waited with weapons and magic Nasir couldn't touch. Where an army of Ghuls itched for any excuse to execute him.

Rage rippled through his veins, the same bitter anger he felt whenever he thought of his captors, whenever he pictured the sorceress who'd trapped him to begin with, whenever he felt the firebrand opal brush the base of his throat. But he tamped down the urge to annihilate, just as he did every day, knowing succumbing to the rage now, before he'd had time to formulate his plan, would do nothing but get him killed.

His gaze swayed back to the wall, and his thoughts drifted to the Ghuls who'd visited his cell earlier. The highborn and the female he'd dragged in behind him. The female hadn't been branded with the slave tattoo, so the Ghul couldn't have been her master. Which meant she'd been there by choice, regardless of the little act she'd put on. Was she his lover? His mate? Nasir didn't know—nor did he care—but some instinct deep inside said whatever the two had planned for him couldn't be good.

The slaves finished their treatment of his injuries and turned Nasir for the door. Just as he'd predicted, there would be no bath for him today. Which meant someone wanted him to remain filthy. His newest punishment for remaining alive? To be treated as a rat instead of only caged like one?

They marched him down the long stone corridor back toward his cell. Guards in heavy armor with wicked blades were positioned every twenty feet, preventing any hope for escape this day. Heavy steel doors marked the openings to cells Nasir imagined were just as dank and depressing as his. He had no idea how many others were imprisoned here, but knew there had to be many. Every time they threw him into the arena, there was another djinni ready to gut him, as if they had an endless supply of slaves from all six tribes, just waiting to make their mark.

The slaves pulled him to a stop outside his door. The two guards stationed out front stepped to the side, then the one on the right unlocked the door and pushed it open. Darkness beckoned, as did the ever-present scent of mildew and filth. From the corner of his eye, he saw Malik, his trainer, striding his direction down the corridor, speaking in hushed voices with a highborn—the same highborn who'd visited Nasir earlier.

The guard shoved him into his cell and yanked the door closed. A clank echoed through the room, followed by muffled voices from the hallway, but Nasir couldn't hear what they were saying. Then footsteps receded until all that remained was silence.

Normally, a *mu'allim* spoke with his *sahad* after a match, but Nasir had yet to see Malik since killing that Shaitan. Another oddity.

Nasir pondered what that could possibly mean as he moved toward the dark corner of his cell. He didn't bother to light the one lone candle he was given, nor did he lie on the dirty mattress. Instead, he eased down to rest his back against the cold, unforgiving stone wall.

Comfort was something he didn't require anymore. There was only one thing that sustained him these days. Only one goal left to achieve. He drew his legs up, rested his elbows on his knees, and stared into the darkness as three words revolved in his mind.

Three words he repeated to himself over and over, day and night, so he wouldn't lose focus. Three words he would one day soon turn to reality.

Kill them all.

༄

Kavin's stomach was so tight she was sure she was going to throw up.

After Hana's little warning in the baths, she didn't know what to expect. Nerves ricocheted through her body as the slave girl dressed her in a light blue gown. The dress was like all the rest she'd been given since coming to Zayd's harem, the material expensive, the bodice work detailed. But she knew it wouldn't look as extravagant and pristine when the monster was done with her. And that, she supposed, was the purpose of getting all gussied up. So the *sahad* could tarnish the dress just as he was going to tarnish her, thereby knocking her off any pedestal she foolishly thought she belonged on.

"You're ready," Hana announced, stepping back to admire the way the expensive fabric draped across the floor.

Kavin steeled her nerves and lifted her chin. Though her stomach churned with fury and fear, she wasn't going to break in front of this girl again. She knew her earlier show of emotion was exactly what Zayd was waiting for, that he *enjoyed* her suffering. At this point she couldn't stop what was about to happen, but she had enough self respect left not to give him the emotional breakdown he desperately wanted.

Hana opened the door and motioned Kavin through. On shaky legs that were thankfully hidden behind the skirt of her gown, Kavin stepped from her room into the sitting area of the harem.

Several other *jarriah* were draped over the opulent, gem-colored furnishings, their gowns as expensive and regal as the one Kavin wore, their slave-band markings an in-your-face reminder of what Kavin had to look forward to when she completed her test.

Three *jarriah* lounging in the room looked her up and down with smug expressions, then resumed their conversation as if Kavin had never entered. But the fourth, a brunette on the far settee, wearing a gold gown and dangling gold earrings, smiled sadly. And in her eyes there was pity.

Kavin looked quickly away and drew a deep breath for courage. Three guards and a male dressed in commoner's garb, his chest covered by a leather breastplate and a whip tied at his hip, waited on the far side of the room.

It was all Kavin could do to walk across the marble floor without collapsing into a puddle. When she reached the males, she recognized the commoner from the arena. He'd stood near the gates, watching the fight with a keen eye. He stepped forward and took her hand.

His skin was shades darker than hers and warm. And his eyes were gentle. "My name is Malik, and I am to escort you to your test."

Rape. Kavin wished they'd all just call it what it really was, but she knew better than to say so.

She nodded once—the best she could do—and moved away from Hana, letting the male in the breastplate lead her out into the corridor.

The female chatter from the salon slowly receded as their steps echoed down the opulent hallway with its arched ceiling and towering columns. Two guards walked ahead, one at her back. Malik held her hand, never once letting her pull away as they made their way out of Zayd's garish compound and stepped into the sunshine.

The glare blinded her, and she held up a hand to block the sun's rays. Warmth beat against her skin, reflected from the dust beneath her feet, but she barely felt the heat of midday as she was loaded into a carriage. Thoughts spun out of control as Malik climbed in after her, and her pulse raced when the door snapped closed. Then the carriage jolted forward, winding its way through the bustling streets of Jahannam.

Free djinn could teleport through open air, but not slaves. So everyone they passed knew what she was. From the garishness of Zayd's carriage, most of them knew where she was going and why.

Her stomach rolled. Every turn of the wheels brought her that much closer to her fate, sent her heart rate skyrocketing. Sweat broke out on her skin, ran down the line of her spine, and gathered at the small of her back.

Once, she'd thought the stately buildings and old-world architecture of this city were charming. Now all she could focus on were the guards stationed on the roofs they passed, the wall that surrounded the city and kept its inhabitants locked inside, and the stark difference between the commoners on the streets and the highborns like Zayd who occupied the garish towers around her and commanded others to do whatever the hell they wanted.

"…remember that and you'll be fine."

Malik's voice cut through her frantic thoughts. Unable to steady her rapid breaths, Kavin turned his way. "Wh-what did you say?"

Malik squeezed her hand. His hair was short and dark, his body lean and muscled. This close, she could see that he wasn't wearing a shirt under his breastplate, and along the edge of the leather that covered his left shoulder and upper arm, the distinct black flames of the slave marking peeked beneath his armor.

He wasn't a commoner after all. Her gaze shot to his face once more. He was a slave, like her, being ordered to do someone else's will. And though his eyes were kind, they also hinted of secrets she didn't want to know. "I said, the Marid looks imposing in the arena, but in the cell, he'll seem even more so.

Weakness is your greatest enemy. Remain strong, and you'll be fine."

Fine. Yeah, right. She was so far from fine it wasn't funny.

Kavin focused on the seat ahead as the carriage rolled down the cobblestone streets and finally slowed to a stop.

The door pulled open. Her stomach flipped like a fish out of water as Malik tugged on her arm, pulling her to her feet. She stepped out into the fading sunlight once more and squinted. The stone-and-wood walls of the arena rose to the sky, but unlike in the busy streets behind them, there were no commoners milling here. No shopkeepers trying to hock their wares. No vendors selling steamy food as there were no fights scheduled for so late in the day. Just more guards, more armor, and more weapons reminding her she was as much a prisoner as the *sahad* who waited for her.

She couldn't focus on any one thing as she was ushered through the main door and drawn down a long hallway. They pushed her onto a lift, pulled her into a dank hallway, dragged her along the same stone floor she'd traveled earlier with Zayd. But this time, the moans in the cells around her, the dripping water, the scent of rotting flesh drove the anxiety higher up her throat until it was all she could do not to scream.

Finally, they pulled her to a stop in front of a steel door protected by two males. The guards who'd escorted her stepped back, their spears clicking against the ground. Her heart pounded against her ribs so forcefully she was amazed they didn't crack. At her side, Malik turned her to face him. "Remember, do not show weakness."

Do not show weakness. Right. Like she could do that.

She swallowed hard. Her pulse was a whir in her veins as the guard turned the key in the lock. As she faced the door once more. A click resounded through the dingy corridor, then the heavy door swung inward, the darkness inside looming like a menacing shadow, beckoning her forward to meet her fate.

Her legs shook. Her breaths grew shallow and uneven. Perspiration dotted her forehead and slid down her spine.

This is not my life. Hysteria built in her chest. *This is not my life!*

"I'll come for you when it's over." With a gentle hand, Malik pushed her forward.

Kavin stumbled, caught herself from hitting the ground face-first. At her back, the cell door snapped closed with an ominous boom, blocking out all light, all freedom, all hope.

A sob caught in her throat as she gripped the cold stone wall and turned to look into the darkness. Fear shook her whole body. Her frantic gaze darted from side to side, searching for the monster, but she couldn't see even a foot in front of her. Nothing but silence echoed in the musty space, sending her heart rate into the out-of-this-world range.

Long moments passed. She tried not to move. Tried not to breathe. Prayed he couldn't see her as she couldn't see him. Prayed he wasn't really in this pit and that someone, somewhere had made a mistake.

This is not my life!

And then she heard it.

The draw of air.

The rasp of breath.

The shuffle of cloth as something big moved directly in front of her.

Chapter Three

THE FEMALE WAS BACK.

Sitting in his corner, Nasir had seen her clear as day when the door had pushed open. Curly, auburn hair that hung to her shoulders, pale skin, a light blue gown that screamed of her status, and the stark look of fear in her eyes before darkness had fallen once more.

Fury built inside him, morphed to a rage he couldn't control. Because he was imprisoned here. Because they were fucking with him now. Because he'd been trapped by that bitch of a sorceress in the first place. Because Ghuls—her violent, depraved, repulsive people—had destroyed everything he'd once loved.

Thankful that this time they hadn't chained him, he lurched to his feet and stalked across the barren cell. Then he grasped the female's neck in a move she couldn't track in the dark.

"What the fuck are you doing here?" he growled.

"Pl-please!" she rasped, clawing at his hand.

"This is not a game. I am not some puppet." He squeezed, the red rage of retribution controlling him. "You and your mate chose the wrong fucking cell, female."

She choked. Sputtered. Coughed as his fingers pressed harder against her neck. Her fingernails dug into his forearm, but he barely felt the pain. Her pulse beat beneath his skin, started to slow. What little air was getting through rasped out of her lungs. Something warm and wet dripped onto his hand.

"This is not who you are."

The voice—Talah's voice—echoed through the room. Nasir's head jerked up; he glanced around the darkness of his cell, searching for her. But just as in the arena, she wasn't there.

The female pawed at his arm, this time with less force, a fraction of the fight she'd shown earlier. "Ple-please," she rasped one more time. "He's not my mate."

"This is not who you are, Nasir."

His attention swung back to the female he held pinned against the wall. Then his gaze dropped to his hand, wrapped tight around her throat, ready to squeeze out what was left of her life.

His skin grew hot, and the air tightened in his lungs. What the hell was he doing? This wasn't him. This was the killer the highborns had created in the arena. This was…the way a Ghul would react.

He released her. Moved back quickly, feeling as if he'd just been sucker-punched. His head spun. The room tilted. Riding a wave of nausea, he stumbled until his spine hit the far wall, then sank down to the ground, dropping his forehead in his hands.

Talah's voice echoed in his mind, dimmer this time but still there, and he tried to conjure her face but couldn't. His memory of her was slowly fading. And though he fought to keep her close, he was afraid he was waging a losing battle. Feared, more than anything, that once she was gone for good, he'd lose the fight for his sanity and truly become the monster the Ghuls were grooming him to be.

Fabric rustled, and rapid breaths crossed the space, echoed near his ears. "Please," the female rasped again. "Please don't hurt me."

Stomach still swirling, he lifted his gaze, peered across the cell. He could see well in the dark, had spent months getting used to it. But she probably couldn't see more than a foot in front of her.

She'd dropped to the floor, was sitting against the far wall, her knees pulled up to her chest, her shaking arms wrapped tight around her skirt, her hair a wild tangle framing her face. And her eyes... He couldn't miss them. Wide, the whites clearly visible, reflecting a terror he knew she wasn't faking this time.

He didn't know who she was or why the hell she was here, but he didn't care. She was Ghul, and for him, that was all that mattered.

He pushed to his feet, then receded back into his shadowy corner. "If you stay exactly where you are, Ghul, and don't move, then perhaps I'll let you live out the night."

ఴ

A loud metallic clank startled Kavin out of a restless sleep.

She jolted from the floor, scrambled to her feet. Held up a hand to block the glare from the corridor spilling into the musty cell.

Freedom. She blinked into the light. *Oh, Allah, at last.* They'd come to rescue her from this hellhole.

She didn't care who was out there. She lurched through the open door and the promise of fresh air. Of safety. A sob echoed in her throat as light blinded her eyes. Strong arms closed around her. Followed by a gentle voice echoing from above. One she recognized from yesterday.

"There, there, *jarriah*. All is well."

Malik. He'd brought her to this pit, but she didn't even care. He was strong. He was warm. He was comforting against her cheek in a way she didn't expect and didn't want to analyze.

She closed her eyes as the sting of hot tears burned her eyelids. The cell door clanked closed behind her, echoing like a cannon through the space. Her heart raced with relief. With joy. With the fact she'd survived. Elation carried her so swiftly she didn't even worry about the guards watching her or that her mental undoing would eventually reach Zayd's ears.

All she cared about was that she was *alive*.

Hands braced against her upper arms, Malik pushed her back, stared down at her. Realizing how foolish she must look, Kavin dropped her head into her hands, tried to get in control of her emotions. Not only had she survived a night in the pits, the monster hadn't touched her after that first instance. In fact, she hadn't seen or heard from him since. She didn't know why he hadn't raped her, but she was so very thankful for his disinterest now.

Feeling stronger, she swiped at her eyes, tried to smile for Malik's benefit. But when she lifted her gaze to his, she didn't see concern or curiosity in his dark eyes. She saw fury.

His jaw clenched so hard it was a slice of stone beneath his skin. His mouth cut a tight line across his tanned face. With two fingers, he tilted her chin up, studied her neck. Realizing there must be marks, Kavin gently touched a fingertip to the cool skin, only to cringe when pain shot through her body.

"I thought he had more restraint than a common animal." Before she could tell Malik she was okay and that nothing else had happened, his head snapped up, and he looked toward the guards behind him, the ones who had also escorted her to the pits the day before. "Take her back to the harem at once."

One guard grasped her arm, pulled her away. But Kavin heard the venom in his voice. And the promise of retribution. "Wait. Malik—"

"It's all right, *jarriah*," he said as the guard dragged her down the hall away from the cell, his voice softer but still teeming with disgust. "I'll make sure he's properly rewarded for his behavior."

Kavin tried to look behind her, but one guard tugged her forward while another blocked her view. At her back, she heard the Marid's cell door clang forward, followed by Malik's voice, shouting, "Get up, maggot. Your *mu'allim*'s here to teach you a thing or two about respect."

Kavin's pulse raced as the guards hauled her from the dungeon of the arena, out into the early morning sunlight, then shoved her into a waiting carriage. Malik had used the word *mu'allim*. He was the *sahad*'s trainer, not just any common slave. As the cart rocked across the street and the city sped by her window, she remembered seeing him near the gates of the arena, watching the Marid's match with… What had she seen on his face that day? Not just interest but…pride.

If he'd trained the Marid, of course he'd have a vested interest in the *sahad*'s wins, but *mu'allim*s trained more than one *sahad*. And pride… That was something else altogether different.

Her mind spun as the carriage came to a stop, as the guards opened the door and tugged her from inside. Light blinded her as she stepped onto the street. She felt the questioning stares of vendors and commoners as she moved, knew she had to look a mess and that most had probably already figured out what she was and where she'd been, but she barely cared. There were too many questions running through her head. Too many unexplained oddities she wanted to understand.

Oddities? You just survived being raped, and you're worried now about the beast who nearly killed you?

She gave her head a swift shake and stepped into the opulent building that belonged to Zayd. But while the lift jostled her and the guards upward, she thought about the Marid. About why he hadn't killed her. Why he hadn't raped her. And though she knew it was useless, she couldn't stop wondering who he had once been and how he'd been captured in the first place.

The guard to her right set the crank and locked it, bringing the lift to a stop. Then he muscled the gate open and stepped back. Hana was right there to greet them. She took Kavin's hand and pulled her into the harem. "Come. Quickly. He's waiting."

Kavin stumbled forward. She'd lost a shoe somewhere, and her bare foot landed hard on the polished marble floor, sending a jolt through her body. The brush of cool air told her the soft blue gown was ripped near her shoulder. Belatedly, she was aware of dozens of eyes in the room—other *jarriah*—but this time, she didn't see pity on their faces. She saw concern.

Her mind a thick soup of haze, she was pulled down a hall and into her suite of rooms. Relief washed through her when she eyed the plush furnishings, including the soft bed she'd slept in the last few weeks. But it quickly turned to unease when Zayd rose from the wingback chair near the fireplace and turned to face her.

Approval flashed in his eyes as he looked her over from head to foot. Then his gaze fixed on her neck—on the bruises she knew he could see—and a smug grin creased his face. To Hana, he said, "Remove that soiled gown."

Shock rippled through Kavin. In the two weeks she'd been in Zayd's home, he hadn't once touched her anywhere but on her arm and face. And she'd never been naked in front of him.

Before she could protest, Hana ripped the gown from her body, the tearing fabric echoing in the vast bedroom suite. Kavin gasped. Cool air rushed over her skin, tightening her nipples, sending a shiver through her entire body. But she didn't cover herself. She knew better.

Eyes hot and predatory, Zayd stepped close. His hot breath washed over her skin while he looked down at her bare breasts, as he slid his gaze to her belly, then finally all the way to her sex. His jaw clenched, and her stomach tightened at what he was seeing. Fear flitted through her veins over what he was thinking.

Then she saw it. Disapproval—stark and violent—flashed in his eyes. He'd expected the rest of her body to be bruised like her neck. Had *wanted* it.

"Zayd—"

His fingers were against her sex before she realized what he was doing. Before she could stop him. She sucked in a frantic breath, threw her hands out to push against his arm. Screamed, "No! Stop!"

But as quickly as he'd touched her, he withdrew, and when he eased back, she didn't just see disapproval in his eyes, she saw disgust and bitter rage.

To Hana, he growled, "Hold her arms."

He knew she was still a virgin. Panic welled in Kavin's chest as Hana stepped behind her, gripped both of her arms, and wrenched them behind her back. "Zayd, wait—"

"Don't fight," Hana whispered near her ear, just as Zayd's open palm connected with her cheek.

Pain spiraled through her face, the force of the slap spinning her head to the side. She gasped at the blow, gave her head a shake, tried to think clearly. "Zayd—"

Another hit. This one across her abdomen. With something thin, made of leather. A blinding burn erupted across her flesh, exploded through her belly. She nearly went down, but Hana's strength kept her from hitting the floor.

"You failed, *jarriah*. Failure is not tolerated. You will be punished."

He hit her with the leather again and again, across her breasts, her stomach, her thighs. She grunted through the pain, through the red welts forming across her skin. Her stomach hurt so bad, she absently wondered if he'd broken something inside her, then knew if he had, he wouldn't care.

"Release her," he barked.

She hit the floor at his feet, tried to move back but needed to catch her breath first. A white towel landed near her hands. Limbs shaking, she reached for it.

Zayd's boot covered the towel before she could get her fingers around the cotton, then he knelt in front of her face. Those eyes, the ones she'd at first thought were handsome, focused on hers with a menacing glare that sent a tremor down her spine. "If even a *sahad* in the pits of Jahannam won't fuck you, you're of no use to my harem. Do whatever you must to get the monster to use you, or I'll leave you in the pits to rot right along with him."

Fear and disbelief rushed through Kavin. He was sending her back? *No, no, no...*

He ran a finger down her still-stinging cheek, something he'd done several times since he'd bought her, as if he were admiring a sculpture or favorite possession. And though she fought it, Kavin trembled all over again.

"So beautiful..." Carefully, he tilted her face up to meet his gaze. Only this time, when she looked, she didn't see fury in his features any longer. She saw truth. A bitter truth that chilled her to the bone.

He leaned in close to her ear. "And if, on the fifth day, *jarriah*, you've still failed? I'll have you beheaded in the city square for all to witness. After I've sufficiently punished you myself."

Chapter Four

Nasir ducked out from beneath Malik's attack, swiveled, and nearly missed being skewered. Unlike the wooden training sword he used, his *mu'allim* wielded a steel blade, one that could inflict serious injury. And seeing how his trainer's deeply tanned features were currently twisted in a fit of rage, that possibility didn't look far off the mark.

Breathing heavily, Nasir swung out, his fake sword clanking against Malik's real one with a deafening clap. Dust blew up from the training circle, flew into his eyes. He blinked twice, dropped to the ground, and rolled away from another near-fatal blow.

"Get up!" Malik roared.

Nasir scrambled to his feet, his sandals skidding on the loose sand of the training arena, and tried to catch his breath. Crouched, ready to deflect whatever Malik threw his way, he swiped at the blood and sweat that dripped into his eyes and blurred his vision. But his trainer came at him again and again, never giving him time to orient himself, never giving any explanation for the intensity of the exercise. And as he fought simply not to be fileted, Nasir knew this was more than a simple lesson. This was retribution for what had happened in his cell last night.

Firebrand

Malik swung out again, and Nasir dodged another shot to the ribs. But before he could strike, Malik held out his left hand, and a surge of energy shot from his fingertips, slamming into Nasir's chest, sending him flying back ten feet through the air to land flat on his back with a crack on the hard ground.

Stars fired off in Nasir's line of sight. The training sword fell from his hand. He shook his head to clear his vision, then stilled when the tip of Malik's blade pressed against his throat.

"That, *sahad*," Malik said, glaring down at him, "was a warning. My magic is not completely bound here, like yours. Where I come from there are penalties for what you did to that female."

Malik withdrew the blade, stepped over Nasir before he could answer, and headed for the arched doorway on the far side of the ring. To the guard standing at the door, he barked, "Get him cleaned up and dump him back in his cell. And only half rations for him tonight."

Slowly, Nasir sat up, rubbed at his still-swimming head. Dust and sand flicked from his hair, rained down his shoulders. Every inch of his body hurt from the workout, but thankfully, no one besides his guards had seen his *mu'allim* kick his ass. Because he was the champion of Jahannam, he trained alone. He lived alone; he ate alone; when it came time, he'd die alone. Remembering what he'd done to that female last night without so much as a second thought, he knew being alone was best for everyone.

He pushed up on his knee, cringed at the pain in his side. One look told him it wasn't a pulled muscle as he'd thought. Blood dripped down his hip and onto his leg. Shaking off the sand, he picked up his training sword and hobbled toward the guards.

"*This is not who you are, Nasir.*"

"It is fucking now," he growled under his breath, not even slowing this time at the sound of Talah's voice ringing in his ears. It was time he stopped fighting who he'd become. The sooner he let go of Talah and a life he'd never return to, the more Ghuls he could kill. And before the sorceress who'd sent him to this hell called him back, he planned to take out as many Ghuls as he could.

His side pinched as he bathed. While they allowed him to clean himself this time, no one offered to stitch the wound. Another punishment, he realized. If he caught some deadly infection in his filthy cell, no one would care. After covering the gash as best he could with a clean piece of cloth, which he tied around his torso, he dressed in a new pair of black pants, then headed for the door. The guards parted. In the dank corridor, the smell of food being delivered to different cells pulled a growl from his stomach.

More tired than hungry, all he wanted was to fall onto his uncomfortable mattress and go dead to the world. Between the female trembling in his cell and Talah's voice haunting him half the night, he'd been bleary-eyed and on edge by morning. But oh so thankful when he'd finally found himself alone. Until, that was, Malik got hold of him.

He stopped in front of his cell, took the tray the guard handed him with its measly rations. As the guard pulled the cell door open and smirked, Nasir wondered what—besides his latest beating—the fucker could possibly find amusing.

The cell door clanged shut behind him. The soft scent of roses filled the air.

And then he knew.

A single candle burned on the table beside his bed, sending flickering orange light cascading over the stone walls. Red hair spilled across his pillow; bare feet rested near the foot of his bed. But it was the slim female curled up on his dingy mattress, wearing nothing but a black gown bunched around her thighs, her hands tucked up near her face, her eyes closed as her chest rose and fell with her steady, sleep-filled breaths, that drew his steps to an abrupt halt.

※

Kavin's eyes flew wide at the loud clap somewhere close.

She jerked upright. Disoriented from sleep, she blinked several times and tried to figure out where she was. Cold stone walls, one flickering candle, an uncomfortable mattress beneath her, and...*oh, shit*...an enraged *sahad* glaring from above.

"What the fuck are you doing here again?"

Kavin's pulse shot up, and she swallowed hard, scrambled back. But the bed was pushed up against the wall, leaving her trapped.

"I..." *Don't show fear.* Malik's words from yesterday flitted through her mind, searched for footing, finally latched on tight when terror wanted to drag her under. "I...I was sent to you."

His dark eyes narrowed. "By whom?"

He didn't know? Her foggy mind spun, and she remembered Hana telling her that Marid didn't keep *jarriah*. That the *jarriah* test was Ghul alone. "I...I'm your reward," she stammered. "For your recent victory."

He stared at her so long her heartbeat sped up until it was a blur echoing in her ears. Shit! Had she really just said that? Her hands shook, and she balled them into fists against the dingy mattress, hoping he wouldn't see.

"You're a reward?" he asked skeptically. "From whom?"

"From…" What should she say? She looked around, frantically searching for an answer, and caught sight of the metal tray of food at his feet. The tray he'd dropped against the unforgiving stones to wake her.

Malik was right—she'd realized his logic after Zayd had hit her, but this cemented it. The only way she was going to survive this new life was to never show fear—in front of Zayd, in front of whomever he sent her to, in front of this *sahad*. It was a long shot—thinking he might treat her differently if he believed she was here by choice rather than as a punishment—but at the moment, it was the only option she had left.

She lifted her chin and prayed it was too dark for him to see it shaking. "From the highborns."

"The highborns don't care about my victories. They'd just as soon see me dead."

That was true, but she grasped on to another truth. One he likely didn't know. "The females… They root for you. For the *sahad* who wears the fire opal."

His cold stare burned into her from across the space. So unfriendly, so calculating, she was afraid he was debating whether to kill her now or let her live a few more measly minutes. She balled her hands together in her lap. Tried to keep them from trembling. Tried like hell to be strong, as Malik had told her to be.

"I don't believe you," he finally said, his low voice cutting through the silence, sending a shiver down her spine. "You don't have the slave marking."

She didn't. And he obviously didn't realize she just hadn't been branded yet. Which meant she was right. He didn't know what she was.

A tiny flicker of hope burst to life in her chest as her gaze lifted from those massive hands at his sides, up his bare arms and shoulders, and finally to his chiseled face, illuminated by the flickering candlelight. If he didn't know she was a slave and instead thought she was a highborn who'd volunteered to be his reward, he'd likely be gentler with her. Maybe he'd even let her live.

That hope spread like wildfire all through her body. It wasn't the best solution, but it was better than being brutally raped. She'd survived Zayd's temper tantrum. Yeah, her skin still burned from the beating, but she now knew she could survive anything this Marid did to her, so long as he didn't kill her. Because she wanted to live. Now more than ever. It might be years—even eons—before she found a path to freedom, but she was determined to do just that. Screw her parents who'd sold her into slavery and already forgotten her. She was the only person who cared about her. And it was far past time she stopped worrying and started strategizing.

Slowly, she pushed up from the stained mattress and stood in front of him on legs she hoped he couldn't see trembling. This close, every flexing muscle beneath his skin, every ounce of waiting power was visible. And she could smell him. Not disgusting and revolting as he'd been before, but clean, male, strangely...enticing.

She gave herself a mental slap. Yeah, at first she'd been mesmerized by his show in the arena and, like other females who'd watched his fights, couldn't deny he was the perfect male specimen, all sculpted lean muscles and brawny sinew. But she wasn't attracted to him. He was simply the first hurdle on her path to freedom.

"I'm not a slave," she lied, praying he'd never learn the truth. "And I volunteered to be your…prize."

His eyes narrowed once more, but she didn't let it deter her. This was the only card she had to play, and she'd bluff all the way to her grave if she had to. "I thought I made it perfectly clear yesterday that I don't want you."

Fear flashed through her when she remembered his hand around her throat. Fear she hoped didn't show in her eyes. Thankfully, the bruises were small and, in this light, probably not even visible. Steeling her nerves, she moved a small step closer, even as the heat of his body encircled her and that intoxicatingly fresh scent she now knew was all him left her light-headed.

"Your wants are of no concern," she said. "And you're lucky the highborns didn't kill you for the way you treated me last night. They're giving you a second chance. It goes without saying that a gift like this can't—and won't—be refused…slave."

She didn't miss the sharp burst of anger that rippled through his eyes at her use of the word "slave." But she also saw the bitter bite of truth when he realized she was right.

Fear and hope swirled together in her stomach. The trap was laid. Now she just had to go in for the kill.

Could she do this?

Her nerves jangled. Her stomach tightened with indecision. For life? For freedom…?

Yes. Reality settled like a granite stone in the bottom of her stomach as she stared into his dark, unreadable eyes, giving her a courage she'd lacked before. A courage she'd need if she wanted to win this game. She could do this. To stay alive, she *would* do this.

She took another slight step forward, lifted a hand, and slowly rested it against his rock-hard chest. He didn't move a muscle, only stared at her with hard, onyx eyes she knew she'd remember forever. But heat and life pulsed beneath her palm, warming her from the outside in, amping that courage from the ground up.

Gathering every ounce of strength, she whispered, "The easiest way to get rid of me, *sahad*, is to take the gift now."

Chapter Five

Nasir's heart raced beneath the highborn's hand.

He was male, and she was as close as any female had been in months, so it made sense he'd react to her. But even with his djinn powers bound, he could tell something was off.

Gone was the scared and timid female he'd spent a long and miserable night locked with in this cell. Gone was the one who'd cowered from him when the Ghul had brought her to view him that first day. Unlike before, now she stood proud and confident, her head held high, her chin jutted out in challenge. But there was something in her eyes…a spark of unease, a hint of worry…and the slightest tremble to her lower lip that told him she wasn't quite as sure as she wanted him to believe.

The contrast sent questions swirling through his mind. Was his humiliation some new perverse form of amusement to the Ghuls? Had she been sent here to break him mentally since they couldn't break him physically in the arena? Disgust rolled through his stomach. They could beat him. They could make him fight. But he wasn't going to willingly be manipulated. Whoever she was and for whatever reason she was here, he didn't care.

He closed his hand over her wrist, then whipped her around so her back was plastered to his front and his arms were closed around her, locking her against him.

"Sahad—"

"Listen to me very carefully, female," he said into her ear, ignoring the soft curves of her ass pressing into his groin, the heat from her body radiating into his, and the silky smooth feel of her bare skin against his. "I don't care what you or your highborn friends have planned. I'm not a pawn in your fucking game. And I won't be told what—or who—to do."

He released her, flinging her around to face him once more, then stepped back. Surprise—and yes, a new shot of fear—widened her eyes. Her balance went out from under her, and she dropped onto the mattress with a grunt. "But you can't—"

Definitely not as confident as she wanted him to believe.

"I'm also not in the mood to talk." Nodding toward the food he'd dropped when he'd walked in and seen her sound asleep on his bed, he said, "If you're hungry, eat. You've already ruined my appetite. But stay the hell on your side of the cell. And when they come for you tomorrow, make sure you don't return."

He blew out the candle on the table beside the bed, then moved into his corner and lowered himself to the blanket on the floor. Pain radiated up his side, and he was so exhausted all he wanted was sleep. But he knew he'd get neither relief nor rest with the female in his cell. Not tonight, anyway.

For several long moments, silence echoed through the room, then the springs on the bed creaked, and very quietly, whispered words echoed through the room. "It's not my game."

He wasn't sure if she'd said them or if he'd imagined them, but he didn't care. His eyes slowly adjusted to the darkness. Only a sliver of light splayed under the cell door, illuminating a mere few feet, but he could see that the female had ignored the food he'd offered and lain back down. Except this time—though she was once again on her side with her hands tucked up near her face—her black dress completely covered her legs, and her eyes were wide and, very definitely, not the least bit sleepy.

He closed his eyes to block her out, leaned his head back against the stones, and saw her determined eyes in his mind. Green eyes, he'd noticed in the candlelight, like shimmering emeralds. Followed by the drape of curly red hair around her shoulders, the neckline of her black dress dipping low into seductive cleavage, and the strap on her shoulder falling to her upper arm, all but begging to be tugged off. With his teeth.

Fuck, this was going to be a long-ass night.

He swiped a hand down his face, brushing away sweat that had gathered on his brow. If they'd handpicked her to mess with his head, they'd done one hell of a good job in the selection. It wasn't just that she was hotter than sin—smooth features, a slightly upturned nose, mesmerizing eyes, and a body he already knew was made to be touched—or that he'd been without female companionship for ages. It was the fact she vacillated between confident and afraid, that she stood her ground even when she wasn't sure of his reaction. That she'd come back at all after what he'd done to her yesterday.

She had to be stupid, brainwashed, or simply fucked in the head.

It's not my game.

An odd sensation rolled through his belly, stopping his train of thought. Had she come by choice? Or had she been forced? His mind spiraled back to that first day, when the Ghul had pushed her forward. The amusement the male had exuded; the fear radiating from her. Was she as much a chess piece in all of this as he was?

Except...that didn't make sense. She was Ghul. Not only that, she was a *highborn* Ghul.

Not all Ghuls are evil.

His own words washed over him like a wave cresting the shore, sending foreboding trickling down his spine. As the female's shallow breaths across the room gave way to longer, deeper ones, his memories drifted back to those last few moments he'd spent with Talah. Standing on the cliffs behind her house, overlooking the sea. The salty air blowing her long, dark hair back from her face.

"You worry too much, Nasir."

"This is my father's war, not mine. If it were up to me—"

"If it were up to you, there'd be a treaty. But your father is right. The Ghuls don't want peace. War is the only solution."

"Not all Ghuls are evil, Talah. Like us, like humans even, some are good and some are bad. War is not the way to solve our differences."

Her expression said she didn't agree. But she smiled up at him in that placating way he'd come to dread and lifted her fingers to his cheek. "Forever the pacifist. You have a gentle spirit, Nasir. If anyone can see the good at the heart of a person, it's you."

He wasn't sure of that. But he closed his eyes, leaned into her touch, wanting to be comforted by her words. He'd preached about tolerance and acceptance, and now he was doing the very thing he'd argued against. He still believed peace was possible, even if his father disagreed, but because he was second in line to the throne and a general in the king's army, he had no choice. That didn't mean he was naïve enough to think that there wouldn't be consequences, though, or that he'd escape unscathed.

His eyes popped open. "Come with me to the castle. Until I can convince the king to stop this asinine war, you'll be safer there."

"Nasir—"

He ground his teeth together. "Don't feed me arguments about not wanting to live with me before we wed or your work at the infirmary, Talah. Just humor me in this."

She sighed, stared at his breastplate marked with the golden flame of the Marid tribe. Bit her lip as she debated what he hoped was a losing argument. Just this once, he needed her to acquiesce and not be so damn stubborn.

Finally, she sighed. "You're impossible, Marid."

"You're not the first to tell me that."

"All right," she said, looking up. "But not today. I have to let the others know I'm leaving so they have time to find a replacement at the infirmary. At least, temporarily." Her gray eyes sparked. "This doesn't mean we've agreed to anything, though, or that I've decided."

Relief washed through him as he dragged her into his arms. He could live with that. So long as she was safe, he'd have time to find a way to convince her she couldn't live without him. "I'll send castle guards to escort you tomorrow."

He kissed her, slowly, gently, with every bit of passion he had in him, and when he eased back, he saw the doubt in her eyes. Doubt he planned to alleviate the moment he returned from this useless battle his father was sending him to.

He skimmed a finger down her soft cheek. "I'll always keep you safe."

Her brow furrowed. "I know you think you will, Nasir, but you can't. And I don't need anyone to keep me safe. Death comes *to us all at one point. You can't stop it any more than I can. And I wouldn't want you to."*

Regret burned hot behind Nasir's closed eyelids, but he fought back the emotions struggling to shatter the shell he'd built around himself. So many times he'd thought about dropping his sword in the arena, of giving up and letting the Ghuls win so he could join Talah in the afterlife, but something always held him back. Though it went against everything he'd once been, he wouldn't rest until every last Ghul was destroyed. And not until he found a way to kill the sorceress who'd commanded the Ghuls to pillage Talah's village in the first place.

The female on his bed sighed. Opening his eyes, Nasir looked her way, fighting back the resentment at her presence. Thankfully, she was still asleep. He watched a wayward curl brushed her cheek and fall over her mouth, her slow breaths fluttering the lock of hair against her lips, reminding him of Talah's hair blowing in the breeze that last day.

What would Talah have done if she were in this female's place? If she'd been thrown in here with him, would she have stood her ground or backed down? He'd been drawn to Talah's gentle spirit, her willingness to help those less fortunate, but she'd never been a fighter. In fact, the biggest regret he had was that he'd never taught her how to protect herself so she would've known what to do when those Ghuls attacked.

The female shivered, and Nasir looked down at the blanket he was sitting on with a frown. He already wasn't getting any love from Malik. If the highborn died from exposure in this freezing cell, not only would his *mu'allim* be after him, the Ghuls would flat-out execute him, no questions asked. And while death didn't scare him in the least, it wouldn't help him achieve his goal of revenge.

Pushing to his feet, he gripped the blanket and stood upright. His head spun, and the room tilted. Bracing a hand against the wall to steady himself, he told himself it was lack of food. He eyed the tray across the room, the metal picking up the light from under the door, and thought about eating. Then his stomach rolled, stopping that thought dead in its tracks.

Sleep was a better idea. He shuffled across the floor, tossed the blanket over the highborn, and swiftly tugged it up to her shoulders. But before he could get a step away, she sighed, snuggled deeper into the cotton, and licked her plump, pink, perfect lips.

His gaze drifted over her features. So different from Talah's. Freckles across the bridge of her nose, a mole near the corner of her right eye, high cheekbones, and just the slightest dimple in her chin. With her pale skin and those startling eyes, there was no denying that she was…exotic.

The word revolved in his mind the longer he stared at her, unable to look away. He'd seen hundreds of Ghuls since he'd been here, but none of the females, slaves or free, had been as enticing as her.

She sighed again, the sound jolting him out of his trance. Enticing? Shit. He smacked the palm of his hand against his forehead and turned back for his corner.

"Not exotic," he mumbled. "Stupid." It was more than possible the highborns were setting some kind of trap for him with her, and he was even more determined now not to fall into it.

He lowered himself back to the cold floor, shifted against the stones, and cringed at the sharp shot of pain in his side.

Glancing down, he realized the bandage he'd wrapped around his torso was soaked with blood.

Fucking fabulous. Just what he needed. But there was nothing he could do about it now except wait until morning. Closing his eyes, he tried to rest.

Sleep came fitfully. His side burned, his legs ached, and he felt as if he'd been through a meat grinder, thanks to Malik's workout. He shivered, wrapped his arms around himself, shifted deeper into the corner and tried to find warmth as the hours ticked by. But even as he drifted between sleep and consciousness, images wafted behind his eyes. Talah's dark hair blowing in the breeze, her olive skin, her gentle smile. Images that slowly morphed until her eyes were no longer gray but sharp, green gems, her hair a drape of wavy red, her lips not curved in sweet compassion but plump, erotic…tempting.

Lips that moved, speaking to him in a voice not from the past but from the present.

※

Crouching in the corner of the cell with the lone candle she'd lit flickering light over the stone walls, Kavin cringed. Sound asleep, the *sahad* was like dead weight, and just lifting his elbow made her muscles strain.

His eyes were still closed, his head resting against the wall, but his skin was burning hot to the touch. She'd tried to ignore his murmurs, hoping he was simply dreaming, but the longer they'd gone on, making zero sense, the less she could. Especially when she realized he must have given her his blanket sometime in the night.

She didn't owe him anything. He'd made it perfectly clear he didn't want her around. But she couldn't ignore him either. So she'd lit a candle, climbed out of bed, and crossed the floor. And now her stomach was tossing on a sea of unease at the bright red blood staining the bandage against his ribs.

"You're impossible to fight with, Marid," she whispered.

His eyes popped open. His body jerked. Then his hand closed over hers against his elbow.

Kavin gasped, tried to pull away. His grip was strong, locking her in place, reminding her of the night he'd held her against the wall. Fear threatened to push in as he stared hard into her eyes, his gaze clouded and unwavering. But instead of being filled with venom—as before—this time, his eyes looked haunted, not those of a killer per se, but of a man who'd seen too much, lived through too much, and was fighting to cope with the fallout.

Silence stretched between them. Her heart raced beneath her breast. He wasn't a man, and she was foolish to think him anything but the monster she'd come to know. But...as his fingers seared her skin, as his gaze bore into hers, tension and something Kavin hadn't felt before—some electric and overpowering current—charged the air.

Her pulse picked up speed as she stared into his hard, dark eyes. Her adrenaline soared. Before she could figure out what the odd sensation was, he let go and dropped his head back against the wall with a groan.

Relief spiraled through her—or was that regret? Her head was so jumbled she suddenly didn't know. Rubbing her hand over the spot he'd just held, she tried to make sense of what had just happened. Couldn't.

"Allah," she muttered, noticing the sweat beaded his brow, the pale and clammy skin. He wasn't just injured, he was sick. "You need help."

"Don't want help," he whispered, eyes closed. "'Specially not yours. Just want to be left alone. Alone is…safe."

Emptiness rippled through Kavin's chest. An emptiness she'd been fighting since the moment her parents had sold her to Zayd. One that had grown and multiplied exponentially with every second she'd been locked in this cell, wondering—dreading—what would happen next. "Being left alone isn't safe," she whispered. "It's the greatest form of torture there is."

He didn't answer. Didn't even move. And suddenly, fear for her own safety mingled with urgency for his. If he died from infection now, she was all but dead. *Jarriah* did not get second chances in the test, no matter the circumstances.

She pushed to her feet, bent and slid her arms under his, careful not to touch the wound on his side. "Come on, get up."

His big hands landed against her shoulders. He rolled his head against the stones. The groan that echoed from his chest told her he still didn't want her help, but he shifted his feet under himself, regardless.

"Come on, Marid," she ground out, pulling as hard as she could. "I can't do this on my own."

Somehow she got him up, braced his back against the wall, and leaned against him to keep them both upright. He had to weigh twice what she did, and he was burning up with fever. She grunted, pulled, and eventually maneuvered him toward the bed. With a groan, he dropped onto the mattress, flopped over onto his back. Blood trickled down his skin from beneath the thin, red-soaked bandage.

Her stomach rolled again, but she ignored it, instead propped his tree-trunk-like legs up onto the mattress, pulled the blanket out from under him, then draped it across his body. Peeling back the cover near his wound, she dropped to her knees, steeled her courage, then slowly untied the bandage from his torso to get a good look.

His hand snaked out again and wrapped around her wrist with stunning force. And just as it had before, electricity arced in the air between them, sent a thousand vibrations all along her skin, and pulled a gasp from her lips.

Her gaze darted to his and held. To eyes that should chill her to the bone but suddenly didn't. Because this close, she saw something else lurking in their depths. Something she'd missed before when she'd been too scared to think. The same emptiness that consumed her. A hint of vulnerability she hadn't known was there.

Her breath quickened. Her skin tingled as if it were coming to life. So many times he could have truly hurt her but hadn't. Even that first night, he'd let her go. And though he held her tightly and could easily snap her wrist with barely a flick of his hand, she somehow knew he wouldn't.

Words formed in her mind. Words she didn't even know if he could hear in his current state, let alone understand. Words she suddenly needed to say. "I-I'm not here to hurt you, *sahad*. I only want to help."

"You can't help me," he muttered. "No one can. Not anymore."

His gaze never left hers, and energy vibrated through her entire body under his blinding stare. Energy she felt all the way to her core. In the silence that followed, his ominous words settled in the air around them, reminding her what Hana had told her in the baths.

"*Marid mate for a lifetime.*" Followed by the news that the death of a warrior's mate was the only thing that could turn him into a monster.

Was that what he was doing? Battling to avenge his dead mate? Questions she hadn't thought to ask before circled in her mind. Then mixed and swirled with the image of him, dangerous and magnificent, fighting to the death in the arena.

Her skin grew hot. A low ache gathered in her chest. Though she fought it, compassion spread through her veins, trickled to her belly. Suddenly, he wasn't the beast the highborns made him out to be. He was nothing more than a slave fighting to stay alive, just like her. Fighting to defy those who wanted to see him dead.

That was what she needed to do, she realized. Purpose rippled through her as their gazes held. A purpose that gave her strength, one she'd been lacking since being brought to Jahannam. Zayd could take her body; he could even take her freedom, but she wouldn't let him break her spirit. No one could take that from her. Not unless she let them.

"Let me try," she whispered, wanting—no, *needing*—to help him for reasons even she couldn't totally understand.

His eyes searched hers. For truth or lies, she wasn't sure. But something shifted in the air between them in that moment. Something she felt all the way to her toes.

He slowly released his grip, turned his head away, and closed his eyes. And as her chest thrummed with the weight of what had just passed between them, Kavin swallowed hard and reached for the bandage again.

The cut was deep, the edges puckered and swollen. She didn't see any signs of pus—which was a good thing—so she recovered it. But her hands were shaking when she pushed to her feet, then pressed the back of her hand against his forehead.

"Allah…" Urgency shifted to panic. She crossed for the door and pounded her fist against the cold steel.

"I know you're out there," she hollered at the guards. "If you want the *sahad* to die on your watch, continue to ignore me."

Metal scraped metal as the slot in the door was pulled open, and the guard's grim face filled the hole. "We don't answer to *jarriah*."

"You'll answer to this one," Kavin snapped. Fuck the guards. Fuck what Zayd would think when he heard what she'd done. Fuck them all. "The *sahad* is sick with fever and infection. I need bandages and medical supplies."

"Why should we care?" the other guard sneered, stepping up to the opening in the door. "One less Marid to worry about."

"You'll care because he's the champion of the arena. And if the highborns find out he died because of your neglect," she lied, "you'll be executed. Or better yet, tossed in the arena yourselves."

Fear flashed in both their eyes, followed by the brutal rush of resentment. But Kavin barely cared. So long as they bought in to her bluff and were motivated to get what she needed, that was all that mattered.

The opening in the door snapped closed, and muffled voices echoed from the corridor, followed by the sharp clomp of footsteps quickly moving away. Drawing a deep breath, Kavin turned back for the bed.

The *sahad* shivered, so she pulled the blanket up to his chin, tucked it around his shoulders. His eyes were closed, his chest rising and falling with labored breaths. In the dim candlelight, she stared down at his face, which suddenly looked childlike and innocent as he tried to sleep, not harsh and cold as it had before. Her gaze drifted over the dark lashes feathering the soft skin beneath his eyes, to the chiseled cheekbones, the weathered skin, the stubble along his square, strong jaw, then finally to the full, masculine line of his lips.

Lips, she could now imagine, that had once been used for kissing, not doling out harsh words and threats.

He stirred, tried to roll to his side, winced in pain but still didn't open his eyes. To ease him while they waited, she sat on the side of the bed and brushed damp locks back from his heated skin. "Shh...just rest."

The muscles around his eyes relaxed as she began humming a song she remembered her mother singing to her when she was little, and he seemed to drift back to sleep. Relief spread through her again as she continued to stroke his hair, then her gaze drifted down his neck to the fire opal at the base of his throat.

The gem was mesmerizing, catching the candlelight and making it dance as if it had a life of its own. Pulling the cover back, she ran her index finger across the smooth stone edged all in gold. Heat gathered beneath her skin, the sensation so startling it cut off her humming mid-song.

Where had he gotten it? Why did the guards allow him to keep something of such value? She knew the highborns all wanted it, had heard whispers in the harem that if a highborn's *sahad* killed him, the gem would then belong to them. But so far that hadn't happened. He'd destroyed every opponent they'd tossed at him.

Another image of him arcing out again and again with his swords in the arena flashed in front of her eyes, the stone as much a part of him as he fought as his hair or eyes or teeth. Was that how he stayed alive? Did the gemstone give him some kind of power?

"Who are you?" she whispered.

He didn't answer. She didn't expect him to. He was lost in some fever-induced haze, but that was okay. Probably better, actually. Because, based on the way she was now feeling toward him, if he turned that dark and dangerous gaze on her again so soon, she wasn't sure what she'd do.

Hinges creaked, and metal groaned. Kavin looked up sharply just as the door was pulled open and a guard stepped in, a square box in his hand. "This will have to do." He dropped it at his feet, then moved back. "See to it he does not die."

He was gone before she could answer, the lock clanking loudly in his wake. Slowly, Kavin moved away from the *sahad* and crossed the floor, then lifted the box and opened the lid.

Bandages, medicine, ointment for the wound. Relief was a welcome yet disturbing feeling.

He wasn't going to die. Not tonight, anyway.

Chapter Six

SOMEONE WAS HUMMING.

Nasir wrestled from a deep and clouded sleep and slowly opened his eyes to blink up at a stone ceiling.

Awareness seeped in. Candlelight illuminated the ceiling above, the rock walls around him, and the dirt floor below. A shiver ran down his back as realization came crashing in. He was in his cell in the pits of Jahannam, lying on the uncomfortable mattress with a blanket pulled up to his chest, darkness surrounding him as always. Except…

Somewhere close, the sweet, gentle notes of a song he didn't recognize met his ears. The melody pushed the darkness to the wayside, dragged his thoughts from despair and pulled them toward the light. Tipping his head, he looked toward the candle's flickering flame…and the redheaded female sitting in his corner, wrapping what looked like strips of fabric into a ball.

Something warm rolled through his chest. Something he hadn't felt in a very long time. Something that nearly stopped his breath.

Her head came up. The humming stopped. She stared at him a long beat but didn't speak. And in her hypnotizing eyes, he couldn't read her expression.

"You're awake," she finally said.

Weird images passed before him. Her arms around his torso. Her lush, tempting body pressing into his. Her leaning over him, the soft curtain of her hair tickling his cheeks. And concern across her mesmerizing face when she'd swiped a cool cloth over his forehead and whispered, "The worst is over. Rest now."

She pushed to her feet, smoothed out the black skirt of her dress, looking nervous and unsure and way too damn gorgeous as she took a hesitant step his way. "How do you feel?"

Nasir's pulse picked up speed, and his skin tingled. How did he feel? Hot. Achy. And oddly…aroused. Especially with the way she was looking at him. But why was she asking? Why would she care?

She moved to the foot of the bed, the candlelight flickering over her cleavage, drawing his gaze, making his skin that much tighter. "You've been asleep almost a full day. Your *mu'allim* was here. He brought herbs to break the fever. It looks like they helped."

He'd been out a full day? And Malik had been to see him? Confusion swept through Nasir's hazy mind as he tried to look away from her tantalizing breasts.

He pushed up on his hands, worked to sit upright. The female rushed over. "Here, let me help."

His adrenaline surged, and he sucked in a breath, knowing he should say no, yet not able to get the words out of his mouth. She set the ball of fabric—no, bandages—on the foot of the bed and gripped his arm in her dainty hands, her skin silky soft against his, her heat and floral scent making him light-headed. Sweat beaded his brow as she helped move him back so his spine was against the walls. And wicked heat flared all through his body at her touch. A touch he wanted to go on feeling. Even knowing he shouldn't.

Talk, dammit. Get your brain back online.

"What—" His voice was thick, raspy, not his own. He cleared his throat. Tried again. "What happened?"

"Infection," she said, finally letting go and moving back. Relief and disappointment swept through him all at the same time, confusing him even more. "From the wound in your side. I stitched it closed and bandaged it with what they gave me. But it was really the herbs your *mu'allim* brought that made the difference."

"Why?"

"Why?" Fine lines formed between her brows. Sexy lines. Lines he suddenly wanted to kiss from her forehead. "Because you needed them."

He shook his head. No, she wasn't following him. And he couldn't believe where his fucked-up thoughts were heading. "No, why *you*? I didn't ask…for a highborn's help."

Her mouth snapped closed. And her pretty green eyes went flat. The way they had when he'd told her he wasn't going to be a pawn in her game.

Except…as he stared at her and his mind turned over images of her tending his wounds, humming to help him relax, brushing the hair back from his face…he had a strange feeling it might not be her game either.

Which…didn't make any more sense than the reason she was still here now.

"I didn't want to be responsible for the great champion's death," she said in a tone that matched her lackluster eyes.

Yeah, but she wouldn't have been. She hadn't cut him. He'd gotten that injury in the training ring.

He rubbed his suddenly throbbing forehead. Man, his mind was still in a fucking fog, and everything seemed off.

"There's water if you want it," she said in a softer tone. "On the table next to the bed."

The bed he'd given her. He looked down at his legs, covered by the blanket he'd tossed over her the night before—hell, he wasn't sure which night now—then to the table where a tin cup sat.

A strange buzz started in his ears, seemed to spread to his chest. Why did she care if he was thirsty or not? Why did she care if he lived or died? He'd all but tried to kill her, then belittled her when he'd found her in his cell again, making it more than clear what he thought of her. What could have possibly compelled her to stitch his wound and tend him in illness?

Because that was what she'd done, he realized as memories of her whispered reassurances and silky fingers skimming his skin spiraled in and clamped on tight. She'd not only treated him, she'd sat beside him, kept him warm…comforted him with her touch and voice and presence.

A Ghul.

A *highborn* Ghul.

A really sexy, way-more-enticing-than-she-should-be highborn Ghul.

Nerves kicked up in his chest, sent his heart rate pounding. He tried to make sense of her actions. Couldn't. Tried to think logically. Came up empty.

Nothing seemed right. Everything was wrong. And yet… somewhere, in the back of his mind, a voice whispered, *Yes. Remember who you are, Nasir.*

His gaze slowly swung back to her, and before he could stop himself, he asked, "Why—why did you stay?"

She bit into her bottom lip, a move that was so damn sexy, blood rushed to his groin. But she didn't immediately answer as her gaze drifted to his feet, covered by the blanket. And reflexively, his toes tingled as if she were seeing them. Touching them. Caressing them with those fingers he remembered sliding across his skin last night.

"I—"

The door creaked open before she could answer. Her head turned that way, soft curls falling over her shoulder as she moved, drawing his attention to the creamy skin of her collarbone, then lower to the soft swell of her breasts. His cock grew hard beneath the blanket, and disappointment whipped through his veins when the guard entered, interrupting them, because he'd sensed she was about to tell him something important. Something he needed to hear. Something that would change things between them forever.

The guard moved to the side. Nasir looked over as his *mu'allim* stepped into the room.

Malik wore his traditional leather breastplate that fit his sculpted muscles, his hands clasped behind his back, his shaved head reflecting the dim candlelight. "You look better."

Nasir ground his teeth against the dull pain in his side and pushed up higher in the bed, trying not to look like such a pussy. Trying to get the raging libido that seemed to come out of nowhere under control. "How long was I out?"

"About thirty-six hours. You should have alerted the guards that the wound was deeper than originally thought. It won't serve you to die in here." Before Nasir could ask what he meant by that, Malik nodded toward the highborn and added, "You have the *jarriah*'s quick thinking to thank for your speedy recovery. By the time I came for you yesterday and realized the severity of your wound, it would have been too late."

Jarriah. Nasir looked back toward the female, standing at the foot of his bed, suddenly studying the floor with great interest while twisting her hands together in front of her. The male who'd brought her to see him that first day had called her *jarriah*. The word was foreign to him—of Ghul origin—but something in his gut told him to find out what it meant. That it mattered. That it was the key to what seemed so off about her.

Her…

He didn't even know her name. In all the time they'd been locked up together, he hadn't asked. Hadn't thought to ask, because he hadn't wanted to see her as anything other than his enemy. Now he couldn't stop wondering if that was true. Now he wanted to know everything about her—who she was, where she came from, and most of all, why she'd saved his life.

Not all Ghuls are evil.

"Get up," Malik said, reaching for the cover and pulling it back. "Rest is over. You need food, then we have work to do." He wrapped his hand around Nasir's bicep and helped haul him to his feet.

Malik handed him off to the guards, who, thankfully, were more gentle than normal. His head swam, but he was able to stand without crumbling to the floor. At his back, Malik said, "The servant is waiting outside to check you, *jarriah*."

"There's no reason for that, *mu'allim*," she replied in a quiet voice. "Nothing has…changed."

"Nevertheless, she must do as she's been instructed." His voice softened. "I'll be back to speak with you later."

"Thank you, *mu'allim*," she replied.

Check her? More questions swirled in Nasir's mind as the guards herded him toward the door. Light burned his eyes as he stepped out into the corridor, but he caught sight of the slim brunette wearing the traditional gray servant garb with the slave band tattooed across her right bicep.

The girl didn't make eye contact with Nasir, just nodded once to Malik, then disappeared into the cell, but whatever was said inside that room was too quiet to be heard. And as the guards ushered him down the hall, Nasir couldn't stop wondering what was really happening.

He was bathed, his wound tended and re-bandaged, then he was taken to the dining hall, which was empty, as always. From the courtyard beyond the high windows that let in only light and the blue of the sky, the crack of training swords slapping against each other echoed, telling him the rest of the *sahad*s were being put through a grueling workout in the baking heat of the sun.

A ripple of contempt washed through him. As champion, he never trained with the others—a luxury, he was told. But he knew the truth. His isolation was just one more way the Ghuls could punish him for being Marid. One more way they tried to break him. They were smarter than he'd given them credit. Torture was one thing, but loneliness…

"Being left alone isn't safe. It's the greatest form of torture there is."

His pulse picked up speed. The fork stopped halfway to his mouth. He wasn't sure when the female in his cell had said those words, but he knew they'd come from her. He could hear them now, in her sweet, tempting voice, as surely as he could suddenly hear the pounding of his own heart.

"Rise, *sahad*."

Nasir looked toward the doorway where Malik stood with his hands clasped behind his back, his mouth set in a grim line. Behind him, two guards waited.

"I want you in the training ring in five minutes."

Malik stepped out; the guards moved in. As Nasir lowered his fork and rose from the empty table, his mind spun with images, words, questions he couldn't answer. If the female in his cell was highborn, she wouldn't know about torture. She wouldn't know loneliness. She wouldn't have cared for him in any illness. And she definitely wouldn't be lingering in his dank, depressing cell right this moment.

"*He's not my mate…*" "*I was sent to you…*" "*Let me help you…*"

His pulse picked up speed. His heart raced beneath his ribs as he walked his tray across the room and set it on the high counter that adjoined the kitchen, then turned back toward the guards. There was only one answer that made sense.

She wasn't highborn.

The guards led him to the indoor training ring, smaller than the arena but with enough room to spar. His legs ached, and he was weak from the infection, but as he stepped into the center of the arena and the guard to the left handed him a wooden sword, he didn't care. All he cared about was learning the truth.

"Leave us," Malik said to the guards. They exchanged confused glances—they were always on hand to watch Nasir, even during training, because a Marid could never be trusted—but when Malik shot them a try-to-defy-me look, they both shrugged and exited, the heavy door clanging closed behind them.

Malik clasped his hands behind his back, the fingers of his right hand closed tightly around the hilt of his sword. "Do you feel rested, *sahad*?"

"Yes," Nasir lied, knowing not to show weakness. In the arena, weakness meant death. In the training ring, it translated to punishment. He grasped his sword tighter as Malik circled around behind him. His *mu'allim* was legendary for attacking when least expected, and, considering how scattered Nasir felt right now, he needed to stay on his toes.

"Honesty between teacher and pupil is the only bond we have, *sahad*."

Shit, Malik knew he was lying. Nasir tensed.

"However," Malik went on, moving around Nasir's right and coming back to stand before him, "considering the circumstances, I'm willing to overlook it. Just this once. I sense your question. Ask it."

Nasir looked up sharply. A *sahad* was never supposed to question his *mu'allim*, in anything. But he wasn't about to waste the opportunity, because he might not get it again. "The female in my cell. You called her *jarriah*. It's not a word I know."

"No," Malik said, circling once again behind Nasir. "Nor should you. It is not of our language. It is a Ghul word."

Our language? Nasir's brow dropped low, and more questions swam in his mind, but before he could ask them, a shot of understanding rippled through him, allowing him to see clearly, as if a veil had just been lifted. When Malik moved in front of him once more, Nasir's eyes opened wide. "Holy Allah... You're—"

The curtain dropped swiftly, blocking Nasir's senses. Malik stared hard into his eyes. "I am your *mu'allim*."

No, he was more. The air left Nasir's lungs on a whoosh. Malik was Marid, just like him.

"Not all your djinn powers are blocked, *sahad*," Malik said in a low voice. "Only the ones they fear you will use against them. You've been so focused on death and killing that you've overlooked what is at your fingertips."

What did that mean? "But how did you—"

Malik resumed his circle. "I was once a *sahad* like you. I developed the powers I was left with. And I learned to block certain things from those around me."

His heritage. He'd blocked who he was so the Ghuls he served didn't know he was Marid. Nasir remembered stories when he'd first arrived, about the *mu'allim* who trained the *sahad*s. He'd been here for ages—no one knew quite how long— had started as a fighter but had eventually worked up to his elevated status of *mu'allim*. Was it possible the current highborns controlling the city didn't know Malik was Marid?

"To answer your question," Malik went on, "*jarriah* is a Ghul word which means concubine."

All his questions about Malik came to a screeching halt. The female in his cell was a pleasure slave? He knew Ghuls kept them—hell, his brother Tariq had been imprisoned as one—but the thought the redhead was one made even less sense than the idea Malik was Marid. "How…? Why…?" He shook his head to try to clear it. Didn't work. "But…she doesn't bear the slave band."

"No." Malik said. "Because she's yet to complete her test."

"What test?"

Malik stopped in front of him. "Females newly turned of age come into the harem untouched. Before being granted full access to their masters' luxuries, they have to prove their worth. Each is sent to the pits for a night. If she survives, she goes back to the harem remembering there are much worse things in this life than serving the pleasures of one or many highborns. If she does not survive the encounter…well, then she's deemed unworthy, and her body is disposed of without the ritual burial."

Bile rushed up Nasir's throat. Even Ghuls had very finite burial ceremonies to ensure a djinn soul crossed to the afterlife. To be denied that rite—in any tribe—was a punishment reserved only for the worst of society. But the knowledge her life had so little value was quickly blanketed when he realized just what his part was in this whole sick scenario.

He swallowed hard. "She was sent to me to…"

"Yes. For her test. But you've yet to cooperate. Which is why she still remains."

Cooperate. A civilized way of saying he'd yet to rape her. Sickness swirled in Nasir's stomach as he stared down at the sand beneath his feet. He'd known highborns were malicious, but this…to torture one of their own in such a way by casting her into the pits with a *sahad* who hadn't touched or smelled or tasted a female in months simply to terrorize her into submitting…

"Why me?"

"That's a question only a highborn can answer," Malik said as he continued pacing. "To be honest, as champion, I'm surprised you haven't been used before this. The question isn't why, but what are you going to do about it?"

What was he going to do? Malik sounded as if he were asking what Nasir was going to do about a broken sword. They were talking about a person, for shit's sake… A fellow djinn, regardless of her race.

He swiped a hand across his suddenly sweaty brow. What was he going to do? Holy hell, he wasn't going to rape her, that was for damn sure. He had no intention of doing anything the highborns wanted him to do. If they thought he was defiant because he stayed alive, then they hadn't seen anything yet. There was no way he was touching that poor girl.

"A *jarriah* gets only one test," Malik said. "They will not give her to another. If you're thinking you won't comply in an attempt to snub the highborns, then I must tell you, it won't work."

Fuck them. There had to be a solution to this nightmare. Nasir's skin grew tight as his mind spun. "How long?"

Malik came around his right side again then stopped and regarded him with steely eyes. "She's been given five days to complete her test. Two have already passed."

That sickness swirled and circled in his stomach. "And on the fifth? If I don't…comply? What happens then?"

"You mean if you don't use her before the allotted time is up?" Malik tipped his head. "Then she will be executed."

Chapter Seven

Kavin looked up sharply as the cell door opened, then pushed to her feet as Malik stepped into the room.

"*Mu'allim*," she said, bowing her head. Light from the corridor spread over his muscular body, highlighting his brown skin and warrior clothing. Even though he was technically a slave and bore the marking, he was of a higher class than her. Everyone was of a higher class than her, even the guards.

She pushed that depressing thought away as he scanned the room and asked, "The servant is gone?"

"Yes, *mu'allim*."

He nodded, then gestured with his hand. "Come."

Surprise registered. Were they letting her go? Or had Zayd finally decided she was a failure and was having her executed before waiting the allotted five days?

"*Mu'allim*?" she asked hesitantly, her pulse suddenly racing with a mixture of horror and sickness.

Malik's face softened, and he motioned again. "It's all right, *jarriah*. We're just moving you to a different cell."

Hesitantly, she stepped forward, then faltered at what that meant. "But I...I'm not supposed to go with a different *sahad*." If she did, it was as clear as declaring failure. And if Zayd found out...

"No, you misunderstand, *jarriah*. We're moving you both to a new cell. One that is a little…cleaner…because of the champion's infection. He'll join you later."

Kavin's brow furrowed as she moved into the brightly lit corridor and blinked against the light. That made sense. Sort of. They couldn't very well let the great champion die of mistreatment. If they did, the guards, even Malik, would be in serious trouble with the highborns. Though she knew it would thrill them to see the champion die, they wanted it to happen in the ring, where they could wager against him and turn a profit from his death. "Y-yes, *mu'allim*."

She followed Malik down the corridor, around several corners, into a section of the dungeons she didn't recognize. No dripping water echoed here or ran along the floor. The doors were wood, not steel, and light filtered in from windows spaced high along the walls.

Malik stopped in front of a thick wood door, pulled out a heavy key ring, and turned the lock. The hinges groaned as he pushed the door open, then stepped aside so Kavin could pass.

She drew in a sharp breath when she moved inside the cell. Only…the word cell didn't seem to fit. The room was twice as big as the one she'd been in. Yes, there were bars on the high windows along the far wall, but there was light. Blessed sunshine reflected off the white walls, gave the room a warm, airy feeling. To the left, a rectangular tiled bath already filled with water was sunk into the cement floor. To the right, a double bed with real pillows and more than one blanket sat pushed up against the wall. And on the bedside table, several candles of differing heights and thickness waited for nightfall to be lit.

It wasn't luxurious by any means. Compared to her rooms in the harem, this one was sparse and empty. But considering she'd just spent the past two days in the dark and cold, the light, the promise of a real bath, and the thought of sleeping on a pillow seemed like heaven.

Unable to keep the tears from her eyes, she turned toward Malik. Wanted to give him a hug but knew better. "Thank you."

He nodded, then motioned toward one of the guards who'd followed them down the corridor. "Bring the *jarriah* fresh towels and bathing supplies."

The guard's disapproving gaze flashed from Malik to her, but he turned for the hall without questioning and disappeared.

Malik looked back at her. "Rest and refresh. You deserve as much after your service to the champion. The *sahad* will be brought to you after his training is complete."

Kavin blushed at his words, but he didn't seem to notice. Or if he did, he didn't react. He bowed once more, then stopped at the door. To the remaining guard, he said, "Bring her whatever she asks for."

The heavy door clanged shut, leaving Kavin standing alone in the middle of the room. And though her pulse raced at the thought of the *sahad* being returned to her, this time it wasn't entirely from fear. Excitement rippled through her veins as well. Excitement at seeing him again, at talking with him—she'd liked talking with him—at ignoring what Zayd wanted her to do and just being herself.

If she only had a few more days left, there were worse places to spend them. She was determined to make the most of what little time she had.

She moved toward the bath, pulled her skirt up, and dipped her toe in the water. Then smiled because the liquid was warm. She could already imagine it sliding over her body, caressing her tired muscles, and reinvigorating her with life.

The door clanged open, causing Kavin to jump. The guard who'd gone for towels dropped supplies on the floor at her feet. "Enjoy your bath, *jarriah*."

The way he snarled the last word sent a chill down her spine, but he left before she could respond. And as the key turned in the lock, she breathed out a sigh of relief.

Yeah, there were a lot worse ways to spend her last few days. If the *sahad* didn't want her, well, at least the fact she was still with him meant no one else could touch her either.

She moved the supplies to the edge of the tub, then tugged off her dress, dropped it on the cement floor and stepped down into the bath. A groan slipped from her lips as she lowered herself into the water and the warmth cradled her sore muscles and battered skin.

Most djinn healed quickly, and she was no exception. The lash marks across her breasts and stomach from Zayd's temper tantrum were nearly healed, and they didn't sting much, but she didn't forget they were there, or how she'd gotten them.

Reaching for the bath salts the guard had brought in, she sprinkled some into the water, then leaned back against the edge of the tub and let her legs float while her mind drifted. Images of the champion filled her mind. His powerful muscles flexing as he fought. The lines of his hard body pressing into hers as she'd hauled him to the bed in his cell last night. The look in his eyes when he'd gripped her wrist. Followed by the pain she saw lingering there. Pain she knew all too well.

Her heart bumped, a reaction she knew could do more damage to her than anything Zayd had planned. She was romanticizing him now, this *sahad* who was supposed to rape her. And yet, he hadn't. He wouldn't. She was as sure of that as she was the fact she'd soon be executed. But…she was no longer afraid of him. She was curious. The only thing she wanted before she died was to know more about him.

The cell door clanged open again, and her eyes flew open in surprise, her legs dropping down to the bottom of the pool in an attempt to hide her nakedness. But instead of the champion, what stared at her was the same guard who'd dropped her bathing supplies against the floor and sneered her way.

A menacing heat rolled through his eyes. One that shot Kavin's anxiety through the stratosphere. She inched back in the tub, recognizing the predatory look in his eyes. The malice. The intent.

The door slammed closed behind him. And a depraved grin spread across his dark face. "All alone. And naked." He crept closer as his eyes raked her body. "If the *sahad* won't fuck you, it's time someone else did, don't you think?" His beady eyes narrowed as he reached for the buckle at his waist. "You can thank me later."

Oh, shit.

Terror whipped through Kavin's entire body. She glanced right and left, searching for anything to use as a weapon. The guard wasn't armed, but she knew he could easily overpower her. And would.

No, no, no. Not like this. If it was anyone other than the *sahad*, she'd be executed on the spot. She wouldn't even have these last few precious days.

He moved closer as he pulled his belt through the loops and dropped it on the floor with a clank. Her legs tensed, her adrenaline pulsed. Her only hope was to get across the room, to maybe use the candles as a weapon…or something from the bed? A spring…anything?

Shit. Oh, shit.

If she screamed, anyone walking by would just assume the *sahad* was finally giving her what she'd been sent here for. The guard slinked around the far side of the tub, pulling off his armor as he moved until he was dressed in just the black pants and thin shirt he'd worn underneath. And as Kavin watched with wide eyes, her hand inched out along the edge of the bath, her fingers wrapping around the jar of bath salts.

Her heart raced while she waited for him to move closer still. He toed off his shoes, his eyes never leaving her, then he stepped down into the pool, obviously not even caring about his pants. "Come here, *jarriah*."

Kavin breathed hard. Waited. And just before he reached her, she hurled the contents of the jar into his eyes.

He swore, his hands rushed to his face, and a menacing roar erupted from him. She didn't wait to see what he'd do next. She rushed through the water to the other end of the pool and tore across the floor toward the bed.

"You bitch!"

She scrambled over the bed, then bent down and grabbed the frame, flinging the bed up and over onto its side as a barrier. Metal clanged against the cement floor. The guard found his footing, pushed his legs through the water. "You'll pay, whore. I was going to go easy on you, but not now."

Kavin's adrenaline spiked. She grabbed a candle from the table beside her, then pulled her arm back and hurled it toward him as hard as she could. It hit him in the forehead. His head snapped back, and his feet faltered. He swore again. Kavin reached for another candle.

But before she could grasp it, he was over the bed, his hand tightening over her wrist, the other closing around her throat. "Fucking bitch!"

Her eyes flew wide. He slammed her back against the cement wall. Pain spiraled out from her skull, radiated through her body. Air choked in her lungs while he squeezed. The candle fell from her hand.

He released her wrist. Reached for the button on his pants. Spots fired off behind Kavin's eyes as he continued to squeeze her throat, cutting off her air. She lifted her leg, tried to knee him in the groin, but he moved out of her way. Tears rushed to her eyes. She swung out with her arms, tried to pry his hand free, but he was too strong. Gasping, she struck his face, clawed at his eyes. But nothing stopped him.

No, no, no. Not like this...

His pants dropped. He pushed her legs wide. A sob caught in her throat as her vision came and went.

Somewhere close, metal clanged. Followed by a voice. A male, familiar voice. "You son of a bitch."

The pressure around her neck released. His body was pulled from hers. Sucking in air, Kavin dropped to the floor, her hands rushing to her throat, her body convulsing as she tried to breathe.

Slowly, she became aware of a struggle in front of her. Looking up, she watched in wonder and surprise as the champion towered over the guard, clutching his shirt in one hand, slamming his fist into the guard's jaw again and again and again. Chest heaving, he finally stopped and dropped the guard to the ground, but there was no missing the hatred in his eyes as he stared down at the bloody mess at his feet. "If you touch her…if you so much as look at her again, I will fucking kill you. I don't care what they do to me. I'll find a way to rip your miserable throat out."

The guard's eyes were filled with stark, raving fear as he scrambled back, pulling up his pants in the process. Voices echoed from the hall, and Kavin looked that way just as another guard and the champion's *mu'allim* moved into the cell.

"What's the meaning of this?" Malik demanded.

The *sahad* didn't answer, instead tore a blanket off the bed and turned toward Kavin, draping it over her naked body.

His eyes met hers briefly. Hard, cold, enraged eyes. But lurking inside them, she saw what she'd seen earlier. Compassion. Strength. Resolve.

Her breath caught.

He moved in front of her, putting himself between her and the others. "The guard tripped."

The room spun as Kavin looked from the *sahad* to Malik and back again. She knew what he was doing. If he was found guilty of attacking a guard, he could be punished, or worse, executed for the crime.

Malik glanced at the overturned bed, then to the guard's bloody face and finally to his armor, belt, and shoes strewn across the floor. His gaze snapped back to the guard, and in his eyes, malice burned hot and bright. Malice that made Kavin swallow hard. "Is this true?"

The guard opened his bloody mouth to answer, but a low growl from the *sahad* drew his attention. Fear rushed back into his eyes as he stared at the champion. After several long beats, he swallowed hard and slowly nodded. "Y-yeah. I tripped."

Malik looked toward Kavin for confirmation. Unable to bear his gaze, she shivered and glanced down, wrapping the blanket tighter around her. To the guard behind him, Malik barked, "Gather his gear. And take him to the infirmary."

The second guard's eyes were wide with disbelief, but he did as Malik instructed. As the two shuffled out of the room, Malik said in a softer voice, "*Jarriah*, are you okay?"

Shame burned hot through Kavin's veins. Shame and anger that she was here, that others had to see her like this, that she was at the mercy of all these males. She nodded, unable to muster up the words.

Silence echoed through the room, then Malik's shoes sounded, followed by the snap of the cell door closing.

Relief pulsed through Kavin as she fought back the tears suddenly burning behind her eyes. She'd lived. She hadn't been raped by that guard. But her chest rose and fell with quick breaths as if she were still in the midst of the attack. Why was she about to lose it *now*?

Metal groaned as the *sahad* tipped the bed back onto its legs, but Kavin barely cared. Her entire body shook, sending a chill over her skin and a sob rushing up her throat.

"It's over now." The *sahad*'s voice was soft. Close. Comforting. And then his arms were around her. Lifting her from the floor, cradling her gently against him, carrying her toward the bed.

She didn't fight him. Didn't even think to. All she could do was focus on breathing. On slowing her pulse. She sank onto his lap as he sat, and when he tugged her face down to rest in the hollow between his throat and shoulder and rubbed his hand up and down her back and hip and leg, she let him.

"Shh…you're okay now. No one's going to hurt you."

He'd saved her. The thought revolved in her mind as her adrenaline rushed out on a wave. Not only that, but he could have been executed for doing so. The reality of that stole her breath all over again.

His body was warm against hers. Warm and big and a thousand times stronger than that guard's, but she felt safe with him. Safer than she had with anyone else…ever. And she couldn't stop thinking about what he'd just done.

Slowly, she swiped at her eyes, then finally lifted her head to look up. His square jaw was covered in a thin layer of scruff, his skin was the color of caramel, his eyes a rich ebony. And his hair, black as night and hanging almost to his shoulders, looked so soft she had the sudden urge to run her fingers through the thick locks. "Wh-what is your name?"

The words were out before she could stop them. Before she could *think* to stop them. His eyes widened slightly, but he didn't let go, didn't pull away, didn't stop his hand running across her back, sending delicious shivers through her entire body.

"Nasir." His lips—his very masculine lips—drew her attention, made her wonder what they felt like. What they tasted like.

"Helper," she whispered, recognizing the meaning. "Your name is very much appreciated today."

"I'm no hero, *jar*—" His words cut off abruptly as his brow dropped low. "I don't want to call you that. What is *your* name?"

"Kavin," she answered, relieved he didn't want to use that word. Relieved she didn't have to hear it.

"Isn't that usually a boy's name?"

"My father wanted a son." He'd gotten her instead. Then had easily gotten rid of her.

She pushed that unwelcome thought aside as his gaze ran over her features. And her stomach tightened while she wondered what he saw.

Did he see a pleasure slave? A Ghul? Or did he see simply a female in a horrific situation?

"Fitting too," he finally said in a quiet voice. "It means handsome. Though I think in this case, I'd use beautiful instead."

Warmth bloomed in her belly. Warmth and something else…a tingling that started in her chest, moved up to encircle her breasts and made them ache, then spread slowly down to settle like a heavy weight between her legs.

Need—a need she'd never experienced before—rushed through her body, calling to her in a way that left her breathless. She wanted to run her hand over his hard jaw, to brush her thumb across his lips. To know what he felt like—just once. Was afraid of what he'd do if she tried. "Th-thank you. For what you did."

"I'd have killed him if I could."

She should be scared—that cold look she recognized from the ring was back in his eyes—but she wasn't. After everything she'd seen these last few days, she knew he wasn't the monster the highborns made him out to be. He wasn't even close. "Why didn't you?"

"Because then I'd be thrown in isolation, or worse. And I wouldn't be able to protect you. The same way you protected me last night."

Oh…

That warmth shifted to something hot and insistent. She pressed her knees together to stop the ache building to explosive levels between her thighs. And this time, when the urge to touch him hit, she lifted her hand without thinking. The blanket fell to her waist, but she didn't stop it. The need to feel his skin beneath her hands was too strong.

He tensed when her fingertips brushed his jaw. Realizing what she'd done, she pulled her hand back. "I'm sorry. His blood…you had a smudge."

His hand captured hers before she could lower it, but there was no pain in his grip. Only a tingling she felt all the way to her core. "Don't…stop. I…like your hands."

Her pulse picked up speed. Was he saying…?

His eyes darkened, and as she watched desire bring a flush to his skin, her heart pounded hard. He placed her hand against his cheek again. Tingling sensations rushed through her flesh. And when his gaze dropped to her breast, visible with the blanket open at her waist, her nipples tightened until another wicked shot of heat arced all through her pelvis.

"I'd like to help you, Kavin," he said in a gruff voice. "To thank you for helping me."

He was asking permission. Never, not in a million years, had she imagined this was how it would happen.

Her entire body tightened at the erotic implication of his words. At what she imagined him doing to "thank" her. At what he would ask of her when that "thanking" was done. But there was no fear. No revulsion. Only…excitement. An excitement that told her this was right.

"Yes," she whispered.

His eyes grew even darker. Beneath her, the muscles in his legs tightened as his arms closed around her back.

She wasn't going to die. As he lifted her from the bed and carried her toward the pool she'd just been in, that realization settled in. Followed by the chilling reality that when this was over, she'd be sent back Zayd. And the *sahad* who'd saved her in more ways than one would forever be a memory.

Chapter Eight

Nasir wasn't sure what he was doing. Certainly not anything he'd planned. But seeing that guard attacking the female...*Kavin*...it had unleashed something inside him. Something he thought had died long ago.

Heat pulsed through his groin as he lowered her to her feet. She clutched the blanket around her while he tugged off his sandals, then reached for a towel from the edge of the bath. Holding it up to shield her body, he waited while she dropped the blanket at her feet, then tucked the towel around her breasts.

Her eyes were wide and curious while he moved down into the warm water, still wearing his pants, and held a hand out for her.

She hesitated, then finally relaxed when she realized he wasn't insisting she lose the towel. Slowly, she stepped down into the bath, the cloth hitting high against her legs, drawing his attention to the toned, creamy flesh of her thighs. Making him hard with just a look.

If ever there was a time when a female was more vulnerable, he couldn't imagine it. Her fear was long gone. Her gratitude for what he'd done so palpable, he sensed right now she'd let him do anything to her that he wanted. But he didn't want to be like her highborn. Didn't want her to look upon him as she had that guard. What he wanted—for reasons even he didn't understand at the moment—was to see her tempting lips turn up in a smile. To learn more about who she was and where she'd come from. To—for a moment—find a peace he'd been lacking for way too long.

She lowered herself into the water and sat on the seat that ran around the inside of the bath. Her gaze strayed to the bandage on his side. "What about your wound?"

"It'll be fine." He clenched his teeth as he eased down into the water, ignoring the burn in his side, then reached for a washcloth from the edge of the bath. After wetting the corner, he swiped the dirt and blood from her face. Blood, he was thankful to see, that wasn't hers. "I think that guard will think twice about touching you again."

"Thanks to you."

His gaze skipped from her cheek to her eyes. Soft, hypnotic eyes, as green as the foam that rolled along the shores of his homeland. Reaching for her hand, he held her fingers up so she could see the bloody nails where she'd clawed at the guard's eyes. "No, Kavin, thanks to you. If you want, I can show you just where to strike to protect yourself from another attack."

"You can?"

One corner of his mouth curled at her surprised expression. "If you know where weakness lies, you can take down anyone, even someone twice your size."

"I think…I'd like that. Yes," she said more confidently. "I would."

A shadow passed over her eyes, one that made him wonder if she was thinking about the highborns who'd enslaved her. Or of the djinn who would touch her and use her for their own perverse pleasure once she was finally free of the dungeons.

He tamped down the anger that thought conjured as he washed her hand, gently rubbing soap over her nails, removing any sign of that guard's touch, then moved to her arms. In the silence between them, he was aware of every breath she took, of the way she watched him, of the scent of her skin—lavender and honey—so intoxicating he was amazed he hadn't noticed it before.

"Where did you get that?"

"What?"

"This necklace." She leaned forward and ran her fingertips over the fire opal at the base of his throat. And as if she'd touched him, warmth spread beneath the gemstone and into his chest, then lower, flooding his belly and groin.

He sucked in a surprised breath and looked down. She was studying the gem, not him, continuously rubbing her fingers over the opal as if it alone held her focus. But the contact made his entire body twitch and tingle with the need to feel her hands on his bare skin. And suddenly, he wanted her attention off the opal and directed only on him.

"It's so beautiful," she whispered.

"I'm bound to it." Was that his voice? It didn't sound like him. It was deep, gravelly, aroused. He cleared his throat, tried to kill the lust now simmering hot inside. Couldn't.

"How?"

Holy Allah, this close, when she tipped those eyes up, he realized just how mesmerizing they really were. Like miniature swirling galaxies, alive with light and life. A light he'd gone so long without.

"I was captured by a sorceress who bound me to the opal."

"A sorceress?"

He nodded, not entirely sure why he was telling her the truth, needing to share it for unknown reasons at the same time. "One who commands an army of Ghuls."

"Zoraida?" she asked in surprise.

"You know of her?"

Eyes wide with wonder darted back to the opal. But she didn't touch it again. And his pulse beat hard, waiting. *Wanting...*

"I've heard stories. About her power over those in the Wastelands."

"Where are you from?"

"The Northern Rim. My parents were...are"—she corrected—"farmers. They live in a small village. As children, we were taught to be on the lookout for Zoraida or any from her army."

"And you've never seen her?"

"No. The only outsiders we ever encountered were..."

Her words trailed off, and a bleak look filled her soft eyes as she focused on the waterline at his bare chest.

Highborns. She didn't need to say the word for him to understand. "How did you end up in Jahannam?"

She sighed, a heavy sound he felt in the bottom of his own chest. "Zayd—the highborn who brought me to you that first day—came through our village. I was selling vegetables in town with my younger sister. As soon as I recognized him for what he was, I knew we needed to leave. My sister and I rushed home. But he was already waiting."

Of course he would have been. Nasir had noticed the way the highborn had eyed her in his cell. A predatory look of ownership. The prick had seen Kavin for what she was—beautiful, young, and innocent—and pounced.

"My powers weren't very strong then," she went on. "I'd only just learned to teleport, wasn't very good at it, and my younger sister had yet to come into her gifts. If I'd been thinking, I'd have taken her somewhere else, but I was afraid. And I thought we'd be safe at home."

"What happened then?"

Kavin continued to study his chest. "My parents spoke with him in hushed whispers. He kept looking at my sister, and I was afraid he was there for her. She was only a child. And then my father announced that I would be leaving with Zayd."

A trick. The highborn had pretended to be interested in the child to get Kavin's parents to offer her instead. The entire thing singed a new path of anger through Nasir's stomach. That a parent could so easily give up one of his own… That the highborns in this land had the right to take anything they wanted…even a person…

"My mother told me I had to go willingly. That if I didn't, they'd take my sister too. And she assured me I'd be safe. So I went. Even looked at it like it was an exciting adventure. Zayd was…pleasant, at the start. And the city was so different from what I'd known. But then…then he brought me here." She sighed again and lifted her arm from the water, looking around the barren room. "To all of this. I don't even know if they miss me."

Pain radiated from her body as she lowered her hand into the water. A pain that rivaled his own. She'd been enslaved just as he had been. But in her case, it had been done by those who were supposed to protect and love her. Something that was a thousand times worse than what he'd been through.

"Zoraida captured my older brother, Tariq," he said before he could stop himself. Before he even thought to try. "As heir to the Marid throne, we were frantic to find him."

"Heir? Then that means you're—"

"Was. Here, I'm nothing more than a slave. No different from you."

Her gaze searched his, soft, so full of emotion, the hard, protective barrier he'd built around himself slowly started to crumble. "Do the highborns know? About your lineage?"

"I don't think so. If they do, they've never said. But then, Zoraida banished me here out of anger, so I'm not sure how much she communicated to them."

"How?" she whispered.

"Tariq had been missing for more than five years. We didn't know if he was alive or dead. When we got word her army was ravaging the Wastelands, I went in the hope I could learn something about his status. I did, all right. Too much."

To keep the anger at bay, he went back to cleaning her arms, and noticed, as they'd talked, that her towel had loosened until the wet cloth was barely covering her breasts. His pulse picked up speed, and that arousal he'd felt before came back swift and strong. "She'd bound Tariq to a fire opal, just like this one, and was sending him to the human realm to corrupt the souls of mortal women. For all the shit her army is doing, Zoraida needs those souls to fuel her immortality. She'd sentenced him as a pleasure slave."

"Like me," Kavin said softly.

He didn't want to think about that. Didn't want to think about Kavin being subjected to the same things Tariq had been. Forcing the unwanted images aside, he rubbed the cloth down her arm, swiping away blood and grime, bringing back the pink hue of her skin that was so damn alluring. "She knew my brother and I would search for Tariq. He was refusing to do her bidding any longer, so she set a trap."

"For you?"

"And our younger brother, Ashur. The bond between brothers in our tribe is strong. She threatened our lives if Tariq didn't do what she wanted. And with all three heirs to the Kingdom of Gannah under her control? She knew it wouldn't be long until her army was strong enough to challenge our tribe once and for all."

"I'm so sorry."

Her sympathy touched him in a way her gentleness hadn't before. He brushed his fingers up her arm, ran the washcloth across her collarbone, and his stomach tightened all over again at the way she drew in a breath and seemed to lift into his touch.

"I don't know what happened to Tariq," he said, trying hard not to look at the towel, now just barely covering her nipples. Hard, pert nipples, the tips of which he could see through the wet cloth whether he tried to or not. The tips of which he suddenly wanted to draw into his mouth again and again. "Something happened between them—I'm not sure what—but she became enraged and banished me to the pits in retaliation. I don't know what happened to Tariq or Ashur."

She leaned forward to run her fingers over the opal once more. A touch that this time sent ripples all through his groin and vibrations straight into his cock. "And this?"

He swallowed hard. Allah, but he wanted this female. He didn't even care that she was Ghul and he was Marid and that they were trapped together in this cell. He wanted to lose himself inside her and forget about sorceresses and wars and the arena that had become his one and only solace. "It means I'm still bound to her."

"So if you were to ever get free of these pits—"

"She could call me back at any moment."

Her eyes lifted to his. Eyes he wondered if he could see forever in if he looked hard enough.

"It seems we're both trapped in a prison," she said softly, "even outside these walls."

"It seems we are."

Her gaze slid back to the opal, but this close, all he could see and feel and smell was her. Her chest rose and fell with her shallow breaths, and when water rippled near the tips of her breasts—her *bare* breasts—he realized the towel had slipped to her waist, and that she hadn't stopped it.

"What would you do if you only had a few days left, Nasir?"

Spend them with you. The thought came out of nowhere, slammed into him, and stole his breath. Beneath the water, his dick tightened to painful levels. "I would make them matter."

Dark lashes fluttered against her creamy skin as she looked up. "I would too."

A thousand words hovered between them. Questions and answers he didn't want to voice. But only one thing registered. Only one thing *mattered*.

He eased forward until his chest brushed the tips of her bare, enticing breasts. Lust, white-hot and overwhelming, arced between them, encouraged him. She didn't ease away. Instead, her hands landed gently on his biceps, and her fingernails dug into his skin in such a deliciously wicked way, blood pounded in his cock.

"If I had only a few days left," he whispered, "I would want to spend them pleasuring you."

Approval flared hot in her gaze, and her nails dug in deeper to pull him even closer. So close her legs opened and her thighs brushed the outsides of his.

"Yes," she whispered. "Yes, I would want that too."

They weren't talking in hypotheticals anymore. And knowing she—maybe even he—likely did only have a few days left, he intended to give her exactly what they both wanted.

He closed his arms around her, drawing her tight to his chest, then lowered his mouth to within an inch of hers. "Let me pleasure you, Kavin."

Chapter Nine

SHE SMELLED LIKE VANILLA AND honey.

Nasir wasn't sure if it was her perfume or shampoo or what, but he loved the scent. And the soft, supple feel of her bare breasts pressing against his chest.

He waited, wanting...*needing*...her approval before this went any further. And when she whispered the word *yes* and lifted her mouth to his, victory ricocheted through him.

His mouth lowered to hers. Warmth and life tingled beneath his lips. Her fingers slid into his hair, then she tipped her head. And when he licked at the seam of her mouth, she opened without hesitation. Let him in. Gave him his first taste of something rich and exotic and hypnotizing.

Someone moaned. He wasn't sure if it was her or him, but he didn't care. All he could focus on was the slick wetness of her mouth, the way her tongue languidly stroked his, the way her breasts tickled his chest.

"Kavin..." He lifted one hand to cup her face, to tip her head the other way so he could kiss her more deeply. So he could taste another inch of her.

She scooted closer, more fully onto his lap, until the heat of her bare sex rested against his fly. The towel fell from her body to float in the water behind her. And everywhere, her heat consumed him. Entranced him. Overwhelmed him.

His lips slid from her mouth to her jaw, then trailed hot kisses across to her ear. She sifted her other hand into his hair, groaned, and tipped her head, offering more. Offering anything he wanted. And the way she rocked against his lap, rubbing against his throbbing cock, nearly did him in.

He wanted to hear her pleasure, wanted to feel it himself. He lowered his head, cupped her right breast, then lifted it toward his mouth. She answered by easing back just enough, then moaned all over again as his tongue brushed her wet, tight nipple.

"Nasir…" Her fingers tightened in his hair. Her hips pushed against his again.

He licked all around the areola, then drew her breast into his mouth, suckling as he'd wanted to do, until she dropped her head back and moaned long and low in ecstasy.

Blood rushed to his groin. Sent a blinding desire roaring through his veins. With one arm locked around her waist, he pushed out of the water and moved for the steps. Setting her down on the edge of the bath, he laid her out on the cool tiles and moved to her other breast.

She was responsive in ways he didn't expect. Passionate in ways he couldn't predict. As he continued to lick and nibble and revel in the sounds she made, something in his chest broke open wide. A part of himself he'd closed off when Talah had died.

He didn't want to examine what was happening to him. Didn't want to think. He just wanted to *feel*.

"Your skin is so soft," he mumbled as he slid his lips from her breast to her stomach, tracing a line of wet kisses to her belly button. "I want to taste more of you. I want to taste all of you."

She drew in a sharp breath. Pushed up on her elbows and braced her feet on the steps beneath him. When he nudged her knees apart, she didn't stop him, but he felt her gaze on him. And when he moved his mouth lower, across her belly, he looked up and watched her eyes widen and darken with lust.

A jolt of arousal sent his pulse skipping. He looked down at her body laid out before him, at the triangle of red curls, then lower to her sex, already glistening with her arousal.

He palmed her breast with his right hand, slid the other down her belly, and parted her with his fingers. Then groaned long and low when he finally saw all of her.

Pink. Wet. So damn tempting it was all he could do not to rip off his pants and drive into her.

She sucked in a breath. Held very still while he looked his fill. As a *jarriah* in training, he knew she'd likely been instructed—at least academically—in all manners of pleasure. But from the hesitation on her face, he was sure this was the first time anyone had seen her. Knew this was going to be the first time anyone touched her. And the knowledge of that sent a thrill through every inch of his body.

He lowered his head and, slowly, stroked his tongue up her cleft. Then groaned all over again when he reached the swollen nub of her clit and she shuddered.

"Nasir..." Her head dropped back. Instinct took hold. She lifted her hips, seeking more.

He did it again, this time circling her clit with his tongue and finally suckling until her whole body trembled.

"Oh…"

"Feel me, *rouhi*. Feel me licking you. Tasting you. Feel me pleasuring you with my mouth."

She moaned. Lifted her hips again and again while he lapped at her. And, as her arousal grew, he felt it everywhere. In his cock. In his skin. In his soul.

He pinched her nipple as he circled and swirled. Lowering his other hand, he brushed his fingers against her sex. She was wet and dripping. And so very hot. He wanted nothing more than to slide inside her, feel her clench around his fingers, but didn't want to do anything to give her master a reason to take her from him. At least not yet.

"Let go, *rouhi*." He blew hot against her mound, rolled her nipple. "Let go and come for me."

She gasped. Tightened her muscles. Panted on the verge of blinding ecstasy. He lowered his mouth to her clit once more and suckled as he continued to tease her breasts. As he drove her wild with his fingers. With his lips. With his tongue.

Her whole body tensed, and she cried out. And as her release consumed her, he rode it with her, licking her gently, drawing out every ounce of pleasure he could, enjoying it through her, in a way he'd never known before.

She fell back against the tiles, twitched from the aftermath. Lifting his head, he looked up her gorgeous body to make sure she was okay. Her chest rose and fell with her rapid breaths. Her skin was slicked with sweat, her eyes still closed, her cheeks flushed and hot. But when a slow smile began to curl her tempting lips, he knew she wasn't just okay. She was sated and relaxed, enjoying a satisfying post-orgasmic glow.

Sheer pride rippled through him. That he'd done that to her. That he'd been the one to give her pleasure no one else ever had.

He pressed his lips against her lower belly, then kissed her higher, moving back up her body as he crawled out of the water and eased over onto his side next to her, marveling at the way she didn't flinch from his touch. At the way she sighed in complete contentment.

His fingers grazed her right breast, and she trembled again. Bracing himself on his elbow, he looked down at all her luxurious hair laid out beneath her, wondering how he could have thought she was a highborn that very first day. Wondering how the hell he hadn't seen the goodness inside her. It was his anger, he realized as he took her in. All that pent-up fury he'd shielded himself with after Talah's death. He hadn't thought Ghuls were all evil before that day. Hadn't ever expected it would take a slave—a Ghul slave—to show him they weren't all evil now.

"Did you enjoy that, *rouhi*?"

Her eyes fluttered open. Glossy, seductive, radiant eyes met his. Eyes that drew him in and pushed all other thought right out of his head. "Yes," she whispered, brushing her fingers against his arm. "Very much."

"Good. That's what I wanted."

He lowered to take her mouth. Intended it to be a gentle kiss. But when she threaded her fingers into his hair and dragged him closer, all that pent-up arousal pushed his need right back to the forefront.

Her mouth... Her breasts pressing against his bare chest... The way she lifted her leg and parted her thighs, inviting him, luring him, drawing him closer to all her succulent heat...

"Kavin," he managed, trying to pull back from her lips, failing miserably. His cock was so hard against her thigh, his need so great, he didn't know how much longer he could resist.

"I want you, Nasir. I want to feel you inside me."

Oh, Allah. So did he. So much so he could barely see straight.

It took every ounce of strength he had to ease away. "I... can't."

"But I thought—" She looked down her body, to her bare hip, where his throbbing erection pressed hard and hot and so eager to get inside her. Then her gaze snapped back to his. But this time, it wasn't brimming with desire; it was laced with confusion. And disappointment. A whole lot of disappointment that speared straight to his chest. "I thought you wanted me," she said in a small voice.

He hated that look of rejection on her face. He was responsible for that. After the way he'd treated her before... After the things he'd said... But he could change it now.

Brushing her hair back from her face, he leaned down to kiss her lips again. Gently. Sweetly. Over and over until she opened and slid her tongue into his mouth, drawing him deeper into something he knew he'd never escape. His blood was a roar in his ears once more. His cock so hard he hurt. But his suffering was worth it if it killed the worry in her eyes.

"I'm not ready to share you," he said against her lips. "I don't want them to take you from me yet."

She eased back, stared up at him with even more confusion. But swimming in her sea-green eyes, he saw heat. The same heat burning him from the inside out. And followed quickly on its tail, a burst of tenderness that softened her entire face.

"Oh, Nasir," she whispered, running her palm against his stubbly cheek.

His chest tightened. A sensation he hadn't felt in so long he wasn't sure what was causing it. But he liked it. So much that even though he knew this was futile, that eventually she'd be taken from him or one of them would die, he turned his lips into her hand, kissed her palm, then closed his eyes and hung on to the feeling.

Not of despair and misery but of hope. And the promise of a tiny speck of blessed light instead of all the wretched darkness he'd been living with.

She pushed him back so he was sitting, then moved into the water. Surprised, he looked down at her. At the wild tangle of red hair around her flushed face. At the same hunger he felt reflected in her eyes. She knelt on the steps, gorgeous and naked and *his*, and when she pushed his legs apart, then ran her hands up his fabric-covered thighs, sparks of heat ricocheted right up his legs and into his groin.

"I want to pleasure you, Nasir. The same way you pleasured me."

He sucked in a breath. Unable to move. Unable to think. Unable to do anything but stare. And want. And lust.

"I want to feel you against my tongue," she whispered, reaching for the button on his pants. "This time, I want to taste *you* come in *my* mouth."

※

Kavin's pulse beat so hard she was sure Nasir had to hear it.

Did he want that? Did he want her to touch and taste and pleasure him the way he'd pleasured her?

He'd said he wanted her. His words from moments ago—his reason for not claiming her—still rippled through her chest, sending warmth to every nerve ending in her body. No words had ever meant more to her. But did he want her mouth on him right now, the way his had been on her?

Please say yes. Please say yes…

For reasons she couldn't explain, she was dying to see all of him, to feel him with her hands, to taste him with her tongue. Though she'd never felt the urge before, right now, she *needed* to make him feel as good as he'd made her feel. Craved it in a way she'd never craved anything else.

"Nasir?" she asked hesitantly when he only continued to stare at her with those heated, dark eyes. Eyes that sent desire skipping right back through her veins, mixed with a wariness she knew he saw.

"It's been a long time for me," he said in a low voice. A sexy voice. An oh-my-Allah, I-could-come-again-just-listening-to-that-voice voice. "I'm not sure that's a good idea."

"I want to." He didn't stop her when she unhooked the button at his waistband. And she took that as her sign, slowly sliding the zipper down his fly. "I need to."

He tensed when she pushed her hands beneath his waistband, one on each side of his hips. His skin was warm against her palms, the muscles bunched below so damn alluring. Bracing his hands on each side of him, he lifted for her, letting her slide his thin black training pants past his hips and down his thighs.

His erection sprang up, so thick, so hard. And then it was her turn to draw in a sharp breath. Her hands faltered as she looked her fill. He was bigger than she expected—thicker, longer, darker at the tip—but it didn't frighten her. If anything, the sight of him so aroused excited her. She drew in his scent—musk and man and need. Licking her lips, she dragged his pants the rest of the way off and tossed them onto the tiles beside the bath, then wondered—imagined—how he would taste in her mouth, how he would *feel* sliding inside her body.

Her pulse raced. Leaning forward, she braced her hands on his thighs and felt him tense all over again.

A smile curled her lips. He liked her touch. As much as she liked his. She tipped her eyes up to his. "You may need to help me a little. I've never done this."

His eyes darkened, and he drew in another deep breath as she leaned forward and extended her tongue, licking just the very tip.

He was warm and hard and just the slightest bit salty. An interesting and unusual taste. But when he groaned low in his throat, she lost her inhibition and leaned closer still, running her tongue along the underside of his head, then opening and wrapping her lips all the way around him.

She knew, of course, what to do. As a *jarriah* in training, she'd seen pictures and drawings of the various sex acts. She'd even, secretly, been shown a live encounter between a *jarriah* and a highborn. A visual that had left her sick to her stomach at the thought of being forced to do any and all of the things she'd witnessed. But this wasn't forced. And this didn't leave a pit in the bottom of her belly. In fact, as she moved her lips lower, suckled, and drew back, her own arousal increased, until she had to press her thighs together to assuage the ache growing once more between her legs.

Nasir dropped his head back and closed his eyes. With his hands braced against the tiles, his torso tipped back, and his face angled toward the ceiling, Kavin had a great view of his body. Chiseled, hard, so incredibly perfect, he looked as if he'd been carved from stone. As she continued to work him over with her mouth, just as she'd seen that other *jarriah* do, she remembered how it had felt to have his hands on her body as he'd licked her. Growing more confident, she slid one hand up his belly and lightly pinched his nipple.

He moaned in response and lifted his hips, forcing his cock deeper into her mouth. "Oh yes, *rouhi*, that feels so good. Flick the tip with your tongue when you pull back."

His words inflamed her, excited her, aroused her to explosive levels. She eased back, ran her tongue all along the head, just as he'd said, then took him deep in her mouth once more.

"Allah," he whispered. "Just like that. Deeper."

His fingers threaded into her hair, massaged the back of her scalp, applied just the slightest amount of pressure so she drew him deeper. Easing back again, she looked up to see his reaction and realized he was watching her through dark and hooded lashes, his eyes as smoldering as she'd ever seen, his face flushed and sparkling with a thin sheen of sweat.

She was making him feel as good as he'd made her feel. But it wasn't enough. The need to make him come, to make him lose control just as he'd done to her, overwhelmed her.

She refocused on her task, tightened her lips, lowered, and took him even deeper, until he brushed the back of her throat. And when he groaned again, when he lifted his hips again and again as if he couldn't stop, she didn't let up. She drove him closer to the edge with her mouth, raked her fingernails across his balls with one hand, and pinched his nipples with the other.

"*Rouhi...* Allah, you need to stop. I won't be able to hold back much longer."

She didn't want to stop. She wanted to taste all of him. And the strain she heard in his voice told her he didn't really want her to stop either.

She continued to suckle him, pushed his hands away when he tried to ease her off his cock, then took him as deep as she ever had. And then she swallowed again and again until her throat worked around his length and he groaned long and low.

"You feel so good, *rouhi*. Oh yes, keep swallowing, just like that. Fuck, I'm gonna come. Do you want me to come in your mouth?"

He grew even harder, thrust deeper, faster. She looked up, continued to work him over with her lips and tongue and throat in answer, continued to give him everything he'd given her. His hand tightened in her hair; his eyes glazed over. Then his entire body trembled.

A growl burst from his chest just as his cock twitched in her mouth. "I'm coming."

His seed burst across her tongue, filling her mouth with a salty sweetness she loved. She swallowed, drawing out his orgasm, watching as it overwhelmed him, consumed him, and left him as boneless as hers had left her. His hand dropped from her hair to the tiles. His muscles quivered as he braced his weight against his arms. Only when she felt him soften slightly against her tongue did she finally let go.

He blinked several times, seemed to have trouble focusing. Then finally rasped, "By Allah. Where did you learn to do that?"

Heat burned her cheeks as she eased back to sit on her heels in the water. She knew his question wasn't meant as an accusation, but it hit her as such, dousing the arousal she'd felt before and reminding her just what she really was. Suddenly very aware of her nakedness, and his, and the fact that, even though he'd just orgasmed, his erection was still hard and big, lying against his thigh, she swallowed, then lifted her gaze back to his face. "I… They make all of the trainees…watch. I've never done that before, though. I mean, that was the first time I…"

She clamped her lips together before the words could get all the way out. Sickness flooded her belly, a sickness she'd kept at bay by not thinking too much about the future. But now…

He was in the water before she saw him move. His arms wrapped around her body, drawing her close, his lips closing over hers to kiss her crazy all over again. And as he held her, as his strong, muscular body pressed against her and his tongue stroked hers in that wicked, erotic way as it had before, it pushed away the dark thoughts and drew back every inch of that desire she'd felt before. When he'd pleasured her. When she'd pleasured him.

A devastatingly handsome smile turned his lips when he eased back from her mouth. A smile that made him look years younger and so full of life, it stole her breath. "I've been trying to plot my revenge against the highborns since the day I was brought here. But you just proved pleasure is the very best revenge there is."

She wasn't sure what he meant by that, but she didn't dwell on it, instead brushed the dark hair back from his face so she could see his eyes better. "You're not upset?"

"Why would I be upset?"

"Because they're right. I just demonstrated I can be as big a"—she fought back the hitch in her voice as she looked down at his chest—"whore…as the others in the harem."

"*Rouhi*, look at me." He tipped her chin up with his finger. "Did I force you to do anything you didn't want to do?"

"No."

"Did you enjoy it?"

Her cheeks heated all over again when she remembered his mouth on her sex, when she remembered how hot he'd been against her tongue. She glanced at his lips. His luscious, sweet, tempting lips. "Yes."

"Then you're not a whore."

"But some *jarriah* in the harem enjoy what they're made to do." Her stomach rolled when she remembered Hana telling her that many *jarriah* learned to crave what the highborns did to them, alone, in multiples, whenever and wherever they wanted.

"Enjoy or tolerate, because they don't know any better?"

Slowly, her gaze shifted to his eyes. His soft, fathomless eyes. "Are you saying they lie?"

"I'm saying they're not given a choice. You are. With me, here, now, everything is up to you. You are not one of them, *rouhi*. With me, here in this cell, you're mine, and I am yours."

Warmth unfurled in her stomach. A warmth she felt all the way to her toes. *Rouhi*… He'd called her that several times now. Did it mean the same in his language that it did in hers? She wanted it to. She loved the thought that he was calling her "his soul." Because that was how she was suddenly thinking of him.

He was not at all what she'd expected. He was kind and sweet and so damn sexy she could barely believe she'd once thought him a monster. She knew it was silly to romanticize what was happening between them. He'd told her—flat out—that pleasure was a form of revenge. But she didn't want to be just another way for him to get back at the highborns who'd imprisoned him. She wanted to be more. She wanted to be *his* in every sense of the word.

As he lowered his head and kissed her again, she cupped his face, opened for him, and drew him into her mouth and heart and soul. His erection pressed against her thigh, sent a jolt of arousal rushing through her veins all over again. Told her, oh, yes, he wanted her as much as she wanted him. And though she was desperate to feel him slide inside her body, she knew he wouldn't—at least not yet.

But that was okay with her. Because she didn't want to give him up yet either. If he took her—*when* he finally took her—she'd revel in the moment and carry it with her for the rest of her life.

However long or short that might be.

Chapter Ten

A CRASH SOMEWHERE CLOSE JOLTED NASIR from sleep. Confusion hit as he blinked at the sunlight streaming into his cell, reflecting off the white walls and bathing the entire room in warmth. But it was quickly replaced with a wave of heat when he registered Kavin's naked body pressed tight against his under the threadbare blanket.

A smile curled one side of his mouth when he remembered carrying her from the bath to this bed last night, laying her out, and pleasuring her all over again with his hands and mouth, then falling asleep in her arms when they'd finally both been breathless and exhausted. The way she'd given herself over to him touched him in a way he couldn't define. Touched him in a way no one else had ever done.

His smile faded. He stared across the room at the shadow of the bars high on the wall above his head and thought of Talah. If she were still alive…if she were at home, waiting for him, would he be feeling what he was right now?

His heart thumped hard as he looked down at Kavin, her face resting gently on his chest, her hand over his heart. He'd loved Talah, had wanted to spend his life with her, but it had always rubbed him the wrong way that she'd never been able to commit. Even right up until that last moment they'd spent together, something had been holding her back.

Did he feel differently about Kavin because she needed him in a way Talah never had? Or was it something more?

His mind was a sea of confusion. He didn't know what to think. What to feel, for that matter. Something had happened to him yesterday—something he hadn't expected. And now, all he could think about was finding a way to spend more time with Kavin. To figure out what it was about her that touched him. It didn't matter that she was Ghul and he was Marid. All that mattered was that he wasn't going to be satisfied with only two more nights. He wanted weeks. Months. He wanted…

Years.

Holy Allah…

His pulse picked up speed as a rush of emotions pummeled his chest from every side. Revenge and hatred were no longer fueling him. What now gave him life, what breathed air into his lungs, was the thought of freedom. With Kavin. And a life free of war and prisons and the horrors he'd lived with for so long.

"Yes. Yes…this is who you are, Nasir. Remember it…"

Talah's voice, as strong as he'd ever heard it, faded slowly until it was only a whisper in his mind. Until he didn't need it anymore to drag him back from the darkness.

Pulse pounding, he looked back down at Kavin, at her sweet, succulent lips, at the tangled red hair around her face. At her delicate, porcelain skin. At the bruises around her neck and down her arms where that guard had held her, then to the fading lash marks across her breasts. Marks he'd noticed last night and had wanted to ask her about, but hadn't because he didn't want to ruin the moment. But seeing them now, in the light of day, a burst of anger whipped through him. Anger, surprisingly, that he could control. Anger that gave him purpose. A purpose he'd been lacking since being enslaved.

Voices echoed from the hallway.

The guards, he realized. Coming to drag him to his daily training. He only had seconds before he'd be separated from Kavin again. Hopefully for only a few hours.

"*Rouhi*," he whispered, gently shaking her.

Her lashes fluttered, and she groaned. But when she focused, those jade-like eyes of hers darkened with desire just as they had last night. Then her lips turned up in such a provocative way, he swelled against her thigh.

"Good morning," she whispered.

"A very good morning." He leaned down and touched his mouth to hers. Electricity arced between them, a shock that rippled through his groin. He wanted nothing more than to lose himself all over again in her kiss, but forced himself to pull away. "Your servant will be here to check you anytime."

Her smile faded as he eased up to sitting. She moved next to him and brushed the hair back from her face. "I almost forgot about her."

He hadn't. Suddenly, anything that had to do with Kavin was foremost in his mind. "I heard the guards outside. They'll be here soon."

He climbed out of the bed and walked to the bath, where he picked up her dress and his pants from the ground. When he brought them back to her, he didn't miss the way her cheeks flushed as she studied his naked body.

Heat rushed through his veins, reigniting that arousal he'd been fighting all morning. "Do you like what you see, *rouhi*?"

Her cheeks turned bright red, but she tipped her face up to his, not trying to hide her interest in the least. "Very much."

Blood rushed to his cock, made him hard all over again. He dropped the clothes on her lap, then leaned down and kissed her, pressing her back into the mattress, thankful for the scraps of cloth preventing him from taking what he so desperately wanted. "Don't tease me. Not yet."

He nipped at her bottom lip, loving the way she tasted, the way her silky fingers raced over his bare back. Somehow, he found the willpower to push away from her body and drag his pants on. She sighed and pulled her dress over her head. But her eyes stayed locked on his abs and—he was pretty sure—his hips. Making him that much harder.

While he tried not to notice, she pushed from the bed and let her skirt fall down her legs. "Will you tease me again tonight? Or will you…you know?"

He buttoned his pants. "Will I what?"

She smoothed out her dress, then sat again. "You know… take me."

The hitch to her voice froze his hand against his waistband. And the thought of doing just that, of lifting the dress she'd just put on and pushing deep inside her body, inflamed him from the inside out. "Do you still want me to?"

Her chest rose and fell, the soft swell of her breasts dragging his attention from her face to her body. Her gorgeous, beautiful body no one but he had touched. "Yes," she whispered. "More than I ever expected."

Guards and impending servants forgotten, he dropped to his knees in front of her. The need to make her his in every sense of the word burned hot, but he fought it back. Because what he wanted now wasn't just her body. He wanted her soul too.

When they were eye to eye, he brushed his fingers against her cheek. "Kavin, I want that too. Desperately. But when we make love, it will be on our terms, not on some highborn's."

Her brow furrowed as she searched his eyes. "But if you don't... Before the days are up...he'll...he'll have me—"

His heart cinched down hard, a heart he hadn't felt in so long he was almost shocked to know it was still there. A heart she had reawakened. "He won't. I won't let him."

"But how will you stop him? If the allotted time passes, and I'm still a virgin—"

"I won't share you."

"You won't be able to stop him. We're both just slaves."

He squeezed her hand resting in her lap, wanting, *needing* her to believe in him in a way Talah never had. "I will keep you safe, Kavin. Trust me. I'll find a way."

She stared into his eyes with that unreadable expression so long he wasn't sure what she was thinking. And he held his breath and waited, wondering if she'd brush him off the way Talah had. Wondering if he was destined to repeat all the mistakes of his past...losing not only what was left of his heart but of his mind too.

"I do, Nasir," she finally whispered. "I trust in you."

His heart swelled, seemed to grow inside his chest. He dragged her face toward his and kissed her deeply, knowing this female—this Ghul, of all people—was the only person who could bring him back from the brink of despair. He wouldn't fail her. This time, everything would be different.

The jangling of keys just beyond the door drew him back and away. Nerves vibrating, he crossed to the other side of the room, then eased down to sit against the cool ground so the guards wouldn't know what had happened between them. But as he propped his arms on his updrawn knees, he chanced a peek at her. At her flushed cheeks, her swollen lips, and her soft, soft eyes. Eyes that were watching him, just as he was watching her. Eyes filled with emotions he hoped mirrored his own.

The cell door clanged open, and two guards stepped into the room. Two new guards Nasir had never seen. Followed by the slave girl he'd glimpsed yesterday.

Options raced through his mind. Thoughts, scenarios, escape plans he knew he could never make work. Followed by Malik's words in the training circle.

"I was once a sahad *like you. I developed the powers I was left with. And I learned to block certain things from those around me."*

In an instant, he knew how they were going to break free. The only catch was time.

Nasir glanced at Kavin. They had two more nights together—two more full days, if he got through his training quickly and Malik let him off easy. On the third, her highborn would be back for her. If they worked hard, they had enough time.

He just prayed Kavin was strong enough for what lay ahead.

※

Kavin watched as the guards hauled Nasir to his feet and took him out of the cell for his daily training routine. He didn't glance back at her, and though she knew why, a tiny part of her couldn't help but be disappointed.

The door clanged shut, and then she was alone with Hana.

Hana clasped her hands behind her back, her long dark hair pulled into a tail at her nape. "You look like you had an interesting night, *jarriah*."

Heat rushed to Kavin's cheeks. Could the slave girl sense what had happened in this room? She brushed the unruly curls back from her face. Told herself no one knew but her and Nasir. But even just thinking about what they'd done, remembering how his mouth had felt on her breasts, on her belly, on her sex… Warmth pooled in Kavin's stomach and sent a bittersweet ache between her thighs.

She lowered her hands, clasped them in her lap, trying not to give anything away. "I'm fine."

"Hm," was all Hana said. But the look on her face told Kavin the slave girl didn't believe her. She held out her hand. "Come."

"Come?" Kavin asked, looking up in surprise. "Where?" The last few times Hana had appeared in the pits, she'd checked Kavin, then returned to the harem to inform Zayd his *jarriah* was still a virgin.

"Your master has requested you."

A burst of fear rippled through Kavin as she stood on suddenly shaky legs. No, this wasn't right. Zayd had said she'd stay until she either completed her test or was executed. "Wh-why?"

"Why is of no concern to you. Your master is waiting."

Kavin's nerves were a quivering mass of fear and apprehension as she stepped toward the door. Outside, a guard from the harem waited, kicking Kavin's worry up another massive notch.

She followed Hana out of the pits and into the sunlight toward the carriage. The guard's ominous presence at her back did nothing to settle her fears. As they traveled the cobblestone streets of Jahannam, Kavin tried to figure out what Zayd could possibly want with her. Memories of the last time he'd called her back—after that first night with Nasir—spiraled through her mind. His rage at her failure. His promise of punishment should she fail again.

"I will keep you safe, Kavin. Trust me. I'll find a way."

She closed her eyes as the carriage jostled her against the seat and fought back the despair. How could Nasir keep her safe when he was locked in the pits and she was…here?

The carriage jerked to a stop, and the door was pulled open. Bright sunlight burned her eyes as she climbed out and was escorted to Zayd's compound. Towering palms and brightly colored flowers greeted her as she stepped into the garden, but she barely noticed the beauty. All she could think about was Zayd, and what he had planned for her next.

The harem was just as she remembered when they stepped off the lift, posh and overdone in vibrant colors. Several *jarriah* lay draped over the velvet couches in low-cut, revealing gowns, just waiting to be summoned. To be used. And moans, hinges creaking, and the undeniable sounds of sex could be heard from a room down the narrow hall to her left.

Kavin swallowed the bile rising in her throat and glanced away from the curious eyes. She knew she had to look a sight after days locked in Nasir's cell. And thanks to that guard who'd attacked her last night, bruises covered her neck and arms. Did the other *jarriah* think she'd been raped? Was that what Zayd would think too? Was that why Hana had brought her back?

When Hana motioned for her to follow, Kavin didn't look back at the females she felt watching her every move. Instead, she steeled her nerves as she was led down a dimly lit corridor toward Zayd's private rooms at the end of the hall.

Hana knocked on the double doors. Kavin's stomach tensed when Zayd's voice called, "Enter."

The doors opened, and, pulse pounding, Kavin followed Hana into the opulent, blue room with its leather furnishings and heavy draperies. A cluster of couches flanked the enormous fireplace. Across the expensive rug, a canopied bed, large enough to comfortably sleep at least four, sat against a wall. To her right, seated behind his enormous desk, Zayd eyed her with…approval.

"My, my, my," Zayd said, leaning back in his chair. "Look what the cat finally dragged in."

Kavin's pulse shot up, and sweat slicked her skin as the guard stepped back toward the door, joining his place next to the first, blocking her only exit.

"Strip her," Zayd said to Hana.

Kavin's heart pounded against her ribs as the slave girl tugged the straps of her gown down her arms. The thin garment slipped free of her body to pool at her feet, leaving her standing before Zayd, completely naked.

This is not my life…

She closed her eyes tight. Tried to stay calm. But her pulse was a roar in her ears and that voice screaming, *Run!*, *Escape! Now!* was all she could focus on.

Hana stepped back. Kavin knew not to cover herself, but her stomach caved in, and every muscle tightened as Zayd's chair creaked. Tearing her eyes open, she watched as he rose from his chair with a licentious grin and walked around the ornate desk.

What would he do when he realized she was still a virgin? She swallowed hard as his gaze slid from the bruises at her neck, down her breasts, to the marks on her arms. And her stomach turned when he looked to her hips, and, finally, to the thin patch of hair covering her sex.

"Well, *jarriah*," he said in a low voice. A sickening voice. "It looks like you were finally used well."

This is not my life!

She knew not to fight him. Knew there was nothing she could do. But bile welled in her throat when he placed his hand on her shoulder, when he dragged it down her arm, then cupped her breast as if he owned it. And when his hand trailed down her stomach, she clenched her teeth to keep from pulling her arm back and pounding him in the jaw.

Nasir. Think of Nasir. She closed her eyes. Breathed hard and fast through her nose.

"Slave," Zayd barked. "Come here."

She sensed Hana move close. Braced herself for the girl's small hand, relieved it would be her checking for the confirmation Zayd so desperately sought, instead of him.

"Well?" Zayd asked, his voice strained with excitement, his hands continuing to cup and fondle her breast in a way that made her want to vomit.

Hana's hand pulled away, and she pushed to her feet on a sigh. "She is still a virgin, master."

For several seconds, nothing happened. No sound. No reaction at all from Zayd. And then she felt the heat of his body, so close Kavin sucked in a sharp breath and dragged open her eyes.

A fury she'd never seen coated his features. A malicious look that sent ice to the pit of Kavin's stomach.

"Still you fail me," he growled. "Perhaps the problem is you just don't know what's expected of you."

No, no, no... He can't. He wouldn't...

He jerked his gaze away from her and nodded toward the guards.

Footfalls echoed across the marble floor. Terror pushed a cry up Kavin's throat. But hands didn't close over her as she expected. The guards didn't touch her. Instead, they grasped Hana at her side and jerked the slave girl around until she was standing in front of Kavin, her eyes wide with fear, her chest rising and falling with her own shallow breaths.

Zayd moved behind Kavin and breathed hot against her ear. "Maybe what you require, *jarriah*, is a demonstration."

Oh, Allah...no.... Servants were not to be used like that. There were class systems, even amongst slaves.

His hair brushed her neck as he nodded at the guards over her shoulder, and Kavin stared in shocked fury as the guard on the right grasped the neckline of the slave girl's dress and ripped it right down the front, as if it were made of paper.

Hana cried out. Her dress fell open. The guard's meaty hands grasped her small breasts in their bruising grip. Hana whimpered, jerked against the other guard, but he was too big, his hold too tight. Sickened, Kavin slammed her eyes shut and tried to look away, but Zayd growled in her ear, "Watch."

"Please don't do this to her..."

"You do this to her, *jarriah*. By your repeated failure. You are responsible." His fingers closed around her jaw, turned her back to look. "Open your eyes."

She did as he said, not because she was afraid for herself, but because it was the only thing she could do to help Hana. "Take me instead. I'll do whatever you want."

Hana whimpered as the guard continued to maul her. Tears streamed down her face as she struggled.

"Whatever I want?" Zayd asked with interest.

"Y-yes."

Zayd didn't answer. And as the seconds ticked by with nothing but the sound of the guards' heavy breaths and Hana's muffled sobs, Kavin was afraid to wonder what he was planning next.

Finally, he said, "You'll stop fighting the *sahad*. Tonight."

"Yes," she whispered. He didn't need to know she didn't have to fight Nasir. Unlike Zayd, Nasir would never lay a hand on her in anger. But sickness brewed in her belly at the knowledge that after Nasir did take her, she'd be right back here where Zayd could do anything he wanted to her.

"Stop."

Relief whipped through Kavin as the guards dropped their hands from Hana's body. The girl fell to her knees on the floor, her body shaking, her face flushed and lined with tears.

This will be me...

"You'll let him fuck you tonight, *jarriah*, or I'll give this girl to the guards permanently."

Hana whimpered, but Kavin couldn't read her expression because Zayd's fingers tightened until pain shot through her jaw. She twisted his way to alleviate the pressure, until his enraged face and eyes brimming with retribution filled her vision and nearly stopped her heart.

"And you, *jarriah*," he said in that menacing, vile voice. "If you fail me again, I'll toss you into the arena with the other *sahad*s and let them gang rape you."

Hana gasped, and terror raced down Kavin's spine as she swallowed hard beneath his hand. He'd do it. She didn't doubt that for one minute. He'd find the most perverse and humiliating way to punish her, and he'd get off not only by ordering it but by watching too.

"After, that is…" He eased his grip and brushed his knuckles against her sore and aching jaw. "I've had my fill of you."

He leaned close to her ear. So close she couldn't see him anymore. But she felt him. Everywhere. And her heart rate skyrocketed at the promise she heard in his voice when he whispered, "And when they're done desecrating your body, then I'll kill you myself, just for the fun of it."

Chapter Eleven

Nasir paced the confines of his cell.

Yesterday, the new room had felt airy and light, and a thousand times bigger than the dank cage he'd been locked in before. But today, it was too small, too tight and—he paused and looked up at the fading rays of sunlight filtering through the barred window high on the wall—too empty.

Where the hell was she?

He scrubbed his hands through his hair, tried to stay calm. Failed miserably. When he'd left Kavin to begin the days' training, she'd been with the slave girl. The one who'd come to check her each morning. Hours had passed since then. He'd expected her to be here when he returned. Wanted to tell her what was happening tomorrow. Needed to start working on developing their gifts as Malik had done. It was their only hope of breaking free of this place once and for all.

But if the highborn took her already…

His feet stilled. And a trail of fury burned straight through his gut. But it was quickly doused with reality. No, she was still a virgin. She hadn't completed her "test." Highborns were nothing if not predictable. They followed their own twisted rules and rarely shied from them. She had at least two more days before her time was up—two more nights. Which meant she'd been taken somewhere else. By some*one* else.

A wave of unease swept through him as his gaze snapped to the door, and he thought of the guards on the other side. Two new guards who hadn't stood watch over him before.

He hadn't seen the guard who'd attacked Kavin last night. Didn't know where he'd gone or if he was coming back. But if he'd touched her again... If he'd so much as looked at her—

The heavy door swung open. And a wave of red hair and black silk filled the space. Relief was swift and consuming. So overwhelming he didn't even care that someone had pushed her into the room, that she was stumbling forward. Instinctively, he caught her around the waist, dragged her close as the cell door clanged closed behind her. Drew in her sweet scent as if it were his last breath.

"*Rouhi...*"

She trembled. Gripped his arms. Then turned her face into his bare chest and held on tight.

He closed his eyes and reveled in the softness of her skin, the silkiness of her hair, and the warmth of her body, reminding him he was alive. Even in hell. But when warm wetness trickled across his chest, he realized she was crying.

"*Rouhi?*" He pushed her back so he could see her face. Tear tracks lined her cheeks, sending his anxiety up all over again. "What happened?"

"No-nothing. I'm f-fine."

She wasn't fine. She was scared to death. He ground his teeth to keep from frightening her more. But if that guard had come back and touched her... "What did they do?"

"Nothing. They didn't do anything…to me." Her eyes welled with tears, then she collapsed against him in a fit of sobs that squeezed his chest like a vise. "Oh, Nasir."

Questions revolved in his brain. Emotions closed his throat. Without knowing what had happened, how could he help her? He didn't know what to say, what to do. Only knew…this was the first time in his entire life he'd ever felt utterly and completely helpless.

His eyes slid closed. He held her tight. He couldn't lose her. Not her too…

When her trembling eased, he swallowed hard. He was afraid to hear the answer but knew he had to ask. "Tell me what happened."

She sniffled, drew in a deep breath. Seemed to gather herself as she eased back and looked up. Her green eyes sparkled with unshed tears when she said, "The servant girl—Hana. She saw my bruises…from that guard. She must have thought you'd…" She swiped at the tears on her cheeks. "I'm sure Zayd told her if there was any sign I'd been hurt to bring me back. So she did. Took me to the harem. To him."

Rage welled inside Nasir, the bitter urge to decimate that had kept him alive in the pits this long, but he forced it back and waited, knowing he needed to give her time to tell him. That he couldn't force it out of her. But his stomach pitched and rolled at the thought of the highborn looking at her. Touching her. And when she pushed out of his arms as if she couldn't stand the thought of him holding her while she relayed the horror, he knew that was exactly what the son of a bitch had done.

"He was elated by my bruises. But when he found out I was still a virgin, well, let's just say he was *not* happy. Irate, actually."

She brushed the hair back from her face, and he caught sight of the purplish marks against the soft skin of her throat. Marks that asshole took pride in.

"I thought he was going to hurt me. When I saw his eyes, I thought he was going to kill me. But he didn't. He knows my weaknesses better than I do."

She looked up, and in her eyes there was pain…and a whole lot of anger he hadn't seen from her before. "So he had his guards hurt Hana."

"The slave girl?"

"I tried to stop them, but he wouldn't let me. They ripped off her dress, then put their hands on her. And she was so scared." Her voice hitched, and a soul-deep sadness replaced the anger. "I tried to look away, but he—Zayd—he made me watch."

He caught her just as another sob racked through her. One he felt through every cell in his body. Holy Allah… He'd known the highborn was depraved, but this…

"I…I couldn't let them rape her."

A chill spread over his spine. "What did you do?"

"I…I promised him…" She rested her cheek against his chest, drew in a breath, let it out as her fingers splayed across his pec. "That by tomorrow I'd have completed my test."

Tomorrow…

Shock rippled through Nasir's body. No, tomorrow wouldn't work. It didn't give him enough time to teach her to harness what few powers the highborns hadn't bound. It didn't give them time to plan an escape. It was too soon. He needed more time. Needed more of *her* warming and bringing him back to life in a way no one ever had.

"No." He swallowed the growing lump in his throat. Forced back the panic. "No," he said louder. "You have two more days. Two more nights. The rule with the test is five days. Malik said its tradition. That it doesn't change."

She pulled back and looked up. "Don't you see? If I hadn't agreed, he wouldn't have let me come back to you. He'd have broken the rules and sent me to another *sahad*, or worse, he'd have taken me himself. I read it in his eyes. He doesn't care if I live or die anymore. He just wants to humiliate and use me however he can, and hurting Hana was simply part of that."

Her lashes dropped as she looked back down at his chest. "At least this way we get to say good-bye. At least this way, I can always remember—for however short the rest of my life may be—that you were the first." She looked up again and whispered, "The only one I've ever wanted. If, that is, you still want me too."

Emotions stole through him, overwhelmed him, consumed every part of him. Then pushed out all rational thought until there was only need. And heat. And a desire like nothing he'd ever felt before.

He lowered his head and took her lips, then groaned when she opened instantly to let him in. Her mouth was wet and inviting, her skin dewy and so damn soft. Her arms circled around his neck. And her body—her lush, curvy, incredible body—pressed up against his, igniting an arousal he couldn't fight back. Not anymore.

"*Rouhi*." He changed the angle of the kiss, cupped her jaw, and slid his tongue over hers again and again and again until her taste made him light-headed. "I want you. Allah, I've wanted you since the first moment I laid eyes on you. So much I can barely breathe from the need."

She groaned, and her lips turned greedy against his. Hard, tight nipples covered by the thin fabric of her dress abraded his skin. And the heat from her pelvis so close to his sent stars firing off behind his eyelids.

"Nasir..." She threaded her fingers into his hair, continued to drive him mad with her mouth. "Please... Please... I need you...inside me."

Yes. Yes. Yes... Why had they waited? That was what he wanted too.

He growled his agreement, trailed his hands down her slim back, and cupped her ass, lifting her easily. Her legs slid around his waist, her arms more fully around his shoulders. And her mouth, her soft and succulent mouth, never left his as he turned and carried her toward the bed.

This wasn't about fulfilling some command or doing what either of them had been *ordered*. It was about need—primal, voracious, all-consuming erotic need. The kind that couldn't be denied. Not anymore.

He lowered her to the bed, braced a hand against the blanket, and swallowed her moan of excitement when he eased on top of her. She kissed him deeper, spread her legs, lifted them around his hips. Arched into him so he could rub against her.

Oh, but the sounds she made...

It was all he could do not to lift her skirt, free himself, and thrust deep inside her. But he didn't want that for her this first time. He wanted to tease her. To arouse her to never before known heights of pleasure. To make her remember this wherever she went from here.

Emotions tightened his throat, but he pushed them aside, focused on her. He licked into her mouth, nipped at her bottom lip, then trailed kisses across her jaw to her ear, where he blew hot, then nibbled at the tender flesh until she groaned.

She shivered, sifted her fingers into his hair. "Nasir…"

He loved the sound of her voice. Loved when she said his name. As he sucked at the sweet column of her throat, she arched into him. The hard nubs of her nipples grazed his naked chest. Amped his need higher still. Pushing the strap of her dress down, he kissed her shoulder, repeated with the other, then tugged at the garment until her beautiful breasts were finally freed.

"By Allah," he whispered, easing back and looking down. The tips of her nipples were pink, like sweet, rich cherries, ready to be picked. Enjoyed. Devoured. "You are so beautiful." He slid down her body, cupped her left breast with his palm, lowered and laved his tongue across the nub until she groaned. "I want to make love to your breasts with my mouth. With my cock…"

Her brows drew together, her gorgeous face flushed with her arousal, her breaths shallow and excited as she watched him. "Can you do that?"

He cupped her other breast, squeezed them together so he could lick first one nipple, then the other, and groaned at the thought of pressing his cock between the two succulent globes. Of her tongue flicking out to lick the tip. Of his seed spraying over her creamy skin as he came.

"Oh, yes, *rouhi*. I can."

"Does it…feel good?"

His lips curled. He took her entire areola into his mouth and suckled until she dropped her head back and moaned, then released it to lave the pink tip with the flat of his tongue. "Yes. It feels extremely good."

She lifted her head, blinked twice. "Okay. Do it."

"What?"

"Make love to my breasts."

He froze. He'd only been teasing. Easing back up her body, he kissed her lips. "Not now. This is about pleasuring you."

She gripped his pants at the hips, preventing him from moving. "Then pleasure my breasts. I want to do everything with you, Nasir. I don't want someone else to be the first at anything."

His eyes held hers. And in the silence, he realized she was serious. And that she'd accepted what she would become after tonight.

※

Kavin held her breath and waited.

Had she said the wrong thing? Was she asking too much? Did he not want her that way?

Unease stole through her, turned her pulse to a roar in her ears. She searched Nasir's chiseled features for any sign to his thoughts but came up empty. As the seconds dragged out, she knew only one thing. She wanted Nasir in every way imaginable. With a fierceness that had no bounds. Wanted this night to be the one thing she'd carry with her into the afterlife.

"Kavin," he whispered just before lowering and taking her mouth.

Relief pulsed in her veins as she opened for him, as she tasted him again and gripped his shoulders to hold him tight. His weight pressed into hers, his body so hard and muscular and covered with a thin sheen of sweat that only excited her more.

How could she have ever been afraid of him? How could she have thought him a monster? She'd been so blinded by perception, she'd wasted precious days with him—precious hours—when they could have been doing this instead of ignoring each other in the tight confines of his cell.

She groaned as he kissed her deeper, as his tongue swept along her teeth, her tongue, her lips. He nibbled at her bottom lip, pressed his erection against her hips, moved his hand from her breast down her waist to her thigh, where he tugged up her skirt until she felt cool air brush her sex.

Nerves and excitement swirled together in her belly. His mouth moved to her jaw, her ear, her throat. She shivered, loving every rasp of his teeth, anticipating every press of his flesh against hers. But she wanted what he'd described earlier. Wanted everything. "Nasir…"

"Time for that later," he mumbled against her throat, working his way down to her breasts again, pushing her dress up higher. "Need to taste you."

She closed her eyes, let her head fall back, and ran her fingers through his shoulder-length hair as he laved her nipples, then moved down her belly. And groaned when his bristly cheek brushed her belly button.

Memories of his mouth, of his tongue, of his fingers pleasuring her whipped through her mind, sent a tremor through her body. Who was she to argue if he wanted to taste her first? Who was she to—

Her whole body vibrated when his tongue raked her clit, sent blinding pleasure all through her limbs. Words died on her lips as she shifted her legs wider, as she lifted her hips and groaned when he did it again. A tidal wave of desire swept over her, a craving that grew with every expert flick of his tongue and brush of his fingertips. One that built like a growing fire until it exploded through every cell in her body, turning her vision a blinding, glaring white.

"That's it, *rouhi*," he whispered against her overheated flesh. "Come for me."

Her orgasm stole her breath, shook her body, robbed her of every thought. As the aftershocks rocked through her and she slowly started to come down the other side, she felt Nasir's lips pressing whisper-soft kisses against her belly and hips, felt his thumb against her clit, sending delicious shivers through her all over again.

She blinked, stared up at the water-stained ceiling. Slowly recognized her surroundings. But words wouldn't come. Gently, Nasir moved back up her body, but his fingers continued to stroke her, to tease her slowly, to drive her wild all over again.

"Allah," he whispered as he kissed the corner of her mouth, her cheek, her chin and nose. "You are so gorgeous when you come. The way you give yourself over to me so easily. No one's ever done that."

"No one?"

"Not the way you do." He slid his fingers lower, against her opening, rubbed gently. "You're so wet. I want to make you come again. I want to feel you all around me."

She ran her arms up his shoulders. Oh, she wanted that too. Wanted him taking her. Claiming her. Finally making her his.

She lifted her mouth to his. "I want you inside me."

He groaned and wrapped his arms around her while he stroked his tongue over hers again and again. Her hands streaked down to his hips, and she gripped his ass, pulling him in while she lifted, rubbing her sex against his rock-hard erection.

"Kavin… You make me so hot."

She loved his admission but sensed a hesitation in him. The same hesitation that had been there from the start. One that kept him from sliding off his pants and giving her what they both so obviously wanted.

He didn't want to hurt her. The realization hit her as he nipped at her bottom lip, as he pressed—gently—against her naked sex. Even now, when he was so hard he had to physically be in pain from the ache, he was holding back.

Tenderness squeezed her heart. Brought tears to her eyes all over again. This *sahad*—this djinni—who was supposed to be a monster, was the sweetest, sexiest, most amazing creature she'd ever met.

She hooked her leg over his hip and easily rolled him to his back. Straddling his hips, she eased back and looked down at his face.

Passion flushed his cheeks crimson as he brushed her hair back from her face. His lips were swollen and wet from her mouth. And there was so much need swirling in his eyes, she knew she'd remember it forever. Also knew that, no matter what, coming here, being sent to him—as horrific as it had been at first—was the best thing that had ever happened to her.

She pushed up so she was sitting on the rigid bulge of his arousal and tugged her dress up over her head, then tossed it on the floor.

His hands landed on her bare thighs, but his gaze stayed locked on her body. And as his eyes darkened, power pulsed in her veins. A power she'd never felt before. A power she possessed because of him.

"*Rouhi*—"

His hand cupped her breast, sent tingling sensations all through her torso. But she ignored it, instead focused on his waistband and the pants that were preventing her from reaching her destination.

Flipping the button, she scooted back, then pushed her hands inside the waistband and dragged the garment down his body.

He drew in a breath as she dropped the pants on the floor, then climbed back over him. Her gaze locked on his erection. Heavy. Hard. Pulsing. So very ready for her.

She wrapped her hand his shaft, reveled at the way he trembled, at the thickness in her palm, at the bead of fluid on the dark, purple tip. Lowering her head, she drew her tongue across his erection, tasting him, loving the way he groaned and flexed his hips, seeking out her mouth.

She took him deep, remembering how it had felt when he'd thrust into her mouth, how he'd tasted when he'd come. Her own desire amped as his eyes closed in a pleasure that darkened his features.

"Kavin…"

He was lost. She knew it wouldn't take much to push him over the edge. But this time, she wanted to go over with him. Releasing him, she climbed up his body until her hands were braced on each side of his head and she was straddling his hips, his cock sliding through her wetness, making her shiver with the promise of impending pleasure.

He looked up with those fathomless eyes as he rested his hands on her hips. She pressed forward, just a touch, until the tip of his cock was braced at her opening. Braced to take her.

"Kavin…"

She lowered and took his mouth, just as her body took him in. She felt his hands at her waist, pressing against her in an attempt to hold her back, but she didn't want that. She wanted to feel all of him. Hard. Hot. Deep. She wanted to know what it felt like to finally be his.

She pushed her hips down hard. Then gasped at the burn and tight fit she felt everywhere.

Holy shit... She pulled her mouth from his and dropped her forehead against his shoulder.

His arms closed around her; his breath feathered her temple. "Breathe, *rouhi.*"

She was trying to, but Allah, it hurt. More than she'd expected.

He kissed her temple, her cheek. His hands cupped her face as he pulled her mouth back to his. And then his leg was hooking over her hip, and he was rolling her to her back once more. A tear slipped from her eye, trailed down her temple. He kissed it away, moved back to her mouth, and kissed her again and again, until the burn turned into a dull ache, one that wasn't so bad.

"So beautiful," he whispered as his hand cupped her breast. "So incredibly sexy."

She lost herself in his kisses, forgot about the ache, and knew only his mouth, his tongue, his body pressed into hers. That and the delicious heat, suddenly reigniting as his hands and mouth moved over her again and again.

"You feel so good around me," he whispered, kissing the corner of her mouth, her jaw, her earlobe until she shivered. "So tight. So perfect."

His husky words, his heated breath, and the way he seemed to know just where to touch her all coalesced until need overruled discomfort. Until desire replaced hesitation. She wrapped her arms around his shoulders and groaned as he pinched her nipple, sending electric sensations straight to her sex. Easing her knees up, she lifted her hips, wanting...more. But he drew away. And the friction of his cock sliding out of her body caused a shiver to rush through her all over again. One followed by a gasp because it felt so good she didn't want him to leave her...ever.

She gripped his shoulders, tried to pull him back. Couldn't talk because his tongue was still deep in her mouth. And then he was there, pushing deep once more, making her groan at the erotic sensation, slowly increasing his thrusts until she was meeting every one and moaning when he hit that perfect spot.

Oh... This was what she'd wanted. This hard, full ache that made her entire body tingle. He pulled back, pressed in deeper. Bracing his hands on the mattress, he lifted his upper body from hers, keeping them joined only at the hips.

"Look, *rouhi*," he said in a thick voice. "Look at me taking you. You're mine. Just mine."

Kavin gripped his forearms, glanced down her body to where they were joined, and watched as his cock disappeared inside her sex, then pulled out again, shiny from her arousal, only to disappear once more.

The visual was so erotic. Seeing what he was doing to her while feeling it at the same time... Her vision blurred. And his one word...*mine*...locked inside her mind.

Her skin grew hot. Tingles rushed through her whole body. She dropped her head back and groaned.

"Yes, Kavin. Yes...come with me."

Her orgasm plowed into her. Swept her under. Consumed her from the inside out.

She felt him shudder. Heard him call her name. But it was distant. Muffled. All she could focus on were the rolling vibrations devouring her. Everywhere.

Slowly, sound returned. Her chest rose and fell with her uneven breaths. She heard Nasir's heavy breathing. Registered his weight pressing her into the mattress and the slick skin of his arms against her hands.

Wow. That had been…better than she'd ever expected. Hotter, more intense, a thousand times more exciting than she'd imagined it could be. And when she thought of the way he'd called her his…

A smile curled her lips. She wrapped her arms around his back, kissed his temple. Kissed it again and shivered when she realized he was still inside her.

"I'm hurting you," he mumbled against her shoulder.

She locked her leg around his hip before he could pull away. "I like you right where you are."

He chuckled, then turned his head to press a gentle kiss against her throat. "Forceful all of a sudden. What have I done to you?"

"Not nearly enough." She smiled as he lifted his upper body from hers so he could see her eyes. Trailed her hands up his strong chest to cup his face, then lifted so her mouth was next to his again. "I told you I wanted to try everything."

His eyes darkened as she kissed him. But he didn't kiss her back. "Kavin—"

"Don't think, Nasir." She licked the corner of his mouth. "We don't have time for thinking."

"There are things we need to discuss."

"Later." She hooked her leg over his and rolled him to his back once more. When she was on top, she braced her hands on his chest and grinned down at him. "Right now, I want you to make love to my breasts like you talked about earlier. And then I want you to make me come all over again. Any way you want."

"Any way?"

Her smile widened as she watched whatever worry had stopped him before dissipate. She lowered her lips to his. "Every way, *sahad*. Tonight I'm yours."

Chapter Twelve

Nasir lay on his side, his head perched on his hand as he stared down at Kavin, lying on her back on the narrow mattress, her face tipped his way, her eyelids closed in sleep.

Her chest rose and fell with her deep breaths, and the sheet lay low across her naked hips. Arousal stirred in his veins as his gaze swept the length of her body, but he fought it back, instead brushed a lock of curly hair from her cheek, marveled at the softness of her skin.

Asleep, she almost looked angelic. Which, considering she was djinn, wasn't a great stretch. Angels and djinn were both created by Allah at the same time, before man. And since they were both supernatural beings, it made sense her beauty could best that of any angel. But where angels lacked desire and free will, djinn were creatures of choice. Sometimes that free will led them down a dark path, as it did many Shaitans and Ghuls and Infrit and…even himself. But sometimes it led to light and illumination and the sweetest feelings one could ever know.

Emotion stirred within him. Ones he hadn't felt in years. Ones that were stronger than what he'd known before. He'd been fighting to stay alive since being brought here because he knew doing so enraged the highborns. But now…

He swallowed hard and trailed his finger across the corner of her mouth. Now he had something more important than revenge. More important than his own desire to live. Something deeper, he realized, than what he'd shared with Talah.

Her lashes fluttered, almost as if she sensed him thinking about her. And as her sleepy eyes opened, a slow, easy smile spread across her luscious lips. Lips he wanted to kiss and lick and taste all over again. "You're not sleeping."

"I don't need much."

She skimmed her hand over his bare chest, her touch igniting a rush of tingles he felt everywhere. "What have you been doing?"

"Watching you."

She rolled her eyes in such a seductive way he wanted to kiss the expression from her face. "That can't be very exciting."

"You were quite entertaining."

"I was?"

"You're talkative in your sleep."

Her eyes widened. "I was talking? What did I say?

He placed a hand on her hip, rolling her easily toward him. "Something about baths and water and *more*. I'm pretty sure you were moaning."

Her cheeks turned bright pink, and she dropped her head against his chest, tucking her hands up next to her face. "How embarrassing."

He chuckled and ran his hand up her naked spine. "You make the sexiest sounds when you're enjoying yourself. What were you dreaming about?"

For a heartbeat, she didn't move. Then she eased back just enough to lift her face to his. "Um. You. And the bath we took the other night."

His blood heated. "You liked that, huh?"

"I loved that," she whispered.

His pulse picked up when she lifted her mouth, when her lips skimmed his. And when her sexy little tongue licked across his bottom lip, the way he'd done to her earlier, he opened. His hand flexed against her hip as her tongue snaked into his mouth, as she tasted and explored, as she groaned and scooted even closer.

He wanted nothing more than to flip her to her stomach and wedge himself so deep inside her she forgot everything but him. But they had things to discuss now that she was awake. And even though she clearly wanted him again too, he didn't want to hurt her. She had to be sore, and though he'd been gentle before, the next time he wasn't entirely sure he could go slow and easy. Not with the raging hunger for her still burning inside him.

Breathless, he forced himself back. "Don't look at me like that, *rouhi*."

"Why not?"

"Because it makes it very hard to resist you."

"I don't want you to resist me. I want you to take me again. I want you to"—she bit her lip—"fuck me."

He sucked in a breath at the visual her words created. "*Rouhi*—"

She leaned in and kissed him again. A kiss that left him light-headed and achingly hard. Then she sighed. "If you really want me to stop teasing you, I guess I will."

Never stop. Ever...

She rolled away, then scooted back until her ass was nestled against his groin and her back was plastered to his chest. "How's this? Better?"

His hand landed on her hip again. He looked down at her pale skin pressed up tight to his much-darker flesh. Felt the curve of her sweet ass against his throbbing erection.

Yes. No. Allah, he couldn't think when she was so close. "Um..."

She giggled, tucked her hands under her head. "I like it." On another sigh, she relaxed against him. "Why do you think your *mu'allim* gave us this room?"

At the moment, Nasir didn't care. All he could focus on was the press of her ass against his cock. The way the slightest shift of her hips made him want to groan. The smile in her voice as she teased him. Sliding his hand across her bare belly, then up to cup her breasts, he lowered and pressed a kiss to her throat. "I don't know. But I think he likes you."

"He does?"

"Uh-huh." He nipped at her ear. "Kicked my ass when he thought I'd hurt you. That's how I got the wound."

She looked over her shoulder. "From Malik?"

"That surprises you?"

Her brow furrowed, then slowly, she laid her head back down on the pillow. "Yes, actually. I'm nothing to him. Why would he care what you do to me?"

He pulled her tighter back against him, loving the heat of her body against his groin, even if it did ignite him to within degrees of boiling. "I heard a story right after I came here. About a great *sahad* who'd been champion for over a hundred years."

"That's a long time."

"He was an animal. Decimated anything they threw at him. Other *sahad*s would tremble simply at his name. The way the story goes, he and his lover had been captured together. He'd been sentenced to the pits, and she…well…she'd been of such blinding beauty, she'd been taken to the harem."

Kavin's upper body turned back toward him. "But if she wasn't a virgin—"

"I don't think it mattered," he said softly, kissing her nose. "A slave is a slave. If they'd wanted the female, they'd have taken her." Sickness rolled through his stomach at the thought, but he forced it aside. "The way the story goes, she couldn't handle it. Life without him. She killed herself before he could figure out a way to free her."

Kavin's eyes slid closed, and she turned back, lowering once more to the pillow. "I know this story."

"You do?"

She nodded, but he couldn't see her eyes. Couldn't tell what she was feeling. "I heard about her in the harem. It was a warning to me, I think. But I didn't know about the *sahad*. He went on to fight?"

"They say he fought for her, even in death. That it gave him power to defy his captors."

Silence settled between them, then she said, "Do you believe that's true?"

He thought about everything that had happened between them since the moment she'd been brought to him. What he'd been before, and what he was now. And felt those emotions roll stronger through his chest. "I believe love is a powerful force. It can give you strength you didn't know you had. Sometimes when you need it most."

She was silent so long he wasn't sure if he'd said the right thing or not. Then, quietly, she said, "It was him, wasn't it? The *sahad*? It was Malik."

He tightened his arm around her. Pressed his chin against her neck. "I think so. I don't know for sure, but when he thought I'd hurt you…I've never seen him so enraged. Females in our tribe, they're worshiped, not treated as property."

"Our?" She turned her head again. "Are you saying—"

"Malik is Marid. He showed me that day. He keeps his lineage carefully cloaked with magic, so the highborns won't know what he is. But if he was that champion… A hundred years is a long time. Unrest in the ruling class here is high, especially with the wars the Ghuls wage. It's entirely possible the highborns in control of Jahannam now are not the ones who were in control when he was first brought here as a slave."

"Why would he stay? If it's true…if he's risen to the rank of *mu'allim* and he's harnessed his magic, he could easily escape."

"I don't know." But Nasir had an idea. He guessed Malik stayed because it was the only way he could be close to his love, even after all this time. And because training others to stay alive was one more slap in the face to the highborns who'd imprisoned him from the start and taken his heart.

"I think this is his room," Nasir said, tucking his chin against her again, holding on to her warmth. "I think he wanted you to have something nicer than that cell of mine for your first time. It's not a palace, by any means, but it is a hell of a lot nicer than that cave."

She lowered her hand to his against her belly and squeezed. "I would make love with you in a cave. I'd make love with you anywhere."

Arousal stirred in his groin again at her words, and warmth encircled his heart. "You have to admit the bath, though, is a nice perk."

She chuckled, and the sound was so sweet it eased the tension in his chest. Eased the worry over what he had to do tomorrow.

Silence settled back between them. Then, very softly, she said, "When I was in the harem, the others would talk about you. They say those from your tribe tend to be of even temperament. That it takes a lot to push a Marid from soldier to *sahad*. That most don't survive, because killing isn't in their blood. But Malik became one. And so did you. So I'm just wondering… who did you lose?"

Nasir's hand paused against the underside of her breast. "What makes you think I lost someone?"

Kavin shrugged but didn't turn to look at him. "You talk about love as if you know. And being with you these last few days, I know you're not a monster. Not like the highborns would have me and everyone else believe. You don't like the killing. And yet you do it."

Surprise rippled through him. That she was so easily able to see to the heart of him when no one else ever had. Not even Talah.

"So who was she?" Kavin asked softly.

He swallowed the lump in his throat as he trailed his finger up her bare arm, then back down again. He'd never told anyone about Talah. Not even his brothers. But he didn't want to keep anything from Kavin. Not now. "A caregiver. She worked with children injured and orphaned in the wars. Helped rehabilitate them and find homes."

Kavin was silent beside him, the only sound the gentle push and pull of her breath while she waited for him to go on. And the fact she wasn't pushing spurred him to continue. "We got word Ghuls were heading toward her village. I was being sent out with the army to meet them. I told her to go to the castle—that she'd be safe there. She agreed, reluctantly, but said she needed to arrange for someone to take her place at the infirmary. I wasn't happy about her delay but agreed to give her the time. I left a guard with her and resumed my post. She never made it to the castle." His throat grew thick as he stared at a mole on her shoulder. "A band of Ghuls we didn't know about attacked from the north before she could get away."

Her hand closed over his against her arm. "I'm so sorry."

Talah's face flashed in his mind. Smiling and waving as he left, her long dark hair flying behind her in the wind. Rolling her eyes at what she considered his overprotective nature. Never knowing it would be the last moments of her life.

"It wasn't your fault, Nasir."

Kavin's breath against his cheek brought his eyes open. She'd turned to face him, her eyes warm and shining with unshed tears, her hands resting gently against his chest. Emotions stole through him. Emotions that were so much stronger than he'd felt with Talah they took his breath away.

"I don't fight to avenge her death," he said in a thick voice. "The Ghuls who manage the pits are not the ones who killed her. I fight—I fought—because it was all I had left. Until I met you."

Her entire face softened. And those eyes that before had simply glistened, now filled with tears.

He kissed the tip of her nose. Kissed the teardrop that slipped from the corner of her eye. Kissed his way down to her mouth, then finally pressed his lips against hers. Softly. Gently. Hoping she could feel every emotion stirring inside him.

He wrapped his arm around her, dragged her body closer, then rested his forehead against hers. "It's crazy—all of this. But in a few short days, you've changed everything for me. You made me remember who I was. You gave me a reason to want to live. I'm not going to let them hurt you. I'll do whatever it takes to protect you."

Her mouth closed over his so forcefully it tore a groan from his chest. She pushed him to his back, climbed over him, kissed him again and again and again as if she couldn't get enough.

The sheet fell away, leaving her bare and beautiful. He trailed his hands up her hips, positioned her so she was rocking against his cock, right where he wanted her most. Eased up to kiss her deeper. "Mine," he mumbled against her lips. "You're mine."

"Show me," she whispered, lifting then lowering to take him so deep they both groaned. "One more time. Show me that I'm only yours."

Chapter Thirteen

Nasir waited until Kavin fell asleep again, then gently eased out from under her.

His body still vibrated from the most amazing orgasm; his heart pounded hard at the things she'd whispered as they'd made love. But it was what he had to do next that left a hole the size of a crater in the bottom of his stomach.

He pulled on his pants and crossed soundlessly toward the door. Once there, he rapped on the hard wood once, knowing the guards were out there keeping watch.

"What?" a voice called from the other side of the door.

"I have a request," Nasir said quietly.

The small rectangular slot in the door opened, just enough so Nasir could see the guard's dark eyes. "What kind of request?"

"I want to meet with the female's master. Before my fight."

The guard turned to look toward his companion, just out of Nasir's line of sight, and relayed the message. When he turned back, he said, "He'll not agree."

Nasir ground his teeth. "If he wants the fire opal around my neck, he'll agree."

Surprise reflected in the guard's dark eyes. His gaze snapped to the opal at Nasir's throat. After several long seconds of silence, he harrumphed and closed the window with a snap.

They hadn't said no. Nasir turned slowly and looked toward Kavin on the bed. This was his only shot. They had to take the bait. All the highborns wanted the opal. They'd tried to take it from him when he'd first arrived but hadn't been able to remove it from his neck. None knew where it came from, but they lined their *sahad*s up to fight Nasir in the ring because the one who killed him would then own the mysterious opal. So far, none had been successful.

He crossed back to the bed, sat beside her, and brushed the curls back from her face. She lay on her stomach, her arms up near her head, her eyes closed in deep sleep. He hated to wake her, hated to start this day that would likely be his last. But he didn't want her master to find her naked in his bed. Didn't want to give the son of a bitch any reason to hurt her more than he already had.

"Kavin, wake up." He ran his hand down her hair, across the smooth skin of her back. "Wake up, princess."

He'd like nothing better than to make her his princess. But that was another life. Not this one. The best he could hope for was that once she was free, someday she could find happiness. And maybe remember what little time they'd been able to spend together, even if it was in a hellhole.

She grunted, stirred, finally blinked and looked up at him with that sleepy, sexy, so-damn-erotic look, he wished he could see it again. Tomorrow morning. And the morning after that. Thousands of mornings after that.

He forced a smile. "Good morning."

Her eyes widened, then she jerked up on her hands and looked toward the window above them. "It's morning?"

She knew what this morning was going to bring. He just hoped he was able to stop it.

"Kavin, we need to talk."

She flipped to sitting and pulled the sheet up around her, her wide, very aware eyes looking all around the room.

He picked up her dress where they'd dropped it last night and handed it to her, trying like hell not to let his own fear show. "I'm fighting today."

She stopped her frantic movements with the dress around her neck. "What?" Her gaze dropped to his side and the wound that was still red and irritated, but, thanks to her, closed. "You're still weak from your injury. They can't make you fight yet. They—"

"They can do whatever they want." He helped her pull the dress down. "I'm a slave, remember?"

"But—"

He captured her hands before she could push from the bed. "It's my job, *rouhi*."

Her eyes hardened, and he watched determination creep across her perfect features. "Then kill them. Kill every single one they throw at you."

Allah, he loved this female. It wasn't even a question anymore. And it didn't matter that she was Ghul and he was Marid or that they'd only known each other a few days. He loved her more than he'd ever loved anyone before. And he knew, without a doubt, that he was making the right choice. "I need you to do me a favor."

"What?" she asked quietly.

He drew a deep breath, one he hoped would give him strength, but realized in the silence between them he didn't need. He already had it, because of her. "If something were to happen to me, Malik will take possession of the fire opal. Whatever happens then, do as he says."

"I don't understand."

No, of course she wouldn't. And he couldn't tell her. Because if she knew, she'd try to stop him. He tightened his hands around hers. "Just promise me you'll do as he says."

"Nasir—"

Footsteps echoed out in the hall, followed by voices. Several.

Nasir's pulse sped up. He was running out of time. The one commodity he'd had more than enough of up until now.

He leaned in, kissed her when her frightened eyes darted toward the door, then rested his forehead against hers. "You were right, I hate the fighting. More than anything about this place. But I'll do it for you. I'd do anything for you. I can't ever thank you enough for bringing me back from the brink."

Tears welled in her eyes as the voices grew louder outside. She ran her hand down his cheek. "Oh, Nasir. I—"

He didn't let her finish. He closed his mouth over hers as keys rattled in the door and kissed her one last time. Drew her deep into his mind and heart and soul where she'd live forever. Then gathered every ounce of strength he had left and pushed from the bed to cross to the far side of the room. Away from her. Away from probing eyes he didn't want to witness their last moment together.

He watched as she swiped the tears from her cheeks, then squared her shoulders and stared at the door in silence. And he remembered what she'd told him last night. How she'd sacrificed herself for the slave girl that son of a bitch highborn had threatened.

She was stronger than he'd given her credit for that first day. In so many ways—in all the ways that mattered—tougher than him, because he knew whatever happened, she wouldn't lose herself the way he had. Awe rippled through him. Awe and wonder and pride that curled one side of his lips. He had nothing to offer her, and she had no reason to want him, but she did. And he was the luckiest son of a bitch for having known her.

The door pushed open, killing his smile. The guard moved out of the way, then bodies filled the space. His *mu'allim*. The slave girl who'd repeatedly come for Kavin. And finally, the piece-of-shit highborn who owned her.

The highborn's hard gaze snapped from Nasir, leaning against the wall near the bath, to Kavin. And when he took in her rumpled hair and the indent on her cheek from a fold on the sheet, a malicious grin spread across his disgusting face.

"Take her back to the harem," he said to the slave girl.

Kavin didn't speak as the girl slowly approached the bed. But their eyes met. And something Nasir couldn't read passed between them.

She pushed up on shaky legs. Every instinct said to reach out for her, but Nasir held his ground and resisted. Because if this didn't go as he hoped, he didn't want to do anything to give the highborn any more reason to punish her.

Please, please, please let him take the bait.

The highborn watched her leave the room, and when he looked back at Nasir, victory flashed in his dark eyes. A victory Nasir wanted to smash to ruin with his fists.

The highborn smirked. "It doesn't look like I need to ask if she finally completed her test. Tell me, was she good? All that fire inside her, I bet once you finally got a piece of her, she was a mighty fine fuck."

At his side, Malik shifted his feet, clasped his hands behind his back in clear discomfort, but didn't so much as utter a sound.

Nasir ground his teeth to keep from popping the dickhead right between the eyeballs. He could take this fucker out in ten seconds, snap his neck, save their realm from his torment, but if he did, he'd be condemning Kavin. And nothing was worth that. "I'm willing to make you a deal."

The highborn snorted and turned for the door. "I don't make deals with slaves."

"You'll deal with this slave. I'm offering you the opal."

The highborn paused at the threshold, glanced back over his shoulder with curious eyes. "What kind of deal?"

He had him. Relief filled Nasir's chest. Now he just had to hope Malik backed him up. "I'm scheduled to fight the Shaitan today. The one that arrived last week. If you can arrange it so I fight your Infrit instead, I'll guarantee your *sahad*'s victory."

"*Sahad*," Malik muttered in warning. But Nasir and the highborn both ignored him.

Interest flared in the highborn's eyes as he turned back to fully face Nasir. "Why is the great champion suddenly suicidal? What's in it for you besides death?"

"Peace of mind."

The highborn's eyes narrowed. "How so?"

"If you arrange it, the fight is yours. And the opal. But only if you grant the *jarriah*'s freedom upon my death."

"By Allah…" Malik muttered.

The highborn stared at him so long Nasir wasn't sure what he was thinking, then a slow, shameless smile spread across his face. "She got to you. I knew she was of great value the first time I laid eyes on her. You did too, obviously."

Nasir wasn't about to discuss Kavin with this prick. He clenched his jaw without answering.

Take the deal. Take the deal. Take the fucking deal…

The highborn rubbed a hand across his chin. "What guarantee do you have that I'll hold to my half of the bargain? Once you're dead, the opal belongs to me anyway."

"Not exactly. My master is one of great power. In her stead, my *mu'allim* has the final say in all matters pertaining to me. The opal's bound to me by magic—and only he has the power to give it to you once I'm dead. As soon as he has confirmation the *jarriah* is free of you and this city, he'll hand it over to you."

The highborn turned to Malik. "Is this true?"

Malik's jaw clenched. And anger brewed in his gaze as his eyes held Nasir's. "Yes," he said without turning toward the highborn. "It is true."

The highborn didn't look pleased when he faced Nasir again. "So I arrange the change to the fights, you die in the arena, then I free the *jarriah*, and the opal is mine."

"And the glory for taking out the great champion," Nasir added, knowing that would seal the deal. "Imagine the envy you'll be amongst the other highborns."

He hadn't meant to sound as if he was mocking the son of a bitch, but he was, and the highborn knew it. His eyes narrowed and filled with contempt.

Take the deal. Take the damn deal…

Seconds drew out in silence. Long, agonizing seconds in which Nasir held his breath and waited. And hoped. And prayed.

Finally, the highborn said, "Fine. You have a deal. Just make your death look good. If you go down without a fight, our deal is broken. Die like the champion you are, or I'll fuck that bitch a hundred ways to sundown."

He turned for the door.

"Don't touch her," Nasir said in a hard voice. One that stopped the highborn's feet. "If you or anyone else does before I'm dead, the deal is off. And I'll find you from the grave. I guarantee it, you prick."

The highborn didn't turn. Didn't look Nasir's way. But the tightening of his shoulders told Nasir he'd heard the threat loud and clear. He stomped out of the room without another word.

When the highborn's footsteps could no longer be heard echoing from the corridor, Malik barked to the guards, "Out. Both of you."

The guards hesitated, but when Malik shot them a hard glare, they scrambled out the door and closed it at their backs.

In their wake, Malik's eyes blazed. "What the fuck was that? Are you mad? What the hell are you thinking?"

Nasir sagged back against the stone wall, his heart racing with the remnants of an adrenaline rush that was now leaving him weak. And hopeful. "The only thing I can do."

"The Infrit hasn't been trained yet. He's no match for you on a good day. He's insane, I'll give you that, but you could take him down with your eyes closed."

Nasir ran his hand through his hair, remembering Kavin's fingers doing the same last night. He drew a deep breath, knowing he was doing the right thing, and met Malik's hard eyes. "I'm saving the female I love. I know you would have done the same if you could."

Malik's jaw tightened. Then he muttered, "Motherfucker. She's a Ghul. You barely know her."

His *mu'allim* wasn't changing his mind. "You saw the same strength in her I did. If you hadn't, you wouldn't have helped her."

Malik's lips thinned. But behind the spark of fury in his eyes, Nasir saw he agreed. "She won't let you do this."

"She's not to know." Nasir straightened from the wall. "I want her out of this hellhole, Malik, and I'll do anything to set her free. But I need your help. This will only work if you agree. I know you don't want what happened to your female to happen to her."

Malik's eyes were as hard and cold as Nasir had ever seen them. Everything hinged on his support. If he was pissed Nasir hadn't consulted him about his plans, if he'd lost his compassion after all these years as a slave, Kavin was lost.

"She wasn't just my female," Malik finally said in a low voice. "She was my wife. And yes, I'd have done anything to free her, even give up my own life for her, if I'd been able to."

Nasir's pulse pounded hard as he waited. As he hoped.

"I'll help her," Malik said softly.

Relief was as sweet as wine, zipping through Nasir's veins. He reached out and clamped a hand over Malik's shoulder. "Thank you."

"Don't thank me yet." He nodded at the opal around Nasir's throat. "That thing is bound to you by magic. I don't know if I'll be able to direct it."

On this, Nasir knew he was safe. When I'm dead, the chain will release. It binds me to a sorceress, one of great power."

"A sorceress?" Malik asked in surprise.

Nasir nodded, not about to get into the hows and whys of how that had come to be. "Whoever wears it will be bound to her will, as was I. I don't know why she's waiting, but at some point, she'll call the opal back. And with it, the bearer."

A slow smile slinked across Malik's weathered face. One Nasir had never seen. One that lit up his eyes and made him look years younger. "Clever move, *sahad*."

One corner of Nasir's mouth curled in response. In a matter of hours, he'd be dead, Kavin would be free, and that prick master of hers would be Zoraida's next slave. There would be justice this day.

He dropped his hand and focused on Malik's eyes. "Let's hope so. Now, tell me about the Infrit I'm to fight."

༄

Kavin's hands shook as she bathed quickly and dressed in the gown Hana held out to her.

She stood in the center of the marble bath in her suite at the harem as the violet silk slid down her body. Behind her, Hana smoothed out her skirts and closed the few buttons at the back. They hadn't spoken as Hana had escorted her back to the harem, and every time Kavin had tried to meet the girl's eyes, she'd looked away. But Kavin had too many other things to worry about than what the girl was thinking or feeling. All she could focus on was the fact Nasir was fighting today.

Her pulse picked up speed, and her hands trembled as she waited for Hana to finish. She didn't care what Zayd did to her anymore. Hadn't thought once about facing him again after her night with Nasir. She just needed to know that Nasir was okay. She needed him to live.

"There," Hana said in a quiet voice. "You're done."

Kavin turned to face the girl. Her eyes were downcast, her hands clenched in front of her. Kavin knew she was thinking about what had happened yesterday in Zayd's room. Remembering the story Hana had told her before she'd been sent to Nasir, Kavin couldn't stop her heart from going out to the girl. "They won't touch you again. I made sure of it. You don't have to worry."

"I..." Hana's voice broke, and when she lifted her eyes, they brimmed with tears. "Thank you. I don't know how to repay you. I acted so superior to you before, and I shouldn't have. I... we're all just slaves."

Nasir had told her the same thing. But Kavin didn't believe that mattered. Not anymore. "Hana—"

The door to the bathroom pushed open. Kavin whipped around to find Zayd standing in the doorway, eyeing her with hard, cold, unreadable eyes.

"You're escorting me to the arena today. Your *sahad* is fighting, and I'm told it's going to be a spectacular show. One you won't want to miss." To Hana, he said, "Be sure she's properly made up. I want everyone to know she's my newest *jarriah*. Including the great champion."

The way he snarled the last words set Kavin's nerves on edge. What had been said between them after she'd left Nasir's cell? The victory in Zayd's voice was more than just gloating over the fact she was finally his. Something else was going on.

"I'll do whatever it takes to protect you."

A shiver of foreboding rushed down her spine as Hana tugged her toward the vanity. "Come. We don't have much time."

Kavin's head spun as she sat on the tufted ottoman, and Hana began fiddling with her hair. But all she could see were

Nasir's soft eyes. All she heard was his gentle voice. Telling her again and again that he wouldn't let anything happen to her.

She gripped Hana's hand so hard the girl yelped. "Listen to me. You said you didn't know how you could repay me. I know how you can. But I need you to do it now. You have to go to the pits. You have to find the *sahad*'s *mu'allim* before the fight."

"But the master said—"

"Fuck Zayd!" Kavin said, squeezing Hana's hand tighter, causing the girl's eyes to go bug-wide. "I don't care what he said. Nasir's planning something. And I can't—won't—let him do it. Hana, you're the only one who can stop this. He doesn't deserve what's about to happen to him any more than you deserved what those guards did to you. All life has value. Regardless of tribe or race or gender. Please…please do this for me."

Fear rushed over Hana's face but was slowly replaced with a strength she seemed to pull from the very heart of her. She swallowed once and nodded. "O-okay. Tell me what you want me to do."

Options, scenarios raced through Kavin's mind. How could she stop this? She didn't even know what Nasir was planning, but she had to prevent him from doing something that would get him killed. Would Malik listen to her servant? And what if he bought into the same bullshit the highborns had been spewing for years—that all *sahad*s were the same? Monsters better locked in cages. Sent to fight like dogs. He worked with them every day. He knew way more about them than she did.

Her adrenaline surged. She had to try. She just hoped Nasir was right and there was a shadow of the djinni Malik had once been somewhere left inside him. "Get me paper and pen. And hurry."

Chapter Fourteen

Nasir paced the stone cell beneath the arena and shook out his arms, his legs, tried to relax his muscles in anticipation of what was to come.

Booms echoed from above, followed by shouts and cheers as the crowd grew more excited. His was the main event. The last fight of the day. So far, four matches had already been completed. From the sounds of the fifth, he'd be up in a matter of minutes.

"Death comes to us all at one point. You can't stop it…"

His feet paused on the hard stones. Talah was right. He couldn't stop it. But he could delay it…at least for Kavin.

His heart warmed when he thought of her, easing the anxiety inside, telling him no matter what, this was the right choice. The only choice.

The door to the cell pulled open just as he was remembering her fingers on his skin, her lips against his, the breathless sound of her voice last night when they'd made love. He turned to find Malik's grim face staring at him from across the room. "They're ready for you."

His pulse picked up speed. He drew in a deep breath, nodded once, and stepped toward the door.

At the archway, Malik stopped him with a hand on his arm. Right over the slave marking branded into his skin. The one he'd gotten when Zoraida had first banished him to the pits. At the time, it had been the worst sentence he could imagine. Now he was so very thankful for the time he'd spent here.

"It's all arranged," Malik said in a low voice so the guards couldn't hear. "After the fight, your body will be brought to me. When I have confirmation Kavin has been freed, I'll give the opal to Zayd."

Gratitude tightened Nasir's throat. "Thank you."

"Don't thank me. If it were up to me, you wouldn't be going through with this asinine plan. You do more damage to the Ghuls alive than you ever will in death."

In that moment, Nasir knew he'd been right as to why Malik stayed in this hellhole. And why he'd taken a special interest in Nasir from the beginning. Without Malik's training, Nasir would have been dead weeks ago.

Malik moved out of the way. Nasir's skin tingled as he stepped out into the corridor where the guards waited to escort him to the arena. In a rush, he thought of his parents in Gannah, of his brothers—Tariq and Ashur, still imprisoned by Zoraida. He didn't know what had happened to them after he'd been brought here, didn't know if his kingdom was doomed to fall or if war had finally reached its gates. All he knew for sure was that Malik was wrong. His death would prove that one life was not more important than another. It didn't matter that Kavin was Ghul, female, or a slave. Her master would forever know that her life had value.

His feet faltered when he spotted the slave girl who had repeatedly come to his cell for Kavin, and his adrenaline surged as he looked past the girl for Kavin's red hair. But the hall behind her was empty. Only the drip of water and the muffled roar of the crowd above met his ears.

He looked back at the girl. Wary eyes met his. She chewed on her thumbnail, then turned away so he couldn't see her face.

A shiver of worry rushed down Nasir's spine as the guards pushed him forward. "Come on, maggot. They're waiting for you."

Nasir's adrenaline surged as they forced him away from her. What was she doing there? Had she come to tell him something? Where the hell was Kavin?

His pulse was a roar in his ears by the time he reached the gate to the arena. The cheers were louder, the chant, "*Marid! Marid! Marid!*" echoing in his ears.

He held his chained hands in front of him, waited while the guard unlocked his cuffs, then took the two swords they held out. The gate opened. Instinctively, he stepped back as a bloodied, decapitated body was pulled through the opening.

He couldn't be sure since he wasn't allowed to train with the others, but he was pretty sure that was the Shaitan he'd been scheduled to fight.

Who was he? What had he done? He didn't deserve to be condemned to this hellhole any more than Nasir did. Any more than Kavin did. Any more than any of them did.

His heart pounded hard against his ribs. The roar of the crowd grew louder. The guard to his right hollered, "Go!" and opened the gate wide.

Nasir stepped into the arena, frantically searching the stands above for Kavin. Multicolored scarves billowed in the air. Angry and excited faces stared down at him, mouths open as they screamed his name, arms raised as they pumped their fists as if *they* were the athletes about to fight.

He couldn't find her.

Anxiety rippled through his veins as he turned a slow circle, looking, searching, *needing* to see with his own two eyes that she was alive. That she wasn't hurt. That the son of a bitch hadn't harmed her.

Kavin…

The crowd grew more excited at his back. Without even looking, Nasir knew the Infrit had been brought into the arena, but he couldn't stop looking.

And then he spotted her. Five rows up, to the left of the main gate. The same gate he'd just walked through.

Relief swirled in his blood as he took her in. A lavender gown graced her curves, her red hair piled on her head in some fashionable updo, and she was wearing way more makeup than he'd ever seen—painted up like a porcelain doll. But even though her face was lined with stress and worry, to him, she'd never been more beautiful.

He drew in a deep breath. Then another. Locked eyes with her and hoped she heard his thoughts even though he couldn't say them aloud.

I love you.

Her eyes softened, and then her face tightened, and her mouth opened to…scream his name.

It took a split second to realize she was seeing something over his shoulder. On instinct, he lifted his swords and whipped around. The Infrit was coming right at him, a menacing fury alive in his black eyes, his hatchet swinging out in an arc, ready to take Nasir's head in one fell swoop.

The crowd exploded in exhilaration. Nasir lifted his sword to block the blow. Metal met metal, the clash echoing through the air to fuel their cheers. Nasir ducked under the Infrit's hatchet, somersaulted across the sand of the arena, and jumped to his feet.

The Infrit was bigger than Nasir expected, at least a foot taller than him and a good fifty pounds heavier. Long dark hair hung to the middle of his back, and his skin was shades darker than Nasir's. But he was slow, his size no advantage. Not when Nasir was so easily able to avoid each blow and dance around the giant.

If you go down without a fight, our deal is broken.

From the corner of his vision, Nasir caught sight of Kavin's frightened face as his sword clapped against the Infrit's weapon. Of the tense features of her master lounging next to her, waiting, watching, expecting.

Nasir focused on the Infrit with renewed purpose, braced his foot against the giant's belly, and shoved hard, sending him staggering back. Before the Infrit could right himself, Nasir arced out with his blade and caught the djinni across the ribs.

The Infrit roared. His eyes widened with shock and pain, then dialed in on Nasir with a menacing rage. He found his footing and charged.

Shit. Nasir shuffled backward. The Infrit swung his weapon. Nasir deflected it with his sword, but the Infrit was stronger, and through sheer muscle strength knocked the sword right out of Nasir's grip. The weapon flew through the arena to land on the sand some fifteen feet away.

Pain radiated up Nasir's side. A quick look down confirmed he'd torn his wound open. He might not have to make this look good after all. Tossing his remaining sword to the other hand, Nasir eased back several steps. "Come on, you brute. Is that all you've got?"

The Infrit's eyes turned red. He growled, then swung out with his blade. Nasir jumped back. The tip of the Infrit's weapon caught him across the belly. Blood welled, but it wasn't deep. Nasir shifted to the side and caught the Infrit across the right bicep.

A howl echoed from the Infrit. When he turned, Nasir ducked his head and did a forward roll right through the giant's legs, then sliced into the djinni's flesh, just above the knee.

Blood gushed. His wound wasn't deep either, but it was enough to bring the crowd to their feet. They screamed as the Infrit dropped to his knee. Sweat dripped into Nasir's eyes as he circled around the giant, looking for an opportunity to let the *sahad* get the upper hand.

"Make your death look good."

He intended to. As the giant slowly pushed to his feet, Nasir glanced at Kavin in the crowd. Worry shone in her eyes. Worry and fear and love. A love that would carry him into the next world, wherever that may be.

He drew a deep breath, turned away from her, and watched as the Infrit rose to his full height, easily seven feet tall. At one point, back when he'd been just a soldier, he might have been scared by this beast, but not today.

"They're waiting for you to die, Infrit," he said, mocking the djinni, knowing it would fire him up and give Kavin's master exactly what he wanted. He turned the hilt of the sword in his hand. "Can't you hear them?"

"*Kill! Kill! Kill!*"

"You're wrong, Marid," the Infrit growled. "They're waiting for *your* death."

Instead of swinging out with his weapon, the giant charged. Nasir barely had time to brace himself. The Infrit plowed into him, hurling his body back and to the ground. Nasir landed with a grunt on his back. Pain radiated up his spine. He tried to lift his arm, but the Infrit was suddenly above him, pressing against Nasir's stomach, holding him still.

"Don't move," the giant growled.

The crowd gasped, then went eerily silent.

Confused as to what was happening, Nasir looked down, and his eyes widened at the crimson blood spilling from his belly around the Infrit's weapon sticking straight out of his gut.

How...? When...?

His gaze lifted. He didn't feel as if he'd been skewered, but then maybe he was in shock. This was what was supposed to happen, but why all of a sudden didn't it feel right?

"Don't move, you asshole," the Infrit growled again. "I'm trying to help you here."

Help him? Did he know about the deal? Had Malik told him? Nasir's head grew light, and he tilted his chin up so he could look into the crowd. Kavin was somewhere behind him. He wanted to see her face. Needed to look upon her one last time...

"Stay down," the Infrit said in a low voice, his hand pressing harder into Nasir's shoulders. "If you know what's good for you, you won't move until we tell you to."

We?

Nasir stopped searching for Kavin and instead looked at the Infrit, pushing off him, dust and sand kicking up around his feet. The giant turned toward the crowd, held his arms out wide, and roared through his victory.

The crowd remained eerily silent.

The Infrit dropped his arms, turned and picked up Nasir's sword, which was lying on the ground a foot from his hand.

And as Nasir watched the giant lift it over his head, readying the killing blow, his instincts screamed *Get up! Defend yourself*! But then he thought of Kavin. Of everything she'd done for him. Of the fact that without her, he'd still be only a shell of the djinni he used to be.

He drew a deep breath. Readied himself.

The Infrit grinned. The fucker actually grinned. "Watch this."

Then he turned toward the crowd, zeroed in on something above Nasir and hurled the sword as hard as he could.

Right toward the area where Kavin was standing.

Chapter Fifteen

"No!" A red haze descended over Nasir's vision. He lurched to his feet and threw his weight into the Infrit. The giant went down with a grunt, sand flying out all around his sweaty body. Nasir nailed him hard in the jaw with his fist, then scrambled to his feet, searching, looking...

Spectators screamed. A mass exodus was taking place in the stands. He couldn't find Kavin. If the Infrit had hit her...

And then he saw her, being dragged by the hair up the steps toward the upper concourse, fighting against the hold her master had on her while frightened spectators rushed around in a frenzy.

She was alive. She hadn't been hit. She...

The highborn paused at the top step and shot Nasir a brutal glare. Kavin screamed, but it was the blood welling from the highborn's shoulder that stopped Nasir's breath. Blood from the wound the Infrit had inflicted when he'd hit the piece of shit with Nasir's sword.

Holy fuck...

His muscles bunched. He looked down at his own body, and his eyes widened when he realized there was no gaping hole. No injury from the Infrit's weapon other than a few scratches.

Shouts and the sounds of heavy footfalls drew his attention toward the main gate before he could figure out what was happening. At least twenty guards were spilling into the arena with weapons drawn.

Shit. *Shit!*

He searched the ground for his other sword. What the hell had the moron done? He'd tried to kill his own master in front of the entire city. They were both going to burn for this. It didn't matter what had happened during their match or who'd thrown the blade into the crowd. If the guards didn't kill them first, the highborns would execute them both simply for the fun of it. And Kavin…

He caught sight of his sword halfway across the arena just as the giant was pushing himself to his feet.

"Some gratitude you've got," the Infrit growled.

"Gratitude? Fuck that." He had to get to Kavin. He had to find her before…

His feet skidded to a stop near his weapon. He picked it up, then froze when the gates on the other side of the arena opened and at least thirty *sahad*s—djinn of all races—each armed, their eyes glowing hot with the promise of retribution, filled the space. *Sahads* led by Malik.

Nasir stared, unable to believe what he was seeing. Before he could ask what the hell was going on, the Infrit picked up his weapon, lifted it over his head, and yelled, "For freedom!"

The pack charged right by Nasir, weapons and fists and bodies clashing with the guards in an echo that filled the arena and drowned out the screams of spectators still rushing out of the stands.

Malik met him in the center of the arena, lifted his sword, and took down a guard just before he reached Nasir.

"What the hell is happening?" Nasir yelled over the roar.

Malik kicked the guard to the ground and pulled his bloody sword from the guard's belly. "Something that should have happened long ago. Find her. Get her the hell out of here before they send reinforcements."

Nasir's chest grew tight as things suddenly made sense. They'd done all this for him. Malik had cast an illusion spell to distract the crowd. Then he'd rallied the *sahad*s—djinn who didn't even know Nasir personally, who hated his race—and staged a revolt.

His head swam with the impact of what they were doing. Of what would happen to them all as a result.

Malik grasped his shoulder, dragging his attention back to his *mu'allim*'s face. "Find her and get the hell out of here. But when you're free, make sure you tell the others…anyone who will listen, all the tribes…what's happening here. I should have done that long ago, but I couldn't. Be stronger than I was, Nasir." His eyes hardened as the battle raged around them. "Then bring your army back and shut this fucking hellhole down."

Wide-eyed, Nasir nodded.

Malik took a step back. Lifted his sword. Screamed, "Go!"

Then he whipped around and swung out at a guard only feet behind him.

Nasir's adrenaline surged. And as the sounds of war erupted around him, he thought of Kavin. The need to find her squeezed his chest like a vise, pushing out all other needs. Grasping his weapon, he raced toward the stands and easily scaled the ten-foot wall. His thighs burned as he ran up the steps and out the archway he'd seen Kavin and her master disappear through, but he ignored the pain and focused only on her.

The hallway was filled with terror-filled highborns, both male and female, rushing every direction, trying to get out of the arena. Only slaves had their powers bound, which meant these djinn could teleport if they wanted. But not through solid stone walls. They had to be outside first.

Nasir searched the frightened faces, then zeroed in on a dark-haired male he'd seen sitting near Kavin and her master. He pushed through the crowd and grasped the jacket of the male, jerking him around.

The male's horror-filled eyes met Nasir's. "Don't...don't...don't hurt me."

"Where did they go?"

"Wh-who?"

"The highborn who was struck and the *jarriah* he was with. Where the fuck did they go?"

The male's eyes shifted, then he pointed to a corridor at his right. "Th-through there."

Nasir shoved the male to the ground and sprinted for the archway. A stone stairwell disappeared into darkness. Nasir skipped steps, rounded the corner, then drew up short when he heard a scream.

"Let...*go* of me!"

Kavin...

His heart pounded against his ribs. He tightened his grip on the sword, clenched his jaw, and silently moved toward the sounds.

۩

Pain rippled through Kavin's scalp and raced down her spine. Zayd jerked her around by her hair and all but dragged her through the dark and empty tunnel that ran beneath the arena. The guards were all above them. There was no one to hear her call for help. No one to save her.

"You fucking bitch!" Zayd screamed. "Did you think you and your pathetic lover could win? That you could beat me? He's dead now, no thanks to you and your asinine plan. And you…" He shoved his shoulder hard against the door that led to Nasir's cell…the cell where they'd made love…then threw her into the room by her hair. "You're about to get exactly what you deserve."

Kavin yelped. Her shoulder and hip slammed into the stone floor. Pain ricocheted through her body, sent stars firing off behind her eyes. She grunted, tried to get up, but Zayd was right there, lifting her by the shoulders and slamming her back down against the floor. "Look at me, you bitch!"

Hair fell into her face. Kavin tried to look up at him, but her vision swam, the pain in her skull and back so strong, it was all she could feel. And Nasir…

Her breath caught on a sob. She hadn't intended for any of that to happen. She'd only wanted Malik to stop the fight. To keep Nasir from doing something stupid in his attempt to save her. And now he was…

Her chest squeezed so tight she could barely breathe. The memory of all that blood spilling from the wound in his belly overwhelmed her.

Oh, Allah. *Oh, Allah…*

Zayd's open palm connected with her cheek. Her head spun around, hit the stone floor. But she only minutely registered the blow. All she felt was the wretched, blinding pain near her heart at what had happened to Nasir. Of the thought of him bleeding to death up there on the sands of the arena right this minute.

"Look at me!" Zayd roared again. "I want you to see my eyes when I show you just what you really are."

"Take your hands off her."

Zayd stilled. Kavin's eyes popped open at the sound of the voice. Nasir's voice.

Slowly, Zayd shifted to look back to the door, and Kavin lifted her head, then peered through watery vision toward the archway. Toward Nasir, standing in the opening, gripping his sword in two hands. His eyes blazed; his body was covered in dust and sweat and only the faint stains of blood. But there was no gaping wound. No blood spilling from his belly. No sign of death as she'd seen in the arena.

Relief and confusion swam inside Kavin's heart and mind as Zayd spun in front of her. Muttering words in the Ghul language that Kavin had never heard, he gripped the sword that magically appeared in his hand. "You think you can take me, slave? I was a warrior before I came to Jahannam. And my magic isn't bound like yours. You're fucked. And so is this slut."

"I think you're a coward," Nasir said, stepping fully into the room. Without taking his eyes off Zayd, he said, "Get up, *rouhi*."

Kavin swallowed hard and scrambled back against the wall. And noticed, for the first time, the blood welling from the wound in Zayd's shoulder. Things had happened so fast in the arena she hadn't realized he'd been hit.

Zayd moved in front of her. "I'm going to enjoy gutting you. But I'm not going to kill you quickly. No, I think I'll keep you alive long enough to watch what I do to this whore."

Nasir's jaw clenched. "Then get on with it, Ghul."

The way he snarled the last word wasn't lost on Kavin. And fear gripped her chest when she watched Zayd's shoulders tighten, when she heard him mutter words in the old language again, when she saw the second sword appeared in his other hand.

Zayd swung the swords like a pro, took a step to his right. Kavin's breath caught as she pulled her legs in close and watched. Waited. Prayed.

Zayd swung out with his right hand, then his left. Kavin gasped as Nasir barely missed being decapitated, then lifted his own sword, stopping the downward slice of Zayd's.

Muscles in his arms and legs flexed as he pushed hard against Zayd. Zayd was as big as Nasir, and as muscular. And he had the power of magic on his side. Fear burned a hole straight to her stomach as the two struggled for control. Just when she was sure Zayd was going to win, Nasir lifted his foot and shoved his sandal into Zayd's gut, knocking the highborn back two feet.

Zayd stumbled, tried to right himself, but his feet slipped on the edge of the bath and then his body fell into the water with a splash. A sword flew from one hand, clanked against the stone wall.

Nasir was right there, charging through the bath, water spraying up and around his legs as he grasped Zayd by the shirt-front and jammed the hilt of his sword in Zayd's face.

Zayd's head whipped around; blood spurted from his mouth. Nasir's eyes were wide with retribution and rage as he slammed the end of the sword into Zayd's face again and again.

Kavin pushed to her feet, her heart pounding hard as she watched. She'd never seen Nasir like this. Not just enraged, but the bringer of death, in all its gruesome forms.

No. Her breath stuttered as she remembered back. She had seen him this way. Once. In the arena. That last fight. Just before

Zayd had taken her to his cell and turned her over to him. She'd watched—in horror—as he'd decimated that Shaitan as if he were nothing.

"You were right, I hate the fighting. More than anything about this place. But I'll do it for you. I'd do anything for you."

"Stop!" Kavin took a step forward. "Nasir, stop!"

Nasir's arm stilled on the upswing. He turned his head to face her. Zayd's blood was splattered all over his face and bare chest, and there was such fury in his eyes. Fury she didn't want to see there, not because of her.

"Please, stop," she whispered, stepping toward him, wanting the Marid back she'd fallen in love with. Not this killer. Not this person he didn't want to be. "Just…stop."

Nasir's eyes were as black as she'd ever seen them, and a shiver of fear ran through her as she reached out, as she touched his arm, because he looked like the monster she'd encountered in his cell that first day. But they'd come so far; she'd learned so much. And she believed deep in her heart he'd never hurt her.

"Please," she whispered. "Please, just…let go. He can't hurt us anymore. He's nothing."

Nasir glanced down at her hand on his arm, seemed to be in some sort of rage-induced haze as he slowly shifted his gaze to her eyes as if he didn't recognize her, then looked to Zayd's bloody and bruised face.

Kavin held her breath. Waited. Was so afraid if Nasir killed him this way, it would cross a line they couldn't come back from. She needed to know the djinni she'd fallen in love with was inside him somewhere. That he could pull *himself* back from the brink if he needed to.

Then Nasir released his hold on Zayd's shirtfront. Zayd hit the water with a splash, sending droplets all over the stone floor. Nasir's sword fell from his hand, clanked against the ground. And then his arms were around her, pulling her close, his face sliding into the hollow between her shoulder and neck to breathe warm against her throat.

"*Rouhi...*"

Relief pulsed through every inch of her body, swept her up in a tidal wave of emotion that poured through her. She slid her arms around his shoulders, held him tight. Closed her eyes and just breathed.

He'd done it. He'd saved her. And himself.

"I'm here," she whispered. "I'm right here."

He eased back, looked down at her. Blood and dirt stained his handsome face, but the rage was gone. In its place were the soft, sweet, gentle eyes she'd come to love. "Thank you," he rasped.

Tears burned her eyes. She was just about to tell him he had no reason to thank her, when she caught sight of movement behind him.

Zayd lurched to his feet in the bath. Blood ran like rivulets down his face. He gripped the sword in his hands and lifted it over his head.

Things happened so fast, Kavin barely tracked them. She screamed Nasir's name, pushed him away from her, then reached down for his sword, which he'd dropped at their feet.

She thrust out before Zayd could. The tip stabbed into his chest, his forward momentum forcing it deep. Zayd's eyes went wide. He stumbled back. Kavin gasped and let go of the blade.

Then his body fell into the bath again with a splash that sent half the water spilling over the sides and onto the stone floor.

Silence descended. Then Nasir looked her way. "Holy shit."

Kavin's own eyes were wide with shock. She hadn't thought. She'd reacted. Her pulse shot up; her adrenaline peaked, then plummeted. She stumbled back a step, but Nasir was right there to catch her.

"Breathe, *rouhi*."

She gripped his arms, focused on the draw and pull of her lungs, was relieved when Nasir stepped in front of her so she couldn't see what she'd done.

"That's it." He rubbed a hand down her back. "Allah, you've got more fight in you than I ever expected. Remind me not to piss you off."

A laugh slipped from her lips. One she didn't expect. One that pushed aside the horror and brought her around to what mattered most. Hands resting against his strong chest, she looked up into his eyes and tried not to be gripped by fear all over again. "How are we going to get out of here? The guards are busy in the arena, but the city walls—"

"I'll show you."

They both looked toward the door, where Hana stood with her hands at her sides, bitter victory on her face as she stared at Zayd's dead body in the bath.

Seconds passed in silence, then she finally met their eyes. "So long as you take me with you."

Kavin sagged against Nasir as she looked up at him. "Take me away from here. Away from death and dying and slaves and highborns. Please. I don't care where we go, I just need…"

Her chest tightened with the weight of everything that had happened, cutting off her words. Of what *could have* happened.

Then his mouth was on hers. Claiming hers in a swift, fierce kiss she felt everywhere. Banishing the fear, telling her this—the two of them together—was all that mattered. And when he eased back, the smile that curled one side of his mouth was so damn handsome, it softened everything inside her. "Your wish is my command, *rouhi*. And just your luck, I know the perfect place for us to go."

Chapter Sixteen

As they stood on a bluff overlooking Gannah, the salty breeze whipping the hair back from their faces, Nasir wondered what Kavin was thinking.

The tall spires of a city he'd loved since he was a child sparkled in the late afternoon sunlight. Palms waved in the air, mountains rose to the north, and the sea filled the horizon beyond. Below them, past the city walls, his people—his tribe—milled about the streets, shopping, working, *living* as they did every day.

He saw home. He saw safety. He saw people removed from war and suffering who had no idea just what kind of horrors were being unleashed in Jahannam. But he'd made Malik a promise. He'd tell them. He'd make sure they all knew it wasn't just those from his tribe who were being imprisoned. It was djinn from all tribes, from all races, from every part of their world. And it was time it stopped.

Kavin leaned against his side. "What if they don't let us in?"

He glanced over her head toward Hana, and read the same worry in the young girl's face that he heard in Kavin's voice. They were both Ghul, about to enter a city they feared would despise them on sight. But Nasir knew differently.

He tightened his arm around her. "You brought their prince home. I don't think they're going to care if you're Ghul or Shaitan or even human."

She looked up at him, and, as the sun warmed her features, he remembered how scared he'd been as they'd fled the arena. Getting out of the tunnels had been easier than he'd expected. But out in the open, he'd been so afraid they'd be recognized. That he'd lose her so close to freedom. But Hana had known a secret passageway under the city walls, and with the guards distracted by the revolt, they'd slipped away quickly and easily.

It had taken three days to reach Gannah. Though his powers had returned once they'd been free of the confines of Jahannam and he could have teleported home, both Kavin and Hana had been imprisoned so quickly after reaching adulthood, they'd yet to develop their gifts. But that would soon change.

"You sound so certain."

"I know my people, *rouhi*. You're free. No one will hurt you here."

Uncertainty filled her eyes as she ran her fingers over the opal at his throat. "Freedom means nothing to me unless you're here to share it. What about this?"

He'd thought the same thing more than once. Wherever the sorceress was, she could call him back at any moment. He had no idea if his brothers were alive or dead, if she was using them and biding her time with him. But he was done living his life under the control of others.

He turned her, wrapped both arms around her back, reveling in the warmth of her body, the feel of her skin, her love that had reminded him who he was—who he *wanted* to be. "We'll worry about that if it happens."

"But—"

He pressed his finger against her lips. "She hasn't contacted me in months. I don't know what happened to her, but I'm not going to live my life in fear. I want to spend it with you. However long that may be. Nothing in life is certain, Kavin. All I know is that I love you. Right now, that and what we do to stop the torture in Jahannam is all that matters."

Her eyes softened, and she lifted her mouth to his when he lowered to kiss her, curled her arms around his neck, and held him so tight he felt her everywhere. And though he knew the battle with Zoraida wasn't over, for now he didn't care.

He was back. He'd found his heart and soul and a reason to live in a Ghul. In the most amazing, beautiful, gentle creature he'd ever met. And because of her, he was alive. He wasn't about to waste a moment of the time he'd been given all because of her.

"Come, *rouhi*," he said, easing back, smiling down at her with all the love she'd given him, even when he hadn't deserved it. "I want to introduce you to my parents."

She gripped his hand in hers as he stepped back, pressed the other against her belly, and shot him a nervous look. One that was so damn sexy, he itched to kiss it from her face. "The king and queen? In this?" She glanced down at the ripped purple gown she was still wearing. "Maybe you could take me somewhere to freshen up first?"

He chuckled, waved his hand, and muttered magical words in his language. Her dress transformed into a simple but elegant pale blue gown that hit at her calves and showcased her slim arms and waist.

Surprise lit her eyes as she looked down. "How…?" She glanced up sharply. "How did you do that?"

His smile grew wider. Behind her, Hana chuckled.

"I am full of surprises. Haven't you figured that out by now?"

Her lips curled with a wicked grin that sent heat careening through his belly. A heat he planned to shower on her as soon as they were alone.

She tightened her fingers in his and took a step down the hill, toward their future. "Something tells me life with you will never be boring."

"You haven't seen anything yet, *rouhi*."

Even desire comes at a price...

Possessed BY Desire

A Firebrand Novella

USA TODAY BESTSELLING AUTHOR

ELISABETH NAUGHTON

*For the NW Pixie Girls,
Who threatened an initiation ceremony
but were sweet enough never to follow through.
Love you girls!*

Chapter One

Claire Sampson looked out over the early morning sunrise on the eastern shore of Oahu and lifted the mug of coffee to her lips. Waves rolled gently against the white sand just yards in front of her, and a gentle breeze blew through the palms above as she sipped the steaming brew. But her attention wasn't focused on the serene view; it was locked on the boat, probably a mile off shore, its sails flying as it drifted slowly through the water, cutting a course for more exotic lands. Tahiti, Fiji, maybe even Australia.

Is that where her bottle was headed? Was she wasting time on this Hawaiian island?

Pushing her glasses back up her nose, she turned away from the boat, then headed back inside the bungalow she'd rented while on sabbatical. Officially, the University of Florida thought she was taking time off to research local Hawaiian folklore and its role in the history of the islands, but that was just her cover. The truth was an obsession she couldn't let go, even when her mind told her this kind of search would bring her nothing but trouble.

Ignoring the warning going off in her brain, she set her mug on the old scarred table and slid into the chair. After opening the lid of her laptop, she pulled up the tidal map at Kaneohe

Bay and compared it to the currents and tides she'd been tracking yesterday via the National Oceanic and Atmospheric Administration website. That bottle Mira had thrown into the Columbia River in the Pacific Northwest nearly six months ago had to turn up somewhere soon.

She bit her lip, flipped screens to check another chart. Her money was on the Hawaiian Islands. She knew there was a slim chance that bottle could have gotten sucked up in the Alaska Current and right now might be part of some frozen Arctic ice floe, but something in her gut told her it was going to show up here.

It had to...

Her phone rang, and without looking, she reached for the cordless from the counter to the right. "This is Claire."

"Claire? I'm so glad I found you."

Claire's entire body tensed when she recognized the female voice. "Sura?"

"Yeah, it's me. I don't have a lot of time. They know what you're up to."

Slowly, Claire pushed out of her chair. Though she'd known this moment was coming, the shock of it still caused her pulse to beat faster. "What did you tell them?"

Sura was the only friend Claire had left from her previous life, and from time to time she checked up on Claire—mostly because she pitied Claire. But they hadn't spoken in months, and even Sura didn't totally know what Claire had planned.

"Nothing. I didn't tell them anything. But it was only a matter of time before they figured it out on their own."

Claire's shoulders dropped, and her heart plummeted like a stone weight into her stomach as well, a reaction that stole her breath because it was both new and unexpected. If this was what heartbreak felt like, she couldn't imagine how humans—those who felt the full range of emotions—dealt with it.

She'd been stupid to think the Guild wouldn't catch on, not after the way they'd banished her to the human world, but she'd hoped she'd have time to find that bottle before they did.

No such luck now.

"I'm sure they're already plotting my next punishment," Claire said with more sarcasm than she intended. "Though I can't imagine what could be worse than this. How long do I have?"

"I don't know. But Ridwan is speaking with the others now, and they will be coming for you. "Ridwan. Great. That could mean today, tomorrow, or a month from now. The High Seven didn't view time the same way humans did.

Sura hesitated, then in a low voice asked, "Claire? You feel, don't you? For months I've been wondering what's happening to me but was afraid to ask. Others sense a change too. Some of us…some of us have discussed it. It's happening to all within the Guild except for the High Seven. We all…feel."

The depression slowly slinking over Claire disappeared in a burst of excitement. Was it possible what was happening to her was also happening to others?

"How? Tell me, Sura. I need to know. When did it start?"

"Right before the equinox."

Before the equinox… Claire's excitement rose another notch.

"Sadness, joy, anger," Sura went on, "I feel all of these. I don't know how to describe it except to say its—"

"Freeing."

Sura sighed. "Yes. So freeing. How have we existed all this time without emotion? Why would they take that from us?"

Claire turned to look out over the gentle waves again as a twinge of animosity seeped into her chest. She'd served the Guild for hundreds of years, but one question, one curiosity had gotten her banished. How many others had been banished for this same reason? How many were now feeling something—anything—for the first time?

"Because controlling our emotions binds our free will," Claire said. "We're not supposed to have free will. We're made of light, not fire or clay. If we have free will like humans and djinn, we might choose *not* to serve."

"Yes, but for those who choose to stay, emotions would only strengthen their service. Certainly Allah—"

"This was not Allah's command." Claire had done a lot of research since being banished. And she knew the High Seven were behind this. Knew it in her heart, even if that was a place she'd just come to trust. "Things are not always what they seem. I've learned that the hard way. I'm going to find the other opals."

"That's part of the reason I called."

"To warn me. I know. I appreciate—"

"No," Sura answered, this time in a whisper. "To tell you that your bottle has washed ashore in the Marshall Islands."

"*What*?" Claire's eyes grew wide, and anxiety pushed in from every side. "How do you know? Who found it? They haven't opened it yet, have they? If they do—"

"Relax. No one's found it. Yet. It hasn't been opened. And the High Seven don't know it's washed up either."

"Then how…?"

"We're celestial, remember? We have multiple resources at our fingertips. We just have to know the right questions to ask."

Claire heard the smile in her friend's voice, and it relaxed her shoulders, if only for a moment. "You're celestial, Sura. I'm" —What was the name those romance novels she'd read to try to understand human emotions called it?— "a fallen angel, remember?"

"I hate that term, *angel*. It implies wings and halos. Which we definitely don't have. And you'll not be fallen for long. Especially not if you find the opals before the High Seven find you. You won't have to fear their wrath anymore. They won't be able to touch you."

Power was a tempting thing. For a moment, Claire let herself consider what she could do with the power of the firebrand opals. Thousands of years ago, Ridwan, guardian of the Seven Heavens, bound the celestial emotions in seven firebrand opals, then scattered them in the djinn realm, where her kind were forbidden to cross. They held power, the kind of power that infused djinn and granted them long lifespans. And Ridwan had scattered them there, partly to test and tempt the djinn, and partly to keep the opals safe. But Claire didn't want power. She just wanted to live. Really live. And above all else, she wanted to have choice, something that had been taken from her long before she'd even been created.

"There's no guarantee I'll succeed," Claire said." To find the other opals, I have to cross over to the djinn realm."

"Which you can do, now that you've been stripped of your powers," Sura answered. "Find the shard in the Marshall Islands and summon a djinni to cross over to corrupt your soul. That was your plan, wasn't it? Turn the tides on the pleasure slave? Seduce him into taking you to their realm? We both know your celestial powers won't be bound there. You'll be able to find the other opals and destroy them. From there... Well, from there what you do with that kind of power is all up to you. Your choice."

Claire's heart raced all over again, followed by a wave of nausea. She'd never been nervous before, but now she was. Now all she could wonder was...could she seduce? Would a pleasure slave know what she was? And what if she failed? If what Sura said was true, this wasn't just about her anymore. If she didn't act, the High Seven would find a way to bind what little emotion others in her order had grown used to.

She frowned, because it was easier than stressing about something she feared she'd never be able to do. "You're too perceptive."

"We are not the unintelligent creatures the High Seven think us to be."

"True. But if you've guessed my plan, they have already too."

"So stop stalling. Find that bottle and get on with that seduction. And do it soon. You're the only one who can."

"No pressure there."

Sura laughed. "Who knows? Maybe you'll even enjoy it."

Claire's mind drifted to the books she'd read for research and the fantasies they had sparked—ones she'd never even considered before. She didn't doubt she would enjoy it. Djinn were, after all, wickedly tempting and highly erotic creatures. The question was whether she was strong enough to use that eroticism to accomplish her goal or if she'd fall prey to it.

Because, as with all free will, when a soul walked on the dark side, there was always a chance it might not come back.

"That's good. Touch me just like that, djinni. My, but you have learned a lot, haven't you?"

Ashur lifted his mouth from the breast he was laving and looked up at Nuha, laid out on the bed, her eyes tightly closed, her fists gripping the silk sheets beneath her as he slid his fingers through her wetness.

"I'm an eager student," he answered, dipping inside her heat and pressing his thumb against her clit for added sensation as he searched for that special spot. The one he'd learned could make a female not only come but beg for more. "Especially when it involves one of Zoraida's most accomplished teachers."

Firelight flickered over Nuha's naked body. She groaned, grasped the sheets tighter, and thrust her hips up to meet his downward stroke. The scent of her arousal filled the air. Perspiration dotted her skin. She was beautiful, just as all of Zoraida's followers were—dark hair, coffee-colored skin, flawless curves designed to entice and allure—but he'd never felt anything for her other than duty.

Then again, it wasn't his job to feel. It was his job to seduce. And it was her job to teach him just how to do that so when Zoraida returned from wherever she'd gone these last few months, he could do her will to the fullest of his ability.

Nuha's entire body tensed, and she tightened around his fingers. Her slim body quaked with the power of her release, telling him he'd passed this lesson.

In the aftermath of her orgasm, Ashur petted her gently, bringing her down as he'd been taught. His cock was rock-hard, the blood pulsing hot in his ears, but he knew he'd find no release today. This lesson had been about pleasuring a female without taking anything for himself. As a pleasure slave, it was important he could seduce without scaring his mark. The humans he'd eventually be sent to seduce would be wary at first. Trust came before sex. And getting a female to trust often meant denying the release he desperately craved himself.

Not that Zoraida's instructors didn't bring him pleasure. They had to so he could learn to control his desire. But there was no passion. No emotion. It was clinical at best. And part of Ashur couldn't wait to finally be sent into the human realm on an assignment. To do what he'd been taught with a female who truly wanted him. Maybe even to feel something other than anger again.

A smile spread across Nuha's face as she blinked several times and looked up at the ceiling in the lavish bedroom suite. "You are nothing like your brother, that's for sure. Tariq was the worst student I ever had."

Ashur clenched his jaw at the mention of his eldest brother's name, and resentment slid through his veins. Tariq had always been the selfish one. Even their father, the king, had said Tariq did what he wanted, when he wanted. As heir to the throne, it was his prerogative. But that selfishness had backfired, and eventually it had led to his being imprisoned by Zoraida when he should have been sitting on the throne of Gannah. If it hadn't been for Tariq, Nasir and Ashur never would have searched for him. They never would have been trapped here as well. Nasir would still be alive.

Anger brewed hot in his gut as Nuha rose and dressed. After all that they'd sacrificed for him, where was Tariq? Free. Living in the human world, as if he were one of the lower-life beings, never bothering to wonder what was happening back in the djinn realm. Never bothering to care what had happened to his brothers.

A fact Ashur never forgot.

"A great many rewards come to those who please the mistress," Nuha said as she slipped the purple velvet robe over her shoulder. "Zoraida will be very happy with your progress when she returns."

The red haze slowly cleared from Ashur's vision and a sense of purpose pulsed through him. Pleasing Zoraida was the only thing he cared about anymore. None from his father's kingdom had searched for him after he'd disappeared. No one had tried to save Nasir from the Pits of Jahannam, where he'd died. Zoraida, on the other hand, took care of those who lived up to her expectations. He saw it every day in the faces of those around him. It was the rebels she punished. Those like Tariq, who were selfish and defiant and refused to give in to her will. And in their stupidity, they missed out on the most important things. In her service, there was no pain. Only riches, power, and more pleasure than any djinni could hope to find.

He rose from the side of the bed where he'd been kneeling and watched Nuha tie the robe at her waist, her dark hair falling down her back like a river of black silk. His desire was still strong, but more than anything, he just wanted Zoraida to show the fuck up so he could get on with that pleasuring. And forget, once and for all, a life he'd never go back to.

A knock sounded at the door, and Nuha said, "Enter."

The door pushed open, and a guard stepped into the room, his armor clinking as he moved. But it was his expression that caught Ashur's attention. Pale face. Wide eyes. A *Holy Allah* look that said something big had happened. "Lady Nuha. I was sent to fetch you. She's back. The mistress has returned."

Nuha's head came up, and her own eyes went wide. "Where? When? Have you seen her?"

"Just now, my lady. Downstairs. In the great hall. She's back, and she wants you and the pleasure slave. Right away."

Ashur's pulse picked up speed as Nuha quickly stepped into her slippers. At his throat, the fire opal he wore grew warm.

"Come, slave," Nuha said, moving for the door. "And hurry."

Ashur followed Nuha out into the hall. Candles from sconces on the walls lit the corridor. His bare feet passed over stone as they moved. Zoraida's compound was hidden in the mountains of the djinn realm—where, Ashur wasn't entirely sure, but it was always cold here. Memories of his time in the dungeons flashed in his mind as they descended steps toward the main level, and his nerves shot up at the prospect of seeing Zoraida again. The last time they'd been face-to-face, she'd been ordering his torture, all in an attempt to get Tariq to do her will. Would she send Ashur back to the dungeons, or would she see what he'd become since her absence?

Smooth marble caressed the soles of his feet as they reached the main level. Ahead, double doors were parted to reveal an eerie orange light.

"This way," Nuha said. "Quickly. We mustn't keep her waiting."

His pulse pounded as they reached the doors. The guard pushed them wide, then stood back to let them enter. Across the room, a fire roared in the enormous stone fireplace, and a female dressed in a black gown with pale blonde hair falling down her back paced in front of its warmth.

She turned when she heard them, and her icy gaze landed on Ashur. "He's not bound."

No, *how are you*? No, *You look well*. Ashur swallowed hard, unsure of what to expect.

"No, *sayyeda*," Nuha answered, folding her hands in front of her in respect. "The djinni has learned much in your absence. I think you will be most pleasantly surprised. He's my best pupil."

"Bring him to me."

Nuha stepped aside and held out her hand, indicating he should move forward, but before Ashur could, he caught the look in her eyes. The one that said, *don't fuck this up*.

His heart beat faster. Hesitantly, he moved forward. When he was a foot from Zoraida, he stopped and drew in a breath that smelled like…roses.

She was tall—almost as tall as he—but it was her beauty that grabbed his attention with the strength of a vise. Milk-white skin, flawless features, lips made for tasting and a body that looked as if it had been created solely for sin. Even with circles under her eyes, indicating the length of her journey, she was beautiful. His gaze landed on her abundant cleavage in the dark gown, and the desire he'd been denied reignited in his veins.

Zoraida's blue eyes searched his features, then ran down the length of his bare chest and finally held on the cotton pants tied low at his hips. Without a word, she circled him, and Ashur's pulse skipped while she inspected him from every angle. When she was finally facing him again, she reached out and cupped his groin. "You're hard, djinni."

The shock of her touch made him draw a breath. He wasn't fully hard, but he could be. He wanted to be. "Yes, *sayyeda*."

"Your brother was never hard for me."

No, Tariq was never anything anyone wanted him to be. "Yes, *sayyeda*."

Zoraida's eyes narrowed as she studied his face, but her hand didn't move. He sensed this was a test, and he wanted to pass. Needed to. He willed himself to grow harder but as the seconds ticked by nothing happened. If she'd just move her hand…

As quickly as she'd grasped him, Zoraida let go. Looking over his shoulder toward Nuha, she said, "What is his level of training?"

"Level four, *sayyeda*. He's been an exemplary pupil. A very fast learner. Eager to please."

"Eager to please," Zoraida muttered, looking back at him. "And what of his…defiance?"

"There is none."

"I find that hard to believe, considering the lengths his brother went to defy me." Her expression hardened. "It is because of him I was trapped these last few months."

Ashur swallowed hard. *Fucking Tariq…*

"He has not shown even the slightest resemblance to your last pleasure slave, *sayyeda*," Nuha said. "In fact, his work ethic has been so strong, he's moved ahead of all the others currently in training."

"Ahead of all the rest?" Zoraida asked, still not looking away from Ashur's eyes. "Tell me, slave, do you not seek to destroy me, as your brothers did?"

It was the question he'd known would come. Ashur's pulse skyrocketed.

"Answer me," Zoraida snapped.

He thought of Nasir. Dead in the pits. And Tariq living life as a human without a fucking care. And finally, of his kingdom, which didn't give a flying rat's ass about him. The last remaining prince of Gannah.

Anger brewed hot, but he tamped it down, knowing control would be his savior. He'd learned that here the last few months. *Thrived* on it. "I am not my brothers."

Zoraida's gaze raked his features. She was trying to decide if he was telling the truth or lying. His pulse pounded hard. If she sent him back to the dungeons...

"That remains to be seen," she finally answered. "Tell me, slave. What is your purpose?"

"To serve you, *sayyeda*. That is my only desire."

Her gaze dropped to the fire opal resting at the base of his throat. "And if I asked you to kill your brother in the human realm to prove your loyalty... What would you say to that?"

Kill Tariq? No, he couldn't. He...

Behind him, Nuha coughed. And a visual of the image he'd been shown months ago flashed in his mind. Of Nasir dying in the pits. And of Tariq, smiling and laughing in the human realm with the woman he'd betrayed them for.

He clenched his hands into fists, and the fury born into his tribe from the beginning of time flared hot and bright. "My *brother* deserves to die. If my *sayyeda* commanded it, I would do her will. Gladly."

Surprise rushed over Zoraida's face, and she looked over his shoulder toward Nuha. "No brotherly love for Tariq?"

Ashur ground his teeth. "None. I want Tariq to suffer."

A smile spread across Zoraida's face, one that made her even more beautiful. "I want Tariq to suffer for what he did to me too. But first, I have a more important task for you."

More important than revenge? Ashur's brow dropped low, but he knew better than to ask.

Zoraida stepped back, and for the first time, he noticed how her fragility. As if the journey had robbed her of sleep. The circles under her eyes seemed darker now, her shoulders not as proud. As he studied her, he wondered what she'd meant when she'd said she'd been trapped.

"Before we deal with Tariq," she said, "I need a soul."

Excitement burst beneath Ashur's ribs, overriding his need for revenge. That meant he was finally going to be sent to the human realm to corrupt a soul, which would fuel Zoraida's immortality and make her stronger.

"As you wish, *sayyeda*," he said. "I am here only to do your will."

"We shall see," she muttered. "Though you say you want revenge, I fear the blood of your tribe is still strong."

Panic set in. "No, *sayyeda*. I—"

"So we're going to consider this your test, djinni," she went on. "Shortly, you will be called upon by a human female. Pleasure her in each and every way she requests. And corrupt her soul for my glory. When you are done, *if* you've succeeded with no complications, you will have that revenge we both so eagerly seek. If you fail..." Her expression hardened, and those eyes that had seemed bright and oh-so alluring before turned to hard, icy chips of glass. "I will send you to the Pits of Jahannam, just like Nasir. And you will know pain like you've never imagined. Are we clear?"

Pain versus pleasure? That wasn't even a question. He bowed. "Yes, *sayyeda*. Your wish is my command."

Chapter Two

STOP STALLING…AND GET ON WITH that seduction.

Claire's pulse skipped as Sura's words echoed in her mind. Her friend had told her which atoll the bottle had washed up on in the Marshall Islands, but it had taken Claire a good two weeks of searching the beaches to locate the bottle herself.

Now, with the firebrand opal sparkling under the late afternoon sun, the chain of the necklace falling through her fingers, all Claire could think about was the fact this necklace was linked to a djinni in another realm. A thrill rushed through her when she imagined him wearing one just like it, followed by a gut-twisting shot of nervousness.

Angels and djinn were not encouraged to interact. It was a rule of her order she'd not bothered to question before. Now though… Now she couldn't help but wonder why.

Palms swayed overhead as she ran her fingers along the smooth stone, alive with reds and yellows and oranges. Waves lapped gently against the shore and the white sand was warm beneath her body, but a chill still spread through Claire.

Opening the bottle had been uneventful. She'd expected some cataclysmic event, but the ground hadn't even rumbled. All she'd felt was a whoosh of air, almost like a sigh, and then the amulet had fallen into her hand.

The sorceress was now back in the djinn realm. Claire knew opening the bottle had freed her. But if the laws of the cosmos held true, Zoraida couldn't cross to the human world until the soul of the one who wore the opal was corrupted. Only then could she come here and take Claire's soul. And Claire had no intention of letting that happen.

It's all up to you…

Before any djinn could corrupt her and make her lose all focus except for pleasure, she planned to do exactly what Sura had guessed. She'd seduce him, convince him to take her back to his world, and then she'd find the other opals and set herself free.

Of course, for that to happen, Claire had to put the damn necklace on.

Her skin grew hot, and all kinds of erotic images popped into her mind. Things she'd read in books and seen in videos in the hopes of figuring out what a pleasure slave would expect a human to fantasize about. She had to admit, she'd been shocked. All the popular romance novels seemed to focus on bondage and multiple partners and sex, sex, sex. Was that what human women wanted? Was that what a pleasure slave would expect her to want? Though she had to admit some part of what she'd read excited her, she didn't understand it, nor was she sure she could go through with any of it. She'd tried sex a few times, just after she'd been banished—mostly because she'd been curious about a temptation that got so many humans in trouble—but it hadn't been anything like she'd read. Either she'd done it wrong or she just couldn't be pleasured. Maybe she wouldn't be able to enjoy sex until the opals were finally destroyed.

That thought didn't ease her anxiety. She chewed on her lip, gazed down at the opal, and tried to think logically. She wasn't as unintelligent as the High Seven thought. If anything, she'd discovered just how smart she was since becoming mortal. And even with the myriad emotions running through her, she'd think this through and come out the winner in the end. Because it was the only thing she could do.

So stop stalling and get on with it...

She clasped the necklace at her nape before she could change her mind. If she couldn't enjoy sex, she'd fake it. The pleasure slave bound to this necklace was djinn. He was ruled by his own desires. He'd probably never know the difference.

She drew a deep breath and traced her fingers over the opal as she stared out at the rolling waves and the warm turquoise water of the private lagoon. She'd rented this small hut on purpose. So that whatever happened would be shielded from any prying human eyes. Only about fifty people lived on this atoll—most congregated near the one main village —but still, the last thing she needed to do was expose a djinni to human eyes. If she did, no doubt the High Seven would think of a new torturous punishment for her.

"Come to me," she whispered. "Fulfill my desire."

"Your wish, my command," a voice echoed at her back.

Shit, that was fast. Claire whipped around and squinted up at the shadowy figure. He was tall, but with the sun shining at his back, she couldn't see much else. His voice though... Just the sound of the deep, raspy tones sent a thrill through her entire body.

Which was just downright weird.

She pushed to her feet and faced him. He had shoulder-length dark hair. Tanned skin. Chiseled muscles covered in nothing but lightweight cotton pants. And his face... Her stomach tightened at the strong jaw, lush lips, and piercing black eyes staring back at her.

His master obviously knew how to make a mortal weak in the knees. She'd sent not just a pleasure slave but a pleasure god.

Heat burned Claire's cheeks, and she wiped her sweaty palms on her khaki shorts, feeling suddenly…nervous. She should have done something with her hair. She'd let the unruly curls dry on their own, and she hadn't even run a brush through them yet. At least she'd left the nerdy glasses in her hut.

"Um, hi. I'm Claire."

That was smooth.

One side of his mouth curled, and oh lovely, he had dents in his face. Really sexy, dents that sent flutters all through her belly. "Claire," he breathed. "A very beautiful name for a very beautiful woman."

It was a line. A really bad line. One that should have made her roll her eyes but didn't. Because all she could focus on was the way he said her name. As if his tongue were caressing the syllables. Which made her wonder…what would it feel like to be caressed by that tongue?

Tricky djinni. He was playing her. Messing with her head. Djinn had that power. She wasn't about to fall for it. She straightened her shoulders. *Remember who's in control here.*

She was. She couldn't forget that. She gave herself a mental slap and squared her shoulders. "And what is your name? Or would you prefer I just call you djinni?"

The smile faded, and his brow wrinkled. "You know what I am."

"Of course I do. Do you think I put the opal on and summoned you by accident?"

"I'm…not sure what to think. You are" —his gaze slid down her body— "not what I expected."

Those nerves came back full force. He couldn't possibly know what she was, could he?

No. He couldn't. She tamped down the panic. She was banished. Her powers were bound. He couldn't tell. No one could. Reminding herself of that fact, she realized he was hitting her with another line. The way he was studying every inch of her body, the heat in his stare… He wanted to put her on edge. And, dammit, she was. Her skin heated, and she couldn't help but shift her weight. No human had ever looked at her like that. Like she was a meal he wanted to devour.

Think. Don't let him manipulate you. She tucked a lock of hair behind her ear, took stock of what he was seeing. Definitely not perfection. When the High Seven had banished her to the human realm, they'd picked an unremarkably ordinary human body for her to serve out her punishment. Her legs were too long, her body straight instead of curvy like women should be, her breasts no more than mosquito bites, really. Normally, she didn't care what she looked like, but suddenly she did. Suddenly, she wished she'd taken time to highlight her blue eyes—the only part of her body she truly liked—and put on a skirt instead of the shorts that made her look like a flamingo.

Which again, was just freaking weird. She never cared what she looked like. What was wrong with her?

She shook off the thought. "You still haven't given me your name."

"Curious," he said. "I like that. My name is Ashur. And I have been sent to fulfill every one of your desires."

Ashur… Her entire body lit up like a firework.

She fought back the excitement and nerves that seemed to come out of nowhere and glanced around the small cove. Even though it was fairly secluded, that didn't mean it was completely private. A road ran along the ridge, and every now and then, locals wandered this way to and from town.

She gestured toward her hut on the edge of the beach, surrounded by palms. "Why don't we take this inside and then discuss the details of…"

The words trailed off as heat burned her cheeks all over again. She swallowed hard.

He chuckled. "Your pleasure? Yes, let's. I'm as anxious to get started as you."

The comment caught her off guard. He was anxious? Why?

She looked down at the hand he held out for her even as a tingling ignited in her belly and slinked lower. "Come, Claire. Let's begin."

Begin? Why did that word set warning bells off in her head?

And why, sweet Allah, didn't she care?

※

A jolt rushed through Ashur's entire body when Claire placed her hand in his. He looked up at her face, narrowed his eyes and searched her features for…what, he wasn't sure.

Did he know her? Had they met somewhere he just couldn't remember? He let his senses guide him, but didn't pick up anything unusual from her. She was human, not djinn, so there was a slim chance they'd met before—albeit very slim. In his younger years, he'd crossed over to the human realm a few times, mostly out of morbid curiosity of a race he didn't understand, but when his father had found out he'd forbidden Ashur to cross again. He hadn't been in the human world in years, and judging from Claire's late-20-ish age, that last trip had likely been when she was a child. But still…there was something familiar about her. Something different. Something… enticing he couldn't define.

His mind spun as she led him toward the hut she'd motioned to moments before. The sweet scent of gardenias rose in the air around him. As he followed. Stepping inside, he took in the interior. It was small—only three rooms. An archway opened to a kitchen to his right, and ahead a door led to what he suspected was a bathroom. But the main room of the hut housed a sitting area complete with couches and tables on a bamboo floor, and beyond that a four-poster bed covered in mosquito netting.

He waved his hand, calling up a power he hadn't used in months. Candles on the bedside tables sparked to life and slow music from speakers somewhere in the room filled the space.

"Clever," she said. "I wish I could do that. She turned to face him. Drew in a breath. Blew it out. "So how does this work? Do we just…you know…get down to business?"

She was nervous. Which was good, because it meant he wasn't the only one. Trust before pleasure. The words were engrained in his mind. Even though his stomach churned with excitement, he needed her to relax in order for this to go as planned.

"May I sit?" he asked, gesturing to the couch.

"Um. Sure, I guess." She frowned. "Sorry. It's not every day you summon a pleasure slave, you know?"

He chuckled and eased down onto the cushions. "Why did you summon me, Claire?"

Her cheeks turned the slightest shade of pink, and again he had the sensation that she wasn't what she seemed. She sat on a chair opposite him before he could let his thoughts get away from him. And then he was too entranced by her to do anything but watch the way she twisted her hands in her lap, shifted them to the cushions beneath her, finally sat on them as if she were trying to stop herself from doing something totally out of character. Like grabbing him.

Grab me, maya.

The thought came out of nowhere and sent another jolt through his system. Except this one was heat and life and excitement. And he welcomed it. After all his months of prison and training, he was as anxious to—what had she called it?—get down to business as her.

She wasn't exotic like Nuha, or breathtakingly beautiful like Zoraida, but she was pretty—big blue eyes, wavy auburn hair, and a tiny scar near the corner of her mouth that made him wonder what those lips felt like, what they'd taste like against his tongue. Her body, from what he could see, was long and lean, like an athlete, and he couldn't wait to see more. But the spark he caught in her eyes when she looked at him told him she was sizing him up in the same exact way, and the "more" would have to wait.

"Well?" he asked.

"Isn't it obvious?" she said with a lift of her chin. "What reason does a woman have for summoning a pleasure slave except for pleasure?"

Add quick to her list of attributes. He smiled and relaxed further into his seat. "Most have a reason. A recent breakup, loneliness, general curiosity, even a desire to learn a new technique."

He lifted his brows in anticipation of her answer, which in turn made her roll her eyes, and he found himself laughing. "I can teach you a great many things. Whatever you like. However and whenever. Until you're satisfied. That is my job."

Her cheeks turned even pinker. "I know."

She bit her lip. Seemed to be thinking over what she wanted to say. And as he waited, he realized her reaction was not what he'd expected. Aside from that strange feeling he got near her, he sensed there was something more than mere distrust at the root of her hesitation. "I take it you don't want me to teach you anything?"

"No it's not that. I just...didn't expect the discussion part to all of this."

"You called me, remember?"

"I know I did."

"Then what's the problem?

She pushed from her seat, began pacing the width of the small room. "It's...complicated."

Nuha and the other instructors had told him this might happen. He scooted to the edge of the couch, rested his forearms on his knees. "Is this the first time you've summoned a pleasure slave?"

She shot him a look. "Of course."

"You're nervous. It's natural. Tell me, are you a virgin, Claire?"

"What?" Her feet stumbled, and she almost tripped but caught herself by grasping the back of the chair she'd been sitting in earlier. "No. Of course not. That's a silly question."

But the pinking of her cheeks again told him she wasn't all that experienced either. Perhaps what she needed was a small dose of...honesty.

"What if I told you this was new for me as well?"

Her feet stilled, and she looked over at him with those mesmerizing eyes. "What do you mean?"

"I mean" —*Trust before seduction*— "you are my first assignment."

Her brow lowered, and her mouth dropped open, but she quickly closed it. "You've never pleasured a woman?"

"Not a human woman, no. But do not worry, I'm well versed in all aspects of pleasure."

She moved around the chair, her interest obviously piqued. "How does one go about training for this kind of…assignment?"

"Months of preparation and instruction."

"From whom?"

"Teachers."

She eased down onto the chair again, tucking her long legs under her, honest curiosity lighting her face. "Female djinn? Were they slaves as well?"

He shifted. This was not the direction he'd expected the conversation to go. His anxiety rushed back. "Some were." *Most.* "But that shouldn't matter to—"

"Who do you serve? Why are *you* here, Ashur?"

The question threw him off kilter. She was leaning forward, her face flushed, her eyes wide, eagerly awaiting his response. And another sense that she was not what she seemed rushed through him.

Some instinct deep inside told him not to mention Zoraida or his imprisonment. Carefully, he said, "I serve you, Claire."

Her gaze held his a long beat, and then slowly, she eased back in her seat. "That remains to be seen. What if I'm not satisfied with you? Will your master send another?"

He clenched his jaw to keep the anger at bay. Sending another was not an option. "She won't need to. Trust me. I will be exactly what you seek."

Claire's entire face relaxed. And heat crept across her features—a heat he felt crackle clear across the room. Something had shifted in her demeanor, but he couldn't pinpoint what.

She pushed out of her seat and held her hand out to him, all signs of her earlier nervousness now gone. "Why don't we see if you are? Come. Show me."

His blood pulsed, and he hardened beneath the soft cotton of his pants as he looked at her outstretched hand. This was what he'd wanted—to be sent to a woman who truly wanted him—so why was he hesitating?

Trust before seduction…

Something in his gut told him he was not the one about to do the seducing.

Chapter Three

CLAIRE WAITED FOR ASHUR TO place his hand in hers as she'd done earlier to him. And when he did, the heat of his skin permeated her own, sending another rush of desire coursing through her veins.

He was one of Zoraida's pleasure slaves. She had no doubt now. Djinn, regardless of race, existed in highly patriarchal societies. There was likely not another female master besides Zoraida anywhere in the djinn realm. Did that mean he was Tariq's brother too?

Claire hadn't talked to Mira much in the months since giving Mira the spell she'd needed to free Tariq from Zoraida's hold. Once Mira had trapped the opal in that bottle then accidentally tossed the bottle into the river, Claire had been more focused on finding the amulet than on whom it could be linked to next. But from the few conversations Claire had had with Mira via phone, she knew that both of Tariq's brothers had been imprisoned with him—brothers he was still desperate to free.

She wanted to ask but knew better. In the end, it didn't matter if Ashur was related to Tariq or not. Claire wasn't here because of Mira's new husband. She had other things to worry about.

The look on Ashur's face also warned Claire not to get too personal. He was suspicious of her intentions. She needed to remember not to rush things and let him think he was driving the seduction.

Which meant she needed to be at least a little vulnerable.

She drew him toward the bed, then turned to face him. "You want to know why I summoned you?"

He lifted one brow in question.

"Because I'm tired of going through the motions of life. I want to *feel*."

It wasn't a total lie. It just wasn't the whole truth.

"Any human male could do that for you."

"No, I don't think he could." She knew for certain he couldn't. "I don't want any messy entanglements when this is over. I want to be able to walk away when I have what I want."

He ran his fingers over the fire opal at the base of her throat. "And when will you have what you want, Claire?"

When you take me to the djinn realm.

"When I'm thoroughly satisfied, of course," she said, her pulse picking up. "The ball's in your court now, djinni."

He chuckled. "You play this game well, *maya*. I have one question before we get down to your…satisfaction. Where did you get the opal?"

Her stomach tensed, the nerves warring with the heat swirling in her veins as he stroked the opal. From what Mira had told her about her interactions with Tariq when he'd been a pleasure slave, she knew Ashur wore one too, but his wasn't visible in this realm. When she crossed to his world, she'd see it.

Where did he wear it? What did it look like against his tanned skin? And why couldn't she seem to think straight when he was touching the opal like that? Oh, he was good. His hands weren't even on her skin yet and she was ready to melt.

"*Maya?*"

Princess. He kept calling her princess. She wanted to laugh at the absurdity—she was far from being a princess—but some place inside her warmed to the word. Had he called his instructors that when they'd been teaching him how to pleasure a woman? Or was she somehow…special?

His eyes darkened with desire as he leaned close to her ear before she could tell herself that was a stupid question. His hot breath rushed over the tender skin of her neck, sending a shiver down her back. "You keep me waiting, *maya*. Do you not want my touch after all?

His lips barely grazed the outside of her ear, and heat flooded her veins. She closed her eyes and leaned into him. "No. I mean…yes, I want it."

Ever so gently, he trailed his lips down her neck, a whisper of a touch, until a shiver rushed through her entire body. "Then answer the question."

"I…I found it."

"Where?"

She lifted her chin as he grazed those lips along the hollow at the base of her throat and moved up the other side of her neck. Oh wow. That felt good. Better than she'd expected. He'd obviously been trained well. "On the beach."

"On this island?"

She nodded. Then trembled when he brushed those wicked lips across the skin just below her ear. Lifting her hands, she gently rested them on his chest. His hard, warm, muscular chest. "Yes."

"And how did you know it was linked to a djinni?"

His lips grazed the outside of her other ear. Instinctively, she moved closer, until the long, lean line of his body pressed against hers.

Oh, he was hard. His erection pressed against her belly, telling her he wanted her just as much as she suddenly wanted him. Tingles spread from her belly between her legs. And vaguely she realized she'd never reacted to a human like this. But right now she didn't care. He felt too good. He smelled like musk and citrus, and the heat of his body seeping into hers was making her light-headed. She fought the urge to slide her legs around his hips. Craved the fullness of his erection pressing against her core. Wanted…him, for purely selfish reasons that had nothing to do with Sura and the others in her order.

"Claire?" he asked in a throaty voice. A voice that sent a shudder through her whole body.

"I…I study folklore," she mumbled as he continued to torment her ear. As her skin continued to vibrate. "I'm a professor. At a university. I know the story behind the firebrand opals."

His touch disappeared. Cool air rushed over heated skin. Confused, she opened her eyes and looked up. But his face was no longer flushed with desire. Instead, his brow was wrinkled, his dark eyes searching hers for…*oh, shit*…truth.

"How does a human know of the firebrand opals?"

Shit, shit shit…

"I…" What could she say? How could she cover this? He couldn't know what she really was. She needed…

She needed him as desperate for her as she'd just been for him.

She rose up on her toes and pressed her mouth against his before she could change her mind. His entire body tensed. Djinn reacted to physical contact. It was one of their weaknesses. She'd been taught long ago that they were ruled by their desires, and judging from the erection she'd felt earlier, she hoped that was still true. Hoped it would be enough to distract him from his line of questioning.

When he didn't move a single muscle, she tipped her head, changed the angle of the kiss, and slid the tip of her tongue along the seam of his lips, hoping, wanting, waiting...

His lips parted. In surprise? Bewilderment? Want? She didn't care. She took the opportunity to dip into his mouth and taste him for the first time.

Darkness. Spice. Lust. Sensations bombarded her from every direction. She stroked her tongue against his, moaned into his mouth, felt herself slipping even though he hadn't kissed her back yet.

You may even enjoy it. Sura's parting words echoed through Claire's mind as she continued to kiss him. She knew she shouldn't. Knew she needed to stay in control. But he tasted so good. Felt so alluring pressed against her. Burned so hot where their skin met...

A growl rumbled from his throat, and then his arms were around her, his mouth opening, his tongue taking charge and sliding along hers, his body pressing tightly against hers, just the way she wanted.

Oh yes. He was still hard. Desire beat out curiosity. Her thighs ached, and that place between her legs throbbed in a way it never had before.

He turned her toward the bed. Thought slipped out of her grasp when he reached behind her and parted the netting. She kissed him deeper while he lowered her to the bed, groaned when she sank against the mattress and his weight finally pressed into her.

Yes, yes, this, just this...

Her goals, why she was here, why she'd summoned him seemed to fade into the background. All she knew was his mouth. All she felt was heat and passion and desire. He kissed her again and again, dragged his hand down her side and pushed her shirt up so he could glide the palm of his hand along her rib cage. She shivered, groaned at the warmth and tingles dancing across her skin, gasped when he finally released her mouth and trailed his lips to her ear where this time he licked and suckled her lobe until she thought she'd go mad from the pleasure.

"What are you doing to me, *maya*?" he whispered. "You smell so good. I want you in ways I haven't wanted another."

She closed her eyes, tipped her head to the side to give him more access. Felt the same way. Which was strange. Forbidden. Wrong. "Not even your teachers?"

He nipped her earlobe, then suckled the sensitive spot. "Never my teachers. Not like this."

A thrill rushed through her at his words. It was another line, but this time it didn't bother her. His hips flexed, his hardness pressing against her, and she groaned again, lifting her hips to meet his. Oh, that felt good. He'd barely touched her and she'd already felt more pleasure than she ever had before.

She wanted more. Wanted the pleasure he'd claimed he could give her. Wanted what she'd never had.

"Show me," she mumbled while he trailed his lips down her throat. "Show me how much you want me, Ashur."

With quick fingers, he pushed her shirt up over her breasts, flipped the front clasp on her bra and pulled her torso away from the bed long enough to strip the garments from her body.

She gasped when he released her and fell against the bed. Then groaned when he palmed one breast in his big, warm hand.

"Beautiful," he whispered.

She dragged her gaze from the ceiling to his face. "Small."

He was staring at her breasts, his face flushed with his arousal, his hand moving over her nipple to tighten the tip and make her tremble. "Perfect."

He lowered his mouth to her breast, breathed hot against her skin. She closed her eyes, arched against him. Knew, in the back of her mind, that she was losing control and that he was turning the tables, seducing her. But she didn't care. This felt too good. This felt too right.

Then his tongue stroked her nipple, and the sensation shot straight to her sex. She moaned and arched against his mouth.

"Yes, *maya*," he whispered. "You like that. Don't you?"

"Yes, yes, oh yes."

"More?"

"Much more."

He chuckled, moved to her other breast, used the tip of his tongue to graze the stiff peak, then drew the entire areola into his mouth and finally suckled.

Oh....

Her back arched off the bed; she tangled her fingers in his shoulder-length hair and tugged him closer. He flicked her nipple with his tongue, alternated between sucking and licking. Ran his hand over her other breast until it too was straining for his mouth.

"Ashur…"

"You're so sensitive, *maya*. Do you think you could come like this? With my mouth on your breast? With my tongue licking you here? I bet you could. I bet you could come so hard."

She couldn't speak. Couldn't seem to find her voice to answer his questions. She was pretty sure she couldn't orgasm, but she was enjoying this. And didn't it count that she wanted to? He seemed to be enjoying it too. She lifted her hips, rubbed against his erection as he licked and laved, taking his time, drawing out her sweet torture. Then cried out when he switched to her other breast, suckled hard and pinched the tip of her wet nipple with his fingers.

Electricity gathered in her breasts before she saw it coming, shot straight to her center, and burst with a force that blinded her. It rippled through her limbs, encompassing every cell, causing her whole body to shake. In the distance, she heard his voice calling to her, and she tried to reach for him, but her hands wouldn't work.

And then, before she could stop it, the world went black as if she'd stepped off a cliff and plummeted straight to her death.

ॐ

"Claire, wake up. Claire!"

Ashur's pulse raced as he shook Claire again and tried to revive her. Her body was limp beneath his, her head tipped to the side as if she were unconscious. "Wake up, Claire."

Perspiration broke out on his forehead, and he pushed off the bed, his mind racing with what he'd just seen.

He had to be mistaken. She couldn't be what he thought she was. Her whole body had *not* just pulsed with a light that lit up the entire room.

He tried to move back, but his foot caught in the pool of netting on the floor. His entire weight fell backward, and a ripping echoed through the room. He grappled for the bedpost but couldn't stop himself from going down. The netting tore away from the canopy. Air rushed up his spine. He landed hard on his ass.

He sputtered, fought against the netting that was smothering him like a tidal wave. When he finally found the gap, he ripped it apart and dragged air into his one-size-too-small lungs.

He couldn't breathe. And not just from the netting. Holy *fuck*. She was—

"Ashur?"

He peered up into hazy blue eyes looking down from the bed. Hazy, mesmerizing, angelic eyes. Her hair was a tangled mess around her head, her features relaxed but curious. But all he could see was that weird-ass light. The light that was now gone but had come from *inside* her.

"Don't touch me." He pushed up on his feet. Grasped the bedpost when he swayed.

"What's wrong?" She sat up, lifted her hands to her breasts, covering the sensitive tips he'd just been teasing Tasting. Pleasuring. "Why are you…?"

He recoiled when she reached out to him, and she pulled her hand back quickly, the lazy, sated look in her eyes sharpening. "What's going on, Ashur?"

He crossed to the opposite side of the room, as far from her as he could get. "That's what I'd like to know. Touch the opal."

"What?"

"Touch the damn opal! You're not my assignment. This is a mistake. Send me back to my own fucking realm right now!"

Her eyes grew wide, and she stared at him like he'd gone psychotic. And he felt like he had too, but he didn't care what she thought. Because all he could think about was getting away from her before it was too late. Before—

Her fingertips brushed the opal. And a cloud of black smoke swirled around him. Relief pulsed in his veins when he felt himself flying, but he still couldn't breathe. He needed air. Needed to find out what the hell was going on.

He landed hard against the stone floor of Zoraida's compound, his bare feet and legs taking the brunt of the impact. Air whooshed out of his lungs, and he fell forward until he was on his hands and knees, breathing quickly, the opal around his neck heavy where it lay against his throat.

"You are not expected back so soon. What did you do to the female to make her send you back?"

Zoraida. That was Zoraida's voice coming from his left. Head still swimming, Ashur eased back on his heels and rested his hands on his thighs while he took in his surroundings. He was in the same room he'd been in when Zoraida had told him of his test. Only this time, Nuha was missing. Two guards, whom Zoraida had obviously been speaking with, stood to her right, looking as shocked as she.

Her heels clicked across the floor as she strode toward him, the skirt of her green gown whooshing in her wake. She stopped in front of him and cupped his chin, forcing him to look up at her. "Do not tell me you have failed already, slave. That's a new record. And I had such high hopes for you. I guess you really are like your brother after all."

He jerked out of her grasp and stumbled to his feet. "I am nothing like Tariq. But she…" Anger pulsed deep in his veins, and he threw his arm out to the side. "You set me up to fail."

A bored expression settled across her face. At her back, a fire roared, but it did little to chill the ice washing through Ashur's body. "Pray tell, how, slave?"

He didn't even care if she sent him back to the dungeons. Given the choice between Claire and the dungeons, he'd take the dungeons any day. "*She* is not human!"

Zoraida barked out a laugh. "Not human? Well, what is she? Djinn? Not possible. Nuha was obviously blinded by your looks." She turned. "Guards, this slave is of no more use to me. Take him—"

"She's celestial."

The guards' armor clanked when they both moved forward, but Zoraida held out a hand to stop them. She turned to face Ashur once more. "What did you say?"

He ground his teeth. "I said she's celestial. She had the whole white fucking light to prove it. You sent me there to fail. You know angels can strip djinn of their powers with a snap of their fingers."

Zoraida pressed her fingers to her lips, her gaze roaming the room as if she were seeing it for the first time. "Celestial. When did you sense this?"

Did she really not know? She was acting like this was a surprise. "When she…" Shit. *Awkward*. He squared his shoulders. "When she climaxed."

A slow smile spread across Zoraida's face, followed by a laugh that seemed to grow from her belly in strength and intensity. "She's fallen. She has to be."

"What the hell does that mean?"

"It means, djinni, that her powers are bound on earth." She tapped her fingers against her ruby-red lips again, her gaze far off as if she were looking into another realm. Or the future.

Abruptly, she dropped her hands and faced him once more. "You'll go back. And this time, you will not fail. I want her soul."

"No." He moved back a step. "No fucking way." He wasn't losing his powers to an angel. Zoraida might bind his powers here so she could control her slaves, but he wasn't losing them for good.

Her hand shot out, and an arc of energy ripped through his body, hurling him back until he hit the wall. He slumped to the floor. Pain spiraled up his spine and stars fired off behind his eyes, but he struggled to stay conscious.

She lunged over him, her face no longer beautiful but taut with rage. "Do you think you have a choice, djinni? You are a slave. *My* slave, and you *will* do what you are commanded. Do you think the dungeons were bad? I have the power to make you feel pain like you've never experienced. And though you hide it, somewhere, someplace there is someone you care about. If you fail me, not only will I make your life a living hell, I will destroy theirs. I will make it my life's work. Only then you will know the full extent of my power."

Fear flashed through Ashur. Not for himself—he didn't care what happened to him anymore—but for his parents. No, they hadn't looked for him when he'd gone missing, but he didn't want them dead.

Slowly, Zoraida straightened, but her fury-filled gaze never left his. "Bring me. That. Angel's. Soul," she ground out. "Do whatever it takes. Just do not fail."

Chapter Four

CLAIRE STRAIGHTENED THE BED AND tried not to freak the hell out.

Her hands shook as she smoothed the bedspread, then sank down to the end of the mattress.

She'd sent Ashur back without a fight. Nerves gathered in her belly, felt like a stone weight dropping. Whatever she'd said or done in that moment of release had obviously freaked *him* out. What had happened?

She couldn't remember. All she knew was the way he'd made her feel had been electric. Amazing. The most soul-shattering thing she'd ever experienced. And she wanted to feel it again. Wanted more. Wanted him.

She blew out a breath, combed both hands through her unruly hair, tried to calm the nerves bouncing around in her stomach like Mexican jumping beans. He was good, she had to give him that. Hot. Sexy as hell. And now… Now she didn't know where he was or even if he was coming back. And thanks to her epic lack of self-control, she also didn't know if she'd just ruined her chance to find the opals.

A breeze blew the curtains from the windows, and a chill spread down her spine. Rising, she looked across the sand at the swirling black smoke, slowly fading to reveal the man—*djinni*—once again standing on her beach.

She swallowed hard, and those nerves kicked up even higher. He was back. Why so soon? What had happened in his realm? And what the hell was she going to say when she faced him again?

Heat crept up her cheeks, and a dark craving ignited in her belly. One that left her rattled.

Play it cool. Act like you don't care. Whatever you do, don't spook him again.

She drew in another breath, let it out. Moved to the sitting area of her hut and eased down to the couch cushions while she waited.

Seconds ticked by on the clock in the kitchen, echoing through the small hut. What was taking him so long? What could he possibly be doing out there?

The door to her hut finally pushed open, and she looked up to find Ashur standing in her doorway, his dark hair hanging to his shoulders, his sculpted body taut with tension, his mouth set in a grim line.

One look at his cold, distrustful eyes and she knew. Somehow he'd figured out what she was and he was *not* happy.

She swallowed the knot in her throat and lowered the magazine she'd idly picked up while waiting for him. "I didn't expect to see you so soon."

His eyes locked on hers, not warm and inviting as they'd been before, but icy. "This is not a game, *noor*."

Noor. The Arabic word for light. Except he hadn't said it in an endearing way. No, there'd been very clear contempt in his voice. She'd been right. He knew exactly what she was, and he was pissed. Tossing the magazine on the coffee table, she pushed to her feet. "No one said it was."

"What do you want from me? My powers?"

She should have expected he'd assume that. But it still stung. "I couldn't take them even if I wanted. And I'm no longer celestial. At least not in the literal way. I'm fallen, or hadn't you heard?"

"You lie."

She blew out a humorless laugh and glanced around the barren hut. "I wish I was, but unfortunately, I'm not. I'm as mortal as they come. At least until my punishment is over."

"You were banished? Why?"

It wasn't a question but a demand, and she considered holding back, then figured, what the hell? He was djinn. Seduction was still the best way to convince him to take her to his realm, even if he did know her lineage. But in order to get him to do that, first he had to trust her. At least marginally.

"Because I posed too many questions to my superiors about humans and life in general. So I was banished here, alone, with a few…conditions, to experience it for myself."

"Conditions?"

"The loss of my powers, for one."

"And the rest?"

She bit her lip. Debated. Finally decided a partial truth would do her better than an out-and-out lie. "Free will. Just enough to make me…curious."

His eyes narrowed. "Then why summon a djinni? I'm sure there are plenty of humans who could give you the thrill you're looking for."

She shrugged, ran her hand along the back of the chair cushion to her left. "Why not? According to my superiors, I've already sinned. Why shouldn't I experience the full range of seduction with a being that was created just for that purpose? Humans don't excite me."

His eyes darkened with both heat and danger, and a shiver of apprehension washed through her. She was walking a fine line here. While he was a slave and technically bound to do her will since she wore the opal, it was clear he had very contemptuous feelings for celestial beings. And she'd just gone and revealed that not only did she lack powers but that she was now mortal. For the first time, she considered the possibility that this could end badly for her.

"And you're saying I do excite you?"

Her stomach tightened when she remembered his mouth at her breasts, his tongue laving her nipples, that mind-numbing orgasm. And this time, she didn't need to lie. "Yes. You do."

He was silent so long, she didn't know what to say. But the dark way stared at her and the steady rise and fall of his chest ignited more than just arousal. It sent a shiver of anticipation through her whole body.

"Take off the opal, *noor*."

"What?" Confusion replaced excitement. That was not what she'd expected him to say.

"Take it off, and I'll consider giving you what you want."

This was a change in tactics. "You want me to release you? I already told you I don't have any powers. The opal doesn't change that."

"Then it won't matter whether you wear it or not. Take it off."

She touched the opal at her throat. He was smarter than she'd thought. Humans who wore the necklace couldn't remove it until their wish had been fulfilled, but he knew enough about those from her realm to know that wasn't the case for her, fallen or not.

She considered what he was offering. The only plus to the opal at this point was that it bound him to her, not the other way around. Then she caught the spark of fear in his eyes.

He still didn't believe her. He wasn't planning to give her anything. And if she released him like he wanted, she had no doubt he'd disappear into the mist and she'd never see him again.

"No." She dropped her hand. "I'll not take it off."

His jaw tightened. "This is not a game you want to play, *noor*."

Oh, but she did. And not simply because winning meant she'd be able to pass into his realm. But because being with him, challenging him, made her feel…alive. In a way nothing and no one ever had before. For the first time since she'd concocted this crazy plan, confidence swelled inside her.

A slow smile slinked across her face, and she moved in front of the couch, then eased down to the cushions, draping her body over the seat in a way she knew would entice him.

"I'm not afraid to get burned, djinni. And from where I'm sitting, it looks like you have a job to do." She glanced at his hips, where the stirrings of an erection pressed against the soft cotton of his pants. Oh, he still wanted her. That was another plus in her favor. Djinn, after all, were ruled by their desires.

Dragging her gaze back up to his full lips, she smiled wider and added, "I think it's time you stopped arguing about something we both know you want and got on with it."

Ashur's heart pounded as he stared down at Claire, laid out over the couch like an offering for his most wicked desires.

The months of training, of denial, of sexual frustration coalesced inside him until the blood pounded in his ears and throbbed in his cock.

He gathered his strength. Black smoke swirled around him as he transported his body from the middle of her hut to the beach outside. He needed a minute to think. Needed to get away from her so he could do that.

Soft granules of sand cradled his feet. He breathed deep and looked out over the rolling waves.

She wasn't going to release him—that much was clear. And he couldn't go back to Zoraida until he'd accomplished his goal. But he *wouldn't* open himself to the possibility of her stealing his powers either. His mind swirled as he scanned the water's surface. He wished he'd paid more attention in school. Nasir was the thinker, not him. He had no doubt Nasir would know exactly what to do with a celestial being like Claire.

He tried to recall everything he knew about her realm. Angels had no free will. Each performed a job for Allah. But some could take human form, and sometimes Allah sent them to test souls to see if they could be corrupted. He'd heard stories of djinn who'd fallen prey to these types of tests in the human realm. Djinn who'd gone with the intention of toying with a human soul only to have their powers stripped by an angel in disguise. And the way they'd done so was in that moment when the djinni opened himself up, either emotionally or physically.

Indecision warred as he looked back at the hut. And his entire body hardened when he remembered the way she'd looked at him, the sparkle in her eyes when she'd all but offered herself, the intensity with which she'd climaxed earlier.

Fallen or not, she wanted him. He didn't know if it was a result of free will or simply a test, but maybe…

If she wasn't bound to the opal, then there was a strong possibility she couldn't command him, not like a bound human. Which meant that until he corrupted her soul, he could do whatever the hell he wanted, and she wouldn't be able to protest.

And an idea took root. One that grew in strength and possibility with every second. It was wicked. It was dangerous. But she'd said she wanted to be thoroughly seduced. He knew one surefire way to do that. The only question was whether or not she truly had any powers left.

The only option was to find out for himself.

※

Claire stood at the window and looked out over the empty beach. Where had he gone this time?

With a frown, she flopped onto the couch and stared up at the thatched ceiling. So much for seducing him. She'd done exactly what she'd told herself not to do. She'd freaked him the hell out again.

She closed her eyes. Drew in a breath, let it out slowly. She just needed a minute to think of what to do next, but before she could get a grip on her thoughts, darkness descended, a black cloud that seemed to pull her under. Something in the back of her mind warned now was not the time to take a nap, but she couldn't stop herself from floating.

A haze rolled in, almost like fog. And through the swirling smoke, she saw images. Fantasies. Those things she'd read about in books and seen online since she'd been banished. Wicked things. Erotic things that shifted and changed in front of her. And somewhere close, a voice whispered, *Oh yes, we can do that too.*

She didn't know where the voice came from, but she liked the sound of it. Liked the accent and the way her whole body tingled in response. Liked the heat consuming her skin and the flutter in her stomach that told her something was coming. A darkness she craved. One she didn't even care could just lead to her downfall.

Her body grew light, her mind empty. The couch shifted beneath her, and then air slid along her spine, as if she were moving.

For a moment, her mind recoiled, but she couldn't open her eyes. And then softness cradled her limbs again.

She sighed, snuggled down against the cushions, tried to stay awake but couldn't.

Hours later—it felt like hours later—that same sinful voice echoed close. "Wake up, Claire."

Claire turned her head, tried to open her eyes, but they weren't working.

"That's it, *noor*." Something soft brushed her calf. "Open those eyes for me. I know you're tired, but fight it. I promise it will be worth your while."

Claire rolled her head the other way, tried to stretch her arms out to the side, but met resistance.

What the...?

"Come on." Another flutter of softness, this time against her kneecap. "Come back to me."

She knew that voice. It was rough. Sexy. She'd heard it whispering in her dream. Wanted to hear it again. She flexed her fingers, tried to shift her leg so she could roll to her side, but again met resistance.

The whisper-soft touch traced the inside of her knee, moved down to her ankle and back up the outside of her leg. Tingles ignited all along her spine.

A chuckle echoed to her ears, then the voice—his voice—whispered close, "You like that, don't you? Open your eyes, and I promise you'll like what you see even better."

She fought against the haze. Finally managed to pull her eyelids open. Soft light blinded her. She blinked several times. Strained to see. Slowly, the watery image above came into view.

Wood beams. A flickering, warm light against a thatched roof. And beneath her…silk.

She was in her hut, the one she'd rented in the Marshall Islands. She tried to move her arms again. The bite of rope against her wrists brought her head up.

"There you are."

Her head snapped around. Ashur was standing at the end of the bed, wearing nothing but the same black cotton pants he'd had on earlier. Darkness pressed in from the windows, making her wonder how long she'd been asleep, and candlelight flickered off his muscular torso. But the feather in his hand, the heat brewing in his eyes, and the menacing grin across his rugged face warned her to be careful how she reacted right now.

She tried to move her legs. Rope ground against ankles. She tugged on her arms again, but they didn't budge, and in an instant, she realized she was tied to each of the four corners of the bed. "What—what's going on?"

"You said you wanted to be seduced. I'm only doing what you desire."

Her heart rate sped up, and she watched as he waved his hand over the table to her right. A series of objects appeared out of nowhere. Strange, rubber, phallus-shaped objects she'd only read about but recognized from the descriptions.

Unease shifted through her. She pulled harder on the ropes, desperate to get free. Pain spiraled up her limbs. "Um…this isn't what I had in mind."

He chuckled again, reached over and lifted the slim purple dildo. "No? I think you lie. I think purple was even your color of choice."

Oh shit. She slowed her struggling. Her cheeks heated as she stared at him. He couldn't possibly know about her fantasies. She'd never shared them with anyone. She—

Her unease jumped. "Are you…Ghul?"

He chuckled once more, an arousing yet dangerous sound, one that shouldn't send a flutter through her stomach but did. "No. I hail from the Marid tribe."

She breathed out a sigh of relief. Marid were powerful, yet reasonable when it came to negotiations. They kept to themselves, were considered honorable amongst the djinn race, and they rarely crossed into the human realm unless coerced. It was Ghuls one had to worry about. The most depraved of all djinn, they could read minds. Loved to, in fact, use that strategy to torment humans and decipher a soul's weakness.

"But," Ashur said, his eyes locked on her, his free hand sliding the length of the dildo, "my master has taught me a few very convenient Ghul skills."

Her eyes grew wide as she watched him stroke the dildo as if it were his own cock, and her pulse picked up speed until it was a roar in her ears.

He'd tapped into her fantasies. That hadn't been a dream at all.

Panic set in, spread beneath her ribs. She struggled in earnest against the ropes. "Untie me. Right now. I command it."

He moved around the bed and leaned close to her ear, so close his musky scent overwhelmed her senses. "What was that? I don't think I heard you right. Try again, *noor*. Command me."

There was just enough venom in the way he said *noor* that she knew this wasn't going to be a sweet seduction. He was pissed that she hadn't freed him. And now he was using her fantasies to torment her. Ghul or Marid, it didn't matter. He'd obviously learned more than just pleasure skills from his mistress.

That panic grew stronger, more intense. She willed him to back away, but he didn't move. And then he chuckled once more. A sound that sent a tremor of fear straight down her spine.

"You're not bound to the opal, *noor*. Only me. And that means your seduction is mine to choose."

Oh shit, no...

"Relax," he breathed hot against her ear. "This is about to get fun."

Chapter Five

Claire's heart raced as Ashur leaned back, that victorious grin curling one side of his lips, making her stomach cave with apprehension over what he had planned.

Wide eyed, she watched as he moved back to the table, picked up the feather and a black strip of silk and brought them and the purple dildo back to the bed.

"Easy," he said while she struggled against the ropes. "All you're going to do is hurt yourself."

He was right. If her wrists weren't bleeding already, they would be soon unless she stopped her fighting. She tried to relax, but when he leaned over with the black sash, her breaths grew quick and shallow. "Hold on—"

He ignored her plea, only chuckled again, covered her eyes and cinched the sash tight behind her head.

Darkness descended, and that fear jumped another notch. But there was something else, some craving brewing in her veins. Something she couldn't define.

Sounds echoed through the room—the springs on the bed creaking as he eased off the mattress, the floorboards groaning as he moved around, something clicking on the nightstand, as if he'd set an object down.

Yes, she'd wanted to be seduced, but not like this. Not every fantasy was meant to be lived out. That was why it was a *fantasy*.

"Ashur…slow down a second. I—"

"You're not the one calling the shots here, *noor*. Get used to it." The feather brushed against her kneecap again, and tingles shot up her leg. Hot, sensual tingles that felt so damn good. Way better than they should. She clenched her teeth as the whisper-soft tip moved up her thigh and skirted the hem of her shorts.

At least she was still wearing shorts. "Ashur—"

"Protest, protest, protest. If I didn't know any better, I'd think you were acting."

The feather trailed up her hip, then caressed the bare skin of her abdomen. And those hot, spicy tingles shot to her hips, making her bite her tongue to keep from groaning. "I'm…I'm not."

The feather moved over her T-shirt, sending spirals of heat all along her rib cage. "Your nipples are hard."

"Because I'm cold." *Oh, Allah, that is not from being cold.* "Ashur—"

"I think this shirt is in the way. Don't you?" The feathery sensation left, and then something clicked, followed by the cold bite of steel against her lower belly that made her entire body freeze and vibrate with excitement at the same time. "Hold still. I don't want to accidentally cut you."

Cut her?

Scissors snapped. A rasp echoed to her ears, followed by warm air rushing over her abdomen and the erotic realization that he'd just sliced her shirt open.

"Ashur—"

"Be still."

She sucked in a breath while the scissors moved up her stomach, cutting away what was left of the thin garment. When he reached the top, the cotton fell open, and the gentle breeze washed over her bare breasts, making the tips even harder, sending a shockwave of arousal straight to her sex.

He chuckled again. "Oh, I think you're definitely enjoying this." A click echoed, as if he'd put the scissors on the bedside table; then the tip of the feather tickled her breastbone. "Tell me, *noor*, are you wet?"

She trembled against the sheet. She didn't want to admit that she was, that what he was doing was the most erotic thing she'd ever experienced, and that the longer it went on, the harder it was for her to think straight. Because she *needed* to think straight. She was the one who was supposed to be doing the seducing and commanding, not the other way around. "Ashur, I don't want—"

He trailed the feather to her right breast, circled the entire areola. "You don't? Then use your powers and free yourself."

She stilled. And her breaths quickened as his words permeated the sexual haze settling over her. "I don't have any powers left. I told you that."

"Then you truly are mine to do with whatever I want." His warm breath washed over her other breast, and then something wet and soft—*oh...his tongue*—circled her nipple. "Do you want my mouth here? Like it was earlier? Remember how good that felt?"

Oh, she did. She hitched in a breath and reflexively arched toward his lips.

His mouth curled in a smile as he pressed soft kisses along the underside of her breast. "I'm going to make you beg, *noor*. Have you ever heard of erotic denial?"

She had trouble processing his words. Because all she could focus on was the wicked sensations in her breasts, the jolts of electricity they were sending to her sex and the need for him to suckle her as he'd done before.

The feather trailed down her bare stomach, over her shorts, then brushed the soft skin of her inner thigh.

Her sex quivered, and she arched her back. She didn't even care anymore that he'd tied her down. She just wanted more of that heavenly mouth. Wanted to finally feel his entire body against hers. Wanted him to taste her. Everywhere.

He chuckled again, and heat flooded her veins in response, as if her entire body were on fire. "Answer me, *noor*."

"No." She twisted her head against the mattress, closed her fingers around the ropes leading to the bedposts. "No, I haven't—"

The feather trailed down her inner thigh, then came up again, this time closer to her sex. She groaned, tightened her stomach, tried to lift her hips higher—to get away? To get closer? She wasn't sure—but the ropes kept her in place. His tongue continued to tease a path all around her nipple but never touched it. She couldn't help it. She groaned. Why wasn't he suckling her? Why wasn't he taking her shorts off? Why wasn't he giving her the release he knew she craved?

He kissed her breastbone, dragged his lips down to her belly button and circled the indentation with the tip of his tongue until her clit throbbed. She groaned again. Arched higher. Gripped the ropes tighter. "Ashur, please—"

"It's a heightened state of sexual arousal where release is repeatedly denied," he said. "It can go on for hours, even days." He continued the soft touch at her inner thigh, the brush of his lips at her lower abdomen, right near the waistband of her shorts. "Trust me, *noor*, I've been trained in all forms of desire. Before this night is through, you're going to wish you had released me."

A chill spread through her, and though her body still hummed with heat and need, slowly, the sexual haze cleared. Until thought reformed, and reality settled in hard.

This wasn't about seduction. This was about torturing her until she finally let him go. About corrupting her soul, just as his master wanted.

I can't let him go. I still need him…

A buzzing echoed close. Followed by his sultry voice. "Let's see how hot we can make you with this."

The scent of rubber rose up to her nose. Then something pressed against her shorts, right over her mound.

Wicked vibrations rocked her entire body. She cried out. Lifted her hips. Her frantic thoughts spiraled away, until she couldn't grasp them anymore. Until all she could focus on was the tingling pulses consuming her sex.

He was using the dildo on her. She thrashed against the bed. Lifted her hips, dropped them, tried to rub against the toy. Yes, yes, yes… She wanted to feel it against her bare sex. Wanted him to press it inside her. Wanted the orgasm that was barreling closer with every second.

A sharp ring echoed through the room. Ashur lifted his head from the breast he'd been torturing and pulled the dildo away from her mound. She groaned in frustration as seconds passed in agony.

Finally, he whispered, "Just your phone. Where were we?"

The dildo pressed against her mound once more. Then every muscle in her body went rigid as his teeth pulled the snap free at her waist.

Oh... It was descending again. The haze that made thinking nearly impossible. The dark craving for his sinful touch. The desire to let go, to stop fighting, to give him anything he wanted.

Maybe you'll enjoy it...

Oh, but she was enjoying. Too much. She was on the brink of doing whatever he commanded, giving him anything, promising everything if he'd just slide his hands into her waistband, drag the shorts down her hips, and take her.

A click resounded through the room, followed by, "Claire?"

Her answering machine. Someone was leaving a message. Someone Claire vaguely recognized but couldn't place because every cell in her body was focused on Ashur's wicked tongue now running beneath the waistband of her shorts and that damn dildo pulsing against her clit, making her sweat.

"Oh," she whispered, lifting her hips again to alleviate the ache consuming every inch of her skin.

"Claire?" the voice went on. "It's Tariq. I heard from Nasir. The bottle's been found and opened. Zoraida is free. Mira and I need to talk to you. If Ashur's still alive, Zoraida will most likely be sending him here. We need to formulate a plan. Call us back as soon as you can."

The vibrations suddenly stopped, and the mattress bounced; then air rushed over Claire's overheated skin, making her nipples even harder. The blindfold was yanked from her eyes before she realized what was happening.

Confused, she blinked several times against the flickering light. Looked up and around. But it was Ashur's face hovering above her that brought everything into focus.

"What the hell was that?"

She was having trouble processing. She just wanted him to go on touching her. Why was he stopping when she was so close? "My…my answering machine."

"Not the stupid box," he snapped. He leaned close until his face was centimeters from hers. His enraged face. "What is my brother doing calling you by name?"

※

Her eyes grew wary. "Your…your brother?"

Grinding his teeth, Ashur pushed from the bed and moved away from her. The desire he'd been fighting back while he'd teased her was gone, replaced with a fury that filled the empty place beneath his breastbone and made his blood boil. He didn't trust himself to touch her at the moment. His brother, who'd abandoned him to torture and death and betrayed their race for a human fucking woman, had just left a message on Claire's answering machine.

"How do you know Tariq?" he growled. "What in all of Jahannam is going on?"

Her face paled. "I…I…oh, shit. He's your brother? I…" Her eyes slid closed. "I didn't know."

Yeah, right. "Where is he?"

Her eyes popped open. He couldn't read her expression, but he saw the worry lurking deep inside.

For herself? Or for Tariq? His fury rose higher. He moved back to the bed, leaned over her, willed himself not to snap like a Ghul. "Tell me!"

Her breasts rose and fell with her shallow breaths, but her eyes were wide and—this time—determined. "Release me first."

He stared at her while his blood ran like a river of lava through his veins. She didn't have any powers left—he'd figured that out in the last few minutes—so, bound or not, he was still in control. But at the moment, he didn't give a flying rat's ass about Zoraida's punishment should he fail her so-called test. The revenge he'd been plotting for the last six months was at his fingertips.

He reached for the ropes at her ankles, untied the knots, then moved to her right arm. As soon as her wrist was free, she jerked it toward her body, rubbing the tender flesh against her stomach. He moved around the bed and freed the other side. Ropes dropped to the floor. She sat up and massaged the red marks at both ankles and wrists, then grasped a pillow and tossed it over her body to hide her naked breasts.

He wouldn't feel guilty. She was *noor*. The wariness he'd felt before about her came steamrolling back. Whatever she was truly after—and he had no doubt now that she was plotting something other than simple pleasure—had to do with his brother. And that meant she was not his ally, not his friend, and definitely not someone he should feel anything for, especially desire or compassion.

He perched his hands on his hips and stared down at her. Her hair was a wild mess around her head from thrashing, her skin luminescent in the candlelight. And the soft, sweet scent of gardenias he'd noticed earlier only pissed him off more because it still smelled exotically enticing. "Where is he?"

"He's…" She hesitated, but before he could bark at her again, added, "in the Pacific Northwest. With my friend Mira."

"The human woman," he snarled.

Her head snapped his way. "She saved him. She—"

"I don't care what *she* did." He tugged open the closet door and grabbed a T-shirt from a hanger. "You're taking me to him."

"What?" Her brow dropped low. "I can't do that. We're on an island. In the middle of the Pacific. It'll take days to get there. Flights only leave these islands once per day, and we need to take a boat to the airport first. It—"

"Put that on."

She grasped the shirt he threw at her. "Ashur, be reasonable. Tariq—"

He moved so fast, her head snapped back, and her words cut off mid-sentence. Leaning on the bed, inches from her face, he growled, "Do not *ever* speak to me about my brother, *noor*. Do you understand?"

Her mouth closed, and she swallowed once, the look in her eyes not just surprise but fear. True fear. Slowly, she nodded.

An image flashed in his mind. Of him in the dungeons during the days before Zoraida had disappeared, chained and half naked, recoiling from her fury-induced rage. Scared, beaten down, controlled. Not that different from the way Claire looked right now.

His pulse picked up speed. And something in his chest cinched down tight. A mixture of power and revulsion and guilt that swirled inside his gut to leave him light-headed and… unsteady.

He wasn't sure what was happening to him, but he wasn't about to lose this opportunity. He didn't know if or when it would ever happen again.

Forcing the bite from his words, he leaned back and said, "I don't need boats or planes to travel in the human realm. But I do need you."

Her sapphire eyes shifted from scared to wary, and he straightened his spine, willing himself not to back down. He didn't care if she was pissed. This wasn't about her anymore, and he wasn't going to be distracted by any angel, fallen or not. "I no longer care if you want me, *noor*. You're stuck with me now. We're going to see my brother. And you will be the one to light the way."

Chapter Six

Claire's nerves were a mess by the time she tugged sandals from her closet and slipped her feet inside. Aside from everything that had just happened in this bedroom, now he wanted her to take him to Tariq and Mira? Something in her gut said this was not a good idea.

I want you in ways I've not wanted another.

The memory of his lips forming those words as he'd kissed her earlier in the day came out of nowhere and nudged aside the nerves. Heat flooded her veins all over again, sent tingles to her belly and lower. Standing in front of him, she focused on his black-as-night eyes and tried to find the djinni who'd pleasured her so completely before…before he'd discovered she was celestial. Before he'd realized she wasn't bound to the opal. Before he'd decided to sexually torture her to get her to do what he wanted.

Except…that hadn't felt like torture. The same wicked craving she'd experienced before came screaming back. That had felt…good. Too good. Was she sick in the head because she'd liked being strapped down? What did it say about her that she'd enjoyed giving up control? That she probably would have let him do anything he'd wanted if he'd kept going?

He held out his hand, but his expression was neutral, and she couldn't tell what he was thinking. "Simply think of their location, and I'll do the rest."

Would he have stopped? Would he have given her release, or would he have prolonged the erotic denial, like he'd claimed? She wanted to believe the first, but the darkness in his eyes warned her she didn't know him at all. Even if he was Marid, he'd been imprisoned so long by the sorceress, he could very well be as base as the Ghuls Zoraida often employed.

Unease flitted through her, and she swallowed hard. Knowing she didn't have another option, she slid her hand against his. His fingers tightened around hers, and before she even saw him move, he jerked her around so her back was plastered to his front, and his arms were closed tight across her body.

Heat instantly enveloped her, followed by the familiar scent of his skin—spicy, citrusy, clean. And as if he had some magical control over her body, desire reignited in her core. His warm breath washed over the nape of her neck, sending pinpricks of pleasure all along her skin when he leaned close and said, "Stay close to me. Tariq is unpredictable."

Her mind stumbled. In the six months that Mira had been with Tariq, Claire hadn't heard a word from her friend about Tariq being "unpredictable". But before she could ask what Ashur meant, black smoke swirled around them, and then her feet lifted from the ground. The smoke churned faster. Her hair whipped around her face, stung her eyes. Ashur's arms tightened, and against her ear, he whispered, "Hold on to me."

She grasped the forearm locked tight against her, was happy for the solid presence of his body at her back. As a celestial being, she'd transported from location to location all over the earth, but never in a human body.

A gasp tore from her mouth when her feet hit something solid. Ashur's arms tightened more, and she knew if he hadn't been holding her, she'd have fallen forward. As the smoke cleared, she took in her surroundings and gasped again when she realized they were standing on Tariq and Mira's deck.

Pine trees rose around them, the scent of moss and damp earth strong. And ahead, moonlight shimmered off the waters of Puget Sound, sparkling like a million diamonds under the night sky.

His arms released her, and immediately her body craved his heat. She whipped around and found him already scanning the glass door, peering inside, looking for his brother. But it was the menace in his eyes that sent a jolt of fear straight to her heart.

She grasped his arm. "Ashur, no. Listen. You don't understand. Let me explain things to you before you go inside."

He looked down at her, but the gentle almost-lover she'd touched before was gone. The same fury she'd seen when he'd heard Tariq's voice was alive on his face. "Understand what? That he left me to rot?" He jerked his arm from her grip. "This does not concern you, *noor*. Stay out here until I'm through."

Through? She didn't like the sound of that. Fear turned to panic. "Ashur, wait—"

He yanked the sliding door open and stepped into the house. Claire couldn't see anything past his broad shoulders, but she heard voices. Tariq's surprise. Mira's shock. Followed by Ashur's fury.

"You son of a bitch." Ashur lunged.

A scream ripped through the night air. A grunt echoed. Wood splintered. Glass shattered. Voices hollered.

Claire tore into the room, stumbling across the door track. Light from the large stone fireplace at the end of the great room rippled over Ashur and Tariq, entangled on the floor. A coffee table lay in pieces, broken wineglasses strewn about. Ashur lifted his fist and threw a punch that sent Tariq's head jerking back. Mira, standing near the fireplace, screamed.

Then movement to the right grasped Claire's attention. And she jerked that direction only to see another male—equally as large and dark as Tariq and Ashur—hurl himself toward Ashur's back.

"Let go, Ashur," the male hollered. "Dammit, let go."

Ashur jerked out of his grip, landed another right hook against Tariq's jaw. The male swore, got a better grip on Ashur, and hauled him off Tariq.

Tariq sat up slowly and shifted his jaw from side to side. "I see you've learned a few moves."

"Fuck you," Ashur growled.

Wide-eyed, Claire watched the scene, unsure if she should step in or get the hell away. Sure, Ashur had been pissed at her when he'd found out she was celestial, but that had been nothing like this.

At Ashur's back, the male still holding him murmured, "Take a breath, brother. No one here's going to hurt you."

Ashur's body stilled, and he twisted his head to look behind him, suspicion alive in his features as if he'd just realized there was another person in the room. "N—Nasir?"

The male smiled. And the spread of the lips, the twinkle in the eyes... Even from her viewpoint, Claire could tell he was Ashur's other brother. "That's what people call me."

Ashur's brow dropped low. "What…? I thought… They told me you died in the pits."

"Not dead," Nasir said softly, loosening his grip until he was no longer holding Ashur. "At least not yet. I was rescued."

He glanced toward the archway that led to the kitchen. Ashur twisted to see what he was looking at. And that was when Claire realized there was another female in the room. A redhead with emerald-green eyes, wearing jeans and a fitted white T-shirt, looking almost as shell-shocked as Claire felt. Claire looked to Mira for clues to who the female was, but Mira was too busy checking Tariq for injuries and helping him up to pay any attention to her.

"*She* saved *you*?" Ashur asked, the snarl in his voice reverberating through the room. "She's Ghul."

Nasir's jaw hardened. "She's my mate. And she'll be your queen soon, so watch your mouth."

Ashur's gaze snapped back to Tariq standing on the other side of the room. "What does he mean by 'queen'?"

Tariq swiped at the blood on his lip. When Mira reached up to help him, he whispered, "I'm fine, *hayaati*."

Mira muttered something Claire couldn't hear, but in the glare she shot Ashur's way, it was clear she was as ticked with Ashur as Ashur had been with Claire earlier.

Tariq looked back at his youngest brother. "I abdicated the throne to Nasir. I've chosen to stay here."

Ashur's irate gaze cut to Mira. "With her? A human? You betrayed me and Nasir and our entire kingdom for *her*?"

Fire flashed in Mira's eyes. "Now just a minute—"

Tariq laid his hand over hers, cutting off her words, but his voice held no anger when he said, "Yes. With her. And I'd do it again in a heartbeat."

Ashur looked from brother to brother. And from the hatred brewing in his eyes, Claire had the sinking suspicion what had started to feel like a truce was about to escalate into World War III. "A Ghul and a human? No wonder no one came looking for me. You were both too busy getting fucked by our enemies."

The female in the doorway to the kitchen drew in an audible gasp. Tariq's jaw hardened.

"I don't care what you've been through," Nasir growled. "You will not talk about Kavin that way."

Tension coated every inch of the room. In the silence that followed, Ashur's inflamed gaze jumped from face to face, finally holding on Tariq's bruises. And there was something in his eyes. A mixture of hurt and betrayal and hatred that Claire recognized. Recognized because she'd seen it in the mirror. Staring back at her those first few years after she'd been banished to the human world.

"You don't command me," Ashur said in a low tone. "None of you do. Not anymore."

Black smoke swirled, and voices echoed. But before either brother could stop him, Ashur poofed right out of the room.

Silence descended. And when the smoke cleared, Tariq looked her way, followed by Nasir, whose surprised expression told her he'd just realized she was there.

"I'm sorry," she whispered, not sure what else to say. "I didn't know he was the djinni she'd send. I…" Her lungs cinched down tight and tears she'd never felt before burned her eyes. Tears over what she'd seen and done and was still planning to do.

Tariq let go of Mira's hand and stepped forward. "Claire?"

Outside, a loud noise reverberated, followed by a string of curse words, some of which Claire guessed had to be Marid.

"Sounds like he ran into the trashcans," Tariq muttered.

Claire's pulse picked up speed, and she looked toward the door behind her. "Why is he out there? Why didn't he just leave?"

"He's bound to the opal you wear," Nasir said. When she looked his way, he was staring at the jewel around her neck.

"He can't get more than a hundred yards away from you." Tariq added. "At least until his job is done."

Claire's gaze jumped to Mira's husband, and unease rolled through her belly.

"How did you find the firebrand opal?" Mira asked, her brows dipping low. "I mean, I thought we agreed if one of us found the bottle, we'd alert the others. How did it get around your neck?"

Mira's voice jolted Claire back to the conversation at hand. "It's…a long story."

Nasir sighed and slipped an arm around Kavin's shoulder when she moved next to him. "Until our little brother calms down, time is all we have."

Another string of curses echoed from the dark forest surrounding the house. Claire looked toward the open door again, and her pulse picked up speed.

"I should go talk to him," Tariq muttered.

From the way Ashur had reacted to Tariq's presence the first time, Claire didn't think that was a good idea. Plus, she knew the last person he'd want to talk to would be the brother he believed had betrayed him.

Her stomach grew light. An odd sort of kinship toward Ashur built inside her, one that had nothing to do with the sexual cravings he'd ignited, one that made it hard to draw air. He was djinn; she was celestial. They came from two different worlds and were not supposed to interact. Yet for the first time since she'd been banished—for the first time ever, really—she was drawn to another being. Not because she was commanded, but because she understood exactly what he was going through.

Tariq moved forward, but she held out a hand, stopping him. "No. Don't. I'll go."

"But he—"

She looked back at her friends. "I started this. It's my fault. And now it's time for me to make at least part of it right."

※

Ashur kicked a can out of his path from the trash bin he'd a knocked over. He'd walked a complete circle around the house but couldn't get more than a hundred yards away. That damn opal was keeping him locked in place. And until Claire came out—because he sure as hell wasn't going back in to that house—he was stuck.

Footsteps crunched on the forest floor, and relief seeped in. He didn't need to turn to see it was Claire. He could sense her. Or, at least, he could sense the opal. Which, at the moment, was all he cared about.

"Let's go," he said.

"We're not leaving."

He swiveled to face her. Moonlight shimmered over her, highlighting her hair and skin, making her look—for the first time—like the celestial being she was. "Yes, we are. You don't command me either. Remember that, *noor*."

He brushed past her and headed down the hillside toward the water's edge. With her outside, he could go a little farther without hitting that invisible barrier, and he needed to get as far from this house as possible.

At his back, she drew in a breath, let it out. A chill from the damp forest slid down his spine, but he ignored it. His head was too full of realities he was having a hard time believing.

Nasir was alive. He'd taken a Ghul as his mate. And he was now going to be king of Gannah? Zoraida's henchmen had told Ashur Nasir was dead. Did they not know Nasir was alive? And did he still wear the opal? The same one Ashur wore but which couldn't be seen in this realm?

He stopped at the edge of the water, rested his hands on his hips, and looked out over the shimmering surface. All of it, every piece of it, was Tariq's fault. If he'd done what their father had commanded years ago and taken over rule of their land, he never would have been in that village when Zoraida's army attacked. He wouldn't have been taken prisoner. Nasir and Ashur wouldn't have spent years of their lives searching for him, wouldn't have been captured by Zoraida's goons themselves. Life in Gannah would be as it was supposed to be. Safe. Predictable. *Empty.*

The last lingered in his mind as an owl swooped low over the water. His life in Gannah as the youngest prince had been easy—too easy—even he knew that. He wasn't the heir. He wasn't the spare. He'd done anything he'd wanted, and no one had cared. He'd charmed the ladies, slept till noon, hadn't once worried about responsibilities or expectations or what tomorrow would bring, like his brothers. The biggest complaint he'd had growing up was that his brothers looked at him as the baby and wouldn't take him along on their adventures. He'd hated that. Hated being left out. But he'd never done anything to prove himself worthy of inclusion, now had he?

Not until he'd gone looking for them and had been taken prisoner himself. And look how that had turned out.

"Ashur, we need to talk."

His jaw clenched. He especially hated that the angel was behind him right now, when he was dealing with all this shit and couldn't get away from her. "No, we need to leave."

"I understand you're upset with Tariq, but things are not what they seem."

He whirled on his heel, and all that anger he'd been saving for Tariq was unleashed on her. "How do you know him? Why did he call you? Start talking, *noor*, because I'm not feeling all nice and agreeable like I was before."

Her blue eyes held his, luminescent eyes that seemed to sparkle under the moonlight, but he couldn't tell what she was thinking. Doubted he'd ever be able to. "Mira was bound to the firebrand opal. She came to me, months ago, because she wanted to know if there was a way to free Tariq."

"Why you? Does she know what you are?"

She tucked a lock of hair behind her ear. "No, none of them know, not even Tariq. I'm a history and folklore professor at a university in Florida. She found me through the Internet, knew I'd published research about djinn."

His eyes narrowed. "Why? What is your fascination with my race aside from wanting to steal our powers?"

She breathed out a sigh and folded her arms over her breasts. "I don't want to steal your powers, Ashur. I told you that. Not all celestial beings have ulterior motives."

"And not all Ghuls are depraved."

One corner of her mouth curled. "Nasir's mate is Ghul, and she didn't look overly depraved to me."

She hadn't looked depraved to Ashur either. She'd looked timid and nervous and as shell-shocked as he felt.

He shook off the thought. No matter how she'd *seemed*, she was still Ghul, and he'd spent enough time in Zoraida's dungeons to know Ghuls scraped the bottom of the djinn gene pool. "So she found you. What does that have to do with my backstabbing brother?"

"Ashur." She tipped her head, and pity crept into her eyes. "He didn't forget about you. When Mira discovered a way to free Tariq from the opal, Zoraida showed up to claim Mira's soul. There was a battle, but they won, and they trapped the firebrand opal—this opal" —she touched the gem at her neck— "along with the sorceress in a bottle. But it fell overboard and washed out to sea before they could stop it. Yes, Tariq chose to give up his throne and stay in the human realm so he could be with Mira, but he also stayed for you. Because he was desperate to find that bottle and figure out a way to free you. He couldn't have done that from the djinn realm."

Ashur had a hard time believing what he was hearing. But then he was still having trouble comprehending the fact Nasir was alive. He had so many questions about that—about how his brother had escaped from the Pits of Jahannam and why Zoraida hadn't yet called him back.

Claire moved a half step forward. "Every moment Tariq stays in the human world, he loses his djinn powers and becomes more human. Soon he won't be able to cross back to your realm at all. He's been frantically searching for that bottle since it was lost."

Ashur thought back to the surprise in Tariq's eyes when he'd stepped in the room. Then to the fact his brother hadn't once fought back when Ashur had attacked him. Doubt pushed against him from every side.

Then he remembered the guilt he'd seen on Claire's face when Tariq's voice had interrupted them back on that island. "Why were you the one to find it? And if you know of my brothers and the sorceress, why did you act like you didn't know who I was?"

Unease rushed over her face, and she looked down at the pine needles beneath her sandals. "Because I honestly didn't know who you were when you showed up on my beach. I assumed Zoraida had multiple pleasure slaves. I didn't think she'd send you."

Zoraida did have multiple pleasure slaves. And she probably wouldn't have sent Ashur, but Nuha had advocated for him. The first time in his life he'd strived to succeed at something, and it had turned into this.

Was it a blessing or a curse?

Claire combed her fingers through her hair. "I...Tariq and Mira knew I was searching for the bottle too. But they thought it was because I was helping them. They didn't know the real reason I needed to find it."

His eyes narrowed, and an odd foreboding slid down his spine. "And what is that reason?"

She drew in a shaky breath, then let it out. And as she stared at him in the moonlight, he had the strange sense that maybe this was something he didn't want to know. There were reasons angels and djinn did not interact. Some mysteries of the universe were supposed to remain just that—mysteries. Otherwise, everything a soul counted on could change in an instant.

"You're not the only one who's been imprisoned, Ashur. My people have been enslaved for years. Our prison might not have walls and chains, but it's a prison just the same."

She drew in another breath, seemed to be thinking through what she needed to say, and though he waited, something in his mind screamed, *run away, now*! But he couldn't. Not just because he was bound to the opal around her neck, but because a space inside wanted—needed—to hear what she said next.

"I went looking for the bottle," she continued, "so I could bind a pleasure slave to my will and eventually convince him—you—to take me to your realm. You were right when you said I was after something other than pleasure. I never wanted you. I only want what waits for me in your world."

He should have expected it, but disappointment felt like deadweight pressing down on his chest. All those months of imprisonment. The endless training sessions. The only thing that had kept him going was the promise that at some point, the female who summoned him would want *him*. Request *him*. Need *him*. And here she was telling him even that wasn't true.

He couldn't seem to do anything right. He was also growing slow, because when she moved a half step closer, he realized he'd been so distracted by his thoughts, he'd let down his guard. If she wanted to steal his powers, she could do it now, and he'd barely have time to react.

He tensed, but nothing happened. No magic filled the air; nothing swirled around him. Her face only softened until it was as if…as if she was looking past the djinni he'd become and was searching for the one he'd once been. Or *could* be…

"You were a means to an end for me, Ashur. I never once cared about who you were or what would happen to you when I reached my goal. Until now. Now…everything is different. And I'm going to try to figure out a way to help you. If, that is, you'll let me."

Chapter Seven

Claire waited for Ashur to say something—anything. She was putting herself out on a limb here, and she wasn't entirely sure why. Until a few minutes ago, he'd been a hot fantasy and, like she'd told him, a means to an end. But watching him with his brothers, seeing the way he reacted to them and *feeling* the confusion and agony she knew he was experiencing, something inside her had changed.

It didn't mean she was giving up her quest. And it didn't mean she wasn't still going to try to convince him to take her to the djinn realm. But maybe there was a way for her to get what she wanted and to free him as well. Maybe there was a way they could both win.

Wariness, heat and something dark swirled in his eyes as he stared at her in the moonlight. She couldn't read his expression. His eyes sharpened, then he grasped her at the shoulders and pushed her back against the trunk of a tree. Surprised, Claire gasped and her eyes widened.

"What kind of game are you playing, *noor*?"

Anxiety pressed in, stole her breath. "N-none."

"Then why would you want to help me? You already said you simply wanted to use me, like everyone else. You're celestial, even if you are banished. And I'm…smokeless flame. We do not mix for a reason."

She wasn't sure that was true anymore.

When he tightened his hands on her upper arms, urging her to answer, she gasped. "I know. But..."

"But what?"

"But...when I summoned you, I had very specific reasons. I just didn't expect to feel something for you."

His eyes narrowed. "You feel something for me."

Her cheeks grew warm. "Yes."

"Something like...contempt?"

The sarcasm in his voice made one corner of her mouth tick up. "No. Most definitely not contempt."

"Not contempt," he muttered, his eyes growing even more suspicious. "Why would you feel anything for me? You barely know me."

That was true; she didn't know him. She bit her lip, thought about how to answer without sounding like a lunatic. Realized there was no way to do that, so simply said, "When I was banished, at first I didn't feel anything about it. It was...just the way it was. And I was fine with it. I knew eventually my punishment would end, and I'd be sent back. But then...then things changed and..."

"And what?"

There was genuine curiosity in his question. And when her eyes met his, it was as if he was seeing her for the first time. He needed to know, just as she needed to feel. His reaction spurred her on. "And I was angry. Really angry. The way you were with Tariq just now. I felt betrayed. I wanted to do something to fix it. But you..."

"I what?"

The quickness of his question, the anticipation in his features as he waited for her to go on… It softened her. Right down to her core. No, maybe she hadn't been wrong after all…

"You touched me. Not physically—although you did that too—but emotionally. I knew what you were feeling, because I'd been there too. Ashur, your brothers have been frantic to find you. They never wanted you to be with Zoraida. Unlike my situation, you have family that loves and misses you. I wish I had that. I would give anything for that. You have it, and you're ready to throw it away because you need someone to blame. But sometimes there are no clear answers as to why things happen. Sometimes…they just do."

He didn't say anything, only stared at her with those bewildered and intense eyes. And she wondered if she was making a mistake. If he was truly a lost cause or if the djinni he'd once been before Zoraida had gotten a hold of him was still in there.

"I want to help you," she whispered, not sure where this connection she felt was coming from, but unable to stop it. "Because you shouldn't have to suffer like me. Because…I think at least one of us should be free."

"And what do you get out of this?" he asked in a low voice.

What did she get? She wasn't sure anymore. "Maybe the chance to do the right thing for once."

Though he still held her against the tree, his grip had softened considerably. She tried to read his expression, tried to figure out what he was thinking, but still wasn't any good at it. And then his gaze dropped to her lips, and his eyes darkened even more with a heat that arced all through her pelvis and sent a flutter straight to her belly.

He was going to kiss her. Her heart pounded hard, and warmth slid through her veins. She wanted him to kiss her. Wanted to taste those lips again and explore the depths of his mouth like she hadn't gotten to do before. But not because it might convince him to take her to his realm. No, this time she wanted him to kiss her because *he* wanted to. Because *he* wanted *her.*

Silence stretched like an eternity between them. He didn't move closer. Didn't make any attempt to bridge the gap. Only stared at her lips. Licked his own. The movement making every cell in her body yearn for more. For him.

Finally, when she couldn't take it anymore, she whispered, "Ashur?"

And as if her voice had drawn him back from some mental free fall, his gaze snapped back to hers, and confusion swamped his features.

He let go of her, moved back. Rubbed a hand down his face.

Claire reached for him. "Ashur—"

He deflected her touch, but when he looked at her, there was no more anger in his features. No more animosity, no more contempt. Only…unease. "I need to think."

"Let me—"

He stepped to the side, out of her reach again. "Just…give me some space. I'm trying to make sense of everything and I can't do that with you close like this."

She tried not to be hurt by his dismissal. Couldn't help it. "Why not?"

He frowned. But it wasn't an angry frown. It was a sexy frown. One she suddenly wanted to kiss away. "Do you really have to ask? Shit." He scrubbed a hand through his hair. "I'm not like you. I already feel, *maya*. I may be fucked up, but I'm not a corpse."

Was he saying…?

He'd called her *maya* again. Princess. What he'd called her before he'd discovered she was celestial. Hope blossomed. Hope for what, she wasn't entirely sure. An end to their feud? Possibly. But more than that, she hoped to continue what they'd started back on that island, even though a tiny voice in the back of her head warned that would just create more problems she didn't need.

"Go inside," he said. "I can't go anywhere without you, but I'm not ready to face my brothers yet. And I can't think when you're looking at me like you want to take a bite out of me. Even pleasure slaves have limits."

Warmth unfurled inside her. A lightness she felt all the way to her toes. "I do want to take a bite out of you. I have since the first moment you showed up on my beach. I want to bite and suckle you the way you did me."

A hint of danger sparked in his eyes, followed by an arousal that flushed his cheeks and made her pulse race. "You don't know what kind of fire you're playing with. My desires are dark, not honorable. What I did to you in that hut was only a sampling of the wicked things I want to do to you."

Excitement rushed through her veins, condensed in her pelvis, and left her hot and aching. Even three feet away, with the cool forest air around them, she felt his need. Hard. Hot. So very explosive. But this time, she wasn't scared. If anything, seeing how close he was to the edge of control only heightened her desire and made her want him more. "So do it. Tie me down. Do whatever you want. I want to feel it all. I want to feel you. I trust you, Ashur."

Tension crackled. Heat and need sizzled in his eyes, and his muscles bunched, as if he might just lunge for her. But he didn't move. He was holding back, and she didn't know how to make him take that last step toward her. But this time—for reasons even she didn't understand—she didn't want to force him. She needed him to come to her, willingly.

"Go," he rasped in the silence. "Go before you can't. Go now."

※

I want to feel it all. I want to feel you. I trust you, Ashur.

Ashur couldn't get Claire's words out of his head where he sat on the damp ground looking out at the water. And not just her words. The heat in her eyes when she'd said them. The way her body had been humming with need as she'd looked at him. And every time he thought of the way she'd looked then, he remembered her tied down to that bed in her hut, moaning and writhing against him as he'd tortured her. As he'd pleasured her.

Sweat broke out on his forehead, and he shifted, trying to ease the tightness in his groin. He could have taken her right here in this forest, against the tree at his back if he'd wanted. She wouldn't have protested. And this time, she would have enjoyed. They both would have. But would that solve any of his problems? He still wasn't sure what kind of game Claire was playing. Yes, she wanted him…but to what end?

Something soft landed against his arms. Ashur startled and looked down at the coat lying over his updrawn knees, then toward the face peering down at him.

"It's cold out here," Nasir said, shrugging in his own coat as he tucked his hands into the pockets of his jeans, "and you're half naked. If you're going to sit out here and brood, at least don't freeze your ass off doing it."

Ashur should have known his brother wouldn't leave him alone for long, and the little jolt of happiness at seeing Nasir earlier came screaming back. The one he'd tamped down because he couldn't enjoy it. Every time he'd found something good in Zoraida's prison, it had been taken away again, as if she'd been waiting for a new way to torture him. "I don't brood."

"Yeah, you do." Nasir leaned a shoulder against the trunk of a nearby tree while Ashur slipped his arms into the sleeves of the coat. "Father always called it pondering. 'Ashur's pondering. Leave him alone.' But Tariq and I knew the truth. You were brooding, trying to figure out a way to get around whatever punishment Father had given you for following us and getting into trouble."

Ashur couldn't argue with that. He rested his elbows on his knees and looked out at the sparkling water. He'd spent most of his life chasing after his brothers, trying to be included. Now he wished he'd left well-enough alone. "He send you out here to check on me?"

"Nope. Tariq knows you're pissed and that you have every right to be mad."

Ashur clenched his jaw. Damn right he had a reason to be mad. Except…every time he thought about the way Tariq had abandoned him, he remembered Claire's voice saying, *"Sometimes there are no clear answers as to why things happen. Sometimes…they just do."*

He didn't want her to be right on this one, and he'd never been one to believe in fate and destiny. The world was what you made it. How many times had his father said that to him?

He watched a log bobbing in the water as it drifted by. Did he even have a choice anymore? He was Zoraida's slave now. Slaves didn't have choices. They served.

"I want to help you..."

"About Kavin," Nasir said, his voice cutting through Ashur's confused thoughts. But Ashur was suddenly glad for it, because it gave him something to focus on other than the rapid pounding of his heart. "Yes, she's Ghul. But not all Ghuls are bad as we've been taught to believe."

For the first time, Ashur took a good look at his brother. Nasir's hair was longer than it had been the last time they'd been together and was tied at his nape. The body Ashur remembered being bloodied and bruised from Zoraida's guards was now strong and muscular—more sculpted than it had ever been. But the biggest shock—the one that made Ashur take a closer look, was the fact the pain Nasir had carried with him since the day his betrothed had been killed was gone. In its place was resolve, strength, and an inner calm that seemed to come out of nowhere.

"What happened in the pits?" Ashur asked. "They told me you were dead."

"Who?"

"Zoraida's guards."

"They wish," Nasir scoffed. "Though I nearly was. I stayed alive based on sheer hatred alone. I was assigned a *mu'allim* who trained me, but it was Kavin who kept me from turning into the monster the highborn Ghuls wanted me to be. I wasn't kidding when I said she saved me. She did. Mind, body and soul—in every way a person can be saved."

Ashur could barely believe what he was hearing. But he could tell his brother wasn't kidding. Nasir had always been the most logical of the brothers, and since he'd blamed the Ghuls for his betrothed's death, it was clear he truly loved this Kavin if he'd put aside his hatred for her. "And you're going to marry her."

A sheepish smile curled Nasir's mouth. "I already did. I couldn't wait. Plus, I didn't want any from our kingdom to question her loyalty."

Holy Allah, this was serious. "What did Father say?"

Nasir looked out over the water. "He wasn't thrilled at first. Assumed the same things as you. But then he heard what she'd done for me, and he got to know her." He looked back at Ashur. "I want you to get to know her too, brother. She has a good heart, not like the Ghuls Zoraida so easily corrupts. She's made me see things differently, made me realize that the people we thought were our enemies just might not be. I made her a promise that we'd go back to liberate the pits and free all who are imprisoned there—every race—and I plan to uphold that promise. Just as soon as we figure out a way to break Zoraida's hold on you."

Ashur's mind spun. Everything was out of focus, different from what he'd believed—what he'd been told. He didn't know whom to trust.

I trust you…

His pulse picked up speed all over again, but not because of anything Nasir had said. Because of an angel who was now… He didn't know where she'd gone. Just knew she was close. Close enough to touch if he wanted.

"Tariq's been here, searching for the bottle since the day he was freed," Nasir went on. "It's why he lives on this island in Puget Sound, why he has that sailboat down there at the dock, so he can follow the currents if need be. And Kavin and I have sent search parties to every corner of the realm in the hopes of locating Zoraida's hideout. But we always came up empty. We didn't give up, Ashur. None of us did. Zoraida's greatest weapon is deception. She wants you to think we abandoned you so she can control you. But think logically, brother. Why would we do that?"

Nasir the peacemaker. Not a lot had changed, Ashur realized. Not really. Except...what his brother was saying... It made an odd sort of sense. Zoraida's guards had tried to break him, and when that hadn't worked, they'd pulled him in, trained him, convinced him he was one of them and that his brothers were the real villains.

His skin grew tight, and perspiration beaded his forehead. He looked toward Nasir again. "Why hasn't she called you back? I sense the opal on you, even if I can't see it in this world."

Nasir looked down at his feet. "I don't know. I've wondered that myself. My opal started vibrating yesterday. That's how I knew the bottle had been found and opened in this world. She could drag me back at any time but hasn't yet. Maybe she doesn't know I'm still alive."

Or it could be that she was too weak to go after Nasir just yet. Ashur remembered how pale Zoraida had looked when she'd first reappeared and sent him to Claire, and how frail she'd seemed when he'd gone back.

"That's why Claire's soul is so important," he mumbled, pushing to his feet.

"What do you mean?" Nasir asked.

"Claire isn't what she seems."

Nasir's eyes narrowed. "What is she?"

Something Ashur wasn't ready to discuss yet. Not until he talked to Claire. For the first time, hope ignited deep inside, the thought that maybe she'd been right. Maybe she could help him after all. Of course, that depended on just what she needed from his realm and why she was so hot to go there. "I need to talk to her."

"Tariq's waiting to speak with you."

"He'll have to go on waiting. This is more important." He turned for the house.

"Ashur."

Ashur glanced over his shoulder, and in his brother's expression, he saw just how much Nasir had hoped to be that peacemaker tonight. The rest of Ashur's anger slid to the wayside. "I'll talk to Tariq when I'm done. Okay?"

A slow smile spread across Nasir's lips. "More than okay."

Chapter Eight

CLAIRE ROLLED TO HER SIDE, dragging the blankets with her. The muscles in her eyes tightened as she waited, a sense of anticipation alive inside her. For what…she didn't know.

Slowly, the fog cleared, and she chanced a look down. Her stomach rolled, and her head grew light. She shuffled back, but pebbles and dirt skittered off the edge of the precipice she stood on, skipped over and cracked against the wall of rock forming a sharp drop. Below, the red glow of flames rising up from a river of lava met her view. Yet above, a bright light overwhelming the darkness, blinding in its intensity.

She blocked the glare from above with her hand, turned to look over the edge at the winding river of red below. From somewhere deep inside, an overwhelming urge to step off the ledge consumed her. Happiness was down there. Sadness too. Emotions of all different kinds. Uncertainty. But intermixed…a future.

The pull was quickly blanketed by the need to look skyward, to the light above. And she did. To knowledge. To answers. To enlightenment.

Indecision raced through her. She didn't know where she was supposed to go. What she was supposed to do. Her heart pounded hard, but before she could choose, the fog rolled in once more, blocking both darkness and light.

Claire jerked awake with a gasp and sat straight up. Moonlight filtered through the window, casting an eerie white light across the dark room, but she didn't need to look to know she wasn't alone. She could feel the presence of another. Could feel *him*.

Her gaze darted to the side and landed on Ashur, sitting in the chair beside her bed, a look of confusion across his rugged face.

"Ashur, you scared me." While her heart raced, she tried to slow her breathing. The dream, vision, whatever it had been, felt too real. She chanced a look at the bedside clock and realized she'd only been asleep about an hour.

Just a dream. Darkness and light. Doesn't mean anything.

"What are the specific reasons?"

Her gaze jerked back to his face. "What?"

He studied her carefully. Too carefully. Had he seen what she'd been dreaming? Had he influenced it somehow? "Outside you said you had very specific reasons for summoning me. I think it's time you tell me what those reasons are."

Claire brushed her hair back from her face and scooted up in the pillows, shaking off the last dregs of sleep. Right. Her reasons. She'd been stupid to think she'd skate free of that conversation so easily.

"Well?" he prodded.

Shit, she had to tell him the rest. She'd already vowed to help him. And even though he'd made that comment out in the woods about still wanting her, from his intense expression now she had a sinking suspicion seduction wasn't going to work anymore. If she wanted his help in return, she had to be honest.

She drew a deep breath. "The celestial order is complicated. Years ago, before I was even born, the High Seven trapped the angels' emotions in the firebrand opals. It was their way to control us, to take away our free will and command us at every turn. Then they scattered the opals in the djinn realm, where we cannot cross without an escort. Since djinn and angels don't mix, as you pointed out earlier, that prevented any of us from finding out about them."

"That doesn't answer my question."

Right. His question. "I'm getting there. Even though I'm banished, I've never been able to *feel*. Not the full range of emotions, anyway. It's hard to explain. It's like having a filter. Angels can feel happy or sad for their assignments, but it's never personal. We don't experience emotions like djinn and humans. But then Mira destroyed Tariq's opal, and everything changed. Suddenly the world became a different place for me. Those emotions I felt before became amplified, and for the first time, I knew what it was like to experience joy or heartache for myself, not through someone else. For the first time, I realized what it was like to truly live. And I wanted more."

"More. You wanted to feel more emotions?"

She wrung her hands together and looked down at her fingers. "No. Yes. I mean... You don't know what it's like to be numb on the inside. Emotions... They're like a drug. I summoned you because I want to cross into the djinn realm and destroy the other opals so that not just I but my fellow angels can experience more."

He didn't immediately answer, and when the silence got to be too much, Claire finally looked over. Except, when her eyes met his, she sensed there was something else he wanted to ask her. Something...personal.

Her pulse quickened all over again.

"Why were you banished?"

Surprise registered. And was followed quickly by disappointment because it wasn't the question she wanted either. "I already told you. I wasn't supposed to ask—"

"Don't give me the line about asking too many questions. I may not be celestial, but even I don't believe you'd be banished for that."

Why the hell was he so smart? He was djinn. She'd always been told djinn acted on their base desires. But in the time she'd been with him, he hadn't once done anything she'd expected. She sighed. "Angels aren't supposed to question authority."

"Then why give you a brain?"

He had a point. She frowned. Tried not to laugh. Hated that she wasn't just being honest, she was exposing everything now.

The dream came back to her as she debated what to tell him, but this time it seemed so real, she was sure she could hear the crackling flames. "All angels have jobs. Mine was to test the souls of newly departed. Every soul develops on a path to enlightenment. The good and evil souls are easy to ascertain; it's the ones who skirt the middle line whom I was sent to test."

"How?"

"I was supposed to tempt them. The road to the afterlife, or the chance to go back and try again."

"Reincarnation."

"Not necessarily." It was hard to explain, and she knew she wasn't doing a good job of it. She shifted against the pillows. "You've heard of a person dying, then coming back to life? Sometimes it was as simple as that. For the truly good, it was a chance to make amends. For the ones we were unsure about, it was a test to see what they'd do with extra time. Would they use it for good or evil?"

"So you passed judgment."

"No." On this she was clear. "Judgment is reserved for the High Seven. But if I sensed a hesitation, I had the ability to send the soul back."

"That still doesn't explain why you were banished."

Claire pulled her knees up to her chest and wrapped her arms around them. "There was a man. In his thirties. He'd been walking along the side of a road at dusk and was hit by a car. I was sent to determine if he should be sent for final judgment. I sensed goodness in him, but I also felt his desire to go back. When I questioned him, he told me he needed to go back for his son. The son was four, suffering from cancer, and would likely die soon, and the man claimed there was no other family to take care of him. His mother had passed in childbirth. I knew the man would have easily passed to the Seven Heavens, but I made the decision to send him back."

"I'm guessing your superiors didn't like that decision."

That was an understatement. Claire sighed. "As angels, we're supposed to do Allah's will, nothing more. When I made the decision to send that soul back, I superimposed my will on him. And that decision impacted not only him and me, it messed with the celestial balance. By sending him back, I opened his soul to the possibility of doing evil and jeopardizing his chance to eventually make his way to the Seven Heavens."

She looked out the window toward the moon high above. She'd paid a price for her decision, but as much pain as she knew that man had felt when his son eventually did pass, she took comfort in the fact the boy hadn't died alone. There weren't many things Claire could picture worse than being alone. And a soul as strong and bright as that man's… She had faith he'd find his way back to the Seven Heavens.

"What happened to the father and son?" Ashur asked quietly.

"I don't know." She cut her gaze from the window and looked down at the blankets beneath her bare feet. "I was banished before I found out. Sent here to experience the life I forced that man back to relive. For good or ill."

"To be tested yourself."

A chill spread down Claire's spine at Ashur's words, and slowly, she looked his way. Was she being tested? Was that what this was all about? Not just a punishment, but her being forced to make the conscious decision between good and evil?

"The red swirl of fire, flames, and a heat that can consume every part of you," he said in that same low voice. "Or peace."

He had seen her dream. Or maybe her mind. Claire's pulse picked up. And again, the same feeling she'd had during the dream—that the fire and flames held life and uncertainty and a future for good or bad that she just couldn't see while the light above held clarity—consumed her all over again.

The draw to step off that ledge grew stronger. She lived now, but she wasn't truly alive. Not inside. And that was what she wanted. That was what she needed before she could make her final decision…whatever that might be.

"Life is not all it's cracked up to be, *maya*," he said softly, and for a moment, she wondered if he'd read her mind, but then she decided he couldn't have. Not so quickly and not when she didn't even truly understand what she was thinking. "I, my brothers, the horror strewn across my kingdom from the wars that still rage there, are proof of the harsh cruelties of life. You speak of emotions and living, and yet you don't see what is before you. I live, and I am a slave. In your quest to be free, you could be condemning yourself to this. Trust me when I say slaves are willing to sacrifice everything—including their honor—for peace."

She stared into his eyes in the silence that followed. And as it had when she'd seen his anger, something softened inside her. Shifted toward him. Tugged her forward. "But maybe one can't appreciate that peace unless they've truly lived. As awful as you make life sound, at least you've experienced it. And you've felt. Anger, sadness, hope, despair…love. Those are things I've never truly known."

"Yes, but feelings can be a weakness. Zoraida thrives on them. And they make decisions…faulty. While you seek out emotions, I've learned to lock them away. At least until recently."

The faraway look in his eyes told her he was thinking of his brothers and everything he'd done before and after his imprisonment. What was it like to feel such emotional extremes? To love and hate with such passion? What few emotions she'd experienced the last few months had been minor compared to what he was so obviously feeling.

She scooted to the edge of the bed. Dropped her legs over the side. "You're not with her now, Ashur. You're here."

His gaze slid back to hers. Held. Darkened with a heat that rolled through her belly and brought every nerve ending in her body to life. "So are you."

Her pulse pounded. The air changed. Crackled with both awareness and indecision. Seemed to come to life itself.

Her gaze slid from his eyes to his full, masculine lips, and a flutter ignited deep in her belly. Lips that had kissed her on that island. Lips she'd wanted to kiss her only hours ago in the woods. Lips she needed to taste now.

"We're quite a pair, aren't we?" she asked. "Not all that different really. We both just want to be free."

"And yet neither of us knows if that freedom will save or condemn us."

Her gaze drifted back to his eyes. And the same unease she'd felt when Tariq had mentioned that Ashur was bound to the opal and not her, slid down her spine. One that was quickly drowned out by the fire slowly building in her veins. A fire she had the oddest sensation only he could extinguish.

"The question is, *maya*, just how far are you willing to go to find the answer?"

Ashur knew he was playing a dangerous game. It was after midnight, his brothers and their mates were somewhere in this house waiting to speak with him, and instead of figuring out what to do next, he'd spent the last hour watching Claire sleep, wishing she were anything but celestial. Wishing he could make sense of the images and words and memories swirling in his head.

He didn't know what to believe. Didn't know what was real or a lie. But overriding everything was the desire to touch and be touched. To forget who and what he was, what was expected of him, and what would happen when this night was over.

"Neither of us knows if that freedom will save or condemn us…"

His own words echoed back to him, sent his pulse skipping. In the dim light, Claire licked her lips, and her gaze slid from his eyes to his mouth. And every second that passed with her sitting so close, with her gardenia scent circling around him and the gentle rise and fall of her breasts drawing his attention to the thin cotton T-shirt she wore, he felt his control slipping.

He couldn't think when she was close. Didn't want to think. But he didn't want to take either. Zoraida needed Claire's soul. An angel's soul. He didn't want to be the one to deliver it to her. And that had nothing to do with his own hopes and fears. It had to do with Claire.

She scooted closer, and her knees pressed against the insides of his, sending shivers of arousal spiraling straight up his legs to tighten his groin. "If you're waiting for fear, Ashur, you're not going to find it. I told you before, I trust you."

No one had ever trusted him before. Not his father, not his brothers, not even himself.

He leaned forward in his chair until her heat consumed him and made him light-headed, but still he held back. "And what if I am your test? Are you willing to risk the loss of the Seven Heavens all for one night with me? A djinni? Smokeless flame that could incinerate your light? You know what I am, *maya*. Let's not pretend anymore."

Her gaze searched his face. This close, he could see the flecks of gold and gray in her blue irises. And Allah, he wanted her. Wanted her in a way he hadn't wanted anything or anyone before. But if he corrupted her soul in the name of pleasure, he'd be no better than the Ghuls Zoraida commanded. No better than Zoraida, really.

He didn't want to be like the sorceress. He wanted to be... himself. He wanted to be free. Wanted to find love like his brothers. Wanted to live...like Claire wanted.

Her fingertips brushed his jaw, her touch so wickedly intense, he tipped his head toward her hand before he could stop himself. "You are not evil, Ashur. And the sorceress does not hold sway over you, not unless you let her." Her fingertips left his jaw, grazed the hollow at his throat where the opal should be sitting but could only be seen in his realm. Her touch—so gentle, so soft—sent electrical sensations all through his groin. "I do not believe you will incinerate my light. Not when there is goodness in your heart. Goodness always triumphs over evil. Always."

Her hand slid down to rest over the space holding his heart. And the heat and life pulsing in her palm caused every cell in his body to come alive. "Banished or not, not even an angel can see into the heart of a person, *maya*."

A slow smile crept across her face, and she lifted her gaze back to his. "True, but I know what I feel. And right now, I want to feel you. Around me. Against me. *Inside* me. Not the djinni I summoned, Ashur. Just you."

He stared into her eyes. And beneath the thin fabric of his pants, his cock hardened, aching with the need to give her exactly what she craved. But still he held back. Because his thoughts were jumbled, his emotions all over the map. He didn't know if he should touch her. Didn't know if he'd be able to stop once he started, even if she begged. Didn't know if she was right or he was wrong or if by taking her like they both so obviously wanted, he'd be saving or condemning her after all.

She pushed against him, and he moved back easily. His spine met the chair. Then she climbed onto his lap, and all thought, all doubt drifted away and was replaced by a heat that surrounded him, consumed him and overrode everything else. "No more talking, Ashur. I just want you."

Her mouth pressed against his before he could stop her. Before he could think to stop her. And when the tip of her tongue stroked the seam of his lips, he opened and tasted her, just as he'd wanted to do from the first moment.

"Ahh..." He groaned into her mouth, slid his hand down her side and under her shirt until his fingers found skin, and gave up the fight. She answered by kissing him deeper, laving her tongue against his in such a deliciously erotic way, all he could think about was her tongue licking the head of his cock and what it would feel to have his shaft encased in the warm wetness of her mouth.

She changed the angle of the kiss, leaned closer to press her breasts against his bare chest. He wanted her naked. Wanted this shirt tangled in his hands out of his way. He tugged on the hem, pulled it up. She broke the kiss long enough for him to drag the cotton over her head, then kissed him again before he even tossed it on the floor.

She shivered when he pinched the tip of her nipple. And he groaned as she pushed down on his lap, grinding her pelvis against his throbbing cock. He liked that she didn't need a bra. Liked that her breasts were small and tight and ready for his touch. The reasons he shouldn't have her drifted out of his mind. Confusion seemed to retreat into shadow. She was warmth and heat and light and life. And he was done questioning. Done debating. Done waiting.

With one hand, he gripped the back of her head. With the other, he reached for the button on her shorts. "*Maya...*"

She groaned, then slid out of his grip before he could stop her.

Chill air replaced heat. Confusion thundered back as he blinked into the dark, trying to find her.

Then her fingertips tugged on the tie at his waistband, and he looked down to see her kneeling between his legs, a wicked smile across her lips, desire and need alive in her eyes.

"I want all of you, Ashur." She pulled the tie and reached inside his pants to free his aching cock. "This time, it's my turn to drive you mad with desire."

Chapter Nine

CLAIRE HAD NEVER KNOWN SUCH power before. Not even when she'd held the strength to determine the fate of a soul.

As she looked up into Ashur's dark eyes and slowly stroked his thick shaft, she knew the power women held over men. Knew—finally—just what it was about lust and love that could make a soul forsake everything else.

Was that what this was? Love? A buzz ignited in her head and beneath her ribs while she slid her hand down the length of his cock. His groan told her he liked what she was doing, the sound making her sex clench in anticipation of what he would feel like not in her hand but inside her body. He was big, thick. Mouthwatering. And just touching him like this was distracting her from her thoughts. She barely knew him. Had only just come to understand him. It couldn't be love so soon... Could it?

"*Maya*..."

He was djinn, darkness and flame. She was angel, light and purity. Except...he wasn't all bad, and she wasn't all good as they'd both been led to believe. There were shades of gray within each of them, regardless of where they'd come from.

"*Maya*...that feels so good. If you keep that up—"

She couldn't meet his eyes. Didn't want to think about love. Couldn't. Not yet. Leaning over his lap, she pushed the questions and doubts aside and extended her tongue, then tasted the very tip of him.

"*Maya...*"

The lust she heard in his voice melded with her own. Spurred her on. She took her cues from him, this time circling her tongue around the head and stroking the flared tip until he quivered. He groaned and lifted his hips, so she did it again. He answered by growing harder against her tongue, sliding his fingers into her hair to grasp her skull. But he didn't direct her movements, and deep inside she sensed he was giving her control. Gifting her the one thing he needed to keep at all costs.

Her chest warmed with both power and emotions she couldn't define. Running the flat of her tongue down the underside of his cock, she marveled when his whole body shivered, the way hers had when he'd teased her with that purple toy. And when his thighs tensed under her arms, she knew his restraint was about to snap. She wanted to give him what he needed. Wanted to thank him for making her feel so alive. Closing her lips over his length, she finally drew him deep.

"Claire..." His throaty moan, the way he lifted his hips, the way he filled her mouth so completely drew her own need and desire to the forefront. She took him deeper, sucked harder, released him as he brushed the back of her throat. Her hand slid down to cup his balls, and before he could moan and press into her mouth again, she sucked him deep all over, stroking her tongue along the underside of his cock while she swallowed the head.

His entire body tensed. He thrust deep into her throat, grew impossibly hard against her tongue. She swallowed again and again, didn't stop, even when he tried to push her away. And she felt his release coming, knew the moment every muscle in his body seized that it was consuming him and he was powerless to stop it.

Warmth filled her mouth—salty, sweet, full of heat and life and him—and she swallowed all that he gave her, reveling in the fact she'd brought him to the brink. That she'd given him the kind of pleasure he'd given her. That she'd made him feel alive.

He moaned and pressed deep once more, then relaxed against the chair. Claire released him, eased back, looked up to find him staring down at her with that unreadable expression all over again. And though her body still vibrated with her own need, the way he was studying her spurred a shot of unease straight through her belly.

"I—"

He moved so fast she barely tracked his movements. One second she was on her knees in front of him; the next she was on her back on the bed, his heaving body hovering over her, radiating renewed heat and need. "I am the one who is supposed to be doing the pleasuring, not you."

Relief flooded her veins, and the thrill of his words hardened her nipples. "I don't command you, remember? You wanted me to pleasure your cock. I don't remember you telling me to stop."

A wicked smile curled his lips. One that was so damn sexy, it made her lust stronger, her need hotter. Made her shake with the force of her desire. "There are other things I want you to do to my cock." His gaze drifted to her breasts. "But first I want to taste you. This time all of you."

He lowered his mouth to her nipple, ran his tongue along the tip until she groaned. And the same wicked sensations she'd felt when he'd done this back on that island rolled through her hips all over again. She spread her legs, arched against him. He moved to her other breast, traced the areola with his tongue, drove her mad while his hand slid down her bare belly and finally popped the snap of her shorts.

Yes, *yes*...

He continued to tease her breast. His fingers slid inside her shorts, moved lower. His palm brushed her mound; then his lips suckled hard, and his fingers danced along her slit.

"Oh, *maya*, you are so wet for me." She groaned at his words, at the electrical vibrations rocking her core. He stroked her throbbing clit, slid his hand lower, then finally pressed one finger deep inside.

"So wet and tight," he whispered against her breast. He drew out, pressed back in with two fingers. His hot breath fanned her breasts. Her sex tightened as he thrust in and out. "Tell me what you want, *maya*. Do you want my fingers here, or would you rather have my cock?"

Oh...she couldn't think straight. Couldn't focus on anything but how wickedly good he felt. "Ashur—"

"Tell me. My fingers or my cock." He pressed deep, stroked inside, grazed his thumb over her clit.

"Ah..." Stars fired off behind her eyes, and her climax spiraled close but retreated when he drew away. She reached for him but found only empty air. Blinking, she looked down to find he'd stripped her of her shorts and was staring at her swollen sex.

"Ashur—"

"First with my tongue."

He didn't give her time to answer. He tasted her before she could tell him she just wanted him. And then all she could do was moan. Her head fell against the mattress; she gripped the sheet at her hips and arched against him. He circled her clit, dipped lower, and tasted all of her just as he'd promised. Then he did it again and again until the room spun out of control.

Electricity ripped down her spine, shot outward from her sex, enveloped every part of her. She heard a voice—her own?—call out. Felt nothing but light and ecstasy. For a moment, everything pulsed bright then went dark, and when she finally came back to herself, she was staring up into the most beautiful eyes she'd ever seen.

"That is such a trip the way you come," he whispered. "I want to feel it with you."

"Yes," she whispered, reaching for him. "Yes."

His mouth claimed hers. He nudged her legs apart, and then his cock was sliding along her sex, slick, hot, so very hard she shivered as it brushed her clit. His tongue licked hers, and she tasted him, and her, and a desire like she'd never known. She lifted her hips, felt him press against her sex, lifted more until the thick head pressed inside.

"Ah, Claire…"

"Yes," she whispered. She lifted her hips, lowered, needed him deeper inside. Needed him to move. "Take me, Ashur."

"No." He rolled, pulling her on top. His hands settled at her waist. "I want you to take me, *maya*."

Control. He was giving her that legendary control he'd needed to survive Zoraida's hell. Her heart bumped, and she shifted up on her knees, hovered over him, then slowly lowered until his cock sank deep.

They both groaned. He was so thick and hard… She felt like she would burst. Felt like she could come, if he'd just move…

She lifted, drew away, clenched her sex as she lowered, taking him deep all over again, never once looking away from his eyes. His face grew flushed with need. His eyes widened until she was sure she'd lose herself in their depths.

"Oh, yeah. Just like that," he encouraged. He sat up, pushed her knees wider. "Rub your clit against me. I want to feel your pleasure."

She did as he said, rubbing herself against him with every down stroke. He felt so good. So big. So thick. Her eyes glazed over as she rode him, as she picked up speed. He gripped her ass, lifted and lowered, helped direct her movements. Pleasure arced through her pelvis, every downstroke making her shiver, making her burn hotter. But it wasn't enough. She wanted more. So much more…

"Ashur…"

"I'll take you there, *maya*, don't worry."

He wrapped one arm around her waist, holding her tight against him as he thrust up, and pressed his other hand against the top of her ass. She shivered, groaned, was so very close. His fingers slid lower, down her cleft and against her sex, and then she felt him touching where his cock was entering her.

Feeling him doing that, imagining what it must look like, made her groan. Then his finger, slick from her wetness, slid around her hip and between their bodies to press against her clit.

She drew in a breath. Against her neck he breathed, "Trust me, *maya*. Trust me to make you feel good."

She did trust him. More than she'd ever trusted anyone. And it did feel good. So wickedly good to have his slick fingers pinching her clit, stroking in time to his thrusts, over and over. Felt so right to let go, to give herself over to him…

She relaxed, then groaned when he pushed deep.

"Fuck, *maya*... You're so tight. So perfect. That's it. Ride me. Come with me deep inside you."

Reason and thought fled. All she knew were sensations. Tingles. Erotically charged pleasure she felt everywhere. She was full. So full. About to explode. She burned. She needed. She craved so much more. Her mouth found his. Hot, wet, needy kisses with tongue and lips and teeth, but it wasn't enough. She pressed down against him. His thrusts picked up speed. His fingers flicked faster. She rubbed against him again and again until the creaking bed, until the wet sounds of skin slapping skin, until even his voice urging her on was drowned out by her cry of ecstasy.

Until a wildfire as hot as those she imagined in Jahannam erupted in the room, consumed everything in its path, and incinerated what was left behind.

Just as he'd warned it would.

༄

Claire's heart raced so fast she feared it might fly right out of her body.

Sound slowly returned, and she recognized Ashur's steady breaths below her, followed by the thump, thump, thump of his heart against her cheek. But her skin was still vibrating from that mind-numbing climax, and her head was so jumbled she couldn't think straight.

A soft chuckle echoed from Ashur's torsod, and he pressed a kiss to her temple before rolling her over. "You are never what I expect, *maya*."

Cool air brushed her skin as he rolled her over, as he pulled the covers back, then pulled her into the pillows with him. All sculpted muscle and tanned nakedness, her very own sex djinni sent to possess her.

And that was what he'd done, she realized, swallowing hard. Possessed her in every way possible. She would have done anything he'd asked in that moment of sexual bliss, and she would have begged for more. It didn't matter that they didn't know each other that well or that he was djinn and she was celestial. When she'd told him before that emotions were like a drug to her, she hadn't been kidding. She wanted...*needed* more of what he'd given her like a heroin addict needs a hit. To the point where virtually nothing else mattered. Not her original goal or her fellow angels or even his own safety and freedom.

Sweat slicked her skin all over again, but this time not from passion, from bone-melting fear. Sura had warned her she could lose herself in this quest, but she'd brushed off the warning, considered herself too smart and strong for that to happen. But now...

A lump formed in her throat Ashur snuggling up at her back, his heat overwhelming her once more, igniting a craving that consumed her from the inside out, because now she knew exactly how to sate it.

"You wore me out, *maya*," he whispered. His hand slid across her waist, sending tingles of awareness and arousal straight to her sex. He pulled her back until his groin was pressed against her ass and his body was cradling her from shoulder to toes. Until she had to bite her lip to keep from groaning and rubbing back against him. "I'm too tired to deal with Tariq and the others right now. For the rest of tonight, I just want to forget everything but you. Let me rest for a few minutes; then I'll rock your world again."

Oh, she wanted that too—needed him to roll her to her stomach, lift her hips and sink into her from behind until they both screamed from the sheer joy of it—but...what would that do except draw her closer toward a darkness she was suddenly afraid she might not be able to claw herself free from? What would happen if she gave in to the erotic ecstasy and her soul then became the possession of his sorceress?

Panic spread through Claire. An angel's soul—even a banished one—in the hands of an evil sorceress, would not be good. Her powers might be bound in this world, but not in that one. And if the sorceress gained access to those powers...what would happen to him?

Her pulse raced, and her skin vibrated as Ashur's breaths lengthened and slowed. Options raced across her mind. None made sense. None seemed feasible. Only one stood out as the last plausible solution.

No matter how good he made her feel, no matter what she might be feeling for him after such a short amount of time, she had to get away. She couldn't stay. Not now, when she knew how very dangerous it would be for not only her, but him and his entire realm.

She waited until she was sure he was deep in sleep, then slid out from under his arm and quietly reached for her clothes from the floor. The mattress bounced once as she pushed to her feet, and she held her breath, waited for him to wake, but he didn't even stir. Slipping on her sandals, she turned for the door, then at the last second remembered the opal.

She wasn't bound to it. He was. And the only reason he was with her now was because she wore it. Emotions pinched inside, stole her breath. Only after a few painful draws of air did she realize what she was feeling.

Sadness. Loss. Emptiness. No matter how they'd connected physically, he wouldn't pick an angel for a mate if he could, and if she stayed, she'd only be confusing the high she got from really great sex with the emotions she craved more than life itself. But even more than that, if she stayed, whether she succeeded in finding the other opals or not, she'd be condemning him to failure. And eventually, to torture and punishment, all because of her.

Tears burned her eyes as she looked toward the bed where he lay softly sleeping. She might have been willing to do that once before, but not now. Was it because of love? She didn't know. Wasn't even sure she knew how to recognize love. She only knew one thing for certain. She might not have the power to save herself, but she could give him the chance to be free.

Her fingers made quick work of the latch at her nape, and the cool stone fell into her hand with a soft jingle. She looked down at the red gem in her palm, alive with swirls of orange and yellow, and recognized she was walking away from something she'd wanted longer than she could remember. But for the first time, she knew she was finally doing the right thing.

She dropped the necklace on the bed where moments ago she'd lain, and slipped out the door without another look back. The living room was empty when she reached the end of the hall. A glance at the wall clock told her it was close to 2:00 a.m. Ashur's brothers must have given up on him and gone to bed.

That would make her exit all the easier.

She crossed the living room and hit the kitchen. She didn't trust herself to stick around and wait for a cab. She'd walk the three miles into town and call a cab from there. She didn't even care that the air was cool and she was only wearing shorts and T-shirt. She had to get away before she couldn't. Before it was too late. Her hand closed over the doorknob.

"Where are you running off to at two in the morning?"

Claire's pulse sped up, and her hand froze against the door handle. Turning slowly, she looked toward the dark breakfast nook and made out a shape sitting in the shadows.

"I..." *Shit.* "I wasn't running. I left something outside."

Mira flipped on the lamp over the table. Light illuminated her pink-polka-dot pajamas, her dark hair pulled back in a tail, her raised brow and incredulous expression. "You didn't bring anything with you, Claire."

Crap, she hadn't. Her mind spun for another pathetic excuse.

Mira set her mug on the table. "Everyone's asleep. I'm assuming Ashur is too, or you wouldn't be making your escape now." She winked. "He's hot, by the way. Even with that massive chip perched on his shoulder. Why don't you pull up a chair and tell me how you the two of you hooked up. I've a feeling there's quite a story behind that one."

Unease rushed through Claire's belly, and she glanced toward the hall. That craving was so strong, so all-consuming, she felt an invisible pull to go back to that room, to climb in that bed, to ravish that body that could make her go blind with lust. But she resisted it. She had to if she had any chance of helping Ashur in the long run.

Mira uncrossed her legs and pushed out of her chair. Reaching into the cabinet for a new mug, she said, "So let's start with your research. You were tracking the tides. This obviously wasn't just to help me and Tariq. I want to know why. And just how you were able to find that bottle when we—using all the djinn tricks Tariq and Nasir know—couldn't."

Claire pressed shaking fingers against her suddenly throbbing temples. What the hell was she going to say? While Mira set a steaming mug of tea next to her elbow then slid back into her seat and eyed her, she fought for words she knew weren't going to do anything but make Mira more confused. "I…I thought I could help. And tracking the tides, going to the islands was research I'll use in future papers."

"But you summoned a djinni. You did that on purpose. What were you hoping to do?"

Save my people. But even as the thought hit, Claire knew it was a lie. She might have told Sura that was her goal, but it wasn't. She'd summoned Ashur for purely selfish reasons. So she could find the other firebrand opals. So she could feel. So she could have everything she'd just walked away from.

"I don't know anymore," she managed, staring down at the wisps of steam rising off her tea. "It seemed like a good idea at the time. Now…"

Now everything was wrong. And she didn't know how to fix it. Or even if she could.

She looked up into Mira's clear eyes. "I can't help Ashur. I was foolish to think I could. I have to leave."

"What? You just got here. We need you. I'm awake now because I couldn't stop thinking about it. Claire, no matter what your reasons may have been, you summoning Ashur is a blessing in disguise. Not only do you know the secrets in the Key of Solomon, which you helped me use to free Tariq, but you're now bound to the opal. You can free Ashur yourself."

If only it were that easy. "No, I can't."

"Why not? Of course you can. You just have to do exactly what you told me to do and—"

Frustration pushed Claire out of her chair. She raked a hand through her hair. "Mira, I told you after you came to see me that the words you uttered that day only worked because of one reason. Do you remember that reason?"

Mira's brow furrowed, and Claire could tell her friend was thinking back. Then Mira muttered, "Pure of heart. You told me in that moment when I said the words from the Key of Solomon, I was pure of heart."

"Yes," Claire breathed. "And it was the magic needed to break the chain and free Tariq. But I'm not pure of heart. I wish I were. I wish I could help, but I summoned Ashur for purely selfish reasons, which have nothing to do with him or you or Tariq or the problems going on in the djinn realm. And those reasons haven't changed, not even now. If anything, they've gotten stronger. If I don't go now, pretty soon I won't be able to."

"I don't understand."

No, and Claire didn't expect her to. She looked down at her mug, sitting untouched on the table, much like her heart.

No, that wasn't true. Ashur had touched her heart in a way no one—no angel or human or djinn—had ever done. And that sadness came back, pressing against her from every side. "Even if I was pure of heart, I still couldn't free Ashur. I'm not bound to the opal."

"What?" Mira's gaze snapped to Claire's neck, where the firebrand opal no longer hung. "How did you get it off? I wasn't able to remove it when I had it. It only opened when—"

"When you freed Tariq. I know. But I'm…different. Ashur's bound to the opal, but not me. And I'm leaving now, before it's too late, so you and the others have time to find another woman to give the necklace to. Maybe then she—"

Claire's chest cinched down hard when she thought of another wearing the opal, of Ashur being bound to pleasure someone else. Even though he wasn't hers, the thought of him with someone else sent a path of fire straight through her heart.

Which was crazy, because she *barely* knew him.

She squared her shoulders, reminded herself she was doing the right thing. Even if it didn't feel like it. "Maybe then she can figure out a way to free him. Because I just can't."

She reached for the door. Mira's chair scraped the floor at her back. "Claire, wait—"

She couldn't. Not any more. Tears pushed at her eyes, and an empty cavern was growing beneath her ribs. One she didn't understand but which she feared might swallow her whole. "Tell the others I'm sorry. That I…" She swallowed around the lump in her throat and jerked the door open. "That I'm so sorry. Trust me, you'll all be better off once I'm gone."

Chapter Ten

A COOL WIND BLEW ACROSS ASHUR's face, rousing him from sleep. Groggy, he blinked several times, then peered into shadows and dim light.

He was in some kind of bedroom. Warm sheets cradled his body, a pillow lay under his head, and moonlight cascaded over pale walls on every side.

This wasn't one of his rooms in the castle in Gannah. It wasn't gaudy enough. And it wasn't part of Zoraida's hideout where he'd been imprisoned and trained. It was too soft. It also wasn't that hut where he'd been summoned by an angel.

Claire...

Thoughts, memories, events passed before his eyes. Followed by a rush of heat that started in his belly and burned a path straight to his groin.

His cock grew hard when he remembered Claire peering up at him with need and lust in her light blue eyes, and his groin tingled with the memory of her soft fingers reaching for his drawstring, sliding into his pants, wrapping around his cock and finally drawing him into the warm, moist heat of her mouth.

He wanted her again. Wanted to lose himself in her softness and light. Wanted to sink inside her body and forget everything else—his brothers, his duties, the sorceress.

He rolled, reached for her, but found air. He moved his hand, patted the sheets, finally pushed up on his elbow and looked over to find her gone.

"Claire?"

No answer. No movement. He glanced over his shoulder toward the dark bathroom, also quiet. A frown cut across his face as he looked back where she'd been snuggled against him only hours ago. Where could she be?

A sparkle of light caught his attention, and he sat up. Reaching for the sheet, he closed his fingers around the cotton and pulled it back. Then stared down at the firebrand opal against the mattress in disbelief and shock.

No. She'd taken it off? Why?

He reached for it, hoping it was still warm, that it had just slipped off, that it meant she was still close. Only cold, hard stone met his fingertips.

Before he could process what that meant, a great rumble shook the house. The bed groaned, the walls trembled, and then a jolt of energy whipped through the room. His body lifted then slammed back against the headboard with a crack that resonated through his skull and sent pain firing through his entire body.

Dazed, he slumped to the ground. And then the room filled with smoke and he felt his body flying.

No!

Flying toward a darkness he couldn't stop.

Mira's scream brought Claire's feet to a stop.

She whipped around, was met by a wind that slashed past her face, thrust her hair behind her. Wood splintered, saplings and rocks flew up into the air. The ground shook beneath her feet.

Claire stumbled, caught her balance. Then watched in shock as entire trees were uprooted, their limbs ripped free to thunder to the forest floor. Her mouth fell open, her eyes grew wide. It was like watching a tornado spin around her, a force of nature that didn't usually occur in the Pacific Northwest. Except nothing touched her.

A roar grew from the house. She jerked that direction. Energy pulsed through the building, a blast of heat and light that rocked the entire foundation. Inside, objects crashed to the floor and shattered.

She didn't think. She reacted. Racing back across the damp earth, she jumped over downed logs and debris in her path. By the time she reached the porch, she was breathing heavily. The house had stopped shaking, but when she pulled the kitchen door open, she gasped at the mess of plates and furniture and broken glass strewn across the floor.

A groan echoed at her right. She shifted that way, then lurched into action. "Mira."

Her friend lay at an angle against the breakfast-nook wall. Blood trickled from a cut on her forehead, and her eyes were dazed. Claire stooped to help her to her feet. Footsteps pounded somewhere close. She turned just as Tariq burst into the small room.

"*Hayaati*." Tariq was at Claire's side in a flash, taking Mira from her arms and gently checking her wounds.

"I'm fine, Tariq," Mira said. "I'm fine, really. I just banged my head." She pressed her fingers against the cut. Winced. "What the hell was that?"

"She called him back."

At the sound of Nasir's voice, Claire looked toward the archway where the djinn prince, wearing nothing but pale blue pajama pants, stood in the center of the disaster with Kavin at his side. Both of their faces were pale, their hair a mess, cuts and bruises already forming over their arms and faces where they'd obviously been hit by debris. But when he held out his hand, all the air was sucked from Claire's lungs.

The firebrand opal glittered under the kitchen lights. "This was on the mattress in his room."

Tariq's eyes grew wide, then his gaze jerked toward Claire. "You took it off? How? What did you do?"

"I..." Panic closed in around Claire as she looked from face to face. "I thought I was helping. Giving him a chance. Why would she call him back?"

"Because he failed," Tariq answered. "How did you take it off? And why don't you look as banged up as the rest of us?"

"I—"

"She left," Mira answered quickly. "She was already outside when that—whatever it was—hit."

Tariq moved to the window. "How long?"

Mira glanced toward Claire, then to her husband. "Minutes."

His dark gaze landed on Claire again, and this time, fear pushed in with the panic. He crossed to her, jerked her chin up with his hand. Stared hard into her eyes. "You're not injured. You should be dead if you were outside when Zoraida's fury hit. Entire trees are uprooted out there. What *are* you?"

The confusion filling Tariq's eyes told Claire this time, he wouldn't be deterred. "I..." That energy had come from the sorceress? Because of her? And now…what did that mean for Ashur? "I was just trying to…to help."

Tears pushed against her eyes. And that emptiness grew beneath her ribs. Grew so wide she was afraid it might swallow her whole.

"Holy Allah," Nasir muttered from the doorway. "She's not human. She's celestial. Look at the tear on her cheek."

Claire sniffled, tried to wipe it away, but Tariq's hand grasped her wrist, stopping her. They closed around her, and every set of eyes focused on her cheek. At the tear even she could see was glowing.

"An angel," Tariq muttered, his gaze jumping back to her eyes. "No wonder you knew the secrets of the Key of Solomon." Rage erupted in his irises. "What were you trying to do? Why did you summon my brother? What kind of game are you playing with us?"

"Tariq, stop!" Mira pushed her way between Claire and Tariq, preventing him from grabbing her other arm. "Stop right now. Can't you see what this is doing to her?"

Tariq stared down at her, his gaze alight with anger and malice, but Claire was beyond caring. All she could think about was where Ashur had gone. What was happening to him. And that by trying to do the right thing, once again she'd made the wrong choice.

Tariq's hand released her wrist. Claire slumped against the wall at her back, then slowly slid to the ground. Pain sliced at her. A pain that was a thousand times worse than the emptiness she'd felt before.

"Tariq," Mira whispered. Then, kneeling next to Claire, she softly added, "Claire, tell us what happened."

She didn't know where to start, but before she realized what she was doing, the words were free, rolling, growing, spilling out. About her, about her order, about the reasons she'd searched for that bottle and why she'd summoned Ashur to begin with.

When she was done, silence settled over the shambles in the kitchen. She swiped at her damp cheeks, thankful at least that the words had forced her to stop crying. She hadn't even known she could cry until just now.

"Holy Allah," Nasir repeated. "That's why Zoraida's so pissed Ashur failed. Because an angel's soul is stronger than that of a human."

Tariq looked toward his brother. "That was more than her normal temper tantrum."

Nasir nodded. "She needs the angel's soul to regain her strength."

Claire's head hurt so bad, she was having trouble following the conversation. The brothers seemed to forget there were others in the room. "We don't like to be called angels. It implies wings and halos, which we don't have. We prefer the term celestial. And I don't understand. Zoraida is already strong. She's a sorceress."

"Who's been imprisoned in a bottle for the last six months," Tariq said, finally cutting his gaze her way. "Zoraida gets strength from the souls her pleasure slaves corrupt. Without them, she grows weak, and she's been without for quite a while now. Did Ashur know what you are?"

"Not at first, no."

"But he found out?"

"Y-yes."

"And how did he react?"

Claire swallowed hard and looked up at Tariq, remembering not only the fury but fear in his eyes when he'd realized what she was. "He...he wasn't happy. He made me send him back."

"But he returned, didn't he?"

"Pissed, I'll bet," Nasir added. "Zoraida would have made him come back."

Claire glanced Nasir's way, then looked at Tariq, who seemed just as eager to hear her answer. "Yes," she finally said. "He...he didn't want to have anything to do with me after he found out. At first, at least."

Tariq looked across the kitchen to his brother. "My powers won't be of any help."

"Mine will." Nasir turned his gaze to Claire. "She's the only one who can go after him."

Claire's head jerked up. "What?" She sniffled again. Looked from face to face. "Didn't you both hear what I said earlier? My powers are bound."

"In this world," Nasir answered.

"What does it matter? I'm not a fighter. I wouldn't know how to rescue him even if I could. I don't know the djinn realm."

"We'll tell you what you need to know."

Tariq's eyes were alive with light and excitement, as if things had already been decided. Slowly, Claire braced her back against the wall and pushed to her feet. "I...I'm not the one to do this. Both of you...you should go."

"We can't send ourselves to her lair," Nasir answered. "And Tariq is right. His powers lessen each day he's here. His won't be enough. Not for what you have to do."

Claire wasn't sure what they were implying, but the way Kavin tightened her hand around Nasir's in a protective way told her whatever they had planned wasn't good. "I...I can't get to the djinn realm. I don't even know how."

"You will," Nasir told her. "Once you steal my powers."

"No," Kavin finally interjected. "Nasir, no."

He turned toward his mate, brushed his hand against her cheek and softly said, "This is the only way, *rouhi*. As soon as Zoraida finds out I'm still alive, she's going to call me back. We've been lucky so far. She's been preoccupied by Ashur and the angel, but she's not anymore. I can feel her fury growing through the opal. She'll be coming for me. Soon. This is our only chance."

"But, Nasir..." Tears filled Kavin's eyes. "I can't lose you."

He pressed a kiss to her forehead. "If we have an angel on our side, maybe you won't have to."

They both looked toward Claire. As did Mira and Tariq. And in the silence that followed, Claire's heart sped up. Could she do this? Could she cross into the djinn realm and face down a sorceress? Her powers were strong—when she had them—but she'd rarely used them. And never in battle. Plus, it had been so long... Would she even remember how to use them?

Indecision raced through her mind. But overriding it was fear. Fear of crossing over, of being faced with the firebrand opals, of staring down everything she'd been seeking so long, and losing herself to the darkness for good.

"Please, Claire."

Mira's voice cut through Claire's jumbled thoughts, and she looked toward her friend, her own eyes wet with tears, fear and hope stamped across her face. Then to Tariq, whose expression mirrored Mira's.

"I...I'm fallen. I don't think I can steal any djinni's powers, even if I want to."

"Yes, you can," Nasir answered in a confident tone. She looked his way, saw the determination in his eyes. "Especially if I'm willing to give them to you. With my powers and this opal" —he nodded at the necklace in his hand— "you'll have everything you need to free us all. You're the only one who can."

☾

"You failed me!"

Ashur had seen Zoraida pissed before, but the fury currently raining down on him now was unlike anything he'd experienced before.

She yanked the whip from the guard's hand. The leather whistled through the air and snapped across Ashur's back, lashing through his skin. Burning pain shot all along his spine.

His body jerked. The chains around his wrists bit into his skin. He ground his teeth to keep from screaming out. The whip whirred again, sliced into his flesh over and over until his vision blurred. Until the cell wall drifted in and out of focus and he had trouble deciphering his surroundings.

"You will suffer like no djinni has suffered before," she growled as she struck out. "I gave you a simple job and you failed. Just like your brother. Used by an angel. Conned into giving her exactly what she wanted. You should be disgusted with yourself."

Whir. Snap. Singe...

Claire hadn't used him...had she? She'd wanted to help him gain his freedom. She'd told him she would. But as the whip lashed out again and again, and he winced at the pain, his words—and her words—came back to him.

"When will you have what you want, Claire?"

"When I'm thoroughly satisfied."

He'd satisfied her. He'd felt her release around him, had seen it in the pulse of light emitted from her body. She'd told him she'd wanted to feel, that she'd risked everything for that experience. And then when she'd gotten it, what had happened? She'd climbed out of his bed and taken off the opal that bound him to her.

Was it possible it had all been a lie? Her reason for summoning him? Her story about why she'd been banished? Her declaration that she would help him gain his freedom? She was the first person in a long time he'd felt anything for, but even he'd admitted feelings could be a weakness. That they caused a person to make faulty decisions. He was with Zoraida now because he'd loved a brother who'd betrayed him. Was he stupid enough to have made the same mistake with Claire?

Whip. Snap. Burn.

"I gave you one simple job!" Zoraida hollered. "Bring me the angel's soul. But you failed at even that. You are useless!"

"My lady," one guard gasped in a shocked voice as she continued to beat him. "You'll kill him."

The end of the whip dropped to the stone floor with a slap. And as Ashur hung his head and worked to catch his breath in the pause, he heard Zoraida's heavy breaths at his back.

"Kill him," Zoraida muttered. "That's a brilliant idea, guard. But not here. I think we're going to make an example out of him. Nuha?"

"Y-yes, my lady," Nuha said from somewhere close.

"I think a public execution for this traitor is in order. Those who serve me need to know there are severe punishments for failure. Where is his brother? The other djinn prince?"

"Nasir? You sent him to the pits."

"Call him back. I want him to witness what happens to those who fail me. And then you will take him on as your personal trainee. If he chooses not to serve as my pleasure slave like his brothers, I'll gut him as well and send his head in a box to his father. Then I'll declare open war on the Marid tribe. No tribal prince will best me. Not when I hold the power of the opals. Every Marid will rue the day their nobility went to war with a sorceress."

"Y-yes, my lady."

"And clean up this rat's wounds. I want him looking his best when he's executed. An example for all who dare to challenge me."

The whip landed against the floor with a thud. Footsteps echoed, and Ashur turned his head just enough to see Zoraida pause at the entrance to his cell.

She braced one hand on the bars, drew in a deep breath, blew it out again. But she didn't look good. Her skin was sallow, her dress hanging off her body as if she'd lost significant weight recently, and the line of her shoulders told him the few lashes she'd given him had drained not only him but her of strength.

She left the room in a blur of blue silk. Behind him, Nuha barked, "Guards, release him."

The guards shuffled over and unhooked his wrists. He didn't have the strength to hold himself up. He slumped to the floor as soon as they let go.

"Now wait outside," Nuha ordered.

"But—"

"Now!"

Boots echoed, and then the cell door swung shut. In the silence that followed, Ashur breathed deep, unsure what to expect.

Nuha crossed on silent steps and looked down at him. Then sighed. "Did you learn nothing from me? I told you to please the mistress, not piss her off."

He sensed more than saw Nuha's frown. She knelt in front of him. But she was smart enough not to touch him. "I tried to warn you, Ashur. I tried. Why couldn't you just corrupt the angel's soul like you were sent to do? She's celestial, for Allah's sake. All djinn know not to trust angels. They're evil."

He did know not to trust an angel. Zoraida had warned him. Every authority figure he'd ever looked up to as a child had told him to be on the lookout for celestial beings when in the human realm. And he'd tried to keep his distance from Claire but…she hadn't stolen his powers. And even though she'd left him after the greatest sex of his life, if she'd truly been after the opals like she'd claimed, she could have used him to cross into the djinn realm to find them. And still she hadn't. She'd walked away.

The pain drifted to the back of his mind. He'd spent years feeling left out, unchosen, the third wheel. But with Claire he hadn't felt any of those things. He'd felt…strong. Desirable. Whole. Maybe for the first time ever.

You are not evil, Ashur. And the sorceress does not hold sway over you, not unless you let her. I do not believe you will incinerate my light. Not when there is goodness in your heart. I trust you…

His pulse picked up speed. She had trusted him. That hadn't been a lie. He'd felt it. Not just in her release, but in the way she'd given herself to him. And deep inside his heart—a heart he now knew he did have thanks to her—he was certain that she hadn't betrayed him, not like Zoraida and Nuha wanted him to believe. She'd simply walked away when she could. She'd done what he hadn't been able to do. She'd saved herself.

He lifted his chin. Narrowed his eyes. Peered upon a female he knew intimately from his training but had no desire to get to know personally. Not like Claire. "Evil does not reside within one race. It lurks in the hearts of those who have free will. The sorceress knows this. She feeds on it. And we fall prey to it because we are weak. But no matter what you or her or any of her slaves do to me, I won't be the one to incinerate goodness."

Nuha's face reddened. "Goodness? Stupid, djinni. You think the angel is good? Look around you. If she were so good, she wouldn't have abandoned you here. And thanks to your misplaced loyalty and foolishness, your race will suffer."

His mind drifted to thoughts of his father, the ailing king. Of his brothers, Tariq and Nasir, whom he'd left in the human realm. Even if Nasir was called back to Zoraida, Ashur had faith his brother would fight the sorceress. He'd survived the pits. He was obviously stronger than Ashur had given him credit. And Tariq was free now. If war erupted in Gannah, Ashur believed in his heart that Tariq would return and fight for their people, even if it meant leaving his human mate.

"Goodness always triumphs over evil. Always."

Slowly, he pushed to his feet. Surprised, Nuha rose, her eyes wide as she watched the muscles in his arms flex and strain.

Blood ran down his back, pooled near his feet, but he ignored it. When he reached his full height, he stared down at the dark-haired female and set his jaw. "Zoraida will not win this fight. Even when I am dead, someway, somehow soon, she'll fall. And you'll fall right along with her. Mark my words, Nuha." He leaned close. "You're all about to die."

Chapter Eleven

Darkness overwhelmed the senses. Claire's pulse pounded in the cool night air as she looked toward the dark shape looming in the distance. She wasn't a savior. She'd never been a savior. She was stupid to come here alone, to let them talk her into this. What if she failed?

Panic pressed in, and sweat broke out over her skin. She should turn around. Go back. Tell Nasir and Tariq they had to come up with some other plan because she wasn't the one...

"*Goodness always triumphs over evil. Always.*"

Her words to Ashur, just hours ago, filtered through her mind. And in the aftermath, her pulse slowed, her skin warmed, and somewhere deep inside, a strength she didn't know she had gathered and grew. She stared at what looked like a rock formation against the starry sky but wasn't, and focused on breathing. Inside there were tunnels and caverns and an entire compound hidden from view. Tariq and Nasir had described it as best they could, and thanks to Nasir's powers, which she now controlled, she'd been able to transport to this dark bluff overlooking Zoraida's stronghold without any of her sentries knowing.

She may have failed at everything else she'd ever done, but she wasn't going to fail at this. She couldn't. This was more than helping that man comfort his dying son. This was about saving a life and putting it before her own.

She made her way down the bluff and crossed the small valley toward the mountain of rock. The sky was so dark, she couldn't see much, but she picked her way along the side until she found a gap and stared up at the towering spires of stone.

Focus and control. Those were the words of wisdom Nasir had imparted to her. She had no idea if this was going to work, but it was now or never. On a deep breath, she closed her eyes and centered herself, then imagined standing on the ledge high above.

Air rushed past her face, and then her feet left the ground. She gasped but didn't open her eyes, instead refocused on where she wanted to go. Seconds later, her feet touched down, and a thrill rushed through Claire when she realized she'd landed exactly where she'd wanted to be.

Okay, that was a trip. And something she could definitely get used to. Except…

A burst of flame caught her attention. She ducked behind a boulder and looked down into the crater below. This had to be some kind of ancient volcano. Rock rose up around in a perfect circle. Torches flickered all along the edge of the crater, and in the very center some kind of tall structure had been built in a U-shape. Directly below and in front of it, flames licked up from a gigantic pit dug out of the ground.

Her eyes widened as the flames grew higher, redder, angrier, if possible. Drums began to beat, and from an archway in the rock wall to her right, people—no, djinn—began to file out and form a circle around the flames and structure.

They were chanting. Ancient words in a language Claire couldn't decipher. She watched when a guard hauled a thrashing male from the tunnel, then gasped when she realized it was Nasir. In the time it had taken her to get to this spot, Zoraida had called him back, just as he'd predicted she might do.

The guards hauled Nasir to a pole yards away from the fire and tied his arms above his head, then stepped aside when he was sufficiently bound. He yelled something at them Claire couldn't make out, then spat on the ground at their feet. And as she watched, her anxiety amped. She thought of Kavin, back in the human realm with Mira and Tariq, probably going out of her mind. Of the kingdom of Gannah, which Nasir was in line to rule; about an entire race of people who didn't know her but who would be doomed if she failed.

But the minute two guards hauled Ashur out of that tunnel, his hands chained behind his back, his hard body bare but for the thin black pants he was wearing, all thought slipped out of her mind.

Her pulse picked up speed. Her gaze shot to the structure high above the flames. To the cable that stretched from one side of the structure to the other, and the platform that could be raised or lowered right into the flames.

This wasn't a ceremony. It was a death ritual. An execution. Djinn were said to be made of smokeless flame. They were going to burn him alive. Return him to that from whence he'd come.

Panic spread like wildfire through her body. She looked right and left, tried to figure out how she was going to stop this. Even with her powers and what Nasir had given her, she was only one. There were at least a hundred—probably more—djinn down there. All under Zoraida's spell. Against one sorceress, maybe she could hold her own, but she didn't stand a chance against an entire army.

A burst of crimson as red as blood erupted from the tunnel, and Claire's attention jerked to the female walking toward Ashur, standing at the base of the steps of the mighty structure.

Zoraida.

Claire knew it was the sorceress, even though she couldn't see her face. Power radiated from her small body. Power that—even though she did look frail as Nasir had predicted—was still strong enough to knock Claire and everyone in this place on their asses. And there was something else. Some dull light…

Claire gasped again. Covered her mouth so as not to give herself away.

Suddenly, everything made sense.

Zoraida stopped in front of Ashur. Said something Claire couldn't hear. Then reached out to run her hand down Ashur's cheek. Ashur jerked away from her touch and glared down at the sorceress. And though Claire couldn't hear what he said in return, the way Zoraida stiffened told Claire loud and clear that she'd wanted his fear. Needed it to fuel her strength. But Ashur wasn't afraid. If anything, he looked pissed. And determined. And ready for whatever was to come next.

Claire's heart pounded as she watched Ashur from the safety of her boulder. Awe and admiration rushed through her. Not just because he was the epitome of strength in the last moments of his life, but because he—a djinni—had taught her something even those in the heavens couldn't. That life wasn't just about having fun and experiencing everything temptation had to offer. It was about finding the one thing you were willing to sacrifice everything for. The one person who made you want to be the person you were born to be.

"Take him," Zoraida snapped, her enraged voice rising to Claire's position. "I'm done with this djinni."

The guards jerked on Ashur's arms and hauled him up the steps. Claire's adrenaline shot into the stratosphere as she watched him being dragged to the upper platform. They hooked his arms to chains anchored to a bar above his head, then stepped back. The entire section he was standing on moved away from the structure, gliding along the cable high overhead until he was directly above the flames.

The chanting grew louder. Nasir yelled up at Ashur. Drums echoed in a steady rhythm. In front of the pit, Zoraida's voice rose above the rest. "No life is above the power of the opals. Death to those who refuse to serve."

The chains began to lower. Ashur tensed, looked down at the fire rising below. Claire panicked, looked all around. She didn't know what to do. How to stop it. What would…

Her gaze shot to the sky. And an idea took root, then exploded as if it had a life of its own.

The skies opened, and rain gushed down in huge, fat droplets, quickly dousing the torches and soaking everything in its path.

The drums cut off. Chants turned to shocked gasps. Wood singed, and the fire beneath Ashur went out in a burst of steam.

A furious Zoraida whipped around with wide eyes, searched the crowd, but Claire didn't break focus. She closed her eyes, called upon her powers again, and felt, rather than saw, lightning spear down from the sky, striking one of Zoraida's guards and igniting his body into flames where he stood.

Screams echoed up from the crater. People scattered in every direction, searching for an escape. Claire summoned the lightning again and again. Bolts struck the ground, destroying Zoraida's guards one by one.

"Claire!"

Ashur's voice dragged Claire's eyes open. Nasir kicked out at a guard rushing past. Ashur stood still, staring at her from his perch. And too late she realized the sorceress's eyes were locked on her hiding spot.

"Run!"

Ashur's word barely hit before she dove behind the boulder, but it was too late. Something grasped her ankle, spun her around, and let go. Her body flew through the air. Rain slapped her face. Though she couldn't see where she was going, she knew she was going down. Into the crater. Toward a death she couldn't stop. Fear gripped her, but she focused again. Her body came to a screeching halt just before she hit. She tore her eyes open and looked down. The ground was two feet below her.

She gasped and broke focus. Her body dropped to the hard surface with a grunt.

"You dare to challenge me?"

The enraged voice made Claire whip around. Sweat slid down her brow as she looked up into fury-filled eyes. Scrambling backward, somehow she found her feet.

"You are no threat to me," Zoraida growled. The sorceress lifted her hands, and an electrical force arced from her fingertips. Claire leapt out of the way just before the ground she'd been sitting on burst into flames.

"Claire, run!" Nasir hollered.

Zoraida thrust a beam of energy from her hand. It hit Nasir in the chest. His body shook. He groaned, then went limp against his bonds.

"Nasir!" Claire darted behind one side of the massive structure. Tried like hell to figure out what to do next. She didn't know if he was alive or dead, but she couldn't give up yet. She focused on drawing a bolt of lightning toward Zoraida, but with a flick of her wrist, the sorceress batted it away as if it were nothing but an inflatable beach ball.

"Did you think you could beat me?" Zoraida roared, advancing on Claire. "You're a fool to follow the djinni. He's nothing. Useless. But soon your soul will be mine. And your powers."

Ashur. Maybe if she could free Ashur, they stood a chance. Claire ran behind one of the many support beams holding the structure up, closed her eyes, and imagined Ashur's chains breaking free. Metal jangled above. Flames erupted at her right, and she tore her eyes open and jumped out of the way and avoid being charbroiled.

"Come back here, angel," Zoraida growled. "Give me what is mine." Her arms lifted. Energy arced. Flames ignited near Claire's feet again.

Claire yelped, darted around the other side of the structure.

From above, rattling chains echoed and Ashur yelled, "Claire! Use your light!"

Her light? Claire didn't know what the hell her light would do. Light wasn't a weapon. Her pulse raced. Her mind scrambled for something that would save them.

Zoraida stepped out from behind the stairs. Claire jerked back, scanned the area. She'd worked her way clear around the structure. To her right was the pit. To her left, nothing but sheer rock walls rising up to form the edge of the crater. And at her back, Nasir hanging from that pole. She'd never make it all the way around the pit before Zoraida zapped her.

"Did you come back here to save him?" Zoraida asked with a menacing glint in her eye as she stepped forward. "Did you think you two could live happily ever after?" She chuckled, an evil, sickening sound. "He's a pleasure slave. He's *trained* to make you think he cares. He'd fuck anything I told him to. It's all he's good for." She looked up at Ashur above, struggling with one arm still chained to the cable. "He's mine. Alive or dead, he belongs to me." She turned her dark gaze back toward Claire. "As will you be when I'm done with you."

"Claire!"

The panic in Ashur's voice hit Claire in the sternum. He wasn't breaking free, and she couldn't focus on two things at once.

Her breaths quickened as she shuffled backward. Zoraida lifted her hands. Claire's heart rate sped up. Energy arced from the sorceress's fingertips.

Claire gathered what was left of her strength. Closed her eyes. Focused on light. On purity. On goodness.

"Goodness always triumphs over evil. Always."

"The sorceress does not hold sway over you, not unless you let her."

"Claire!"

Energy snapped. The force hit Claire so hard it stole her breath. And then, as if she were a reflective surface, it bounced off and shot away from her.

A scream rose up in the air. Claire tore her eyes open and gasped when she caught sight of the sorceress's body erupting in flames.

Fire consumed everything—Zoraida's red dress, her blonde hair, her flawless skin. Her screams echoed through the darkness, the flames illuminated from a blinding white light pulsing from Claire's body.

Claire watched in shock, unable to move. The light pulsed from her skin, keeping her immobile, highlighting the horrific scene. The sorceress's screams turned to gasps then groans, then finally ceased altogether. Her blackened body slumped to the ground, and the fire ate up what was left until all that remained was a pile of ash.

The light went out, and, dazed, Claire dropped to her knees.

Chains echoed somewhere above, followed by the pounding of footsteps, but Claire was too exhausted to move.

"Claire! Holy Allah…"

She recognized hands against her shoulders, the softness of skin against her own, of the heat of another next to her as she was pulled close.

"Claire, Claire… Please, talk to me."

Fingertips brushed the hair away from her face. Water droplets hit her cheek. She turned her head and blinked several times to look up into Ashur's worried face. Rain ran in rivulets down his cheeks, and his dark hair dripped across his bare shoulders. He held her in his lap as if she were precious. As if she were his. Her heart—the heart he had awoken—warmed to him all over again. "It's…still raining."

Relief rushed over his features. He closed his eyes. "It never stopped. Allah, I thought that was it." He opened his eyes, but instead of soft and concerned, this time they were hard and focused. "How did you get here? What the hell were you thinking? You could have been killed."

The anger she heard in his voice with the last statement jolted her out of the haze she'd slid into. She tried to sit up but he held her too tightly. "Nasir and Tariq… They helped me. They said I was the only one who could find you."

"Nasir?" He looked up to where his brother was still restrained to that pole. "Shit."

Gently, he set her on the ground, then scrambled for Nasir, unhooking his arms and lowering him to the ground. The two exchanged quiet words, but Nasir seemed dazed. A little of Claire's anxiety eased. Nasir was okay. He was alive. He—

Sand crunched, and feet stopped next to her. Ashur's hand closed over her arm and drew her up. "Allah, I want answers. Why are you here?"

She couldn't read his expression. Was he angry? Frustrated? Relieved? She wasn't sure what was going on, but she suddenly needed space. Pushing out of his arms, she stepped back. Around them, smoke and steam rose from the fires Zoraida had started. From the one Claire had ignited. "Would you rather I hadn't come? You'd be dead now."

He raked a hand through his dripping hair. "I'd rather you were safe. How did you get here?"

"Nasir gave me his powers."

"He *gave* them to you? Just like that?" His gaze flicked to the opal around her neck. The one she'd used to find him.

And suddenly, the frustration in his voice made sense. He thought she'd stolen Nasir's powers. That she'd been the reason Zoraida had called Nasir back. Unease turned to a gut-wrenching disappointment she felt everywhere. Had she thought there might be some kind of happily ever after with him as Zoraida had mocked? Yeah, she had. Even though she hadn't admitted it out loud, she was a fool to think he might want her. One incredible night did not mean there was any kind of future for them. She was still celestial, and he was still djinn.

She had to look away from Ashur. Couldn't face the disappointment in his eyes. Her gaze flicked toward Zoraida's remains. And the fire opal that now sparkled amongst the ashes.

It was there. Just like the one around her neck. Power pulsed from both. Called to her. Begging her to move forward. To reach out. To take. Ashur's anger suddenly seemed unimportant. With Nasir's powers, her own and the opals, she'd be stronger than anyone. Stronger than Ashur. Stronger than the sorceress. Stronger even than the High Seven.

Power had never been her goal. But now, faced with it, her pulse hummed and her fingers ached to reach out, to take what was being offered. To claim. She could make Ashur hers without his consent. It didn't matter if he loved her or not. She could still have exactly what she wanted. That and so much more.

"Claire?"

Ashur looked from the opal on the ground, then back to her. His voice held a note of concern, but all she could focus on was the opal. Two distinct choices spun out in front of Claire. Two very different paths. One toward her celestial life, enlightening but not her own, the other toward power and every pleasure her heart had ever desired.

Her feet moved forward.

"Claire," he said again in a wary voice. "Claire, what are you doing?"

"What I was meant to do," she answered. Her eyes widened and glowed as she looked down at the firebrand opal in the ashes at her feet. "Everything I was born to do."

Chapter Twelve

Light pulsed all around Claire. Her body swirled. She gasped. Felt like she was being tossed on an angry sea. And then everything stilled.

She pried her eyes open, then held up a hand to block the bright glare blinding her tired eyes.

"We've been waiting for you, Claire."

She blinked twice. Recognized the voice. Realized she was home, not back in the human realm, where she'd intended to go when she'd walked away from Ashur and the opal. "S—Sura?"

Her friend chuckled and sat on a bench in front of her. She was in some kind of park. Everything—the grass, the trees, the bushes and flowers—were bathed in white, giving the entire space a calm, peaceful, content feeling. "You passed."

"Passed?" Claire repeated, still trying to adjust to brightness. She's forgotten how consuming the light could be. How warm. How perfect. She'd been away from it so long.

"I lied to you, Claire." Sura pushed her blonde hair over her shoulder. "Our emotions aren't stored in the firebrand opals."

Claire's brow wrinkled. "I don't understand."

Sura smiled. "It's easy if you think about it. You see, you'd been in the human realm long enough, but you hadn't made a conscious decision for good or evil. The High Seven decided it was time to tempt you."

Claire's mind spun. Tempt her? They couldn't. Not one of their own. Could they?

Her gaze snapped to Sura's peaceful face. "So you lied to me? On purpose?"

"I had to. It was your test. And you passed. You gave up power and pleasure for love. You chose the harder path. You did what Zoraida couldn't. And for that, the High Seven have decided to offer you a choice."

Claire was still having trouble comprehending what Sura was telling her. "What kind of choice?"

"One a thousand times tougher than the one you just made." Sura smiled and held out her hand. And though she couldn't explain why, Claire eyed her friend's palm, unsure if she should take it. Afraid if she did, she'd never see Ashur again.

"Come, Claire. And I promise everything will be explained to you. In a moment, you'll no longer worry about what you just gave up."

※

Ashur's head was in a fog.

He stood in the grand ballroom in the castle in Gannah, greeting senators, thanking lords and ladies for their well-wishes and congratulations, doing everything that was expected of him as second in line to the throne, but his mind was elsewhere. His heart…his heart a hard ball beneath his ribs.

"Yes, yes," his father boasted at his side to a senator whose name Ashur couldn't even remember. "We're all so thankful to have him home."

"It's a miracle," the senator said.

"No miracle," his father answered. "I always knew Ashur was destined for greatness." He turned his bright gaze in Ashur's direction. "Savior of not only our kingdom, but our realm as well. The sorceress's armies have scattered to the wind. Thanks to Ashur, this war will soon be over."

Ashur's stomach turned as it did every time his father praised him for defeating Zoraida. The djinni refused to believe what Ashur had told him. That an angel had saved their race, not him. An angel who'd disappeared before he could tell her how thankful he was that she'd come after him. How relieved he was that she hadn't been hurt. How confused he was over her actions.

He caught Nasir's gaze across the room. Dressed in his formal military uniform, standing proud above the masses as he shook hands of those who'd been at the celebration welcoming the brothers home and with Kavin in a pale pink gown at his side, Nasir looked every bit the king he would one day become. Ashur's stomach churned again, and he swallowed hard.

He needed air. Needed a break from the festivities and people. He needed quiet. Needed…light.

He excused himself from the receiving line, and though his mother called out to him in a worried voice, he ignored her and headed for the doors on the far side of the room.

Warmth washed over his face. He closed his eyes while the doors clapped shut at his back. Breathed in the salty sea air.

Behind closed eyelids, he could see the light. Feel it beating down on him. Heating his skin. Easing the ache inside. Allah, how he'd missed the light all those months locked in Zoraida's prison. He'd had a taste of it with Claire. Just enough to make him crave more.

"Stifling, isn't it?"

His eyes popped open at the sound of Tariq's voice to his right. He looked that way, surprised that of all people, it was his eldest brother who'd followed him out.

Since he'd abdicated the throne and chosen to live in the human realm with Mira, he wasn't dressed in a military uniform like Ashur and Nasir. His black slacks and jacket were nice, but amongst the elite in the castle, they signified him as nothing more than a commoner.

Ashur leaned against the railing and looked out at the hazy city below and the sea that disappeared in the horizon. "You could say that."

They'd barely spoken since Ashur's return. So much had happened between them that Ashur didn't know where to start. And because this celebration was the first time Tariq had visited from the human realm since Ashur had been back, they hadn't had the opportunity.

Tariq leaned next to him. "Nasir will make a good king. The people love him. And did you see the way they've taken to Kavin? Even Father's enraptured by her."

Ashur watched a gull swoop over the city. That had been the biggest shock of all for him since he'd been home. Their father, who claimed no race was equal to the Marid, was Kavin's biggest fan. "It's because she's gorgeous. He's always had a soft spot for the pretty ones."

Tariq smiled. "Who would have ever thought it? A Ghul will soon be queen."

Not Ashur. Never Ashur. But then, if someone had told him an angel would save their kingdom from the horrors of war, he'd have laughed in their face.

That hard ball beneath his ribs seemed to grow in size, but he ignored it. "Will you miss it?"

"The ceremonies and duties and never having a moment to myself? Not a bit."

Ashur glanced toward his brother. Tariq meant it. "But you love this kingdom. You always have."

Tariq rested his foot against the bottom railing, his gaze scanning the city. "I still do. But my heart isn't here. And to be a just king, you have to rule with everything. Including your heart. Mine lies in the human world. It always will. I think part of me knew that before. It was why I was so restless. Why I couldn't commit to my duties when Father wanted. I'm not meant to be here, Ashur."

Slowly, Ashur looked back toward the spires of the city, but his pulse sped up. And that hard ball beneath his ribs warmed. Was he meant to be here? He wasn't sure. He felt lost. Nothing gave him pleasure—not seeing his home or being with his family and friends. He felt like a part of himself was missing. And every time he thought of Claire, he couldn't help but wonder if her light was what he was missing.

"You're losing it, aren't you?" he asked, more to distract himself from his thoughts than to hear Tariq's answer. "Your powers? You won't be able to cross here much longer, will you? And even that doesn't change your mind?"

"To love another is to see the face of Allah. Once you've seen that, how can you go back to the way things were before?" Tariq shook his

Firebrand

head. "Father might not agree with my decision, but Mother knows I'd never make a good king now. Not without my heart. And without that, Ashur, we're nothing. Without that, we're as cold and dark as Zoraida. I don't know about you, but I don't want to end up like her. Power, fame, glory… They mean nothing to me. Not anymore."

Ashur's heart beat hard, so hard he was surprised Tariq couldn't hear it. He'd wanted those things before. Power, fame, to be recognized as not just equal but better than his brothers. It was why he'd gone after them both when they'd disappeared. Not simply to rescue them but so that he could be the one hailed hero. So he could have the glory. So a day like this—when the entire kingdom was singing his praises—could happen, and everyone would finally realize his worth.

Only now that it was here, it was meaningless. What did those things matter? He wasn't the savior everyone thought him to be. He was a fraud. *He* had needed saving. Not just physically from Zoraida's hell but emotionally from his own. By an angel who'd poofed out of his life before he could stop her. Before he could tell her what she meant to him. Before he'd realized it himself. And now she was gone for good.

"She went back."

Ashur and Tariq both looked toward the end of the veranda where Nasir stood, the medals on his uniform glinting under the afternoon sun.

"Who?" Ashur asked.

"Claire," Tariq said at his side, turning back to Ashur.

Ashur's gaze jumped to Tariq, and his brow lowered. "What do you mean?"

Nasir moved up on Ashur's other side. "When she left us at the mountain, the High Seven drew her back to the celestial realm. But they gave her a choice. To return to her life before the banishment or to go back to the human realm."

Ashur already knew this—at least the part about her going back to the celestial realm. He'd spent several days searching for her in the human world, much to his parents' dismay. Had needed to talk to her. To find out why she'd left so suddenly. Why she hadn't even touched the firebrand opal she'd been seeking for so long when it had lain inches away at her feet and why she'd given Nasir his powers back. And when he hadn't found her, he'd realized she'd been sent back to her own world.

"She chose the human realm," Tariq said quietly.

Ashur's gaze snapped to his brother. "What did you say?"

On his other side, Nasir chuckled. To Tariq he said, "Told you he'd care."

Tariq smiled, the same easy grin he'd had as a kid when they'd been teasing him. "I said she went back to the human realm. She's mortal now. Like Mira, she can't cross into our world, but she's there, waiting if you want to talk to her."

Talk to her? Ashur wanted to shake her. Find out why she'd saved him and why she'd run. And then he wanted to kiss her until they were both too breathless to argue.

His heart raced, but it was no longer a hard, cold ball beneath his ribs. It was hot. So hot. And pounding hard with the thought of seeing her again.

"Why?"

"Why what?" Nasir asked.

"Why would she choose to stay without the opals?" She'd told him how empty life was without the full range of her emotions. It was why she'd summoned him in the first place. Why subject herself to more of that emptiness?

"That's a question only she can answer," Tariq said.

He looked toward Tariq. "Where is she?"

He smiled again. "Where you first met her."

That beach. In the Marshall Islands. Where he'd only barely restrained himself from ravishing her.

He needed to see her. He couldn't wait. He needed answers. He needed—

He stepped away from the railing.

Nasir grinned and turned his way. "Eager all of a sudden, huh? She's not going anywhere, little brother. Why don't you stay? Have a few drinks. This is your party, after all."

Ashur shot him a look. "Would you stay if it were Kavin?"

Tariq's grin widened, and to Nasir he said, "You were right. I've a feeling Father might just lose his second in line to the throne. You and Kavin better get busy making those babies."

Nasir chuckled, and Ashur frowned as he looked between the two. What the hell were they jabbering about? He didn't care about anything but seeing Claire. He turned for the door. "I have to go."

"Hold up," Tariq called.

When Ashur turned, Tariq stepped in front of him, but the humor was gone from his features when he laid a hand on Ashur's shoulder. "You asked me if I'll miss it. I'll miss this. The three of us, together." He looked toward Nasir, who moved up on his side, the humor gone from his face too. "You already know this, Ashur, but I'll say it for posterity's sake. Blood is stronger than distance and time. Wherever you go, whatever you do, you'll always be my brother. You've spent your life searching for adventure, and I've a feeling you're about to embark on the biggest adventure yet. But I want you to know, whenever you need me, I'll be there for you."

"Me too," Nasir said in a thick voice. "And unlike this one, I can cross realms no problem. So if you need someone, I'm your guy."

Ashur couldn't help it. He chuckled. Then sobered because he realized what they were saying.

They didn't think he was coming back. His heart rate quickened. Was that what he was doing? Was he choosing Claire? He didn't know. He just knew he needed to see her. To talk to her. To bathe in her light one more time.

"I..." His throat grew thick. For so long in prison he'd blamed his brothers for his plight. Blamed Tariq especially, because his eldest brother had been happy and in love when Ashur had been suffering. When in truth it was that love that had saved Tariq. The way love had saved Ashur. "I don't know what to say to you both. 'I'm sorry for being an ass' doesn't seem like enough."

Nasir laughed. Tariq smiled. And the hand on Ashur's shoulder squeezed tight. "How about 'I'll call you.'"

Tariq was giving him an out. Just as he'd done when they were kids and Ashur had gotten in trouble. Tariq had always known the solution. All the tension Ashur had stored in his shoulders released. "I'll call you."

Tariq pulled him in for a tight hug. And Nasir did the same when Tariq let go. When Ashur eased back, both of his brothers' eyes were damp, just like his.

He turned away before he made a fool of himself and said, "I'll tell Mother and Father I'm leaving."

Nasir chuckled again. "Good luck with that. Maybe it would be better if you just escaped unnoticed."

"When Father's fawning all over Nasir's bride," Tariq added. "He'll barely notice your absence then."

"He doesn't *fawn* over her," Nasir said.

"Right." Tariq rolled his eyes. "I'm surprised Mother hasn't decked him yet. Did you see the way he was staring at her breasts?"

"No," Nasir said, shooting Tariq a look. "And how do you know anything about her breasts?"

Ashur smiled. They were back. The brothers he remembered. Always ribbing each other, lighthearted, happy. The brothers he remembered from before the war, before Zoraida's invasions, before their world had turned bleak.

He turned for the double doors but spun back on his heels with one last thought. Pointing at Tariq, he said, "And I am sorry about your house." Then cringed. "I hope Mira's not too upset about that."

Tariq tucked his hands in his pockets and shrugged. "We've been living on the boat. She loves the water. And tight spaces with me. All is good. Besides" —he nodded toward Nasir, who was feigning disgust— "this guy's paying for the remodel. Least he can do for me since I gave him a kingdom and all."

This time, Nasir rolled his eyes. "I'm never going to hear the end of that, am I?"

"Never," Tariq said with a grin. "What are brothers for?"

Sitting in the pink-and-white-striped beach chair in the warm afternoon sun, Claire pushed her toes through the sand and looked out at the gentle waves lapping against the shore. Palms swayed overhead, and a light breeze blew her hair away from her face. The cove was quiet today. No tourists. No locals. Just her and the view she never tired of looking at.

She was going to miss this place. She only had two months left in her sabbatical before the university expected her back, and now that she'd made the decision to stay in the human world, she had to forget about all the plans she'd made for the future and start blazing a new trail. She'd said she wanted to live, really live. Now was her chance.

A heavy weight settled on her shoulders, and she drew a deep breath. Depression, that's what this was. The big letdown. She didn't regret her decision—not now that she knew the truth—but a part of her had hoped this would all end differently. The same part of her that had foolishly thought about a happily ever after with Ashur.

He was free. That should be enough for her. And maybe there still was a happily ever after out there somewhere for her. Though at the moment, she couldn't imagine finding it with anyone else.

Sighing, she closed the journal in her lap and pushed her sunglasses to the top of her head. She'd been out in the sun too long. It was obviously baking her brain. She pushed to her feet, closed the beach chair, and headed for her hut on the far side of the cove. After leaning her chair against the porch, she wiped the sand off her feet and pushed the screen door open.

Then gasped.

Ashur was sitting in her living room, in the middle of her couch. His long arms were extended across the back, one foot was propped on the opposite knee, and an amused expression crossed his handsome face.

"Wh-what are you doing here?" she managed. Oh yeah, that sounded smooth. She swallowed hard.

"Waiting for you. I thought you were going to burn to a crisp out there." He pushed to his feet. "You know, with your light complexion, I hope you're wearing sunscreen."

She could barely process what he was saying. All she knew was the djinni she'd been dreaming about the last week was standing in her living room, his big body eating up all the space as if she'd summoned him. Which she hadn't.

"I don't understand. You should be in Gannah." Her brow lowered. "Why are you here?"

He crossed to her, and her heart sped up. But he didn't touch her like she hoped. Instead, he sat on the arm of the chair closest to her. "I could ask you the same thing."

Her eyes searched his familiar features. Dark hair hung like a fall of silk to his shoulders, and his eyes sparked with curiosity. And those firm lips she'd dreamed about were so close all she could focus on was kissing them again. Feeling them next to hers. Tasting them one more time.

"You didn't take the opals," he said softly. "Why not? I thought that's what you wanted."

She swallowed again. Searched for the right words. Knew she'd never find them. "I didn't go to your world to get them. I went to help you."

"Then why did you leave so fast?"

"Because I was tempted. The opals carry great power. I knew if I didn't leave then, I might not be able to later." She shifted her feet. "I'm not sure if you know this—I didn't until I got there—but Zoraida wasn't just a sorceress. She was celestial, like me. Fallen. And like me, she was tempted by the power in the opals. But instead of fighting that temptation, she gave in to it. Her light turned dark. There was very little of it left in her, but I could still feel it. I knew if I stayed, I'd end up just like her."

"A fallen angel," he said, looking down at the bamboo flooring. "Oddly, that makes a lot of sense." His gaze swung back to hers. "What happened when you came back here? I searched for you in the human realm after but couldn't find you."

He'd looked for her? Her heart bumped, and her skin grew warm. "I...I thought I was crossing back into this realm, but my superiors drew me home."

"To the Seven Heavens?"

She nodded. "It turns out everything I'd believed was a lie. Our emotions aren't housed in the opals. That belief was just the setup for my test. You were right about that, by the way. I was being tested. But not by you. By the opals themselves."

"I don't understand."

Neither had she, at first, but now that she'd had a week to think about it, she realized everything had happened for a reason. "I was banished because I became too interested in life, to the point where that interest was interfering with my job. I'm not the first from my realm to do that. I just didn't know it happens to many of us. So I was sent here, and since I wasn't used to feeling emotions, I didn't really know what to think. Feelings, emotions came on slowly, and it took me a while to get used to them. And with a friend of mine in the realm feeding me information" —she frowned when she remembered discovering Sura had been in on the test from the start "—I honestly believed the angels' emotions were stored in the opals."

"But they're not?"

She shook her head. "The opals were created thousands of years ago, by the High Seven. One for each of the deadly sins the High Seven banished from our order at the beginning of time—lust, gluttony, greed, sloth, wrath, envy, and pride. The power within the opals comes from that—from how each person who comes in contact with them interacts with those sins. In Zoraida's case, her powers grew quite strong because she was impacted by each one. The High Seven scattered some of the opals in the human realm, some in the djinn realm. Even though you have supernatural powers and humans do not, you both still have free will. And the High Seven are always testing mortals. They allowed the opals to exist to see how mortals would be tempted by them."

He frowned. "Forgive me for saying so, but your High Seven sound like a scheming bunch."

She couldn't help it, she laughed. "Yeah, I guess they do. But then that's their job. To see which souls survive temptation and are truly worthy of reaching the Seven Heavens."

"Tariq said they gave you the choice to go back to your realm."

He'd talked to his brother. She wanted to ask if that meant the two had mended their rift. Wasn't sure now was the time. She nodded again. "They did."

"So why are you still here?"

A tingle ran through her belly, igniting a flutter she felt everywhere. Could she tell him the truth? Indecision raced through her mind. Would he think she was a fool? They didn't even know each other that well. But he was here. He'd come all the way from his realm. And he'd said he'd looked for her just after she'd left. That had to mean something, right?

Nerves caused her skin to tingle. But she knew if she didn't take a chance now, she'd never have the opportunity again. And this was why she'd chosen to stay. "Because I wasn't ready to go back. Because—" She drew a breath. It was now or never. "When I was with you, the emotions I felt were too strong to make me consider giving them up. I finally felt alive. Not from any opal, but from you."

His dark eyes searched hers so long, her nerves shot up. What was he thinking? She didn't know. Couldn't read him. If he'd just come to find out why she hadn't taken the opals, he knew now. And yet, he wasn't leaving.

"Nasir said you're mortal now."

Wow, he'd really had quite a conversation with his brothers, hadn't he? She nodded again.

"So does this mean you gave up the Seven Heavens…for me?"

Her pulse pounded hard. He didn't seem excited by the news. She forced herself to nod once more anyway.

"And you can't go back?"

"When I pass from my mortal life, I can. But only as a mortal, not as a celestial being."

"And the High Seven are okay with that?"

"They felt I was worthy of the choice because I passed the test." Or so they'd said. She'd never know what they really thought, nor did she care anymore.

"I never understood how Tariq could give up his heritage to be with Mira, but I think maybe…now I do."

Was he saying…? Claire's pulse picked up speed as he pushed to his feet, as he crossed the space between them, as he took her hands in his.

"I've been searching for a reason to truly live for a very long time. Since way before I became Zoraida's prisoner. I just didn't expect it to come wrapped in the body of an angel."

Every cell in her vibrated. "We don't really like the term angel. It implies—"

"Wings and halos." One corner of his mouth tipped up. "I know. Tariq told me."

He had? Her heart pounded harder. "Ashur—"

His big hands framed her cheeks, tipped her face up to his, sent tingles of awareness all through her skin. "I don't quite know what the future holds, but I do know, if you're here, then that's where I want to be."

He wanted her. Really wanted her. And by staying with her, he was giving up everything too. His life, his home, even his family. Her stomach clenched. "You—you'll lose your powers if you stay in the human realm with me."

A slow smile spread across his face. "Then we'd better make the most of them while we can."

Light and heat flared behind her, and she turned to look toward the bed on the far side of the room. Hundreds of candles of all shapes and sizes lined the tables, the windowsills, even the floor. And on the mattress, the toys he'd teased her with before appeared, including that purple vibrator.

She couldn't stop the laugh that pushed up her throat. She dropped her head against his chest, smiled wide as his arms circled to pull her close. It felt so right to be held by him. So perfect. Why on earth had she ever thought some silly opals were more important than this? "That's not why I chose to come back here, you know."

"But it doesn't hurt, right?"

She smiled wider and wrapped her arms around his waist, loving the way his body fit against hers. As if it were made just for her. "No, it doesn't. I've sort of fantasized about those toys and what you planned to do with them before we were interrupted last time."

He leaned back and looked down. "You did?"

"More than once."

A devilish grin curled his lips. "Then maybe I'd better show you."

His mouth closed over hers. And she gasped, then sank into the kiss. Into him. Into everything she'd never known she'd wanted.

True happiness didn't come from somewhere else. She knew that now. It wasn't found in magical opals or even in a life of ease. It came from within. From finding where you were meant to be. From risking your heart and loving someone more than yourself, even if that love wasn't guaranteed.

When they were both breathless, he eased back. And in his eyes, she knew no matter what their future held, she'd made the right choice.

"I don't know much about being mortal, *maya*."

Maya. He'd called her princess again. Desire shot straight to her center. She stepped back, clasped his hand and pulled him toward the bed. "Don't worry. I'll teach you everything I know. And then" —her lips curled— "you can teach me everything *you* know."

He leaned to her side and pushed the toys to the floor, then lowered her to the mattress. "Your wish is my command."

And as his weight settled on her and she opened to his kiss, she couldn't help but think those were the most perfect words she'd ever heard.

Thanks for reading *BOUND TO SEDUCTION,*
SLAVE TO PASSION and POSSESSED BY DESIRE.
I hope you enjoyed the Firebrand Series!

If you would you like to know when my next book is available, you can sign up for my new release e-mail list at http://www.elisabethnaughton.com. Follow me on twitter Twitter.com/ElisNaughton, or like my Facebook page Facebook.com/elisabeth.naughton1.

Reviews help other readers find books. I appreciate all reviews, whether positive or negative.

To see a list of my other books and to read an excerpt from MARKED, book one in my bestselling Eternal Guardians series, please turn the page.

Read on for a sneak peak at

THERON – *Dark haired, duty bound and deceptively deadly. He's the leader of the Argonauts, an elite group of guardians that defends the immortal realm from threats of the Underworld.*

From the moment he walked into the club, Casey knew this guy was different. Men like that just didn't exist in real life—silky shoulder-length hair, chest impossibly broad, and a predatory manner that just screamed dark and dangerous. He was looking for something. Her.

She was the one. She had the mark. Casey had to die so his kind could live, and it was Theron's duty to bring her in. But even as a 200-year-old descendent of Hercules, he wasn't strong enough to resist the pull in her fathomless eyes, to tear himself away from the heat of her body.

As war with the Underworld nears, someone will have to make the ultimate sacrifice.

Chapter One

SOME NIGHTS, A WOMAN JUST wanted to bash her brain against a wall to keep from screaming. For Casey Simopolous, this was one of those nights.

"Yo, sistah. My tongue's not getting any wetter over here by itself." The blond frat-boy wannabe at the other end of her section threw his arms out wide with a could-you-be-more-stupid? look on his face. "We gonna get those drinks or what?" The two idiots seated next to him at the small circular table laughed and slapped him on the shoulder in a you-da-man move that made Casey grind her teeth together.

Oh, she could think of a number of comebacks for that one, but like the bad girl she wasn't in this den of indecency, she bit her lip instead. She plastered on a smile she didn't feel, dropped off the beers at table eleven and headed toward the troublemakers.

She hefted the full tray over her head as she zigzagged through XScream. Around her, heavy bass echoed from speakers hidden in the walls, vibrating the floor beneath her feet, sloshing her brain against her skull in the process. She had a killer headache, and that low-level buzz she'd been experiencing for the last thirty minutes was wreaking havoc on her usually cool-headed mood. If she hadn't eaten recently, she might have chalked it up to low blood sugar, but since Dana had forced her to choke down a burger during her break, she knew that wasn't the case. And she was tired of trying to figure out just what was wrong with her anyway.

Stop stressing already, would you? Sheesh…

She shook off the thought and picked her way around tables, past loggers and teachers and even the town's mayor. Far be it from her to judge who got their thrills in a place like this. To her right, Anna was onstage, working it for all she was worth, and from the corner of her eye, Casey caught a bra—or was that a G-string?—fly through the air, but she ignored that, too. Just as she did every night.

The college kids who'd been flicking her crap all evening whooped and hollered as they watched Anna turn with a lusty grin, bend over at the waist and shake her size-zero behind. They obviously didn't catch the fact that Anna's seductive wink and lip-licking was motivated by nothing but dollar bills, but then that wasn't exactly a surprise. These three yahoos were anything but Rhodes scholars.

They barely spared Casey a glance as she drew close, which was just fine with her. The micromini schoolgirl ensemble Karl insisted all the servers wear wasn't the most flattering outfit on her five-foot ten-inch frame, and she couldn't wait to be done with her shift so she could get out of it as fast as possible.

She set the first beer on the table in front of troublemaker number one, moved around behind the blond who was shaking his head in a yeah-baby move while salivating over Anna, and reached for the next beer on her tray. But before she could wrap her fingers around the chilled glass, a body slammed into her from the side, jostling the drinks and her and sending frothy golden liquid spilling over her tray.

"Hey!" she exclaimed, trying to right the tray before she lost everything on the table at her side. "Watch it!"

That buzzing picked up in her head, and before the words were even out, a tingling sensation lit off in her hip to radiate outward across her lower back and knock her equilibrium out of whack.

Casey swayed, reached out for the table but only caught the edge with the tips of her fingers. She had a moment of *Oh, crap* as she went down, heard chairs scrape the dingy floor and the college kids' shouts of surprise. But before her body hit the ground, an arm of steel that seemed to come out of nowhere wrapped around her torso, and another darted out to rescue the falling tray.

She didn't have time to do more than gasp. The mystery man who'd nearly knocked her to the ground turned her in his arm as if she weighed no more than a feather and set her on her feet. He handed her the tray, nodded and said in a thick accent, "Excuse me."

And Casey lost all ability to speak.

He was huge. Easily six and a half feet tall and at least two hundred and fifty pounds of solid muscle. His legs were like tree trunks, his chest so wide it was all she could see. And that face? *Greek god* came to mind, with that olive skin, the shoulder-length hair the color of midnight and those black-as-sin eyes. But it was the way he was looking back at her that really threw her off guard. Like he recognized her but couldn't place her. Like they'd met, but the idea didn't thrill him. Like she was the last person on the planet he wanted to be staring at right now.

"Jesus," one of the college kids behind her exclaimed. "Are you brain-dead or what?"

Oh, damn. Those stupid college kids.

She was just about to turn to defuse the situation, but the Greek god beat her to it, shooting them a withering look that could have turned flesh to stone. The kid's smartass mouth snapped shut, and the comments died behind her. Neither of his friends piped up to berate her more.

For the first time all night, a little of Casey's headache dissipated. She wanted to turn and look at the stupefied expressions on the troublemakers' faces, but she couldn't tear her gaze from the man in front of her. He must have noticed her staring, because he cast another bewildered look her way, then gave his head a swift shake and headed off to the other side of the club.

And it wasn't until he was all the way across the room that she finally drew in a breath.

Holy cow. What was that?

Her lungs suddenly seemed one size too small. She sucked in air, rubbed a hand over her brow and tried to regulate her breathing as she continued to stare. He stopped at a booth near the back wall, and though Casey couldn't see his face, it was clear he was talking to someone seated in front of him.

Someone who was female and blonde and petite and who had come in alone a half hour ago, then slinked into the shadows to watch the show.

At the time, Casey hadn't paid the woman much mind—occasionally women came into the club alone—but now she did. Now that *her* hero in black had zeroed in on the blonde beauty, Casey definitely wanted to know more about each of them.

"You gonna stare all night or get busy?"

The voice at her back shook Casey from the fog brewing in her head. Turning, she pulled her attention to the three college kids, studying her like she was a complete moron, their irritation with her obviously usurping the earlier intimidation from her mystery man. The tray wobbled in her hand, but she caught it before the half-empty glasses spilled again.

"So sorry," Casey muttered, grabbing a rag from her tray and mopping up the mess on their table. What was wrong with her? "I apologize."

"Geez," the blond muttered, shaking beer from his fingers. "What are you, mentally challenged or something?"

Casey ignored the comment and finished cleaning the table. "I'll get you three more beers—on the house, of course."

"Damn right," the one to her right snapped, as he turned to look back at the stripper feet from him up on stage.

She ignored that too as she finished grabbing empties, then glanced toward the hulking shadow several tables over.

"Those guys giving you trouble?" Nick Blades asked as she drew close.

"No more trouble than normal." Carefully, Casey picked up the wadded napkins on his table and dropped them on her tray. He was nearly as big as the Greek god, but that's where the similarities ended. Nick's blond hair was cut military short, he sported a series of strange tattoos and piercings, and it was hard not to stare at the jagged scar that ran down the left side of his face from temple to jaw. He always sat in her section, and though she'd told herself a thousand times he was harmless, a part of her just couldn't convince herself of that. She'd been there. She'd seen what he could do. And though she was grateful, she didn't want to see it again.

He watched her carefully, but she didn't make eye contact. "You seemed a bit distracted there."

Casey's hand paused as she thought back to the hulking Greek god, and warmth spread up her cheeks as she went back to cleaning Nick's table. It made perfect sense a guy like that would glance right past her and go after a looker like the woman in the corner. Men didn't generally notice stick-skinny Amazon women when curvy, petite blondes were anywhere close.

"You want another one, Nick?"

At his silence, Casey finally glanced up, and that's when she noticed Nick wasn't watching her but was staring across the club with narrowed eyes and a tight jaw. Staring toward the Greek god and his blonde bombshell. But he wasn't looking on with admiration or intrigue or even jealousy. No, Nick was watching them with malice, and very clear recognition.

Weird. How would someone like Nick know a guy like that? "Nick?"

Nick cut his eyes from the corner, his face turning impassive. "Might as well."

That tingling intensified again across Casey's lower back as she backed away from his table. "I'll get that for you and be right back."

She left him sitting in the same spot and headed for the bar, reminding herself the whole way she didn't want to know what Nick Blades thought of anyone. She had enough of her own problems to worry about. On a long breath, she set her tray on the shiny surface and handed Dana, the bartender, her orders.

Dana pulled the tap and filled three pints for the boys Casey had spilled on moments before. Then she glanced toward the middle of the room. "I see your admirer's here again tonight."

Casey frowned. She didn't like to call Nick an admirer. Didn't like to call him anything, for that matter. But she'd never shared the real reason with Dana, and she wasn't about to now. "I know."

"It's kinda sweet," Dana said. "Though he doesn't strike me as your type."

Casey didn't think it was sweet. Lately it was bordering on creepy. But she shrugged for Dana's benefit. "I don't have a type."

Dana smirked and set the beers on Casey's tray. "And if you did, it definitely wouldn't be the bad-boy biker type."

It got under Casey's skin, just a little, that she was so predictable. "Don't judge a book by its cover, Dana."

Dana pinned her with a look as she poured vodka into a glass and added orange juice from a pitcher. "Spoken like a true bookseller. How's the shop anyway?" She dropped a cherry into the drink and set it on the tray.

"Fine. Not as busy as this place, but then I don't serve up sex between the pages."

"Maybe you should."

Casey couldn't help smiling. "Yeah, maybe I should."

She waited while Dana finished her order, and tapped her fingers on the bar to the beat of Justin Timberlake's "SexyBack." Jessica was onstage now, already shimmying out of her hot shorts, and Nick was barely paying attention. Casey's gaze swept over the room, and for a fleeting moment, she wondered what her grandmother would say if she could see her now.

"*Acacia.* Meli, *what has happened to you?*"
"*Nothing, Gigia. It's only temporary.*
"*It's always temporary with you*, meli."
"You off in a few?"

Dana's voice pulled Casey from her musings and she nodded. "Yeah. Thank God. Fifteen more minutes, then I'm free for the weekend. The bookshop's closed tomorrow and Monday."

"Good. You work too hard, Casey. I don't know how you do it. All day at the shop, nights here. Ease my worry, honey, and tell me you've got a hot date planned."

Casey reached for the tray. "Yeah, with a good book."

"You need to get out more, Case. Find a good-looking guy who'll remind you what life is all about."

Casey thought back to the Greek god. She just bet *that* guy could remind her what life was about.

She shook off the thought as she hefted the tray and turned to leave. "I don't have time for hot dates. I'm too busy."

"After you deliver those," Dana said at her back, "cut out early. I'll cover for you."

Casey glanced back. "You sure?"

Dana shrugged and smiled as she wiped out a glass, her soft red hair glinting under the dim lights. "Yeah, sure. Go on. Something comes up, I'll get Jane to cover your tables."

"Thanks," Casey said on a sigh, feeling suddenly tired.

"One thing before you go. When you get home, would you check to see if I left my phone there the other night when I came over? I can't seem to find it."

"Sure thing. I'll call you."

Dana winked. "Appreciate it. Have a good weekend, Casey. You deserve it."

Casey stopped at the college kids' table and delivered their beers, then glanced toward the back corner. The blonde was pushing herself out of the booth, but she stumbled when her feet met the ground, which was weird because Casey was sure

Marked

the woman hadn't had anything to drink. The Greek god was right there to catch her, though, just like he'd done with Casey.

No, not like he'd done with Casey. Her eyes narrowed as she watched. He was much gentler with this woman. He pulled her close as if she were made of glass and seconds later swept her up in his arms and whisked her out the back door of the club, straight out of a scene from *An Officer and a Gentleman*.

Only this guy was ten times bigger and a million times hotter than Richard Gere ever was.

Warmth rushed to Casey's cheeks again as she watched, and envy—the only word she knew to describe that strange tightness in her chest—stabbed at the center of her. What would it feel like to have a guy like that so focused on her?

The door snap closed behind him, leaving only the darkness and thumping bass of the club in its wake. With a frown, Casey took a deep breath and turned.

No sense worrying about something she'd never have. No sense worrying about something she didn't have time for anyway. She needed to finish her shift so she could get home and sleep off this weird virus she'd been fighting the last few days. Then pull herself together so she could do it all over again Tuesday morning.

She crossed to Nick and handed him his Coke. "I'm heading out, Nick. You need anything else, Dana will take care of you."

He lifted his fresh glass. Long sleeves covered his arms, and the fingerless gloves he always wore kept all but the tips of his fingers from view. "Will do. And Casey?"

She stopped midturn and glanced back. "Yeah?"

"That guy who ran into you? If you see him around town, I want you to let me know."

Casey's brows drew together. "Why?"

"Personal reasons."

Okay, *that* was weird, too.

"And you'd be smart to stay away from him if you do see him," he added in a low tone. "Far away. He's dangerous."

That spot on Casey's lower back tingled again, and she lifted her chin. There was looking out for her, and then there was telling her what to do. And even though something instinctive told her she'd never see the Greek god again, right now, coming from Nick, she wasn't wild about either.

"Yeah, Nick," she mumbled as she turned and headed for the dressing room. "I'll be sure to do that."

※

"Theron, put me down." Isadora's free hand pushed against Theron's chest, but her protest did little more than annoy him.

He wouldn't lose his temper. The fact that he'd spent four days tracking her down was inconsequential at this point. So was the fact that he'd left his kinsmen to come after her. He would simply take her home before the Council discovered she was gone and all hell broke loose.

"Theron, I mean it," she said again, as the door to the human skin club snapped shut behind them and he headed away from the building.

"It's time to go home, Isadora. You've had your fun."

Isadora glanced over his shoulder back toward the building with a defeated look in her eyes. "You don't understand. I need her."

Need *her*? Like hell. He was the only one she needed right now. If her father found out what she'd been up to...

He gnashed his teeth at the thought and kept walking. If it were up to him, no one would know where she'd been these last few days or what she'd been up to. The last thing he—the leader of the Argonauts and a descendent of Heracles, the greatest hero ever—needed was for his warrior brothers to know his future wife had a human-female fetish.

He cringed at the thoughts. Both "human female" *and* "future wife."

Isadora squirmed in his arms again, but finally gave up with a sigh. And that was just fine with Theron. He wasn't in the mood to play nice.

The air was cool, but Theron barely felt it. A muffled thump-thump-thump echoed from the club behind him as he walked. Quietly, Isadora said. "She was beautiful, wasn't she? Graceful and tall. I...I didn't expect her to be so tall."

More frustrated by the second at Isadora's strange behavior, Theron picked up his pace. It wasn't until Isadora sighed again and rested her head against his chest that he remembered how inebriated she was and how tightly he must be holding her.

He loosened his grasp and forcibly gentled his voice, though even he knew it came out rough and stilted. "Isadora, you cannot just run off like this."

"I...I know," she breathed against him, her body growing lax in his arms. She shivered and tried to burrow closer. "I just wish..."

Her fading voice made him remember how she'd had trouble standing in the club. For the first time, he realized there hadn't been a single glass on her table. Not even a watermark from one that had been recently cleared away. Gathering her in one arm, he reached around and felt her forehead. Her skin was cold and clammy.

His aggravation morphed to urgency. She wasn't drunk at all. She was sick.

Skata. He had to get her back to Argolea. Like, *now*. "Hold on to me," he said firmly in her ear, repositioning his arm under her legs again. "I'll get you home."

She closed her eyes and, after a moment of what looked like incredible pain and heartbreak, nodded in what he could tell was great reluctance. "Yes. Yes. You're right. It's long past time. Take me home, Theron."

He took one step forward with her in his arms and felt the air change. It went from moist and warm to frigid in the span of a nanosecond. And he knew without looking that they were not alone.

Four daemons, beasts of the Underworld caught between mortal and god, horns sharp, teeth bared, appeared as if from thin air. One directly ahead, two to Theron's right, one to the left. They had bodies of men, covered in leather and trench coats that flapped behind them as they moved, with hideous faces, something of a mix of lion and wolf and goat.

Isadora's muscles relaxed in Theron's arms. He wasn't sure if she'd fallen asleep or if the sickness that racked her body had pulled her into unconsciousness, but at the moment he didn't care. It was better for her if she didn't see what they faced.

"Release the princess, Argonaut, and your life will be spared," the daemon directly ahead announced in a raspy voice.

A humorless sound bubbled from Theron's chest even as his mind spun with options on how to get out of this one. His kinsmen were nowhere close. He'd come looking for Isadora on his own. "Since when have daemons been known for their mercy?"

The leader growled. "Our mercy is the only thing that will save you. Unhand her. Now. You will not be given another chance."

They were about out of chances, as far as Theron could see. He glanced down at Isadora, out cold in his arms. For nearly two hundred years he'd served his race because it was his duty. Even though it hadn't been his first choice, he'd been willing to marry her if it meant preservation of their world. Tonight, though, he knew he would serve the *gynaíka* who would one day be Queen of Argolea, in order to save her life and that of their people. Even if it meant losing his own.

The two daemons on his right moved closer. Theron closed his eyes and used every ounce of strength within him to form a protective shield around Isadora. The effort drained him of his powers. He had nothing left for the fight to come.

Knowing she was now safe from the daemons, he slowly set Isadora on the ground at his feet. She curled onto her side on the cold asphalt but showed no other signs of consciousness. He rose to his full height of six feet, five inches and stared at the four daemons who still towered above him. "If you want her, boys, you'll have to come and get her."

The one in the middle, who was clearly in control of the others, chuckled, though the sound was anything but humorous. "So arrogant, Argonaut. Even when you're trapped. Atalanta will be most amused by your brashness."

"Atalanta is a petty hag with a perpetual case of PMS. And let me guess... As her number-one whipping boy, you get what?

The right to wipe her ass?" He laughed, though he knew all it did was enrage the beasts in his midst. If he was going to go out, though, he might as well go in a blaze of glory. "Let me ask you this, dog face, just how inconsequential is your race that Hades would so easily hand you off to a bitch on wheels like Atalanta, anyway?"

The four growled in unison. The leader's eyes flashed green. "Taunt all you want, Argonaut. In mere minutes, you'll be begging for us to kill you."

They moved forward in a unit, as if of one brain. And without hesitation, Theron brought his fingers together until the markings on the backs of his hands glowed from the inside out. The portal opened with a flash and closed seconds later, leaving him alone with the daemons in the cold parking lot.

In the split second of silence that settled over them like a dark cloud, fury filled the face of each daemon, followed by a roar the likes of which only a god has ever heard.

"Sending the princess home was the last mistake you'll ever make, Argonaut," the leader growled.

They struck as a pack, taking him down to the pavement hard before he had time to reach his weapons. Teeth bared, fangs unsheathed, they tore into his flesh.

As his back hit the unforgiving ground and the last vestige of strength rushed out of his body, Theron had one fleeting thought.

This was going to be bad. Before it was over, it was going to be very, very bad.

To learn more about Elisabeth's books,
visit www.ElisabethNaughton.com

Praise For

ENSLAVED

"Another winning installment in the Eternal Guardians series will leave you eager for more as the action is unbelievably thrilling and the emotional conflicts are involving throughout. 4 ½ Stars"—*RT Book Reviews*

"Elisabeth Naughton has done it again!! *Enslaved* is filled with action from the very beginning."—*Enchantress of Books*

ENRAPTURED

"Filled with sizzling romance, heartbreaking drama, and a cast of multifaceted characters, this powerful and unusual retelling of the Orpheus and Eurydice story is Naughton's best book yet. Starred Review"—*Publishers Weekly*, starred review

"Creative worldbuilding and ever-present danger pull the reader into this mesmerizing tale. 4 1/2 Stars"—*RT Book Reviews*

TEMPTED

"Endlessly twisting plots within plots, a cast of complex and eminently likeable characters, and a romance as hot as it is complicated."—*Publisher's Weekly*, starred review

"Dark, dangerous, and absolutely addicting."—*NY Times* bestselling author Christina Dodd

"Ms. Naughton has taken the Greek Argonaut myth, turned it on its head, and OWNED it!"—*Bitten By Paranormal Romance*

ENTWINED

"An action-packed creative wonder guaranteed to snag your attention from page one."—*Fresh Fiction*

"Do NOT miss this series!"—*NY Times* bestselling author Larissa Ione

MARKED

"Naughton has tremendous skill with steamy passion, dynamic characterization and thrilling action."—*Publisher's Weekly*

"Elisabeth Naughton's MARKED gives an incredibly fresh spin on Greek Mythology that is full of humor, action, passion and a storyline that keeps you from putting down the book."—*Fresh Fiction*

STOLEN SEDUCTION

"This third book in the Stolen series is full of intrigue, secrets and undeniable love with characters you can't get enough of... an awesome read!"—*Fresh Fiction*

"An adventurous story of twists and turns, this story will keep you guessing until the very end. And the chemistry between Hailey and Shane is sizzling hot. Naughton combines passion and danger in one fast-paced story."—*News and Sentinel*

STOLEN HEAT

"This book has got it all: an adventure that keeps you turning the pages, an irresistible hero, and a smoking romance."—*All About Romance*

"Stolen Heat is an awesome combination of deadly suspense, edgy action and a wonderful romance with characters that you'll laugh, cry and yell with."—*Night Owl Romance*

STOLEN FURY

"A rock solid debut...Naughton's intelligent adventure plot is intensified by the blazing heat that builds from Lisa and Rafe's first erotic encounter."—*Publisher's Weekly*

"Naughton deftly distills deadly intrigue, high adrenaline action, and scorchingly hot passion into a perfectly constructed novel of romantic suspense."—*Chicago Tribune*

WAIT FOR ME

"This book blew me out of the water."—*Cocktails and Books*

"Wait For Me more than met my expectations, it was downright delightfully angsty with a great big dose of scorching hot scenes between two characters who could not have been more made for each other. The unraveling mystery is compelling all on its own but the chemistry between Kate and Ryan will keep you truly captivated."—*Paperback Dolls*

About The Author

A former junior high science teacher, bestselling author Elisabeth Naughton traded in her red pen and test tube set for a laptop and research books. She now writes sexy romantic adventure and paranormal novels full time from her home in western Oregon where she lives with her husband and three children. Her work has been nominated for numerous awards including the prestigious RITA® awards by Romance Writers of America, the Australian Romance Reader Awards, The Golden Leaf and the Golden Heart. When not writing, Elisabeth can be found running, hanging out at the ballpark or dreaming up new and exciting adventures. Visit her on the web at www.ElisabethNaughton.com.

Made in the USA
Charleston, SC
23 April 2013